The Town at the End of the World

The Town at the End of the World

Book One: Founding

Genevieve Carr

Faraway Publishing
Black Mountain, N.C.

In memory of Evi, the one who made me a mother,
and Karen, a storyteller whose story was far too short.

In three words, I can sum up everything
I've learned about life.
It goes on.
—Robert Frost

Table of Contents

Chapter One: March 2034

Irina Karrigan stands on the front porch, gathering the courage to go inside. In her hand she holds a baseball bat; on her back she carries her fourteen-month-old son, Matteo. She takes a deep breath, trying to steel herself, then reaches for the doorknob. The front door is locked, so she uses the bat to smash the cut-glass door window with a practiced swing, then reaches through and undoes the bolt lock.

She sniffs the air and detects the familiar scent of death. She hopes that the house's former inhabitants had the decency to die in their bedrooms. Out of habit, she puts on a pair of rubber gloves, then steps into the house. The houses in this development have four floor plans, and she knows them all, so she already anticipates that her path to the kitchen will necessarily lead her through the open- concept living room. In Irina's experience, living rooms are the second most likely place to encounter bodies.

Unfortunately, the former occupant of this house decided to spend his final moments in the warm embrace of his television. His desiccated corpse is wrapped in a stained blanket on the black-leather couch, the television silenced by the final death of the power grid a year and a half Before.

Irina tells herself that the scariest thing about corpses is that they're a reminder of one's own mortality. A year after the Virus finally extinguished itself by killing 99.99% of its human hosts, this corpse poses no physical threat to her. No virus lives that long, not even the norovirus mutant that lived on surfaces for two weeks and, so far as Irina knows, killed every person except her and Matteo.

She tries to ignore the body on the couch and the pictures on the refrigerator door as she clears the kitchen pantry and cabinets. The house's occupant must have died early in the Pandemic, because the kitchen is still relatively well-stocked with canned and dried goods and even several bottles of

Willamette Valley Pinot Noir. She stuffs everything that isn't too expired into the cloth bags she's brought. Merely glancing at the stamped dates on the packages sends a bolt of anxiety through her. Soon the dried goods will expire like their makers did, the canned goods will run out, and she will have nothing but her own wits to rely on.

She takes several trips to the shopping cart outside, returning until the kitchen is emptied of anything remotely edible.

Matteo begins to fuss, and she sits down in an Adirondack chair on the front porch to nurse him. He cries and pushes against her, as he often does lately. His days of getting nourishment from her are growing short. Finally, he latches, and she stares out at the abandoned desert neighborhood as he nurses. The only sound, apart from his occasional suckling noises, is the soft moan of the chilly, early March wind. Irina is used to the silence, but she still doesn't like it.

Matteo finishes nursing and begins fussing again. Irina whispers to him and kisses his forehead; then she straps him back into the backpack, hopeful that walking will soothe him. Fat rain drops begin to pelt the hungry desert. The clouds stretch back to the horizon, promising something more than a brief shower. Because the gasoline had gone bad the year before, she's forced to walk or bike everywhere, regardless of the weather. There was a time when she would have walked home in the rain without any umbrella, like any self-respecting Oregonian, but now she wouldn't take the risk of Matteo getting a chill. So she reluctantly goes back into the house and searches the coat closet until she finds an umbrella. She nods a farewell to the corpse on the couch and sets off into the rain.

The walk "home" is a cold and cumbersome mile as she awkwardly pushes the cart with one hand while holding the umbrella in the other. As the rain hammers the umbrella, Irina talks to Matteo, partly to break the monotony and partly out of a sense of obligation. Matteo doesn't babble like his older sister, Clara, had. Instead, he stares out at their bleak world with wide, speechless eyes. He only occasionally emits a short, singular utterance. He interacts with his mother, but he's nearly always serious, with none of the silliness that his sister displayed at his age.

Irina, like many mothers, is sure that anything that's wrong with Matteo is her fault. If only she talked to him more. If only she could find the strength and energy to fake joyfulness. She's certain that her own sorrow transferred to him, even before his birth. He was marinated in her grief for nine months, his brain and limbs imbued with her sadness.

Irina can provide him only survival. She can't offer him the kind of childhood she'd given Clara—filled with light and creativity, with days that seem endlessly sunny in hindsight.

Her first pregnancy, eight years before, though wrought with the usual nausea and tiredness, was filled with joy. She'd tracked every milestone, happily charting Clara's growth, secure in her ignorance, certain that nothing could go wrong. Her pregnancy with Matteo, though, was different.

She'd been relieved, then panicked, when she learned she was pregnant with Matteo. She and her husband, Sam, had been trying for a baby since Clara died in the accident seven months before, but as soon as Irina learned she was pregnant, two months after the first reports of the new virus, she realized how unbelievably irresponsible and selfish they had been to create new life when the world was descending into chaos. They'd gone on trying to conceive during those final two months, caught in the same denial as the rest of the world: surely there couldn't be another pandemic, less than a decade after the official "end" of the last world-stopping virus.

Matteo grew in her womb, as governments belatedly declared states of emergency, as air travel was shut down weeks too late, as businesses and doctors' offices shuttered, and as world mortality estimates reached 5%, then 30%; then there was no one left to tally the statistics and report them to the public.

There were no ultrasounds of Matteo. The doctors didn't see people in person anymore, so Irina's prenatal visits were all video conferences. It didn't escape her notice that the doctor, himself, seemed incredulous that she'd chosen to get pregnant during a pandemic. What did he know, she thought, about what it feels like to lose your only child: their specific laughs and cries and shouts, their loves and hates, and to also lose your identity as parent, all at once?

Or perhaps he did know. By that time some people had lost children to the Virus. Perhaps she had mistaken scolding for envy.

Eventually, five months into her pregnancy, even the video visits ceased when the doctors, too, succumbed to the Pandemic.

On January 24, the day of Matteo's birth, it snowed eight inches in Salem, Oregon—an extraordinary amount of snow for the area. Irina went into labor that morning, several weeks early by her calculations.

She spent the day in a state of terror. There was no hospital to go to: the Salem Hospital had closed in mid-September, followed a month later by the Portland hospitals. Irina couldn't call any doctor that might still be left, because the cell phone network had died with the power grid in mid-October. Sam couldn't even engage in his usual favorite form of research, pulling up instructive videos on the internet, because the internet, too, had disappeared with the power grid and cell phone network in a sweeping wave of silence.

The only thing that gave Irina any comfort was Sam's steadfast calm and the fact that this was her second birth. While the snow swirled down outside the large windows of their living room and Irina's labor pains increased, Sam read labor instructions in one of Irina's pregnancy books and fed logs to the fire. As the day grew darker and the snow gathered in drifts on the ground and coated the pine limbs outside the window, the pain became unbearable.

Irina had opted for an epidural with her first birth. She'd never seen much of a point in pain for the sake of pain. It seemed to her that women who would forgo modern medicine were simply trying to prove their own toughness.

"I climb mountains," she'd said with great conviction to the doula during her first pregnancy, when the woman suggested an unmedicated birth. "I don't need to prove how tough I am."

That January night, Irina desperately wished she'd had an unmedicated birth, just so she could anticipate how bad things were going to get. In the absence of a doctor, there was no feedback about how far along in the process she was, no promise of relief or even life at the end of this.

Movie scenes of screaming women in labor had always seemed overwrought to her. But then, in the literal eleventh hour, as she felt her body torn apart, she understood. Suddenly, in a fog of fear and pain, there was Matteo, slick and squirming in her husband's arms. Matteo let out a loud cry, and Sam looked up at her with tears and sudden panic in his eyes. He followed the instructions in the book, cutting and tying the cord, but there was nothing to prepare him for the amount of blood.

"Stitches!" she snapped at him after delivering the placenta. "Get a needle and thread. Sanitize them, and put in stitches!"

He handed her the baby, numbly gathered the necessary supplies, soaked the needle and quilting thread in rubbing alcohol, then balked at the prospect of actually stitching skin. Nothing in his background had prepared him for this. Sam was the kind of man who carried spiders outside, instead of killing them. He was patient with children and kind to animals. He cringed when he saw violence in movies. The vestiges of his Thai mother's Buddhist faith still clung to him.

"You have to," she said, more gently this time. He was crying as he stitched. Outside it snowed and snowed.

+++

Here, now, in Bend, Oregon, she shakes herself from the memory as she hauls the rickety shopping cart up the small hill to the house she's claimed. The rain pounds on the umbrella. Matteo watches with interest, his large brown eyes tracking the small streams that have formed on the street around them.

She closes the umbrella and pushes the shopping cart inside the house. It rattles across the entryway tiles as a brown mutt comes running to them.

"Hey, Buddy," Irina says as he nuzzles her hand enthusiastically, then bolts into the front yard, returning quickly because he hates the rain.

Inside, Irina sets Matteo in his playpen. The fire had gone out while they were gone, and a chill had settled on the house. She relights the fire, then unloads the groceries into the usual cabinets. She sets several buckets and pots outside on the deck to catch the rain and save herself the trouble of carrying water from the stream.

Matteo begins to fuss, then cry. She lifts him into his high chair and feeds him canned peas. She sits down at the table beside him and watches him eat, trying her best to summon up the playfulness that used to come naturally to her. She can't help it, though, that sometimes when she looks at Matteo, she sees Clara—Clara's big dark eyes, her thick black hair. She sees the short arc of Clara's life, her baby smile, her curious eyes, the way at Matteo's age she laughed and babbled constantly, her early clumsiness and later grace. She sees Clara twirling in a circle in the fall leaves on the way to the farmer's market. She hears Clara reciting facts about a caterpillar she'd found, rambling about a nature show she'd seen, asking "Mama, are you listening? You're not listening!" Irina remembers what it felt like before she knew—in her bones,

6

in her every breath, at a cellular level—that children die. She remembers what it felt like to trust the universe, to take life for granted.

It's midafternoon before Irina finally opens up a can of soup for herself and pours it into a pot on the edge of the fireplace. She stares out the window as she eats without tasting. The day has grown darker and even more drizzly. She can barely see the Deschutes River winding its way through the rainy desert below her house.

Irina had arrived in Bend from Salem nine months before, four and a half months after Sam died. The morning before she left Salem, she'd driven her car to the Willamette River, gotten Matteo out of his car seat, and walked to the middle of the Marion Street bridge with him in her arms. She'd stood there in a haze of postpartum hormones, sleep deprivation, and grief, staring at the river below, praying that the jump would kill them both. Something, though—fear or guilt, certainly not hope—had pulled her back from the edge. She'd gotten back into the car, driven home, and packed her things that day. She knew that she had to leave Salem, or she would die. She could no longer occupy the place she'd lived when she was whole and happy. She'd filled up the car's tank with the last of the stabilized fuel and watched her home shrink in the rearview mirror.

When she arrived here, she had spent a few days scouting along the river before settling on this home—mostly because there was a small seasonal stream that ran just outside the yard, joining the river about a quarter of a mile down the hill. Its three fireplaces, fenced back yard, and front porch also made the house inviting. The solar panels on the roof looked promising, but she'd never been able to figure out how to get them to work without the power grid.

In the backyard, she'd found two graves, but the family pictures showed a family of four. Perhaps the others had died in the hospital. Perhaps they'd been buried in shared graves, as family members often were as the infection progressed.

Perhaps the final members of the family had wandered off into the desert when their time came; she'd found the remains of several bodies in the desert scrub since she had arrived here. She was glad to find no bodies inside this house, unlike several other properties she had investigated, and no scent of death or sickness. Aside from the graves, it looked like the family had simply gone on an extended vacation. The car was in the garage, along with several bicycles—one of which even had a child seat for Matteo.

She'd packed up the personal belongings from most of the rooms and moved them into the garage. The children's rooms she left untouched, just as she'd left her daughter's room in her own house. The first floor is more than enough for her and Matteo, who sleeps beside her bed in a portable crib she found at Walmart.

Irina had added a picture of the house's original inhabitants to the flip-book photo frame she'd brought from her own home, though she can rarely stand to flip through it.

The plumbing situation is less than ideal. The toilet has to be flushed with water carried from the stream, and baths are only a weekly affair now in a tub filled with stream water warmed on the fireplace, usually too little water and not quite warm enough. In the interest of efficiency, Irina shares her bath with Matteo, who seems to enjoy it.

Irina lights several candles against the gathering darkness. While Matteo naps, she washes their dirty clothes in the stationary tub, wringing and hanging the clean clothing on a drying rack in the laundry room. She brings in more firewood from the garage, feeds the fire, then settles on the couch with a gardening book, trying to troubleshoot the fungus that's attacking her potato crop. Without being invited, Buddy jumps up next to her, and she's grateful for his warmth, if not his tendency to assume permission.

Matteo is her purpose, but Buddy is her comfort. He was there with her when her child died, when her husband died, when she drove through the mountains to Bend. At first she'd taken him everywhere with her, needing the sense of protection that a dog—even just a medium-sized one—offered. Soon, though, she came to the firm conclusion that there was no one left that she needed protection from, and Buddy was permitted to sit out most of those trips.

Still, she always takes him with her when she goes down to the river. The coyotes have grown braver now that the humans have left the earth. She sees their eyes reflected outside when she shines a flashlight through her front windows. She hears their yips and howls every night, and she sees their paw prints that lead right up to her front door. They seem to be always circling the house, waiting for death, waiting to take over the small piece of the world that humans still hold. She could swear that on one particularly cold night last winter she heard them scratching at the door.

Buddy snuggles up next to her, nosing his way under the blanket she's wrapped around herself. Loneliness settles over her. It's been four hundred and twenty-six days since she had a conversation with another adult.

She takes Buddy with her to the small garden plot she'd planted in the back yard, though he resists the outing because of the rain. The rich green, wrinkled leaves of kale are coated with raindrops. She plucks a few and pulls two potatoes, the best she can expect from an early spring crop. She thinks about trying to find some livestock but figures that most of them died from lack of care. So she'll have to supplement her garden and canned goods with ducks and rabbits that she hunts or fish from the river. Growing up in Utah and learning gardening from Sam had left her with some survival skills.

Inside, Matteo begins crying, and she returns to him, lifting him gently out of the playpen where he's been napping. She soothes him and feeds him, then watches as he toddles around. He bumbles drunkenly between the padded pieces of furniture, finally tripping and landing in her arms and giving her a rare smile. For an hour or so she plays with him; then she pauses to pour herself a large glass of wine and prepare their dinner.

Outside, the rain dies down and the wind picks up. Darkness settles over the desert, unmitigated by electric light or moonlight. She pours another generous glass of wine and slides more logs into the fire. She reads *Little Blue Truck* to Matteo. His eyes grow heavy as he settles against her on the couch. Eventually he falls asleep, sandwiched between her and Buddy, and she carefully moves him to his crib in the bedroom. She lights a candle on top of the dresser and starts a fire in the bedroom fireplace. The wind howls across the top of the chimney eerily, and she shivers.

As the room warms, she washes her face and brushes her teeth. She looks in the mirror—an urge she almost always ignores—and sees a face she doesn't recognize, a cold wraith cast in warm candlelight. Her eyes and lips dip down now. She's grown old in the space of just a few years. There was a time when her face was her pride, when her body had carried her up mountains. But now, at thirty-nine, her face and her breasts sag. Her once voluminous wavy reddish brown hair is flat and shot through with gray. Though she rarely feels hungry, the ribs and hipbones that jut out from her skin tell another story. Her beauty is just one more thing that she's lost, but gazing in the mirror now, she feels it's one thing too many, and a great surge of rage wells up in her.

Why, she wonders, am I still here?

She wishes then, for the millionth time, that she could have curled up in that grave with Sam. Or better, that they had died with their daughter, before their act of desperation bred another human to hold her here once Sam was gone.

There were others who had killed themselves, especially when the infection numbers really started to tick up. Orphaned children and parents who'd buried their entire families. Faced with bottomless grief and the prospect of a painful death, ten or twenty percent of the population decided, simply, to opt out of life. She envies their decisiveness.

"Maybe death isn't that bad," Sam had said to her one night as they lay in bed staring up at the ceiling in the late stage of the Pandemic. "Maybe we reincarnate."

"As what?" she'd asked, "There aren't that many humans to reincarnate into."

"Maybe a deer," he'd said, "or an eagle, or a wolf, or a mountain lion."

Or a coyote, she thinks now. There are enough of them around.

Matteo lets out a little cry in his sleep, reminding her of why she remains here, and she returns to the bedroom and leans over his crib. She longs to touch his face, to feel the warmth of living skin, to be reassured of him, but she fears waking him. So instead she traces the air above him, just close enough to feel his soft breath on her palm. He's still here, against all odds.

She finishes her glass of wine and refills it halfway again, then opens the sliding door and lets Buddy out. She keeps a shotgun in hand, just in case any coyotes have managed to penetrate the back fence. She swears that she sees the glow of at least one pair of eyes out in the desert. She shivers and wraps her arms around her thin frame.

She lets Buddy back in and checks all the locks again, blowing out the candles as she does. She scatters the logs to slow the living room fire, then secures the doors on the fireplace. She takes another glance around the house, unable to shake the feeling that she'll forget something essential. With Buddy at her heels, she returns to the bedroom, gun in one hand and wine glass in the other. She leans the shotgun against the wall beside her bed, then locks the bedroom door, and secures the deadbolt she'd installed herself with the last of the battery in the drill.

From behind the shades of the big bedroom window, she extracts the small solar-charging panel that's hooked to her phone. Despite the weather, there's enough power for her limited purposes. She plugs the headphones in and settles under the covers, sipping her wine. Buddy jumps up beside her and curls up against her legs.

The phone no longer offers the internet or the ability to call a friend; it only offers painful memories. She pulls up the list of albums she downloaded before the networks went down and selects her favorite album, a band that she and Sam had once watched at Red Rocks on a clear, moonless, starry night. They'd sat under a spangled sky, just a little bit drunk, surrounded by music and the slight, ever-present odor of Colorado weed. It had seemed then, just a few months into their marriage, that their entire lives were spread out before them, filled with possibility and promise. That memory still raises goosebumps on her skin. She wonders if any beauty still exists in the world. It probably does, even here in the desert—maybe especially in the desert—but she no longer sees it.

The wine has blurred her emotions around the edges just enough to make them bearable. She opens the photo gallery. Her world—and her photos—mostly stopped on October 8th of the year before the Pandemic, the date she counts as Clara's last day. There are only twenty pictures since then—six from Matteo's birth and one for each month after. She should take more pictures of him, she knows; there's enough battery if she uses the solar charger. Some part of her knows, though, that pictures are meant for posterity, and she doubts very much that they will live long enough for posterity to be relevant. The monthly pictures are an act of obligation.

She scrolls back through the pictures of her perfect "Before" life: gymnastics classes and afternoons at the playground, Sam holding Clara, and Sam holding Irina. There were sunsets on the Oregon coast, bathed in magic-hour sunlight, a day at the riverfront park when Clara and other children splashed in the fountains, a swim lesson at the Y, several birthday parties and holidays, a bike ride with her best friend Kylee, a brief childless getaway to the Grand Canyon. There is a video of Clara laughing, but Irina knows that even with the wine, that would be too much to bear.

She allows herself to grieve, to really feel it, for only the length of the saddest song. Three minutes and twenty-seven seconds of catharsis is all that she permits. She sobs quietly, crushing her face against her hands, begging to open her eyes to another reality or not to open them at all. Then the song ends, and she swipes the tears and the music player away. She pulls up the calendar on the phone and marks an X for the day, wondering how far into the future the phone's calendar will stretch out without the aid of a network connection.

She finishes her wine, blows out the candle beside the bed, turns off the phone, and curls up tightly under the blankets.

+++

The days blur into each other. On April 7, Matteo says his first word: Buddy. He looks right at the dog when he says it, so Irina is sure that he hasn't just randomly stumbled on the sound. She feels a deep sadness that there's no one there to share the moment with her. That night, over her second glass of wine, she recalls Clara's first word: "dada." Irina had been a little sad that "mama" hadn't been her first word, but she was hardly surprised, since Clara had always preferred Sam.

The truth was that Irina had never felt like a good mother. She'd had a miserable childhood herself, so she wasn't actually certain what a "good mother" even looked like. She usually just stumbled along with well-intentioned ineptitude. Sam, however, despite losing his father when he was young, had been raised by a kind and loving mother and seemed to glide effortlessly through parenting without the slightest hint of the guilt and insecurity that Irina felt.

The days wear on Irina, heavy in their repetitiveness. The desert grows warmer. She needs summer clothes for Matteo, so she walks to the Walmart with Matteo in the backpack. She wheels the cart down the empty highway, naming things for Matteo as she goes—car, desert, sky, sun. Sometimes he tries to repeat the words, but mostly he just watches the world. Familiar loneliness settles on her. It's impossible to ignore how alone she is as she passes by the dark store fronts and empty parking lots.

Like most of the stores, Walmart has been looted. Irina bumps the shopping cart up over the lip of a shattered glass sliding door. Inside, the store is dimly lit by opaque skylights, so she turns on a headlamp. She'd visited several months before, so she already expects the shelves to be mostly empty of food and survival-related goods. The children's clothing section, though, had been passed over by the looters. Because most of the stores closed early that first Pandemic summer, the clothing is warm-weather clothing. She fills the cart with whatever 18- and 24-month pants and long-sleeved shirts she can find, mostly things marked with fading yellow clearance tags. She re-checks the food section and finds a few scattered cans and a couple of bags of dried beans. After picking up a few other necessities, she walks back to the entrance. As she bumps her cart over the base of the doors, something catches her eye.

Taped to the outside of the unbroken door to her left is a piece of paper with handwritten Sharpie words.

Do you want to rebuild? Come to Ferndale, CA, a post-Pandemic community. Beautiful views, fertile soil, and a moderate coastal climate. Meet at the Ferndale Library.

She stares at the paper. The edges are barely curled, and the black writing isn't faded. She doesn't recall having seen it when she visited this store last winter. Whoever left it here must have visited relatively recently. For reasons she can't explain, she takes it down, folds it, and puts it in her pocket.

By the time she returns home, she's forgotten about the paper. She doesn't think of it again until she changes into her pajamas, still slightly buzzed from her usual two large glasses of wine.

She pulls the flier out of her pocket and stares at the writing. She thinks that she's heard of Ferndale at some point or maybe even driven by the town. It must be on the California coast somewhere, but she has no idea where.

Anyway, it's irrelevant to her. She isn't going anywhere. Irina refolds the note and puts it in a drawer in her dresser, then goes through her nightly routines, concluding with her allotted three minutes and twenty-seven seconds of sadness, an X on the phone calendar, then blurry oblivion.

+++

May arrives and Matteo finally and decisively stops nursing. The house sometimes gets so hot that Irina has to leave all the windows open, even at night. It makes her nervous. She has pangs of regret about leaving the milder weather of Salem.

Matteo grows increasingly mobile, which poses problems for Irina. She sometimes has to leave him alone in his playpen so she can fetch water, wash the laundry, or hunt for rabbits in the brush nearby. He's also getting several molars, so he often wakes up at night. At mealtimes he cries and rejects any food she offers him. Irina grows even more tearful than usual during the day.

One afternoon in late May she lies on the couch as he toddles around the living room. She's been headachy and exhausted all day. The light from the windows seems like too much to bear, so she closes her eyes for a moment.

When she opens them, he's gone. She must have fallen asleep. She gets up and searches the room frantically. Her stomach drops when she notices that the front door is open. She rushes through it and sees him teetering on the edge of the neighboring house's stoop. She calls his name, and he turns to her. The next few moments are slow motion as he loses his balance and falls down the stairs. There is silence, then a loud cry, then more silence as he sucks in air and lets out an even louder cry. By the time she gets to him he's covered in blood. She tries, unsuccessfully, not to panic. The blood pours out of his forehead and into his eyes and open mouth. He cries and cries. She scoops him up and runs back to her house.

Inside, she cleans him up with a washcloth, revealing a large gash in his forehead. He'll need stitches, though there's no one but her to give them. She feels queasy at the thought. His head continues to bleed.

She realizes belatedly that she should have a needle and thread around for this contingency. There's likely one in this house, but she doesn't know where. She'll need to go to the store and get supplies. The wound is swelling before her eyes, and it occurs to her that she should probably watch him for a concussion, though she doesn't have any clear idea of what that entails.

She straps him into the baby carrier so he's in front of her and she can keep pressure on his wound. He's calmed somewhat, and he stares at her with big brown eyes, bloodshot from crying. She kisses the less bloody side of his forehead. With a word of farewell to Buddy, she departs for a Walgreens she'd seen nearby.

She walks quickly, trying not to jostle Matteo. It's growing late, and her stomach rumbles. She passes the empty houses with their dead lawns and crosses the highway. One of the doors to the Walgreens is already smashed, so she walks easily inside.

The store is torn apart, but after a little searching, she finds a sewing kit and bottle of rubbing alcohol, and she soaks the thread, needle, and scissors in a bowl of alcohol. Matteo fusses, and she opens a box of stale graham crackers from a nearby shelf to placate him.

Then she comes to the moment that she'd avoided thinking about. She'll have to give him the stitches herself. The wound still oozes blood steadily, and she's pretty sure that a gaping cut will create a risk of infection. She looks at Matteo, chewing on the graham cracker on the floor nearby, and wonders how she'll keep him still. She recalls that when Clara had to have one of her fingers glued at the Salem Emergency Room, the nurses had wrapped her up tightly in a blanket to restrain her. Irina searches until she finds a fleece blanket with flowers on it.

"I'm sorry, buddy," she says as she lays Matteo down. He squirms against her as she wraps the blanket around him. He wails loudly. She straddles him. He manages to get his hand out and she has to rewrap him. He looks up at her with terrified eyes, and she blinks back the tears. She has to do this. She dons a pair of rubber gloves and douses her hands in alcohol, then takes the needle and thread out of the bowl of alcohol. She pierces his skin, and he lets out an equally piercing cry. He tries to move his head, so she holds it with her other hand. She gets five messy stitches in before drawing the thread as taut as she can, tying off, then cutting it. She puts a dab of expired antibiotic ointment on his forehead, then covers the cut with a large Band-Aid. He gives her a final look of betrayal, and she slides down on her knees beside him. He tears himself out of the blanket and crawls away from her, still crying. She cries, too, and reaches for him. He moves farther away from her, which makes her cry harder.

Finally, he lets her pick him up and pull him close against her. His cries turn to hiccups, then steady breathing, and she realizes that he's fallen asleep in her arms. She tucks him gently back into the carrier. He stirs a little but falls back asleep with his head against her chest. She kisses his matted hair and sniffles. Then she stands up awkwardly.

She stuffs an armful of first-aid supplies into a plastic bag. It's almost sunset, and golden rays of sunlight are streaming through the westward facing doors, illuminating a piece of paper taped to the unbroken door. In her rush and distraction, she must not have noticed it. It bears the same message as the note she found at Walmart. It's slightly more faded because it's in a less sheltered alcove here.

She stares at it for a moment. Then she goes back into the store and looks for a map. After some hunting, she finds a *Rand McNally Road Atlas* close to the back of the store. She pages through it to California and scans the coast. It takes her a few minutes to find it, because Ferndale isn't a city, or even a large town; it's a tiny dot with small lettering tucked into the Northern Coast of California, south of the Redwood Forest. Irina's hand shakes as it hovers over the paper. She tucks the atlas into her bag and heads home.

That night she keeps a close eye on Matteo, trying to remember the symptoms of a concussion, but he sleeps better than he has in a week, obviously exhausted from his traumatic day.

She takes the piece of paper out of her dresser and unfolds it, trying to discern any new details about it. It's the same black Sharpie message in the same unadorned, typical handwriting.

What if there's a town left? What if there are people there who know more about survival than she does? She allows herself to imagine what that town would be like: a school, a doctor, security, some kind of laws. Maybe farms with livestock and crops, something more than her bare garden, which is usually beset with some combination of bugs and fungus. The people there would know how to keep from going hungry. They would have skills that she doesn't have.

It's clear to her that she can't stay here alone. As Matteo gets older, it will be increasingly difficult to do the things that she must do to provide for him. Right now she can leave him alone in his playpen when she needs to go out, but he's already started trying to climb out of it. In a few months, she's certain he'll figure it out. Then she'll need to bring him with her wherever she goes. How, though? In a year or two he'll be too big for the backpack but still too small to walk very far on his own.

And when he gets older, then what? He's never even seen another child.

She considers the ever dwindling supply of canned goods and her struggling garden. It was foolish to come here to the desert, but she also couldn't stay in Salem. She looks at the flier and she feels the slightest glimmer of something resembling hope.

Tomorrow she'll make a list and pack their things. She can't wait any longer. They need to depart before the summer gets too hot.

Chapter Two

A week later, Irina stands in the driveway beside her bike and trailer. She looks over her list again to make sure that she hasn't missed anything essential. She checks the tire pressure one final time. Satisfied, she straps Matteo into a child seat in the front of the bike and snaps a helmet on his head, despite his protests, then slathers him with mineral sunscreen. Buddy hops into the trailer, and she Velcros it closed. Then she puts on her helmet and pedals away from the place she's called home for almost a year.

The buildings of Bend fade away behind her and are replaced by Ponderosa Pine trees. When she passes by Newberry National Volcanic Monument, she recalls the time that she and Sam had brought Clara here. As a science teacher, Sam had loved Oregon's varied landscapes and amazing diversity of wildlife. He'd rattled off facts about the volcano that she had only half listened to. She regrets the number of times that she had only been partially present in their conversations.

For hours she rides south on the highway through an endless procession of Ponderosa Pine trees and flat terrain, almost unvarying in its monotony. She has only her thoughts and the sound of the wind to keep her company. She sees no signs of other living humans. Even before the Pandemic, this part of Oregon was sparsely populated, though, with only a few tiny towns spread out across many miles of two-lane desert highway. Irina tries to recall the pre-Pandemic population of Oregon. Four or five million people? If the Virus had a 99.99% mortality rate—the last estimate the experts had offered before they, too, succumbed to that probability—that means that only four or five hundred people are left in the entire state. Of course, there were also people like her who avoided getting sick because they had an early warning or premonition. She suspects, though, that by now many people in either category have died of starvation, cold, or suicide.

Irina wonders about her family in Utah, her best friend Kylee, and the other people she loved. She pushes those thoughts away and tries to imagine Ferndale and the people who live there.

After forty miles of unchanging geography, she reaches a place where a river parallels the highway, and she stops and sets up her tent. She refills her water bottle and drops the iodine tablets in, thinking of how far she still has to go and how empty the world is. For a moment, her faith in her plan falters. What if she's taken a deadly gamble, leaving the relative safety of Bend to find that there's no one in Ferndale? She pushes that thought away and reminds herself that her options are limited and she has a duty to try to find a better life for Matteo.

Irina feeds Matteo, Buddy, and herself from the limited food supply she'd fit in the trailer. She lets Matteo explore as the sun sinks toward the horizon. When the sky begins to darken, she dresses Matteo in pajamas and changes the Band-Aid on his forehead. The three of them retire to the tent, and he falls asleep almost immediately. The vulnerability of being alone in a tent makes her anxious, so she turns on a small, dim camping lantern and pulls her favorite book from inside its waterproof bag. She extracts the unopened envelope from inside the book; then she reads the book again from the beginning. Its familiarity soothes her and ties her to her past.

She recalls every iteration of herself that has read this text: the college junior who was assigned this book in Advanced English Literature class and was entirely blown away by it; the first-year law student who was alone and friendless far from home and needed something familiar; the woman in her mid-twenties who needed an escape during her messy divorce; the woman in her late twenties who was falling in love with Sam and would read bits of it aloud to him over their long phone calls; the woman in her early thirties who felt adrift in life and needed this touchstone; and finally the mother who had lost her child and endlessly reread the passage about eternal recurrence—the same passage that has been marked with an unopened envelope since Irina left Salem.

She thinks again of Sam, the person who had taught her how to love. Irina's divorce had been finalized only five months before meeting Sam. She hadn't been ready for anything serious, but Sam was handsome, kind, and friendly. Irina was twenty-seven, but still not over her childhood trauma, so she tested Sam's love routinely with unnecessary arguments, demands, and sudden withdrawals. Sam, though, saw something extraordinary enough in Irina to persist. Irina still isn't sure what it was.

Irina had disappeared without explanation for several weeks after they got engaged. When she finally returned, Sam demanded that they get couples counseling. Sam found a tranquil old man who specialized in a form of therapy that Sam said was "evidence-backed." Irina resisted at first, but when Sam gave her an ultimatum—counseling, or he would break off the engagement—she conceded. Irina has always suspected that it was really her mother-in-law, Pati, who pushed Sam to demand this. Sam was habitually conflict-averse, and his mother was a tough but loving woman who had clawed her way into the male-dominated field of virology. Sam was Pati's only child, and his happiness was paramount to her.

So Irina sat uncomfortably in the therapist's comfortable office, while she and Sam unearthed the miseries of her childhood, the source of her sexual quirks, the reasons for her negative self-image, and the patterns she'd created in their relationship. At the time, Irina felt that every session was focused on her problems, but in hindsight she realizes that there were plenty of conversations about Sam's passivity, his early loss of his father, and his conflict avoidance.

They spent two years in counseling, during which they got married, bought a house, and combined their lives. Together, they built a strong enough marriage to withstand even the eventual death of their child.

She turns to the page with the passage about eternal recurrence, and she whispers it aloud to herself, finding that it still moves her nearly two decades later. She replaces the envelope in the book and puts them both back in the bag; then she checks to make sure that her gun is close by, and she switches off the lantern. As she drifts off to sleep, she imagines Ferndale.

+++

The next day and a half is the same monotonous high desert scenery. She reaches the turnoff for the mountain pass that will eventually lead her to Grants Pass and I5. There's a small cafe and minimart on one side of the intersection and an old, squat motel on the other side. She unloads Matteo from the bike, puts him in the backpack, and breaks down the door to the minimart. Inside are mostly empty shelves. She finds a few cans of sodium-filled food, a couple of bags of rice, and some dried goods that were already nearly expired when the Pandemic started. She loads up the rice and canned goods in her trailer, then checks the cafe, which yields a few institutional-sized cans of beans and green beans.

The motel is shabby but looks like a more comfortable place to rest than spending a second night in the tent. And it seems unlikely to be occupied by any corpses, so Irina kicks in the flimsy door to one of the rooms and drags the bike and trailer inside.

There are no corpses in the room, but it still looks like something out of a horror movie, with decades-old carpet, bowed wood panel walls, and comforters that are probably older than she is. It smells of dust and stale weed smoke, so she leaves the door open to air the room out, while Matteo toddles around the parking lot, chasing Buddy.

Darkness begins to settle over the pine trees, and a chill breeze sweeps across the cracked concrete. She considers starting a fire to cook the food, but after a full day of riding, it seems like too much trouble. Instead, she shoos Matteo and

Buddy into the room and barricades the door with the dresser. She feeds them all a cold dinner, changes Matteo's bandage, wipes his face and hands with a wet rag, and dresses him in his pajamas, then cuddles with him on the bed until he falls asleep beside her. She looks at him in the semi-darkness, hoping that she's doing the right thing for him, that she hasn't taken a deadly gamble that will cost them both their lives.

She's lying awake in bed worrying, when she sees light seeping in around the mostly closed blackout curtains. She sits upright immediately, grabs her gun from the bedside table, and fumbles across the room to the window. She takes the safety off the gun as she peeks carefully through the narrow gap in the thick fabric.

Outside, she sees headlights cutting through the inky darkness as a car creeps up the highway from the south.

What is it doing here? She wonders. How do they still have unexpired fuel?

Then she realizes that it could be an electric vehicle. Maybe someone around here figured out how to make their solar panels work or had an off-grid system to begin with. In this part of the state, populated with "State of Jefferson" flags and anti-government preppers, that wouldn't be surprising.

She briefly wonders if she should go outside and flag the car down. After all, she is on a quest to find other people. Something about it seems wrong, though. It unnerves her for reasons she can't understand, and Buddy obviously agrees. Beside her, his hackles rise, and he lets out a low growl as the headlights sweep the far wall.

Goosebumps rise on her arms as she watches the car slow in front of the hotel. It pulls into the parking lot of the minimart across the street, and two men get out. The sound of their car doors closing seems impossibly loud in the silence of the lonely night. They're speaking to each other, but she can't make out their words. She watches as they enter the same building she'd been in just a few hours before. They emerge with several cartons of cigarettes. The one man opens one of the packs of cigarettes, while the other strikes a match. They both smoke in the moonlit parking lot, just fifty feet from her.

In the glow of the cigarette she can see that one of the men is wearing some kind of hat or helmet with an apparatus that covers part of his face. Irina squints in the darkness, trying to make out what he's wearing. For a moment, he turns toward the hotel, and she ducks quickly behind the curtain and against the wall, though she's certain he can't see her in the darkness. Unless . . . a troubling thought occurs to her. Is it possible that he has night-vision goggles? This seems like paranoia, but they have an EV, so who knows what other technology they have access to . . . .

As though sensing her distress, Buddy growls again. She lays a hand on his back, praying that he won't bark and reveal their presence here. She's glad she hadn't pitched her tent in the parking lot, started a fire, or left her bike and trailer outside, as she'd originally contemplated.

Long minutes pass as she hides against the wall beside the window. She hears their voices grow closer, and fear fills her. Her grip on her gun tightens. There's the sound of wood splintering, and she peeks through the window and sees them breaking into the hotel office three doors down. Irina can see now that the one man is wearing a camo helmet with binocular-like goggles, which she's almost certain are military-issue night vision. Both men have black handguns in holsters at their waists, though they don't seem to be keeping them at the ready. They step into the office.

A minute later they emerge again, shaking their heads. "Should we check the rooms?" the man with the goggles asks.

"Nah," the other replies. "This place is a dump. Let's get going. We'll have better chances in Bend."

In the motel bed, Matteo whimpers in his sleep. The man with the goggles turns toward where Irina is hiding, and she moves quickly behind the wall again, her heart beating. They're only about twenty feet from her. Can those goggles detect her body heat through the curtains? She has no idea what kind of capability military-grade night-vision goggles have.

When she gathers the courage to peek outside again, they're back across the road, snuffing out their cigarettes, and getting into the car. At the sound of their doors slamming, Buddy growls again. Irina puts her hand roughly around his snout to keep him from barking. The car pulls out of the parking lot and continues north in near silence. As it disappears, she breathes a sigh of relief.

Then her fear subsides, and she's left with doubt and regret. Other than the flier, that car was the first sign of human life she'd seen in more than a year. What if there's no one in Ferndale, and she's just let her only opportunity for human companionship literally pass her by?

She spends an hour lying awake in the dark considering this, chastising herself for her self-defeating distrust and fear, hoping that the car will return. It doesn't, though, and she wakes in the morning to the same empty world.

She gets back on her bike and pedals on, up into the mountains, where the landscape finally becomes more scenic with towering conifers and verdant meadows. After another three lonely days, she arrives in Grants Pass, hoping to find some food. She'd only visited the town once, and her memories of it are hazy, so she rides aimlessly, looking for the highway she'll need to follow out of town. As she pedals down a residential street, she hears a gunshot. Then another.

Is someone shooting at her? It certainly seems like it, but she can't see anyone. The houses around her appear to be abandoned, with overgrown yards. Another shot rings out, and she's certain it was aimed in her vicinity.

"Go away!" A gruff male voice shouts. "There's nothing here for you. Go back to wherever you came from!"

She pedals away as quickly as she can, not stopping until she's reached the southwest part of town. The grocery stores here all appear to be looted, so she's forced to break into a house and scavenge canned goods from its cabinets. She's grateful, at least, not to encounter any corpses. She rides south for a few more miles, before pitching her tent in a copse of trees a hundred feet down a dirt road.

Irina wakes at dawn with a terrible urge to relieve herself. She slips quietly out of the tent, leaving Buddy and Matteo behind. She turns from the tent door and freezes as her eyes land on a man standing about twenty feet away, looking right at her. She curses herself for stupidly leaving her gun in the tent.

He's about two decades older than her, with a long, ragged beard and wild blonde hair. He keeps one hand in the pocket of his jacket. Behind him she can see the roof of a farmhouse peeking out from the pine trees. She isn't sure whether it was the evening dimness or her extreme exhaustion that had caused her to overlook the house and the nearby garden plot.

Little mistakes, she reminds herself, are the difference between life and death.

She'd learned this when Clara died. Yet here she is, facing this stranger. He stares at her, and her anxiety notches up under the intensity of his gaze.

"You're on my farm," he says finally.

"I'm sorry. I didn't know anyone was here. I'm leaving," Irina replies, her voice shaking.

"You can stay," he says. "I have breakfast."

"I really need to go," she answers with false calm. Irina knows how to talk a man down. She'd done it with her father. She was sometimes successful and sometimes extremely unsuccessful.

"You can't leave," he says, pulling his hand out of his pocket. She sees the gun too late. He swings it up to point at her. "You have to come with me."

Inside the tent, Matteo is still silent, but Irina hears Buddy's growl. Every inch of her body trembles.

"My baby is in the tent," Irina says, her voice shaking.

He considers for a moment. It's clear he hasn't really planned this out. Finally, he says, "Come here."

Irina knows where this is going, and her body reacts in terror. She begins to cry, and her muscles freeze as he closes the distance between them, his boots squishing in the mud.

"Please," she begs. "Please don't hurt me."

Then, to her great shame, she feels her bladder release. She'd awoken already needing to relieve herself, and her bladder control has never been the same after Matteo's birth.

Now she stands, urine dripping down her legs, snot and tears dripping down her face. A look of shock crosses his face, then sudden awareness. He drops the gun to the ground and buries his face in his hands.

"I wasn't going to hurt you. I wasn't going to . . . I just wanted you to stay. I just wanted . . . . I've been here alone so long. I just wanted you to stay . . . ." He trails off with a strangled sob.

She stands perfectly still, unsure of what's happening, terrified, humiliated, her eyes fixed on the gun he'd dropped. He takes one last look at her, then says, in a choked voice, "Just go."

He flees back to his house, jogging up the steps and slamming the door behind him. Irina picks up his gun with shaking hands. She tries to unload it, but finds it already empty. She tucks it into her waistband.

Inside the tent, Matteo lets out a cry. As she picks Matteo up and straps him into the bike seat, Irina keeps an eye on the house, fearing that the man will change his mind and return. She tears the tent down roughly, stuffs it and her other items into the trailer, and signals to Buddy to get in. Looking anxiously behind her at the house one last time, she pedals as fast as she can down the road.

Two miles away, she turns onto a dirt road and rides a few hundred feet down it, her lungs burning. She leans over and vomits into the bushes along the road. Matteo wails from the bike seat. Irina sobs and coughs.

Her mind spirals. She's the only thing ensuring her and Matteo's survival, and she's terribly incompetent. It's a wonder they've survived this long. She's equipped with skills for a world that has ended. She won't survive in this one. Her stomach twists and her breath feels too short.

She's certain she and Matteo will die soon.

She tries to talk herself down. In a week, she'll be in Ferndale. There will be people who know how to survive. She just has to keep going. Her anxiety ticks down just a little. She breathes deep breaths, like the counselor on the emergency mental-health line had taught her when she had postpartum anxiety after Clara's birth.

Irina had failed Clara. Her death had been Irina's fault. This reminder undoes any progress Irina's made with the panic attack.

She tries to remember what her therapist had taught her about decatastrophizing. But how do you decatastrophize, she wonders, when you're in the middle of the whole fucking catastrophe? Is there a worst case scenario that's worse than this one?

Breathe in, she reminds herself. Hold. Breathe out.

She releases Matteo and gives him an expired cereal bar. Then she pulls out her book, sits on the muddy ground, and begins reading. Her heartbeat slows as she whispers the words aloud to herself. She breathes in. She holds. She breathes out. Slowly, the panic recedes. She feeds Buddy his breakfast and gives Matteo some oatmeal. She considers changing her clothes, but the act of stripping down here in the open feels too vulnerable and dangerous, so she gets on her bike, rides back to the highway, and continues southwest toward Ferndale.

She rides the rest of the day without seeing the scenery. Despite Matteo's howls of protest, she takes few breaks. Eventually he falls asleep, tears drying on his face. That evening she stops at a rundown roadside motel. She kicks open the locked door and drags her bike inside, then barricades the door after her, pushing the entire bed up against it. She barely manages to get Matteo ready and change out of her filthy clothes before falling into nightmare-filled sleep.

The first thing she's aware of when she wakes the next morning is her own stench. She recalls the prior day with humiliation and anxiety as she does her best to clean up with a washcloth and bottle of water, then packs, feeds Matteo, loads up her companions, and pedals off down the road.

The picturesque mountain scenery is wasted on her. She barely eats and stops only for Matteo and Buddy to stretch their legs and have meals. That evening she reaches the coast, and she breathes in the sea air with relief. She's nearly there.

When the road approaches a wide river, she takes a side street down to a lodge along the river's banks. She kicks in the door of the lodge and starts a fire in the fireplace in its spacious living room. Then she gathers the courage to undress and bathe herself and Matteo in the chilly water. It's cold here on the coast, and she has to bring out all of the layers she's brought for him and her. She barricades the lodge door after them; then she burrows down with Matteo and Buddy under several musty blankets. Irina sleeps restlessly and keeps her gun close by.

The following morning as they pass under the boughs of the massive trees in Redwood National Park, it occurs to her that the trees and the rest of the natural world have outlasted the humans. South of the Redwood Forest, the road bends along the coast. The beaches here are dramatic, with huge rock formations just offshore and towering cliffs covered with spindly coastal pine trees.

She wakes early the next morning, sensing that hope is waiting for her close by. That afternoon, Irina sees a column of smoke from a house on a hill a few miles south of Eureka. She stays as far away from it as possible, pedaling quickly and glancing behind herself frequently. The day grows late, and she rides farther than she thought possible, propelled by the desire to arrive at the safety of Ferndale by nightfall.

There are no signs of life on the road into Ferndale. The ribbon of pavement stretches endlessly through fields of greenish-gold grass beneath the setting sun. The deep blue mountains in the distance never seem to get any closer, no matter how long she pedals. It's evening when several brightly-colored, well-maintained Victorian houses appear along the road and grow more numerous as she enters the town.

Suddenly an island of tidy normality appears among the overgrown yards: a library with clean classical architecture and a neatly maintained lawn. Irina gets off of her bike and approaches the entrance with Matteo and Buddy. On the door is a sign with the same handwriting as the folded paper in Irina's bag. It reads:

> *Welcome to Ferndale! Please make yourself comfortable. We will return on Monday/Thursday to meet you.*

Unease sinks into Irina. Aside from this strangely well-manicured library and a few feral cats, the town appears to be entirely deserted. Where is the community that she's seeking?

It's possible that the fliers directed people to the library for screening before they're shown the real town. That's certainly what Irina would do. It's Wednesday night, though, so she figures that she'll get answers soon enough. The door is unlocked, she's tired, and it's growing late. This seems as good a place to rest as any.

The library is small but tidy with large windows and wooden bookshelves. She lets Matteo explore, while she hauls her bike up the wheelchair ramp and through the side door. Then she barricades the side door with a bookshelf and locks the front door. They eat dinner, and Matteo falls asleep in her lap as she reads to him in the growing darkness. She settles him in his little sleeping bag, then turns on her lantern and reads her favorite book until her eyelids grow heavy. She marks her page and lets Buddy outside one final time. Then she falls quickly asleep.

Chapter Three

She wakes to the sound of voices outside. She stands quickly with her finger on the trigger of her gun. Beside her, Matteo stirs. Buddy's hackles go up, and he growls slightly as the lock turns, the library door opens, and a man steps inside. The man blinks when he sees the three of them.

He's handsome, but in an ordinary way—the sort of attractiveness that wouldn't strike a passerby on the street but that a person might notice on the second appraisal. He looks about Irina's age, but his shaggy straight dark brown hair is already graying at the temples and has started to recede slightly in the corners of his forehead. He's only two or three inches taller than Irina's five feet, five inches, with a build of lean muscle—the body of a man who does manual labor every day but with limited nourishment. He has broad shoulders, tanned skin several shades darker than Irina's, a neatly cropped beard, and high cheekbones that are all the more pronounced because of his thinness. His eyes are a striking dark olive green and rimmed with eyelashes that any woman would envy.

He holds nothing but two worn cloth tote bags. Irina starts to raise her gun anyway but stills when she sees a little girl peek out from behind him. The girl is probably five or six with awkwardly cropped bangs and the man's hazel eyes. She looks hesitant but curious, especially about Buddy.

Both of them look well-kempt as though both they and their clothes have been washed recently, and neither looks particularly malnourished—a stark contrast with Irina's gauntness and the obvious fact that she's wearing yesterday's clothes.

The man and Irina stare at each other as the dust motes dance around them in the morning sunlight. His eyes drift to Matteo standing beside her, clutching her leg, and Buddy, who cocks his head at the little girl. Then, finally, he speaks with an accent that's heavy and hard to place. "You found my sign."

Irina nods, feeling anxious and unsure of her decision to come here, remembering the man outside of Grants Pass, the stranger who shot at her, and the mysterious men in the electric vehicle. She knows nothing about this stranger or why he posted those signs inviting people here.

He offers her his hand without hesitation, and she's certain that he checked out from civilization very early in the Pandemic. "I'm Rafael. And this is my daughter, Miranda."

Irina does introductions and shakes his calloused hand, using her firmest, most lawyerly handshake to convey that she's formidable. He winces a bit at the strength of her grip.

"Pleased to meet you all," he says.

Good manners, Irina thinks, a year and a half after the fall of all known civilization.

"You, too," she replies. "Where is everyone? I haven't seen anyone else since I got here."

"Unfortunately, there's no one else yet. I left the fliers in a lot of places I passed through on my ride from Washington a few months ago. But so far, you're the only one who's shown up."

Disappointment fills her, but it's eclipsed by the unease that twists her stomach. She's alone with him—well, not quite alone, because the children are here, but they're hardly able to protect her if he's a threat. As though reading her mind, he steps back further, giving her more space.

"Where did you come from?" he asks.

"Bend, Oregon."

He looks quite taken aback by that. "That's 400 miles!"

"I have a bike. And a gun."

"And a guard dog," he smiles. While they've been talking, Miranda has edged forward, and Buddy has happily met her in the middle, where she enthusiastically gives him belly rubs as he squirms on his back before her. Matteo watches with curiosity.

"Doggy," he says, smiling. "Doggy, doggy."

"Are you hungry?" Rafael asks.

Irina is very hungry, but she's not sure what to make of him yet. He digs in his bag, and her hold on her gun tightens. Rafael pulls out a slightly bruised apricot and offers it to her.

She takes the apricot and bites into it. It's been years since she had a fresh apricot. The sweetness of its orange flesh instantly brings back the memory of the last time she ate one, during a picnic she and Sam had with Clara by the Willamette River, the year before Clara died. She recalls perfectly the quality of the light that day and the heaviness of the cooler she carried as they walked through the green grass. Her eyes well up at the recollection.

Rafael studies her. Matteo begins to fuss a little and reaches out for the apricot with one hand while hanging on her leg with the other. She lifts him up and offers it to him, and he takes a little bite.

"Thank you," she says softly.

"I've been working on clearing out some houses in town, if you want to stay here. You don't have to, though. I know you were probably expecting more people, and I was really hoping there would be more. I guess I should have come down I5 on the more populated side of the mountains and left my signs there."

"Then we wouldn't be here," Irina says. She takes another bite of the apricot, then offers it to Matteo again. "I guess we'll stay."

She knows that she has no other real options. She's exhausted, and her trip here was miserable and terrifying. She hates the idea of continuing to ride through unknown territory with no better destination.

"I'll show you the houses that I've cleared out, and you can pick whichever one you like."

"You live here in town, then?"

"No. My house is about six miles outside of town, along the coast. I only come here twice a week, mostly to keep clearing out the houses and see if anyone else has arrived."

"So I would be alone?" Even though she's skeptical of him, the prospect of being alone seems worse than the prospect of him as her neighbor.

"My home has a small guest house, if you want to stay there instead."

Her uncertainty must show on her face, because he adds, "It's totally separate from the house, and there's a lock on the door. You can bring your gun and your guard dog."

"Okay," she replies after a moment, without her mind ever really giving her mouth permission to accept his offer.

"I have a couple of things to do before I head home. If you want to check out the town, I can meet you after. I also have some more apricots if you're still hungry."

"I'd like to see the town. And another apricot would be great."

He digs in his bag and hands her two more. "If you walk south on Main Street, that's the nicest part of town. I'll find you in an hour or so."

She puts Matteo into the backpack and calls Buddy. As she steps out the door into the bright outside world, Irina sees Rafael pull out several books from his tote bag and begin carefully reshelving them with Miranda.

She follows the road south. The buildings are mostly authentic Victorians, lovingly maintained with colorful gingerbread accents and welcoming wraparound porches but overgrown gardens and lawns with knee-high grass.

Behind a curtain of foliage and a white picket fence, she catches a glimpse of a particularly glorious deep blue-and-red Victorian bed and breakfast. Next door is a small garden with a miniature, child-sized Victorian house, painted gray with vivid accents of yellow, orange, and baby blue. She enters the overgrown space through the gate. Native plants bloom brightly, their orange, purple, and yellow flowers contrasting with their green leaves. In the back of the garden is a small pond, now covered with algae, and a dried-up waterfall. Buddy sniffs the ground around the pond and is delighted when a few frogs hop out.

Irina releases Matteo from the backpack and sits on the ground with him, sharing a meager lunch. Only then does the full weight of her disappointment hit her. She came all this way, only to arrive here and find nothing. Well, not quite nothing—she found a man and his daughter—but not nearly the town she'd hoped for. She rubs her temples and considers her options again. She can leave, but there's no obvious place to go. If she returns to Bend or Salem, she'll face the same problems she'd fled. If she continues south to Sacramento or San Francisco, where the pre-Pandemic populations had been large enough for there to be at least a few survivors, she may encounter more dangerous strangers.

She could stay here in town. Having a neighbor six miles away would give her some security and companionship—assuming that he's trustworthy. Still, though, there's the problem of caring for Matteo alone, while doing what it takes to survive. If she lives in Rafael's guesthouse, they could pool resources and share tasks. He doesn't seem threatening or dangerous. He mostly just seems sad and tired—a state she can relate to. He's also been taking care of Miranda alone, so, like Irina, he would probably appreciate having another adult around to help. But can Irina trust him with Matteo? Is he responsible, kind, patient? He's managed to care for Miranda, but he's still a total stranger.

And Miranda . . . Irina isn't sure how she'll stand being around a girl who's about the same age Clara was at her death. After Clara died, Irina spent her days trying to avoid little girls. She stayed away from the park, the ice cream shop, and the children's museum. She rerouted her path to the grocery store, avoiding the preschools and elementary school. Finally, she took a leave of absence from her job, unable to stand even the children there. Could she really bear to watch another little girl grow up?

And yet, she can't overlook how difficult it is to care for Matteo on her own. Even now, he toddles dangerously close to the algae-filled pond. She gets up and pulls him back.

"We can't do this alone forever," she says, as he kicks and fights against her, trying to return to his adventure. She sets him on the ground, but he continues crying, even as he gets back up and walks toward the pond.

She looks longingly at the bed and breakfast next door, wishing she could curl up in one of its beds with him but knowing that if she did, he wouldn't sleep. Instead he would spend the time either crying because he wanted to be outside or looking for ways to injure himself.

He approaches the pond's edge, and she pulls him back again, feeling a surge of frustration. She straps him in the pack as he tries to wiggle out of her arms; then she hoists him onto her aching back and continues down the road as it transitions into an old fashioned main street with quaint shops on either side. She passes a salon, a bookstore, and even a millinery. A few windows are broken, but otherwise, it would be easy to pretend that she's strolling down the street on an ordinary Sunday morning, waiting for these shops to open.

She turns onto a side street and finds a glorious yellow-and-peach Victorian bed and breakfast a few blocks down. She shudders, though, when she realizes that there are a few pieces of a mostly skeletal human cadaver on the front porch. She supposes that someone had wanted to spend their final moments in the rocking chair and later been disassembled by the scavenging coyotes. Her thin illusion of normality shattered, she quickly turns back to the main street, where she sees Rafael biking toward her, his large trailer clattering behind him. Miranda rides beside him on a smaller bike. Irina is pleased to note that he's responsible enough to ensure that they both wear helmets, and she feels a little more hopeful about the possibility of trusting him with Matteo.

They all turn back toward the library. Rafael walks his bike beside Irina, with Buddy trotting beside them and Miranda riding her bike in circles around him.

"He's been with you the whole time?" Rafael asks, looking at Buddy.

"Yep. We got him for my daughter a few years before the Pandemic started."

If Rafael notices that she mentioned a daughter who's no longer here, he chooses not to comment. Irina is used to that, but isn't sure whether to be bothered by it or not. On one hand, she hates bringing down the conversation by acknowledging that children die, but on the other, sometimes it infuriates her that other people can't bear to even talk about what she has to live with every day.

It occurs to her belatedly that the Pandemic has likely universalized the once exceedingly rare experience of losing a child. After the Pandemic, it's probably more unusual to have not lost a child. In all likelihood, Rafael has also lost a child.

"Miranda has wanted a dog for years," Rafael says, interrupting her thoughts. "We've seen some feral cats, but Buddy is the first dog we've seen since the Pandemic started."

"I guess most of the dogs got trapped in the houses with people who died, and even those who got outside probably couldn't really take care of themselves," Irina keeps her voice down so Miranda doesn't hear her.

"We had lots of feral dogs in Venezuela, but even they relied on human trash to survive."

"You grew up in Venezuela?"

"I left in my 20s, just before the Covid pandemic."

"Why did you leave?"

"Things got really bad there. We couldn't get basic necessities—medications, building materials, even food. Inflation was out of control; our currency was worth less every day. Everything was a struggle. My best friend got arrested by the government for supposedly having some ties to someone who was accused of trying to organize a coup. The government detained him for months, tortured him, harassed his family. When he got out he wasn't the same man. I knew I couldn't stay there. I met my wife, Helena, when she was visiting her Venezuelan grandmother for the summer. That fall, we got engaged and because she was an American citizen, I got to move here."

"Did you lose her in the Pandemic?"

Rafael is quiet for a moment, and Irina is afraid she's upset him. Finally he answers, "She died in the Pandemic. But our marriage was complicated, so I think I probably lost her earlier."

Irina isn't certain how to reply to that statement because they don't know each other well enough for her to feel comfortable asking follow-up questions, so there's a brief lull in the conversation until he looks at the ring she still wears and asks, "And did you lose your daughter and husband in the Pandemic?"

Irina feels a strange, irrational gratitude that he remembered her mention of a daughter.

"My husband got the Virus, but I lost my daughter, Clara, in an accident before the Pandemic."

"I'm sorry," he says, pausing to look at her. "I've lost a lot of people, but I imagine it would be even worse to lose a child."

"It was awful. I keep hoping that it will get better over time, but it's still awful. Matteo helps, though. Clara was our only child, and when I lost her, I felt like I lost everything. Now at least I get to be a mother again."

"Matteo was born during the Pandemic?"

"Yeah. That was irresponsible, wasn't it?"

"I think we do what we need to do to survive. You needed him."

She's amazed to be talking to a relative stranger about this. After Clara's death, Irina's grief was so all-encompassing that it filled any room she was in. Her acquaintances avoided her altogether, and even some of her friends and family couldn't bear to be around her for long.

Only Sam, Kylee, her Aunt Hannah, and a few others had really showed up the way she needed them to.

They both lapse into silence as they walk past the last of the storefronts. "This is a beautiful town," Irina says. "How did you end up here?"

"I came here with my wife a decade ago. When I decided to move south, this seemed like a good option because the soil is fertile and the weather is mild all year round. No need for air conditioning and no threat of blizzards."

"Everything here still looks so normal. A lot of the stores in Bend were looted."

"Some were here, too. But this was a small town, with a lot fewer people. I've been careful not to break any windows or door knobs when I have to get into the buildings, since I don't think we'll be able to get replacements." He pauses as though gathering courage to say something important. "I really am hoping to rebuild this town, to grow a sustainable community here."

Irina isn't sure what to say in response to his optimism, but she's spared the need to reply because they arrive at the library. She brings out her bike and loads Matteo into the bike seat as he howls in protest. Rafael pinches Matteo's toes playfully and makes a funny face to distract him from his brewing temper tantrum. Irina is grateful when it works, then a bit annoyed that she didn't think of it herself.

Buddy hops into the crowded bike trailer, and Irina follows Rafael and Miranda down the road, south out of town. Houses fade into agricultural fields already choked with weeds and wildflowers. A few miles down the road, though, they pass by a small cultivated field of vegetables growing in neat rows. Beside the field is a beige clapboard Victorian house with a sign that reads "Fern Cottage," and behind that, a small orchard. For a moment, Irina thinks this is his house, but they keep riding, following the road toward the ocean. They pass by a wide expanse of beach marked by a sign that says "Centerville Beach" and a large, white concrete cross—some kind of memorial to people long forgotten, Irina assumes. Then their road becomes a bit washed out as it turns south along the coast and into the hills, which glow emerald green in the early summer sun. Pulling the bike trailer up the hills is a strain, but the view makes it worth it.

Irina shivers at the blue infinity of the Pacific Ocean spread out before her. She sees a long stretch of beach and hears the faint crashing of the waves on the shore. A little further along, the road winds down between the hills of verdant grass, and she loses sight of the ocean.

Miranda grows tired and walks her bike. Rafael walks beside her to keep her company. Irina joins them, pushing her heavy-laden bike.

They pass by several pastures pockmarked with the hulking skeletons of cattle that had been penned in and unable to get water. The wasteful futility of their deaths in the face of her own frequent hunger skewers Irina. Rafael sees her looking and says, "I saw some cows in the fields south of here and a couple of horses in a pasture along the river. I wasn't sure how to approach them by myself, but now that you're here, maybe we can work on that together."

The thought warms Irina and not just because having a horse would mean a lot less time pulling a heavy bike trailer.

"I grew up around cattle and horses," she says. "My mother's family had a ranch in Utah. I lived there for a while."

"I've never visited, but I hear that Utah is beautiful," he replies.

"It is. My grandparents' ranch was in southwest Utah, in a place that had pink rock mountains and slot canyons. I loved the desert—the sudden rainstorms, the smell of the sagebrush and juniper, the big skies, the way that the landscape can change completely in ten or twenty miles," she says wistfully. "Whenever I felt sad or lonely, walking in the desert made me feel better."

It occurs to her for the first time that maybe she'd fled to Bend because she was looking for something that had brought her comfort before.

After a while, the forest opens suddenly into rolling grasslands and a view of the sea. Rafael follows a gravel drive up the hill to their left. At the top of the driveway is a large, modern house with three stories of terraces and a wall of windows facing the ocean. There are so many windows that Irina can actually see through the house to the hills on the other side.

"This is your house?!" Irina asks.

"My dream house in my nightmare world," Rafael responds with a sigh. "There's no one here anymore. We may as well live in architectural marvels while they're still standing."

To the right of the house, Irina sees a separate structure, which seems to also be constructed almost entirely of windows. "I guess the people who lived here didn't believe in privacy."

"The guest house had shades, but they were the fancy electric kind that were controlled by a remote, so we'll need to figure something else out. It does have locks, though, as previously discussed," he says with a wry smile.

The gravel driveway ends at a garage with frosted-glass doors. They park the bikes, and Irina releases Buddy, who immediately begins playing with Miranda. Matteo, who has fallen asleep during their ride, wakes and begins wailing. Irina is grateful when his cries turn to whimpers, then giggles as he sees Miranda chasing Buddy.

Irina follows Rafael up onto the front patio, carrying Matteo with her. The three of them sit in the chairs, watching Miranda and Buddy race around the yard. It occurs to Irina that Buddy likes Miranda because he remembers being loved by a little girl. The thought makes her sad. She's never considered that Buddy might also be mourning.

Irina notices a large stone firepit and stack of firewood.

"I like to have a glass of wine and a fire out here in the evenings," Rafael says, following her gaze.

"That sounds luxurious," Irina replies.

"I think it's important to appreciate the little things we have left," he remarks with a serious, almost wistful, tone. "I think we need to try for something more than just survival."

"I can't imagine being happy again," Irina says, shocked at her own candor.

Rafael is quiet for a moment, pondering that. "Neither can I, but I can imagine them being happy." He looks at Miranda laughing with Buddy and Matteo giggling at the two of them.

"How long have you been taking care of Miranda by yourself?"

"Since the very beginning of the Pandemic. Helena, Miranda, and I were taking a week-long vacation at our cabin that June. That Wednesday, Helena got called back to the hospital where she worked. She came back the next day and told us to stay at the cabin for the foreseeable future. I guess she'd seen enough of the Virus to be really scared. For a while she brought us things—food, medicine, gasoline for the generator, even chickens—until she couldn't anymore. I guess she died at the hospital, probably working until the end to try to save anyone she could."

"I'm sorry," Irina says. "It's so hard to take care of a child while grieving."

"It really, really is."

"How did you survive the winter? Can you hunt?"

"I can fish, but I'm a terrible hunter. I tried hunting with a friend years ago, but when the time came to actually shoot the deer, my aim was terrible. My friend, Jose, said that I was 'insufficiently committed to killing.' That observation would later prove prescient, but Rafael isn't in the mood to tell that story right now, so he says, "It was the chickens that saved us. We brought three of them along to Ferndale, actually."

"You carried chickens with you all the way from Washington?"

"I did, in a bike trailer, and I had another trailer with food and camping supplies behind that."

"That's a lot to pull!"

"I had Miranda helping on a tandem bike."

"I can't believe she rode all that way!"

"I wouldn't say she did it happily. There was a lot of whining and a lot of questions about how far we still had to go."

"But you got here."

He smiles. "We did, and now we have even more chickens—two hens plus a whole new brood of chicks and the old rooster. We have eggs and arepas for breakfast every day."

Irina feels a surge of warm familiarity, "My grandmother used to make me arepas."

"Your grandmother was Venezuelan?!" he asks.

"No, she was Colombian. My grandfather was a member of the Latter Day Saints church, and they met when he was on his mission. It was a bit romantic and scandalous, apparently."

"Well, Venezuelan arepas are a little bit different. Better, I think," he smiles.

"I suspect my grandmother would disagree," Irina smiles, thinking of the woman who helped raise her.

Miranda asks for water, and they pause the conversation to go inside. Irina hesitates at the door, unsure of what to do with Buddy, but Rafael calls him in. The front door opens into a bright living room with walls of windows facing the ocean on one side and the hills on the other. In the back of the room is a glass-floored staircase that leads to the open second story and then the third and down to the basement. Upstairs, Irina can see two levels of glass-railing balconies overlooking the living room. On one end of the room is a short hallway with three doors, and on the other is an open-concept, modern kitchen with gleaming, useless appliances and a large glass and chrome table with eight chairs.

The living room is stylishly decorated, with pale wood floors, white walls, and black-and-chrome modern minimalist furniture arranged around a white-stone wood-burning fireplace. On the walls and tables, pieces of art offer bright pops of color.

Buddy makes himself at home on a rug in front of the fireplace, while Rafael pours water from a glass pitcher for everyone. The house doesn't look very childproof, so Irina isn't sure if she should put Matteo down. Rafael seems to sense her dilemma, because he starts clearing breakables off the tables and placing them in the middle of the counter.

"I'll look for some baby-proofing things next time I'm in town," he says, surveying the living room. "There are a lot of sharp edges here."

For a moment they stand, sipping their water, uncertain of each other. Then he offers to give her a tour.

He starts walking up the stairs and gestures for her to follow him. She hesitates for a moment, her old wariness kicking in, but then follows, still carrying Matteo with her. At the second floor Rafael turns down a hallway and opens a door to a bathroom. Irina hangs back, unsure of his intentions. He moves away from the door and farther down the hall so she can look inside.

"It's a bathroom?" she says, confused.

"With a hot shower," he replies.

"How!?" she exclaims.

"I was inspired by the Mexican tinaco. I hoisted one of this house's rain barrels up onto the roof. I pump the hot water to the barrel; then gravity creates the water pressure for the shower."

"But where do you get the hot water?"

"This house, like a lot of houses on the Lost Coast, has a well. I use a hand pump to pump the well water to the basement; then I connect a separate hose with a foot pump to pump the water through some metal coils over the fire pit and up to the barrel. It takes twenty minutes to pump the water; then

47

you have to give it another thirteen minutes to reach the perfect temperature."

"That's brilliant . . . and also very precise. Were you an engineer?"

"I was trained in engineering in Venezuela."

Irina assesses him anew. "Well, you may not be able to hunt, but you have other useful survival skills."

"I can garden, too. You probably saw my garden when we were on our way out of town."

"By the Fern Cottage?"

"Yep. I learned some useful skills while working in landscaping. I've got a garden here too, but the soil's better in the valley."

They retrace their steps downstairs, and he shows her the water pump. "I haven't been able to set up anything similar in the guest house yet, but you're always welcome to come over and get water."

"This is great," Irina says.

"Thanks," Rafael replies. "I hope that you'll be comfortable here."

Their eyes meet for a moment, and she sees something hopeful and fearful in his hazel eyes, something she recognizes well: loneliness.

"You must be tired. I'll show you the guest house," he says. "And I can carry Matteo if you want a break."

Irina initially wants to say no, but something about Rafael puts her at ease, so she hands Matteo over to him. Matteo looks at him curiously, reaching for his face and hair.

"Hi, Matteo," Rafael smiles.

"Ha," Matteo says. "Ha, ha."

The guest house is a smaller version of the modern minimalist ambiance of the main house. There's a bedroom, bathroom, and living room with a fireplace. Rafael helps her carry her bags inside; then he brings her a folded playpen, a jug of water, and a bag of apricots. He sets up the playpen as she watches Matteo.

"I've got a warehouse of goods downtown. As I've cleared out the houses, I've moved useful things there, so if more people do arrive, they'll be able to pick up whatever they need. If there's anything you want, let me know."

"Thank you," she says, "for everything."

"You're welcome. If you need anything else, you know where to find me. And if you want, you can join us for dinner on the back patio later."

He departs, and Irina lies down for a nap with Matteo and Buddy.

+++

After he leaves the guesthouse, Rafael's thoughts continually return to his new neighbor. After two months of checking the library, he'd pretty much given up hope. Once he settled in Ferndale, he realized that it's a long way from anywhere, located in a place that's literally called "The Lost Coast," making it unlikely that anyone would ever make their way to the town.

To find that someone had made that journey is shocking. For it to be a woman about his age is a stroke of amazing luck. Rafael likes Irina's firm handshake and the inquisitive way she observes everything around her. For her to have survived this long on her own shows an admirable amount of fortitude and intelligence. Despite her gauntness and her dirty clothes, he can also tell that Irina is attractive, striking even, with her large dark eyes, dusting of freckles, and long auburn hair.

He's quick to remind himself, though, that she already seems uncomfortable around him, and he has too much at stake to do anything that would make her think he's interested in something more than peaceful and mutually beneficial cohabitation. Irina represents hope for a hundred things that Rafael has longed for—someone with whom he can have an intellectual conversation, someone to help share the burden of the chores necessary to survive in this strange new world, someone to help with Miranda, someone with a complimentary skillset, someone to help keep him sane.

Still, there's only so much a man can do to keep his thoughts in check after several years of celibacy. He reminds himself, though, that this fact alone might cloud his thinking about her. Perhaps it isn't even her, specifically, who interests him. Nearly any woman would attract his attention.

He senses Irina is complicated too—that she has some deeper trauma, even beyond the Pandemic and the loss of her husband and daughter. He has no idea what she's survived or how, but he's noticed her fear of him. Given their isolation, any romantic or even ambiguous overtures on his part would be coercive. So Rafael resolves to keep his thoughts and actions firmly in check. He doesn't need a romantic attachment—he'd never been very good at those anyway—he needs a friend.

He spends the rest of the afternoon watering and weeding the garden, tossing a football with Miranda, and canning apricots, while vegetable soup cooks over the fire. As Rafael lines the jars of apricots on the counter, he looks at them gleaming in the afternoon sun with something approaching satisfaction. This winter will be easier than the last.

The sun is slouching lower toward the sea, when he sets out four bowls and spoons hopefully. He calls for Miranda, and she comes bounding to him, exclaiming something about a bird's nest she'd found in a bush near the house. Her resilience always impresses him. There are days when she's sad or moody, evenings when she wants to look at the few printed pictures of her mother they brought from their cabin, nights when she still has nightmares, but mostly she's happy.

They've almost finished their bowls of soup, when he hears Matteo crying in the guest house. He resists the urge to get up and offer assistance, reminding himself that though he's desperate for company, Irina may want some space. He and Miranda finish their second helpings and agree to go to the beach.

He leaves the pot over the fire and the two bowls and spoons on the table. Then he and Miranda lure the chickens into their coop and gather what they need for the hike. Rafael places a note under one of the bowls on the table. As he leaves, he glances back once more at the guesthouse. He doesn't hear Matteo crying anymore, but he also doesn't see any movement inside.

The trail to the beach is just across the road. Miranda carefully balances on the rocky parts, taking his hand several times as she picks her way over the places where the path has eroded away. The tide is going out, and the wet beach and the surrounding cliffs gleam in the evening light. The course of the stream that meets the sea has changed again since they last visited just a few days ago. It traces a delicate curve through the dark gray sand. Rafael sits and watches Miranda silhouetted against the setting sun as she runs down to the surf, searching for pebbles.

He's grateful for this second chance with her for every day they get to spend together here at the end of the world. He wonders, though, what kind of life is left for her. What if purgatory is the only thing he's saved her for? He sighs. He needs to find some way to bring more people here.

Eventually he gets up and joins her to search for stones in the receding surf. As the sun approaches the horizon, they splash in the cool stream, then sit down on the beach together to watch the sun set.

"I wish Mommy was here," Miranda says. Rafael always feels badly when this topic of conversation comes up. His feelings about Helena are far more complicated than Miranda's are.

"I know," he replies, putting his arm around her. They sit quietly for a while, before turning on their flashlights and heading back up the path. When they arrive at the house, Irina is on the living room couch wrapped in a blanket, looking out the windows at the dark ocean with Buddy curled at her feet.

"Thank you for the soup," she says as they walk in the front door.

"You're welcome," he says. "I'm going to put Miranda to bed; then I'll get a bottle of wine and meet you out on the patio?"

"That sounds lovely."

Inside, by candlelight, he helps Miranda through her usual nighttime routine, then retrieves a bottle of wine from the basement. Irina is drying the clean dishes and pots by candlelight in the kitchen, when he returns to get the wine glasses, and she helps him carry candles and blankets out to the patio, where they seat themselves comfortably in the chairs, and Buddy takes his place at Irina's feet. Rafael pours a glass of wine for each of them.

Wordlessly, she blows out the candles, leaving them in total darkness. He's surprised, but says nothing. Above them, the stars blaze bright without the interruption of civilization.

"I haven't seen stars like this since I camped with my grandfather in Utah," she says.

"You never go out at night?"

"Not since I've been alone."

"You're afraid of the dark?" he asks.

"It's silly, right?" she replies.

"Not silly, just . . . surprising."

"That I've survived alone this long and I'm still afraid?"

"I guess, yeah. How did you survive?" he asks.

"I'm a good hunter," she smiles, "My grandfather taught me while I was living on the ranch. I also had a good stockpile of seeds, canned food, and MREs. My mother-in-law was a virologist, and she persuaded Sam that we should isolate and buy a bunch of things early in the Pandemic, before the shortages and the store closings, back when you could still buy things online and have them delivered. She knew enough about the Virus to tell us how to avoid it—to have everything delivered into our garage, then not to touch anything for three weeks. I thought she and Sam were crazy. They were right . . . , but it didn't save them. She died of cancer because there were no more treatments available, and Sam died from the Virus."

"How did he get sick and you didn't?"

"He didn't get sick until very late," she says. Maybe it's something about Rafael, or maybe it's the wine or the darkness, but she's suddenly ready to tell the story that she hasn't even allowed herself to recall. "I got a really bad infection after Matteo's birth that January. Sam went to the store to get antibiotics, and he made a mistake and touched his face. I didn't think he would get sick—there was almost no one left at that point—but he wanted to take all the precautions. He moved into the neighbor's house."

Irina remembers that week vividly. They would each stand in their respective kitchen windows, facing each other from different houses, holding up the same reused signs to each other: she held up "I love you," and he held up "I love you." She held up "How are you feeling?" and he held up "Fine," until seven days later, when he didn't. He simply shook his head, and she began to sob, holding Matteo to her chest.

"He did get sick. The last time I saw him . . . ," the tears make her voice catch, "he was in the backyard, digging his own grave. I guess he didn't want me to have to do it."

That morning, she'd woken up to the ever-present sound of winter rain and the new sound of a shovel hitting dirt in the yard. From her window she could see Sam standing in the downpour, digging a large hole. He stopped every few minutes to rest, rain running down his face, his chest heaving. He looked cold and sick and haggard. It took her a surprising amount of time to realize what he was doing. He finished the hole that evening, and he set up a small, two-person tent beside it in the drizzling rain. When he saw her at the window, he held up an envelope damp from the rain. He walked over and put it into the mailbox in front of their house. Then he stepped out of the rain and into the tent, and she never saw him again.

Several days later, she smelled the now-familiar stench of death. She'd waited several weeks, then pulled the whole tent into the hole, and covered it as best she could.

"That was just the sort of person he was," Irina says, her voice shaking. "He was so damn thoughtful. He was a wonderful dad and a great husband. He was patient. Affectionate. Kind. He left me a letter, but I've never read it." The envelope still waits, wrinkled and worn, tucked into her favorite page of her favorite book.

"Why not?" Rafael asks, his voice warm in the chilly darkness.

"I remember reading somewhere that 'marriage is a long conversation.' That letter is the last thing that Sam will ever say to me, and I guess I'm just not ready for our conversation to end." She pulls the blanket more tightly around herself as the damp cold of the coastal night sets in.

She draws a deep breath and looks up at the stars. "I can't help thinking that if I hadn't gotten sick after Matteo's delivery, Sam would still be here."

"That's not your fault."

"I guess. I just wish it had been him who survived instead of me." She takes a shaky breath, then asks, "Do you ever wish that you hadn't survived?"

"Well, I sometimes wished I was dead before the Pandemic, and I can't say that the first year of the Pandemic improved my mindset. Lately, though, I honestly haven't thought about it. I wouldn't say I'm happy. Just resigned, I guess. Maybe even content sometimes."

"You weren't happy before the Pandemic?"

"I'd just finished my engineering degree when I left Venezuela. When I arrived here, no one had heard of my college. I couldn't find a job anywhere. I figured that I'd go back to school to redo my degree here, but Covid shut everything down, and the only work I could get was outdoor work as a landscaper. After a few years, I finally got into a college program and was going to start taking classes. But then Helena got pregnant. With her career it didn't make sense for me to keep going to school after we had a baby. I was furious that my life wasn't what I hoped. I felt like people didn't respect me; they assumed that I was uneducated. I worked so hard to get my degree, but they looked at me and just saw a gardener. I know now that it really shouldn't matter, but it sure as hell mattered to me then."

"It's so hard to start over," Irina says softly.

"It really, really is," Rafael agrees for the second time that day, sensing that they understand each other.

They sit in silence for a while, looking at the Milky Way above them. The fingernail moon that rises past the roof of the house does little to diminish the glory of the sky. In this darkness, Irina can even detect color in the stars—red, white, yellow.

"This is how people used to see the stars," she says.

"It's not surprising that ancient people believed in magic and gods and spirits," Rafael says. "It's easy to encounter the numinous under a night sky like this."

"Your English is extraordinarily good for someone who grew up speaking a different language," Irina remarks, only wondering afterward if the statement was a rude assumption.

"I went to a fancy English-language boarding school, where I read a lot of books," he says, apparently unbothered by her comment. "My accent always gives me away, though."

Irina likes his accent, but she doesn't say so, fearing that it will seem inappropriate. She considers the shape of him in the near darkness. Something about him makes him easy to talk to. Perhaps it's his willingness to disclose details about himself or the way he anticipates her needs. She figures that his thoughtfulness is the product of spending two years rearing a child on his own. So much of parenting is recognizing unarticulated needs. Whatever it is about him, she likes it. She'd been disappointed that afternoon when she'd finally wrestled Matteo into a fresh diaper and found that Rafael and Miranda had already left. And she felt a spark of something— pleasure? excitement?—when she saw him and Miranda returning to the house, their flashlights bobbing in the darkness. She realized that she was looking forward to seeing him again.

He is attractive and disarmingly kind. She stops that line of thinking, though, running her thumb over the gold band on her left ring finger. It isn't Rafael, she thinks; it's just that she misses the usually easy companionship of her marriage. She's almost forgotten what it's like to be touched in anything other than Matteo's needy, baby way of grasping her, but to even think of another man touching her feels like betrayal. She summons up a picture of Sam—his lopsided smile and hair that always stuck out awkwardly on the sides—and it easily dispels these ambiguous feelings she has about Rafael. Sam is still her husband. Their conversation isn't over.

"I should get to bed," she says, standing, folding the blanket over her arm, and picking up her wine glass.

"Me too," he agrees, also standing and taking his glass. They walk into the house together, and she moves to wash her glass in the sink that's filled with soapy water, but he reaches for it and says, "I'll get it. You should get some sleep."

As he takes the glass, his fingers brush hers, and she thinks that she sees his eyebrow furrow in the candlelight. The light is dim, though, and she can't be sure that she saw any reaction at all. Her pulse flutters, and she's frustrated at her body's seemingly automatic reaction to the proximity of this man.

"Goodnight," she says and quickly flees back to the safety of the guesthouse, with Buddy on her heels, locking the door behind her.

Rafael looks after her as the door closes, annoyed with himself for making her uneasy. He hadn't meant to react when their fingers touched, but something in his face must have revealed his surprise at the pleasure of even such a slight touch. He reminds himself again what's at stake, and he resolves to do better tomorrow, to give her no reason to suspect that he would ever desire anything more than friendship from her, to find some way to keep his disobedient body in check.

He washes the glasses, brushes his teeth, and falls into bed without even changing into pajamas.

Chapter Four

When she wakes the next morning, Irina is surprised to find herself in the highest thread count sheets she's ever experienced. Matteo still sleeps soundly in the playpen, so she quietly slips out from under the sheets and tiptoes into the living room. The world outside her windows is obscured by fog, as though the guesthouse is ensconced in a cloud. It drifts past, giving her occasional glimpses of the main house, the emerald hills, and the blue sea.

In the bathroom she scrutinizes her reflection in the mirror and sighs. She could use a shower. She feeds Buddy; then he follows her as she slips out the door of the guesthouse into the chilly morning. She props the door open with a rock so she can hear Matteo when he wakes. Rafael has a kettle and two pans on the grate above the fire, one with arepas and the other with eggs. Her mouth waters at the prospect of an actual breakfast. She hears the door slam as he comes outside precariously holding a French press and two coffee mugs. They greet each other as he sets the items down on the table.

With a thick oven mitt, he retrieves the kettle from over the fire and pours the steaming water into the French press. Everything about this feels so normal that she can almost believe she's a guest here at his home on an ordinary weekend morning. She offers help, but he declines, so she sits down at the table. The smell of the coffee tempts her to pour it too early.

"Miranda's still asleep, but we can have breakfast." He moves the skillet with the eggs off the fire and places it on a folded towel on the table. Buddy sniffs at a cooler a few feet away from the table. Irina gets up to inspect it and is surprised to find several sizable fish inside.

"Lunch," Rafael says, gesturing to them.

"You already went fishing?" Irina asks, sitting back down at the table and pouring the steaming coffee into the mugs. She takes a blissful sip. After two years, it's very stale, but she doesn't care.

"I usually get up at sunrise," he answers, shrugging. He picks up the pan and drops the two arepas onto a plate, quickly slices each one with a plastic knife, then slips the eggs inside the sliced arepas, making a sandwich. He hands one to her and takes a bite from the other as he sits down at the table.

"What can I help with today?" she asks.

"I was thinking of expanding the garden since there are more of us to feed. We also need some more firewood." He gestures to a small stack beside the house. "You can take your pick of chores."

"I'll do the garden," Irina says, figuring that task will be easier to manage with Matteo. She can put him in the playpen while she works.

"Sounds good. The tools are in the garage. I was thinking of expanding it by about ten feet, but you don't have to do it all today."

They lapse into silence as they finish their arepas and coffee. The fog starts to clear a little, and the ocean comes into view.

"Can I take a shower during Matteo's nap?"

"Of course!"

Matteo cries inside the guesthouse, and Irina goes to retrieve him, while Rafael begins making arepas for Miranda and Matteo.

When Irina emerges from the guesthouse with Matteo in her arms, Miranda is already dressed and sitting at the table. Irina holds Matteo as he eats his arepa messily. Buddy happily waits for bits of food to rain down around him. By the time they've finished breakfast, the fog has cleared, and the sun is out. Irina moves to take the dirty pans inside, but Rafael stops her.

"Miranda takes care of the dishes," he says. The little girl is already gathering the now cool pans and utensils and carrying them into the house. Irina sets Matteo down on the patio so he can explore. Rafael lifts the French press to offer her more coffee, and she accepts. He fills her cup, then pours the last bit in his cup.

"She's well-trained," Irina observes, watching Miranda.

"That's all Helena. She read a book about how kids should learn to do chores when they're still little, even if they do them badly. She had Miranda helping with her own laundry when she was three. She's broken a few dishes, but there are plenty of dishes left in the world, so I think we'll be fine."

Irina wishes that Helena was here with them. It would be nice to have the companionship of another woman.

"Helena was a good mother," he says, and she hears the sadness in his voice. She has a strong intuition that, like her, Rafael doubts his parenting abilities. It's just a guess, so she says nothing, though some part of her, instinctively, wants to reassure him that he's doing great, especially considering the circumstances.

"It's nice that Miranda can help," she says, sipping her coffee.

"It is," he agrees. "She's able to do basic chores, and she typically listens when I tell her not to do something. I can't imagine how hard it's been for you with a baby."

"It felt impossible. That's why I came here, to be honest."

He nods in understanding. "Even in ordinary times, the first three years are pure survival mode. I don't know how you did it."

"I lived on canned food, wine, and desperation." She isn't really joking, but he chuckles. She considers what he's building here, a clear contrast to her bare, temporary existence in Bend. She lacks Rafael's sense of future, she realizes. She never thinks in the future tense, only present tense and, in her weaker moments, past tense. The future is too large and uncertain, the past too painful, and the present too insistent.

"I should get started on the garden," she says, finishing her coffee and rising from her chair. He watches Matteo, while she gets the playpen and a few toys, then fetches the tools from the garage. Miranda finishes the dishes, and she and Rafael depart on their bikes to find firewood.

Irina cuts the grass near the garden with a manual mower. Then she puts on gloves and begins to hoe out the ground. Within five minutes she's exhausted and, despite the chill of the morning, covered in sweat. Her arms ache from the reverberations of the hoe against the ground. Still, she carries on, eventually falling into a rhythm, pausing to drink from the water bottle that Rafael had thoughtfully left out for her. Matteo babbles happily as he watches her through the mesh side of the playpen. Irina doesn't stop hoeing until her arms are numb. She sits down for a break and realizes that Matteo has fallen asleep. She's alone. The wind moves through the grass; then it stills, and the world around her is silent. Familiar loneliness drives her back to her task.

She looks down the hill and sees Rafael and Miranda returning with a trailer full of firewood. They walk around the side of the house, each carrying an armful, Miranda with small kindling-sized pieces and Rafael with larger ones.

Rafael stops and shakes his head when he catches sight of the garden. Irina pauses, wiping the sweat from her brow. For a moment she thinks he's displeased.

"Good job," he says, finally. He and Miranda stack the logs on the woodpile; then he leaves Miranda behind to help Irina in the garden, while he picks up more firewood. Miranda breaks up dirt clods, while Irina continues to hoe out several more feet of ground. When Matteo wakes up, Miranda plays with him on the patio. Irina pours water for herself, Miranda, and Matteo;

then she sits on the ground with them, rolling a ball back and forth.

Miranda tries to get Matteo to say her name. "MEE-RAN-DA," she repeats, several times.

"Man-da," Matteo parrots back.

"Yes, I'm MEE-RAN-DA!" she says again, as Rafael rounds the corner with an armful of firewood. She points at him. "And that's my daddy."

"Dada," Matteo parrots, and Miranda lets out a shriek of laughter at his misunderstanding, so he giggles and says it again. "Dada."

Irina feels a lance of sadness pierce her at the reminder that Matteo will never call Sam "dada." She tries to correct him, to get him to say Rafael's name, but it's no use. Now that Miranda is laughing, Matteo is just repeating "dada" over and over again gleefully, basking in the warmth of her attention. Rafael finishes stacking the wood and joins them.

"Dada," Matteo says, looking at him. Miranda laughs. Irina flushes with embarrassment at the misunderstanding.

"Sorry," she says, but Rafael just shrugs, returning to the bike trailer to unload more of the firewood and leaving Irina to contemplate the strangeness of their situation. It should be Sam that Matteo is calling "dada," Sam that she's working to rebuild with. Instead, she's going to live with a complete stranger, share a household, care for their children together.

She thinks about this as Rafael cleans and cooks the fish, and they all eat lunch together. She's quiet, replying when he talks to her, but not going out of her way to make conversation. Miranda fills in the lulls with rambling stories about their time in the cabin. She excitedly brings her rock collection outside for Irina's inspection. Irina holds Matteo back as he squirms and reaches out, trying to put the rocks in his mouth.

While Miranda clears and washes the dishes, Irina and Rafael sit at the table watching Matteo play on the patio.

"You got a lot done," he says, surveying the garden. "More than I expected, to be honest."

"What did you expect?" she asks. A challenge.

"Well, I probably would have taken a very long break after I finished about half of that amount. Then I would have switched to an easier task and started tilling again tomorrow morning. Tilling is hard work. How are your hands?"

She holds them up. Despite wearing gloves, her palms are raw. He grimaces.

"Just to be clear," he says, "you really didn't have to do that. You don't have to break your back here. I don't expect it."

"I want to do my share." She doesn't want to be beholden to him or give him any power over her.

He studies her for a moment. Again, he surprises her by reading her mind. "You don't owe me for staying here. I'm just glad to have any help. Really."

She meets his eyes, and for a moment they are both still.

"We really should check out those horses you said you saw," she replies finally. "Tilling a garden would be a lot easier with a horse and plow."

+++

While Matteo naps, Irina takes the first shower she's had in a year and a half. She makes sure the bathroom door is locked, then slips out of her clothes. She scrutinizes herself in the mirror—the now loose skin of her stomach, the breasts flattened by motherhood and malnutrition, the tattoo over her heart. She steps away with a sigh and turns on the shower. The water pressure isn't great, but the temperature is perfect, and the sensation is so pleasant that she sighs. She opens an expensive-looking shampoo from the tiled shelf in the shower

63

and sniffs it, trying very hard not to think about the fate of the woman it had belonged to. It smells of a complex and intoxicating blend of roses and spices. She washes her hair, then uses a matching body wash to scrub away all the grime and sweat from tilling the garden. This simple act, which she had taken for granted every single day of her Before life, now seems like a luxurious miracle.

When she emerges, she feels almost human. She combs her hair, then dresses, and goes back downstairs. Rafael has finished tilling the garden and sits at the table, watching Miranda play with Buddy. Irina retrieves her bags of seeds from inside the guesthouse and sits down beside him.

He sorts through them, impressed with the selection and her careful handwritten instructions on each packet. He notices that she even has several varieties of annual flowers. Irina has maintained these seeds lovingly, knowing that any varieties she loses are likely lost to her forever, now that most commercial seeds are expired.

"Nearly all of these will work here," Rafael says. "But some might require warmer weather to germinate. We can experiment with indoor growing, though. On the top floor there's a room that has lots of windows and a fireplace. Maybe we can set up some pots and rotate them around the room to follow the sun."

"That's a good idea. I also have some wheat that we can plant in the fall, and I know how to harvest and process it." Irina is excited to have something useful to contribute. She'd spent time researching this at the beginning of the Pandemic, before the internet died.

"Great! I don't know anything about growing wheat. We can start planting the vegetables now, if you want." He calls Miranda over, and the three of them begin sowing and labeling neat rows of seeds in the newly tilled garden. Afterward, Rafael hooks a hose up to the rainwater cistern and pumps the water, while Miranda and Irina water the garden. He watches them working together and feels hopeful in a way he hasn't felt in years. It's good for Miranda to have a woman around, and it's a welcome change to have someone else who can help him bear the weight of survival.

+++

That evening after dinner they all sit in the front yard as the sun sets over the sea. Irina wrestles with Matteo in the grass, holding him upside down as he laughs. Rafael sits at the table beside Miranda, struggling to keep her attention on the reading workbook in front of them. Miranda keeps fidgeting and making excuses to get up. Rafael's tiredness and rising frustration are obvious.

When Irina returns from putting Matteo to bed, Rafael is still sitting at the table with Miranda. "We're not done until you at least finish this page," he says with irritation.

"I already did three pages," Miranda whines. "I don't like this. I don't know why I have to do it."

"So you can read books, Miranda."

"Do you want to close up the chicken coop? I can work on Miranda's reading with her," Irina offers. Rafael agrees.

"Let's try something different," Irina says. "I'll be right back."

She goes into the house and picks out *Madeline* from the bookshelf. She spends the next half hour sounding out basic words with Miranda, as she'd done with Clara several years before.

Rafael feeds the fire and sits in one of the patio chairs. For a moment as Miranda reads, Irina forgets that she isn't with Clara. It's so familiar to sound out words with a little girl. As she grows tired, Miranda leans into Irina the same way that Clara used to. Irina longs for the weight of her own daughter in her arms. The page blurs before her eyes, and she looks away to find Rafael watching her. She sees understanding in his eyes. Slowly, Miranda leans further into Irina as her eyes grow heavy.

While Rafael helps Miranda get ready for bed, Irina returns the book to the book shelf. She surveys the strange assortment of texts there. A paperback catches her attention, and she picks it up. It's a marriage self-help book she and Sam had read together.

"Helena and I were reading that when we were at the cabin. We didn't get to finish it, obviously," Rafael says from behind her.

She startles, nearly dropping the book. She feels guilty as though she hasn't just been looking at his bookshelf but peering into some part of his mind.

Rafael continues, seemingly unbothered by her invasion. "I finished it later on my own."

"Why?" Irina asks.

He shrugs. "Reading material was pretty limited at the cabin. Also, I thought that maybe it would help me understand what went wrong with my marriage."

"Did it help?" she asks, setting the book back on the shelf.

"I think I know some of the places where I made mistakes, and where she did too. And the book has made me a better parent to Miranda, actually. A lot of it is just basic stuff— listening and responding to people's attempts to connect, being kind, understanding the deeper beliefs and feelings below the surface." He pauses for a moment, gathering his thoughts. "I think that people—and relationships—are just systems. If you understand the system, you can optimize for better outcomes."

She makes a face that he interprets as something between disbelief and amusement. "That's a very engineer description of the intangible."

"Oh? Hold that thought." He goes to the basement to get a bottle of wine, then to the kitchen to retrieve two glasses. He lights a few candles, pours them each a glass of wine, then sits down in one of the living room chairs and gestures for her to sit in the other. "Explain?"

"People aren't predictable," Irina says. "You can't liken them to machinery. For example, as a parent, you have to know that parenting isn't a system in which you can ensure a particular outcome."

"I can't ensure, but I can optimize. It's probabilistic, not deterministic." He gives her a wry smile that leads her to believe that he enjoys her challenge.

"Let's check in on that in twenty years."

"You're saying that nothing we do as parents matters? It's just chance?" He raises a skeptical eyebrow.

She waves his argument away. "Lots of studies have confirmed that most parenting choices don't matter."

"And yet, I taught my child to do chores, and now she's a child who does chores."

"But that's because she was a child who was predisposed to be amenable to that!"

He narrows his eyes and smirks at her. "I've never asked you what you did for a living before the Pandemic. I bet I can guess!"

She laughs. "You're changing the subject."

He closes his eyes and pretends to concentrate really hard. "You were an attorney, right?"

"If you change the subject, that means I'm right!"

"Just tell me if I guessed correctly."

"Fine, you guessed correctly. But back to people as systems . . . , it's not true! And relationships aren't systems, either. You're reducing the numinous, as you called it, to the blandly concrete."

"Actually, I think you just proved my point, in a way. You said that people aren't systems, but then you suggested that genes determine a person's outcome. So people are systems, just not subject to the particular inputs that we were initially discussing."

She purses her lips. "The point remains, though, that parenting isn't a system you can optimize for, necessarily."

"I'd like to see your studies," he replies with a grin.

"Gone with the rest of the internet."

"If you believe that parenting doesn't matter, then why do you read books to Matteo? Why do you try to teach him new words? Why do you laugh with him?"

He has her there. Her actions are incongruous with her stated beliefs.

She shrugs. "Because maybe I'm wrong. Or maybe the studies don't show everything. Or maybe that's the other intangible part of the system: I love him, and that love makes me disregard rational thought. I think parental love, by definition, is the rejection of rational thought. You have a baby . . . what does that newborn do for you? For the first two months, they don't even smile. Yet you give up sleep and pretty much all normal human functioning for them. You would die for them . . . ."

Her voice catches, and she stops talking. There it is, like a bruise that she sometimes bumps accidentally—a sharp, sudden pain. She looks away in the semidarkness but senses that his eyes are on her.

"I'm sorry," she says. "Sometimes it still gets me."

"Of course it does." Rafael pauses a moment as though unsure of how to proceed. "Tell me about Clara?"

It's a question that hurts but one that Irina often wishes someone would ask her. After Clara's death many people acted as if she'd never existed. If Irina brought her up in conversation, they would change the subject, spooked either by the reminder that children die or the reminder of Irina's unimaginable loss. It stung that Irina was denied even the ability to mutually recollect her daughter with another person. Mutual recollection was the palest imitation of a person but still better than silence.

So she's glad for the opportunity to talk about Clara with another person, even if it's painful.

"She was about Miranda's age when she died. She was smart, joyful, mischievous. Even when she was a baby, she had a sense of humor. She would do things just for a laugh—dancing in her high chair, making faces. And she loved jokes, but she always got the punchline wrong. She liked to chase Buddy around the yard while laughing maniacally. She could go from throwing a temper tantrum to having a laughing fit. She had this dark, incredibly shiny hair and the longest eyelashes I've ever seen. It was hard to get her to ever wear a dress, but she loved to have her hair braided . . . probably just to keep it out of her face while she was having adventures. She had such a big personality. She was so alive . . . until one day she wasn't. It's so hard to believe that someone with so much life can just . . . cease to be."

She stops, embarrassed that she always seems to be crying. She wipes her nose with her sleeve.

"I'm sorry," he says. "Is it hard to be around Miranda?"

"It's hard to be reminded of the things I'll never do with Clara again."

"Is there anything Miranda or I can do?" he asks gently.

"Not really. Everyone told me it would get better with time, but that hasn't been true so far. I feel like I'm stuck in purgatory." She pauses, gathering courage, then continues, "I have a theory that grief is a social process that has to be shared. That's why there've always been mourning rituals—wakes, sitting shiva, funeral processions. These were things people did together to process grief. If you can't grieve with other people, you get stuck."

"That's part of why I want to bring people here," he says. "I think we have to move forward together."

"You're assuming that everyone who comes here will have good intentions, but every additional person is a risk. I was an attorney before the Pandemic—a prosecutor, then an advocate for abused children—and I saw that there are lots of dangerous people in the world."

"I know that. But we can't survive on our own here. This isn't sustainable," he replies.

"Were all of the people you encountered on your way here kind and well-intentioned?"

"Yes, actually. We stopped at a monastery in the mountains near here, and the Brothers there were very kind. They even offered to let us live in their community. We met a couple of other solo travelers and an entire family. We also slept in the basement of a Mennonite church north of Bend. They were very friendly, too."

"I didn't have as good of an experience," Irina says. She tells him the broad details of her encounter with the man outside of Grants Pass—the unloaded gun, his sudden and confusing regret—while sparing him the more humiliating parts of the encounter.

"That's awful, Irina."

"It was terrifying and confusing. I still don't understand what he was thinking. Why hold me up with an unloaded gun, then just run away?"

"I don't think it was rational. He was probably just terribly afraid of being alone again. He was desperate."

"But desperation makes people dangerous," Irina replies.

"That's part of why we have to rebuild something," he says. "If we can create a real town, a place where people are safe and fed, we'll ward off the worst post-apocalyptic narratives. This isn't the kind of apocalypse with warlords and cannibals . . . yet. But it might become that when the resources run out and people are desperate."

Irina sighs. "I understand, but that's a long way off, and as a woman, I have more immediate security concerns that I'm not sure you can really relate to."

"I'm only an inch or two taller than you, Irina, and I'm a terrible shot," he says with a wry smile. "I'm not going to win many contests of physical dominance. My point is that if we're proactive, we can actually make ourselves, and the world, safer."

She purses her lips, and he decides not to press the point. "I won't try to bring anyone here without your approval, but I did leave a lot of fliers, so people might show up anyway."

"I know. I hope you can understand, though, why I'm hesitant about strangers."

"I'm a stranger," he says.

"You're a calculated risk," Irina answers, getting up and bidding him goodnight.

+++

They spend the next day picking and canning the rest of the ripe apricots in the orchard. On Sunday, Irina washes her clothes and Matteo's clothes in the stationary tub in the main house, then hangs them, with Miranda's eager help, on a line in the backyard, except for her underwear and bras, which she hangs in the guesthouse bathroom for the sake of modesty.

Each day has the same weather—foggy morning, clear afternoons that are on the cold end of mild, followed by a chilly evening.

"Did you ever consider moving somewhere warmer?" Irina asks, pulling the blanket more tightly around herself as they sit on the front patio watching the last vestiges of sunset. "Like maybe the Sacramento Valley?"

"You know it gets to be about 100 degrees there in the summertime, right?" he replies.

"True, but at least it gets warm sometimes," Irina grumbles.

"It gets warm here sometimes."

"Are you counting 75 degrees as warm?" she asks.

"I'm counting 70 degrees as warm!" he laughs. "I like it here. I like the scenery, the mountains, being able to sit here and watch the sunset over the ocean."

"The scenery is beautiful. I just wish it was about ten degrees warmer. What was it like where you grew up?"

"Until I left for boarding school, I lived in a small coastal town in the northeastern part of Venezuela. It was oppressively hot and humid all year round."

"Does your family still live there?" She realizes after she's asked the question that even if they did live there Before, they're very likely not living anymore.

He understands what she means, though. "My mother and her aunt were still living there when I last heard from them. I don't really know my father. Well, I knew of him, but we were never close."

In the town where Rafael had grown up, everyone knew Eduardo Cruz; they just didn't know that he was Rafael's father. Eduardo's family owned most of the town of Rio Azul. They were cocoa farmers, descended from the original Spaniards who established the town.

"His family pretty much ran our town. My mother was the nanny for his children until she got pregnant with me. I never knew he was my father until I turned twelve and started to look a lot like him—I've got his eyes, apparently."

They're lovely eyes, Irina thinks but doesn't say.

"My mother convinced him that it would be in his best interest to send me away to that fancy English-language boarding school," Rafael continues.

"That sounds awful!"

"It was even worse than you'd expect. I didn't belong there, and my classmates knew it. I spent most of my time in the library. I'd read about 90% of the school's books by the time I graduated."

"I can't believe your mother sent you away!"

"She thought that it would open up opportunities for me."

It didn't work out that way, of course. When he moved to the United States, he lost his grasp on the future he was promised. But as he reflects on this, while recounting his story to Irina, he feels deep gratitude for the sacrifice his mother made. As a parent, he understands now how difficult that must have been. She loved him deeply and entirely, and she must have missed him terribly when he left, yet she never let her façade of upbeat optimism crack. He wonders if she was as disappointed in his career as he was. If she was, she never let on.

"She didn't want to move to the U.S.?" Irina asks.

"She wanted to move eventually, but not while her aunt, Tia Rosa, was still alive. My mother felt she had a duty."

Irina nods in sympathy. "When was the last time you heard from her?"

"Early September. She said that Tia Rosa had died. My mother didn't tell me she was sick, but I think she was. She told me she was glad that Miranda and I were safe." He sighs sadly.

"I wish that she'd come here to live with us or that I had at least gotten to say goodbye to her."

"I'm sorry," Irina says, knowing the strangeness of that ambiguity. She has every reason to believe that own her family members in Utah are dead, yet she'll never have confirmation either way. Utah may as well be the moon.

"I'm going to bed," Rafael says, getting up. She bids him goodnight, then sits for a few minutes on the patio, surprised that she doesn't feel fearful about being alone in the dark—probably because she knows that Rafael and Miranda are nearby. For a little while, she watches the stars emerge and listens to the night sounds. Then she calls Buddy and returns to the guesthouse, locking the door behind her.

+++

"I'm going to start cleaning out another house," Rafael tells Irina the next morning, after they check the Ferndale library for new arrivals and find it empty, as usual. "You can join me if you want, but you don't have to."

"I'll come with you. But I'll need a playpen for Matteo."

They arrange to meet at a house nearby after he's picked up the playpen. Irina walks down the street with Matteo on her back and Miranda beside her. The morning fog swirls around the Victorian houses like a Halloween scene.

Irina steps up onto the porch of the little green craftsman house and tries the doorknob.

"Daddy makes me wait outside until he checks for dead people," Miranda says, sitting down on the porch steps.

Irina nods, unsure how to reply. So they wait on the steps until Rafael arrives and sets the playpen up on the front porch. He instructs Miranda to watch Matteo as Irina plops the toddler down in the playpen. Matteo fusses, and Irina tries unsuccessfully to placate him with several toys.

"You don't have to do this part if you don't want to," Rafael says. "I'm fine checking for bodies and clearing them out myself. There's another house that's farther along, if you want to start sorting things there."

"It's fine. I've spent the past year scavenging from houses, so I've seen plenty of bodies, and you could probably use the help," Irina replies.

"Well, let's do this then," Rafael hands her gloves, then puts on his own. He tries the doorknob, and when it doesn't open, he pulls out a little kit and jostles the lock until the doorknob twists in his hand, and the door swings open. Irina immediately smells the faint odor of death.

"I suspect this is going to be a bad one," Rafael nods toward the room to the right of them, where toddler toys are strewn around the floor.

"Why are you doing this?" Irina asks. "Why not just leave it? You already have a nice house."

"Because other people will need places to live when they come here," Rafael replies as they walk down the hall.

"What if no one ever comes to Ferndale?"

"Even if no one comes here, I believe the dead deserve a burial. It's wrong to leave people decaying as their houses fall down around them."

"You believe in ghosts or something?" Irina asks as they reach the first door in the hallway.

"I believe in social obligations and, as you put it, rituals of grief." He opens the door and gasps, "Shit."

Irina steps into the doorway beside him.

The room is small, as bedrooms in its era often were. It's painted a sunny yellow that contrasts with the scene before them. On the heavy antique bed are four skeletal bodies, two large and two small—one about Miranda's size, the other about

Matteo's size. The two larger ones are facing each other, with the children wrapped up between them.

"Fuck," Irina says. Tears immediately fill her eyes and her stomach churns. Rafael, too, is blinking back tears. "Suicide?"

"Looks like it." He walks over to one of the two nightstands and picks up the cup there. He peers inside but sees nothing. There are stains from dried vomit on the floor, and the decomposition process has discolored the bed and the floor around it. The horrifying logistics of it make him shudder.

"I hope it was fast and painless," Irina says.

"It almost certainly wasn't. It takes hours to die from overdosing on most medications. Sometimes even days."

"How do you know that?" Irina asks, before really considering the question.

"I told you I was depressed before the Pandemic. I did my research."

Irina files this piece of information away. "What do we do now?" she asks.

"Well," Rafael sighs and assesses the situation, "I guess it makes sense to wrap them all up in the bedsheets and take them out the back door so Miranda doesn't see them."

"Then what?"

"I usually take them to the graves I dug outside of town."

"How many times have you done this?" Irina asks, mildly horrified but also a little impressed at his dedication.

"I've cleared out a dozen houses. Eight of them had occupants. Nineteen people total."

"It'll take you years to clear the town," Irina says.

"Time is something I have right now."

Irina wants to argue with him about the wisdom of spending his days this way, but she senses that he's likely as stubborn as she is.

"Well," he says, "Let's do this. I'll get that side; you get this one."

She grasps one side of the stained, fitted bed sheet; he grabs the other, and they lift together. Irina is surprised by how light it is—just the weight of bones. As they lift, though, the sheet, rotted from the fluids of decay, falls apart, and the corpses fall back onto the bed. Rafael curses before noticing a waterproof mattress cover under the broken sheet. Together they lift that, and this time it holds. Irina gags from the sight of death and rot. Rafael wears a fixed grimace. They walk down to the end of the bed on either side, then come in closer to each other and angle out the door, holding the mattress cover up to keep the bodies inside. They shuffle down the hallway awkwardly, then try to guess the way to the back exit. One wrong guess later, they reach the door. Rafael struggles to unlock it and turn the knob while gripping the mattress cover. He curses again before finally getting the door open, and they carry the bundle out and set it gently on the lawn.

As Rafael props the side gate open, Irina stares at the corpses before her. In a way she envies them—they died together, and they got some choice over when and how. She shudders though, remembering what Rafael said about how long poisoning takes. How painful was it? How gruesome?

Together they lift the bundle, carry it through the gate, and deposit it into a large trailer. Rafael covers the corpses so Miranda won't see them.

"Thank you," Rafael says gruffly. Irina stares after him as he pulls the trailer away. Then she walks back into the house and surveys the kitchen before her. There are no dishes in the sink. Other than the toys they saw in the living room and the thick layer of dust everywhere, the house looks as though someone had just cleaned everything. She walks back to the living room. On the walls are pictures of the family who lived here. A mother, father, little boy, and toddler girl. They grin out from posed, edited photos taken on a sunny beach. She stares at them, feeling deep grief. She walks around the house, taking note of anything that might be useful.

There's a high chair in the kitchen. Irina considers it. Can she use it after seeing the fate of its previous occupant? She decides she cannot.

She checks on Miranda and Matteo. He's fallen asleep in the playpen. Miranda is coloring.

Irina continues to peruse the house. The coat closet and the bedroom closets are full of clothes that look far more appropriate for the cool coastal weather than anything she has. The woman was about Irina's size, and most of her clothes are well-known brands. Irina pulls a few athletic hoodies, some sweaters, and a pair of mom jeans out of the closet in the yellow bedroom. She's uncomfortable with their provenance, but she's unsure if she'll find anything suitable in her size at Rafael's warehouse. She puts the clothing in a small duffel she finds in the closet.

Rafael returns, and they strip the bed and consider the mattress. The mattress cover saved it from any staining, but Irina is sure the smell will linger.

"What do we do with it?" she asks.

"We'll take it out back and let it air out. A lot of the mattresses here had bodies on them. If they aren't stained, I save them. It doesn't make sense to waste anything."

"That doesn't seem sanitary."

He sighs with annoyance. "Irina, we're about one generation away from sleeping on straw mattresses. We can't afford to waste anything right now."

"I wouldn't even know how to make a straw mattress."

"Me either, which is kind of my point. We'll air it out. If it continues to stink, we can junk it. But for now, we're in the business of saving everything in case we end up needing it."

"You really think people will come here?"

"I hope so."

She purses her lips. She doesn't feel like arguing, but her reservations remain. Rafael goes through the medicine cabinets, the cleaning supplies, and the shed in the backyard, boxing up everything useful and loading it in the cart. Irina pulls out a mop from the kitchen closet and mops the bedroom floor as best she can with a little drinking water and some of the cleaning solution under the kitchen sink. The hardwood will never be the same.

Matteo wakes and cries from hunger. Irina feels guilty about leaving him alone for so long, but there's so much work to do. They all sit together on the front porch and eat a modest lunch, then walk together with the cart to the warehouse.

They're walking down a side street off Main when Irina stops and points at a building. "We need to go in there."

"A museum?" Rafael asks.

"Yes! Think about it! The museum might have all kinds of useful things from before there was electricity."

He looks skeptical, but they walk over, and he pulls out his little lockpicking kit to open the door. The space is dark and dusty, but it doesn't smell of death. Irina retrieves a camping lantern from her bike trailer. They peer around in the semi-darkness. The first few exhibits don't seem relevant. There's some milking equipment that looks as if it might be useful one day, though Irina is puzzled about the purpose of several of the items.

She smiles when she comes to a section with a horse-drawn buggy and a plow.

"Deus Ex Machina!" she cries. Rafael's brow furrows. Miranda stops touching the wheel of the buggy and turns to look at Irina.

"What I mean," Irina says, "is that if there really are horses, this is incredibly lucky."

"You think the plow will still work?" Rafael asks.

Irina laughs. "It's a piece of metal affixed to other pieces of metal. I think it'll work. And, if it doesn't . . . ," she looks around, "there are two more here." She continues walking. Miranda and Rafael trail after her. "Fantastic!" she exclaims.

Before them is a blacksmith's forge, with not only the tools but the forge itself.

"This worked," Rafael says, recalling the long-ago trip that had inspired him to travel hundreds of miles to return to this town after the Pandemic. It had been one of the few bright spots in his marriage. "Helena and I watched a demonstration on blacksmithing, here. But we have no idea how to use this."

"You seem good at figuring things out," Irina says.

Rafael recognizes her challenge. "We aren't currently in need of any blacksmithing," he says, "but when we are, I'll do my best." They leave the museum feeling a little better.

"That was a good idea," Rafael remarks.

"I'm surprised you didn't think of it," Irina says.

"I'm very goal-oriented. Sometimes I get my blinders on and don't even look around. I suspect you're better at creative solutions than I am," he replies.

They arrive at the "warehouse," which is really just a bunch of classrooms at an old Catholic school that Rafael uses as a storage area. He shows her the inventory list that he keeps in his notebook and the piles of various kinds of objects: clothing, medication, tools, books, linens, and assorted other objects.

Irina pages through his notebook. "This is impressively organized."

"Thanks," he says, a bit embarrassed at her praise.

They find the things they need, then load them up and ride home.

+++

That evening, Rafael feels lingering disquiet when he recalls the family they found. He senses that Irina does too. So they sit in silence, reading by candlelight.

Rafael puts on his reading glasses and rereads Borges's *Limites* for the hundredth time, immersing himself in the words of his mother tongue. But his mind wanders. He hasn't spoken a word of Spanish since the last conversation he had with his mother that September. He and Helena had never spoken it together because she'd been raised in the U.S., mostly speaking English. It wasn't a conscious decision to fail to teach Miranda Spanish; it was simply inertia. He regrets not teaching his daughter Spanish, though. If he had, at least there would be one other person in the world who could speak to him in the language he still often thinks in, the language that shaped his mind and formed his initial thoughts as a child.

He wonders how many languages have died along with their speakers in the Pandemic. Any small, niche language is likely already gone. Others may die over the course of the next few generations as the limited number of survivors coalesce around common languages. Certainly plenty of people who speak Spanish have survived, but he's unsure if he'll ever meet them. By the time he does, if he does, will he even be able to speak his own language anymore? Will the words flow back to him easily, like a river when a dam bursts? Or will they have to be pulled with difficulty from his memory?

He could still try to teach Miranda, but he struggles enough to try to teach her to read. Just the thought of their reading lessons makes him feel stressed. How is it possible that he hasn't managed to pass his love of reading on to his daughter? Reading is the only thing that made his teenage years bearable.

His thoughts turn to Helena, as they often do when he's feeling melancholy. He presses on that not-quite-healed wound. He misses Helena deeply on Miranda's behalf. He misses her as Miranda's mother, but he doesn't miss her as his wife. Their marriage had been difficult from the start. They'd hardly known each other when they married. In an argument a few months after Rafael moved to the United States, Helena told him that she suspected that he'd only married her for the green card. He denied it at the time, though she was partly right. It hadn't been the only reason, of course—Helena was beautiful, smart, and charming, and he'd fallen for her quickly— but if it hadn't been for the abysmal situation in Venezuela and the promise of a green card, he wouldn't have moved things forward so quickly.

The marriage had declined in correlation with his professional prospects. In the ugliest moments of their fights, Helena had called Rafael sexist outright because he objected to her long work hours and struggled with his failure in the face of her success.

Now he resumes his argument with her ghost. He admits he's guilty of resenting her success in contrast to his failure and of being unsupportive of her grueling, demanding career. He'd been a bad husband—emotionally unavailable for years of their marriage and sexually unavailable for the final year of it.

But had he resented her career because of some outright or internalized expectation of what their gender roles should be? He resented only that Helena's job often left him to take care of Miranda alone, after a long day of physical labor. And he resented Helena's success for the same reason he resented the high school group-chat discussions of his classmates' successes. To avoid seeing the contrast between their successes and his, he had deleted the group-chat app from his phone, but he couldn't escape the contrast with Helena, because she never let him forget his many failures. She was exasperated at his inability to get a better job, his failure to make more of a monetary contribution to their household, his disabling depression. She'd clearly thought she was marrying a different man—a man who would be successful, who would help her finances and her image.

Perhaps he could have seen their situation differently. He could have reframed it: she was succeeding; thus, they, as a team, were succeeding. He doubts, though, that she would have encouraged that framework. Thinking that way would have let him off the hook too easily.

He knows that Helena was successful partly because she was hard on herself. She expected nothing short of the perfection that she embodied: a perfect body, perfect hair, a perfect wardrobe, a perfect 4.0 GPA, perfect family photos. His imperfections had annoyed her at first and infuriated her later.

The only person Helena had ever truly accepted was Miranda. She'd never criticized Miranda, and while Helena often came home late in the evenings, she never missed a birthday, Christmas, or milestone doctor's appointment. He could find many faults in their marriage, but she was a good mother.

Still, he'll always wonder why she didn't stay at the cabin with them instead of returning to the hospital. Despite their marital difficulties, it would have been easier to survive these past few years with a co-parent, and a doctor would be extremely helpful in their current situation.

Yet he isn't certain that they ever truly loved each other. He doesn't know much about love, but he's pretty sure that it requires a level of acceptance of each other's flaws that he and Helena never achieved.

He wonders if he'll ever get a chance to build the kind of companionship that lucky couples have. He doubts he's capable of that. It's a need much farther up the hierarchy of needs, anyway. Right now he's just one step above bare survival.

It's getting late, and he's emotionally and physically exhausted from today's work, so he bids Irina goodnight and goes to bed.

Chapter Five

That Friday while Matteo naps, Irina ladles canned carrots into sanitized jars.

Miranda comes down the stairs, her hair wet from the shower, and asks, "Can you braid my hair?"

Irina nods, wordlessly. She already knows that this will be upsetting, but she sees the hopefulness in Miranda's eyes and can't bear to disappoint her.

She directs Miranda to sit while she gets a brush and hair ties. "One braid or two?" Irina asks.

"Two please!" Miranda answers. Irina parts Miranda's hair and begins the first braid. She recalls doing this many times for Clara. Miranda's hair is finer, lighter, and softer. Irina enjoys the feeling of it in her hands and is surprised to find that she's missed the intimacy of braiding someone's hair.

Irina finishes and ties off the first braid, and Miranda says, "My daddy says mommy used to braid my hair."

"What was your mommy like?" Irina asks, thinking that maybe Miranda, too, would like an opportunity to talk about the person she loved and lost.

Miranda looks down sadly. "I don't really remember. But daddy says she really loved me."

"I'm sure she did."

"I wish she was here." Irina can hear the tears in Miranda's voice, as she winds one clump of hair through the other.

"Me too. I'm sorry that she isn't."

"Do you think I can ever have another mommy?"

"Maybe. I think that's up to your daddy, though."

"Maybe you could be my mommy?"

Irina pauses, unsure of how to answer. Finally she says, "I don't know. But even if I'm not your mommy, I can still care about you, and we can do things together."

"Okay," Miranda says, but Irina can sense her disappointment.

She finishes the second braid and wraps the hair tie around the end.

+++

"Today Miranda asked me if I can be her mommy," Irina says to Rafael that evening as they sit on the patio in front of the fire. It's taken her a glass and a half of wine to work up the courage to have this conversation.

"She told me. I'm sorry about that."

"I think this is confusing for her," Irina says, taking another large sip of wine. Rafael thinks, but doesn't say, that this is confusing for him, too.

"I know," he replies instead.

He hates to ask, but he does anyway, "Do you want to move into town?"

"Do you want me to?"

"Hell no," he answers without hesitation, then catches himself, "not unless you want to."

"I really don't want to take care of Matteo all by myself," she says. He feels, strangely, a bit hurt. Perhaps it shows on his face, because she adds, "And I like living here with Miranda. And you."

"We're glad you're here."

"I think I hurt Miranda's feelings," Irina says softly.

"I think she was a little hurt, but there's nothing you can do about that. She's sad because her mother died. It's been good for her to have you here. She likes spending time with you. Of course she wants to put a label on that, but no one can replace her mother."

Irina knows this from painful experience.

"I lost my mother when I was a little older than Miranda," Irina says.

"I'm sorry," Rafael replies, "What happened to her?"

"Cancer. It started off as colon cancer, but by the time she went to the doctor, it had spread everywhere else. She died a couple of months later."

She's had almost two glasses of wine, so Irina voices a suspicion she's never shared with anyone before: "I don't think she wanted to get better. I think she thought that something serious was wrong, and she chose not to get it checked out. I think she thought it was her ticket out of a miserable life."

"She was that unhappy?" Rafael asks. He understands that wish to simply stop living.

"She was a martyr and my father was a monster. We were all miserable." Irina suddenly stops, wanting to disclose no more. Instead she asks the question that's been on her mind since she found this family in Ferndale.

"You researched methods to kill yourself. What made you decide not to do it?" She realizes after she asks that what she really wants is to hear someone make their best argument for life.

"I think," Rafael says, "That I didn't want to kill myself as much as I just didn't want to be alive anymore. Like I said before, I was miserable when I moved to the U.S. I hated that I didn't have a job; then when I did, it was a job that didn't use any of my skills. I suffered through years of schooling for the promise of a better life, but then when I got here, I couldn't succeed. I did terribly on the SAT when I was trying to get into U.S. universities. And it wasn't the language barrier. My English was fine. It was a lot of pressure, and I've never been good at exams. I'm pretty sure I failed the entrance exam for the boarding school and my college in Venezuela too. Eduardo just paid the necessary bribes to make up for my bad score. I thought I was smart, but there was a number on the page that said that I clearly wasn't. I didn't have any friends here, because I arrived right before Covid. Pretty much as soon as I got here, things went downhill with Helena. I was just tired of living, and I didn't think it was going to get better."

"What made it better?"

"You want the real answer? Or the answer that won't make you second guess your choice to come here?" Rafael has had two glasses of wine too, so he's also in the mood for candor.

Irina feels a zing of anxiety. "The real answer."

Rafael pauses and looks up at the stars above them. "A couple of months after Miranda was born, I went to a voluntary inpatient mental health program. I don't know if it was the newborn sleep deprivation or the fact that I had to drop out of the part-time undergrad program I'd finally gotten into or both, but things got really bad. Helena found my suicide research and threatened to divorce me and fight for full custody if I didn't get help."

"Is that the thing that was supposed to make me second guess my choice to be here?" Irina asks.

"I had to take a leave of absence from landscaping to go to the mental health version of rehab. That isn't making you want to pack your bags?"

"I wish my mother had cared enough to do something, anything, to make her life and mine better," Irina replies.

Rafael feels a rush of relief. He's at least gotten past this obstacle. There's another, more troubling piece of his past that he longs to share with her, but he's fairly certain it will make her pack her bags and leave this town, so he keeps that story to himself.

"It helped, then? The program?" Irina asks.

"It did. It was helpful to be there, every day, working on things. It sounds awful, but it also gave me perspective. I could see that there were people who were much worse off than I was.

"Eventually I got a little better. Then I participated in a medical trial with psychedelics, and that was helpful too. I saw a counselor for a couple of years until the Pandemic started, and that really helped. I realized that I didn't want to stop being alive. I wanted to see what would come next in this story. My story, Miranda's story, everyone's story. It didn't fix all my unhappiness, and I did have a bit of a relapse the year before the Pandemic, but it wasn't nearly as bad."

"I'm glad it helped."

They're both quiet for a minute; then he asks, "Do you think that all the things we've been through helped us survive the Pandemic?"

"I think people always want to create meaning out of suffering, but sometimes suffering is just suffering. Sometimes there's no reason or purpose in it," Irina says. "I'm only here because of Matteo."

He's been honest with her, so she shares something she's still deeply ashamed of. "When Sam died, I almost jumped off a bridge with Matteo. I changed my mind at the last moment. I knew I had to keep living for him."

Rafael looks at her earnestly. "I understand why you thought about it, but I'm glad you didn't jump. The world is better because you didn't."

Irina looks away awkwardly at his earnestness.

Then he says, "I think even if Miranda wasn't here, I would have tried to survive."

"That must have been a damn good inpatient program. Worth every penny."

He smiles a half smile and shrugs. "I still want to know the rest of the story."

+++

After they've finished their chores that Saturday afternoon, they pack a picnic dinner and some blankets and flashlights and hike down to the beach. The morning fog has cleared out and the day has reached a comparatively warm mid-June high of sixty-seven degrees. Miranda stops along the trail to watch a hummingbird eating from a Leopard Lily. Irina, remembering Sam's lessons, tells her it's a male "Anna's Hummingbird."

"He's pretty," Miranda says.

"If you want, we can try to plant some flowers for the hummingbirds in our garden," Irina offers.

"I'd love that!"

"We could also learn about some other birds. I bet we could get some books and binoculars," Irina tells her.

"We've got plenty of binoculars in the warehouse," Rafael says.

"Yes! I want to learn about the birds!" Miranda exclaims. She skips down the path in front of them.

"Sam taught Clara all of Oregon's birds," Irina says wistfully.

"If it makes you sad, I can do it instead," Rafael offers.

"No, I want to. It's a way of remembering them."

The beach is breathtaking—gray sand surrounded by high bluffs backed by green hills strewn with wildflowers. Irina resolves to visit more often.

The blue Pacific inhales and exhales against the land. Buddy chases waves, which thrills Miranda, who runs after him. Rafael lays out a blanket, and Irina sets Matteo down for his first taste of the beach. Unfortunately, he takes a literal taste,

90

shoving sand into his mouth before Irina can stop him. He coughs and sputters, spitting it out on the ground, then quickly grabs another handful and tries to do it again, before Irina stops him.

Irina rolls her eyes. "It's amazing that humans survived as long as they did."

"Toddlers do make a person wonder about that," Rafael says. Matteo toddles toward the stream that bisects the beach, and Irina sighs and gets up to go after him. She pulls him back, and he fights against her, kicking and screaming and arching his back. Irina sets him down in the sand with exasperation. He stares up at her with tear-stained cheeks and indignation until she offers him a piece of apricot.

"I'm not really sure that I like toddlers," Irina says as he chews on the fruit. "Does that make me a bad mom?"

"I can't say that the toddler phase was my favorite either," Rafael replies. "But I'm really enjoying the stage that Miranda is in . . . most of the time. So, no, I don't think that makes you a bad mom. Maybe there's just some other phase that you'll enjoy more. Maybe you'll be the best mother-of-a-teenager ever."

"I doubt that. I didn't even like teenagers when I was one."

He laughs. "Fair enough. Neither did I. What stages did you enjoy most with Clara?"

"I actually really liked the stage she was at right before she passed. Old enough to follow basic directions, little enough to still want to spend time with us. Like Miranda."

"The problem is that in a couple more years, Miranda won't want to hang out with us anymore," he says with a sigh.

"Maybe. Maybe not," Irina shrugs.

"Maybe she'll be the exception," he says.

Irina chuckles. "'My kid will be different: the fiction that underlies every act of procreation."

The day grows late, and they call Miranda back to the blanket for dinner. They eat more apricots and blueberries and a Thermos of bean soup. Irina thinks again about Matteo's nutrition. She's pretty certain that he's not getting enough protein, fat, or calcium, but there's little she can do about it.

The sun sinks down over the horizon, bleeding pink and peach tones into the sky. "I wish that I could paint this," Irina says.

"What kind of painting do you do?" Rafael asks.

"It's been years since I painted anything, but I used to paint landscapes with oil paints," Irina replies. "I wasn't very good, but I did enjoy it."

The sun sinks below the horizon, and they gather their things to go home. Irina picks up Matteo, who's fallen asleep on the blanket beside her, and straps him into the backpack. Rafael offers to carry Matteo, but Irina declines, assuring him that she's used to it. Matteo cries at being awoken, then falls asleep with his head bobbing awkwardly every time she takes a step. They trek back up the hill, flashlights cutting lines of light in the dirt path and the wildflower fields surrounding it.

"Do you want to check out the horses and cattle this week?" Rafael asks Irina as they walk.

"That would be great."

Back at the house, Irina puts Matteo down in his crib, then goes straight to bed, leaving the guest house door unlocked behind her for the first time.

She wakes in the middle of the night to a scream from inside the main house. She's out of her bed in seconds, grabbing her gun, throwing open the guesthouse door, and sprinting to the dark house. She stands outside the back door to the main house, trying to assess the situation. She hears murmured voices inside, and she sees candlelight. She opens the door, holding her gun.

"Rafael? Miranda?" She calls out their names softly.

The door to Miranda's bedroom upstairs is open, and Irina can see the candlelight flickering inside.

Rafael comes out in sweatpants and a t-shirt. "Everything's alright. She just had a nightmare." Miranda appears behind him in princess pajamas.

"I had a dream about the mountain man," she says.

Rafael isn't ready for this conversation, so he shoos her back inside. "It's okay. I'm just going to stay in her bedroom tonight. We'll see you in the morning."

Irina returns to her bed, but she can't shake the feeling of instinctive anxiety that Miranda's scream had created. Finally, she falls asleep just as the first light of dawn filters through the morning fog.

+++

That Thursday, Irina does the inventory while Rafael brings the loads of items to the warehouse. At noon he declares that they've done enough, and they sit outside in the parking lot of the Catholic school and eat lunch.

Miranda shows him the field guide to birds that she and Irina had found in the warehouse. They spot a large blue and white bird and look it up in the book, even though Irina already knows what it is. She lets Miranda find the picture; then Irina reads the name of the bird to her: "Scrub Jay." She flips to the back of the book and reads the page of information about the bird. Matteo toddles over and scares it off; then Miranda lures it back by throwing a blueberry.

They ride on country roads through fields of wildflowers to a place where Irina is thrilled to spot three horses in a pasture several hundred feet away from the road. They get off their bikes, she puts Matteo in the backpack, and they hike through the long grass.

Irina and Rafael lean against the fence, surveying the horses: a mare and a small foal on one side of the pasture, another horse much farther down by the stream that runs through both neighboring pastures.

"Oh, this is even better than I thought!" Irina says with excitement. "That foal is only a couple of months old."

"So?"

Irina smirks at him, "Do I have to explain the birds and bees to you?"

Despite being a 37-year-old man, Rafael blushes. He shakes his head, still confused.

Irina laughs and continues, "There are three horses in the pasture, Rafael. One of them is a foal that was born long after the Pandemic. You understand?"

From behind them, Miranda, who neither of them had realized was listening, pipes up, "Mommy horse, daddy horse, baby horse!"

"Which is unexpected because?" Rafael asks.

"Because most male horses in the U.S. are geldings." Rafael looks uncertain.

"They're castrated," Irina clarifies. Rafael grimaces.

"What does that mean?" Miranda asks.

"It means they can't have babies," Irina says. "But that horse," she points at the lone horse by the stream, "obviously can have babies. Which means . . ."

". . . sustainability," Rafael concludes.

"For at least a while. Eventually we'll need to find more horses to introduce some diversity into the gene pool," Irina says. She looks around at the fence and finds what she expects to find. "We'll need to fix the fence there," she says, pointing to a place where the fence in between this pasture and the next is splintered.

"If they were trying to escape, why didn't they break down the outer fence?" Rafael asks.

"I really am going to have to explain the birds and the bees to you, aren't I?" Irina asks, chuckling.

Is she flirting with him? He isn't sure. He has the brief, immature, and wildly inappropriate urge to respond that he'd like to show her what he knows about the birds and the bees. Then he remembers his age, their situation, and the fact that, after several years, his knowledge of the specifics of the birds and the bees is likely a bit hazy anyway. He bites his tongue.

"He didn't care about escaping," Irina explains. "He only cared about getting to her. But now we have to keep them separated, unless you'd like Miranda to have a demonstration of the birds and the bees."

"Oh, I know birds and bees!" Miranda says. "Irina taught me some birds—Scrub Jays and sparrows and . . . ." She rambles on.

Irina laughs, and Matteo instinctively joins in, shrieking with glee in the backpack on her shoulders. Rafael looks at Irina, doing his best to suppress a smile.

"You're funny," he says. "Comedian is exactly the skillset I was looking for when I posted those fliers. I'm glad we've filled that vacancy."

"Oh, I think Miranda was already doing that job."

"Miranda only recently graduated from thinking that farts and burps are funny, and she still thinks it's hilarious to repeat the same thing over and over again, until I get annoyed. So I can tell you with confidence that until you arrived, the comedian position was still open here in Ferndale."

Irina grins at him. Matteo laughs and waves his arms happily. Miranda continues to list the birds she knows. Rafael rolls his eyes.

"I'll fix the fence," he says.

+++

The next morning, they return to the pasture. Irina assesses the horses for a little while. She's pleased to find that the mare is friendly and even lets Irina slip a halter from a nearby barn over her head. Irina leads the mare and foal into the adjoining pasture so Rafael can fix the fence with pieces of wood he'd taken from another pasture. When he rejoins her and the children outside the fence, Irina says, "I don't think the stallion's going to be good for much beyond the obvious."

"You can't train him?" Rafael asks.

"He's like a teenage boy at the peak of adolescence. He's got only one thing on his mind. Stallions are hard to train, even for people with a lot more experience handling horses than I have. That's why there are so many geldings. He'll be useful to us, though. He has a job: make more horses."

Rafael thinks that this horse is living the dream of many teenage boys. He wisely keeps this thought to himself.

Irina gestures to the mare. "She's obviously been trained and socialized with people. She's friendly and might be useful to us, but teaching her to pull a cart or a plow will take a while, and we can't start until we wean the foal. We should move the mare and foal closer to us and leave the stallion here for now. After we move the others, we can open up the fence between the pastures to give him more grazing space. Once she's settled in a new home, I'll have to wait a little while before I can start separating her from her foal. She needs to trust me." She pauses, considering. "I could really use some horse training books. Do you have anything like that at the warehouse?"

"I don't recall seeing any, but we can look on Thursday. We can also check the Ferndale Library, but selection there is really limited, and this is a pretty niche topic," he replies. "I've been thinking of going to Eureka, though. It's a larger town, so it should have a larger library. That's been hard with Miranda, though, because it will take a day to ride up there, probably another half a day to actually find the library, then a day to get back."

"I could stay with her and Matteo while you go," Irina says. They discuss this for a while and decide to wait a few more weeks so Miranda can become more comfortable with Irina. Irina mentions that they'll also need a horse cart, and Rafael pulls a small notepad out of his pocket. As he flips through the pages, Irina spots sketched diagrams and lots of lists. He scratches a small note in the book.

They sit down in the grass to have lunch. Miranda identifies birds with the book she's brought. As Irina helps her sound out the names, Rafael notices that Miranda is getting a little better at reading. He praises her and thanks Irina again.

On the way home, they stop at a large field where several cows are grazing. Here, too, Irina is pleasantly surprised. She counts two young bulls, four older heifers, and two new calves. She guesses that the bulls must have been calves when the Pandemic started. The thought of having milk for the children allays some of her fears about their nutrition.

"There are more cows spread out around the area," Rafael tells her. "Before the Pandemic, local stores sold bumper stickers saying 'Ferndale is a cow town.' There were thousands of cows. It was part of why I thought to come here."

"That was a good instinct. These cows could mean the difference between going hungry and being well-fed," she says. "We should separate the bulls from the heifers and babies. I can start halter-breaking them after I get the horses moved."

"Have I told you lately how glad I am that you came to Ferndale?" Rafael asks.

She laughs, "Not in so many words. But I'm glad I came here, too."

When they arrive at the house, Irina puts Matteo down to nap in his playpen, then gets her rifle. She stops in the laundry room, where Rafael and Miranda are washing clothes, to ask him to listen for Matteo, then she heads out into the high grass.

When she returns a half hour later, holding a dead rabbit by its feet, Miranda and Rafael are in the yard, hanging their laundry on the line. Irina notices that she sees no boxers or briefs and guesses that Rafael has made the same calculation that she's made: in order to cohabitate together, they'll have to maintain some amount of modesty.

Irina gathers the necessary supplies and lays the rabbit down on the table. Miranda comes over, looking curiously. When she sees the dead rabbit, she frowns.

"You may not want to be here for this part," Irina tells her. Miranda goes to play with Buddy on the other side of the yard, and Irina begins her task. Rafael sits down to watch. Irina puts on a pair of rubber gloves, then cuts off the feet of the rabbit. She lifts up the fur between the rabbit's shoulder blades and makes a small incision; then she hooks her gloved fingers under the skin and pulls it apart. Rafael grimaces, but Irina doesn't flinch. She's done this hundreds of times. Rafael is horrified when she twists its head off.

"If you're going to faint, please warn me," Irina teases him.

Irina continues to process the rabbit, slicing it open and removing the organs carefully. She sets aside the heart and liver for Buddy. Then she rinses the carcass and begins to butcher it.

Rafael is impressed with her stoicism. "I take it you've done this a lot?"

"I used to hunt rabbits with my grandfather when we did the cattle drives. We'd camp with the ranch hands and eat rabbit stew cooked by my Abuela Mariana."

"How often did you visit your grandparents?"

"I lived there after my mother died and my dad lost custody."

As she separates the parts of the rabbit and cubes the meat up for the stew, she says, "One of the ranch hands got my mother pregnant when she was sixteen. They ran off to Idaho and married. He was an alcoholic, though, with a terrible temper. Once she got sick, there was no one to protect me."

Irina drops the chunks of meat into the pot beside her. "One day my teacher, Ms. Keller, noticed my bruises and asked me about them. She told me that when she was a little girl, she'd been taken away from her parents and placed with her aunt. She said that if I told her the truth, my life could get better. So I did. Then children's services got involved, and my father agreed to surrender custody."

She spares Rafael the more gruesome details—the coppery taste of blood in her mouth, the times when her father had come home drunk with his drunk friends, her encounters with his closest friend, the sounds of her father hitting her mother.

Her father is almost certainly dead. She ponders that idea and finds that it doesn't bother her at all.

She pauses for a moment, dropping more cubes of meat into the pot. "I met my grandparents on the day they came to pick me up to take me to Utah. They were religious, and my mother stopped talking to them when she ran away to Idaho. They brought me to their ranch, and I met this huge family that I'd never known. It was totally overwhelming at first. I had a really hard time adjusting."

"Did they raise you in the church?" Rafael asks her.

"No. By the time I arrived, my Aunt Hannah had already defected. It caused a lot of trouble for her in the community and some strife in the family. My grandparents fought about it a lot. I guess in the end my grandmother won out, and they accepted

Hannah's choice. I think for Abuela Mariana it was normal to love someone who didn't share her faith, since none of the rest of her family converted to the Latter Day Saints Church. My grandparents took me with them to the Sunday services a few times, but I really didn't like it, so they let me stay home with Aunt Hannah. It was a little alienating, though, because there were things I couldn't participate in with them."

Irina looks out over the hills toward the ocean. "I still think of Ms. Keller sometimes."

"Did you ever talk to her again?"

"She wrote to me when Clara died. I was touched that she still remembered me. "

Irina looks up at the sky, willing herself not to cry in front of him. "When I worked with child victims, I used to tell those kids the same thing Ms. Keller told me: that their lives would get better. My life did . . . for a while. Until we lost Clara."

He longs to reach out and take her hand, but he's uncertain about crossing that boundary, so he doesn't move.

"What happened to your grandparents?"

"They died a couple of years before the Pandemic, within days of each other. He died of a broken heart after she died of cancer. Even happy marriages always have a sad ending."

"At least he didn't have to miss her for long." Irina knows all too well what he means. "And the rest of your family?" Rafael asks.

"When last I heard, a bunch of them were isolating themselves on the ranch. It's possible they survived. They had the livestock and a pretty large garden."

"I hope so," he replies.

"It doesn't matter anyway; there's no way I could reach them now."

From the other side of the yard, Miranda calls Rafael. He looks at Irina apologetically. "That's alright," Irina says, "I have to get the stew going anyway."

+++

The next morning, Irina treks down to an empty pasture in the valley beside the house. It has shaded areas, a small open stable, and a stream that runs through it to the beach. The grass is overgrown, but Irina figures that the horses can fix that themselves.

While Rafael watches the children at home, Irina walks several miles to the horse pasture. She's successful at putting a saddle on Lily—the name Miranda had selected for the mare—and Lily lets Irina slide up onto her back. Riding brings back pleasant memories of cattle drives through the desert, early morning rides to mountain streams to fish with her grandfather, galloping races down dirt roads with Aunt Hannah.

Irina circles the pasture a few times with Lily. The foal, Sunshine, walks along beside them. They leave the pasture and head up the foggy road into the seaside hills. Lily walks steadily through the clearing mist with Sunshine tagging along.

Irina is impressed with Lily's calm temperament. When she walks the horses past the House by the Sea, Miranda comes out to the road to greet them, carefully reaching up and petting Lily's neck under Irina's supervision.

As Irina watches, she can't help recalling Clara's love of horses. Irina is grateful to be able to spend time with another little girl about Clara's age—to teach her some of the same things she taught Clara, to share that part of herself—but sometimes it still stings that she'll never know who Clara would have become. In some ways, it's healing to do those things with Miranda. In other ways, it's painful.

Irina and Sam had so many hopes and dreams for their daughter; then that entire imagined future had been

101

extinguished with a single mistake on an ordinary October morning.

Chapter Six

The beginning of summer passes quickly. Irina slowly separates Lily from Sunshine: first moving them to neighboring pastures for a little while, then taking Lily out on longer and longer rides.

She separates the cows into two pastures, then uses the milking skills she hasn't used since she was a teenager. As she watches Matteo and Miranda drink the milk, she feels a little bit of anxiety about their calcium and protein intake ebbing away.

The seeds Irina and Miranda planted begin to sprout in the garden. Irina is especially pleased to see the hummingbird-friendly flowers. Rafael finds an old horse-drawn cart in one of the barns at the county fairgrounds in Ferndale. He spends a few mornings repairing it.

Midsummer arrives, and Rafael packs up his bike trailer with camping gear and several days' worth of food. Irina, Miranda, and Matteo watch him bike off down the road after breakfast.

As he pedals away, Rafael feels both excitement and nervousness about being separated from Miranda. This is the first time in years that he's had some time and space to himself. He feels a surge of gratitude for all the ways that Irina has made his life easier. Since she arrived, he's finally been able to breathe a little, to glimpse a future that involves something more than constant struggle for survival and the gnawing fear that he'll fail Miranda.

He admires Irina's resilience and ingenuity, her patience with Miranda, and her dedication to contributing to their household. Her knowledge of horses will make their lives easier, and her hunting abilities will keep them all fed over the winter months. More than that, though, she's brought some humor into his and Miranda's lives, which had too often slipped into melancholy silence before her arrival. He looks forward to seeing her every morning and talking to her in the evening.

Something about her makes him want to be candid. He wants her to know him, and he wants to know her.

He congratulates himself, though, on channeling any ambiguous feelings he'd had toward Irina into a mutually beneficial friendship and co-parenting partnership.

He lets gravity carry him down to the valley without pedaling, enjoying the feeling of the breeze and the sun on his face. He bikes through Ferndale, stopping to put a sign on the library saying that he'll return next week. He rides over the Eel River and gets on the highway toward Eureka.

+++

At the House by the Sea, Irina straps Matteo on her back so she and Miranda can spend the morning gathering more firewood. While he naps, they tend the garden and can string beans. That evening she takes them both to the beach to watch the sunset.

Later, Irina waits in Miranda's second-floor bedroom while the little girl changes into her pajamas and brushes her teeth. It's the first time Irina has ever been in this room. The decor is the same modern, minimalist style as the rest of the house, but Miranda has added her own accents. In a vase on the nightstand is a bouquet of flowers she and Rafael had picked the day before.

Stuffed animals are arrayed on the bed, and framed pictures adorn the dresser.

Irina looks at the pictures and feels a strange twist of jealousy when she discovers that Helena was quite beautiful, with enviously voluptuous curves, thick dark hair, and long lashes. Her smile radiates joy as she holds a tiny, red baby in a hospital bed.

Miranda joins her and says, "That's me and mommy when I was a little baby. And this is me and mommy at the park and me and mommy at Christmas."

Nearby is a picture of Rafael holding newborn Miranda. He looks younger, less thin, without the gray that's shot through his hair now. He's smiling, but the smile doesn't quite reach his hazel eyes. Irina studies his face for too long, realizing with apprehension that she's been missing him all day.

The fifth photo is a professional portrait of the whole family with Helena and Rafael on either side of Miranda, holding her hands. They're all smiling broadly, but to Irina's eye, only Miranda's smile is authentic.

Buddy arrives and the three of them settle into Miranda's bed as Irina reads the opening pages of the first Harry Potter book—a book Irina had hoped to read with Clara. They stop occasionally so Miranda can sound out some of the words. As Miranda snuggles against Irina in the bed, affection blossoms in Irina's chest.

Eventually, Miranda's eyes droop and Irina sets the book aside. Irina says goodnight and leaves the door of the room cracked open behind her as she leaves. She's feeling a little melancholy, so she pours herself a glass of wine. After reading for a while, she brushes her teeth, changes, checks on Matteo in his playpen in the guest room, settles into the guest bed that Rafael had made, and falls asleep.

She wakes to the sound of Miranda's scream. She quickly pulls a blanket around herself and hurries to Miranda's room in the darkness. Irina lights a candle, then climbs into the bed beside Miranda as she used to do with Clara. Miranda snuggles into her.

"I had a dream about the mountain man," Miranda says.

"The mountain man?" Irina remembers Miranda mentioning this after her prior nightmare.

"Daddy shot the mountain man, but he didn't die," Miranda says, sniffling.

"In your dream, you mean?" Irina asks.

"No, when we were at the cabin. He died later. Daddy and me had to leave. Then he died."

Irina feels a little tendril of worry unfurl inside her. Did Rafael kill someone? It seems terribly out of character for someone who blanched when she twisted the head off the rabbit. Has he been hiding this from her? What else doesn't she know?

She reads to Miranda until the little girl falls back asleep. Irina, though, lies awake for hours, wondering what she should do. Should she question Miranda more? Should she ask Rafael about it or assume that whatever he did was reasonable? She falls asleep just before dawn without answers.

+++

Irina spends the next two days trying her best not to think about the mountain man. She distracts herself with chores, a trip to the Fern Cottage garden with the children, and a visit to see Lily and Sunshine. Miranda, thankfully, has no more nightmares.

When Rafael rides back up the driveway just before dinner on the third day, Irina is still not sure what, if anything, she should say to him about the mountain man.

Miranda bursts out the front door and runs to Rafael. He sweeps her up into his arms and twirls her around, relieved to be reunited with her. Miranda excitedly rattles off a list of everything they've done over the past three days as Rafael unloads the trailer.

He immediately feels that something is off with Irina, and it makes him nervous. Her greeting is cooler than he would have expected. He wonders if she's annoyed about how long he was gone or if she's just exhausted from caring for both children on her own.

Without saying much to him, she returns to her cooking on the back patio. He stares after her, puzzled, then finishes unloading the trailer.

He joins Irina on the back patio and offers to help, but she declines his assistance, so he plays fetch with Miranda and Buddy in the yard. When Matteo wakes, Rafael offers to go get him from the guest room, but Irina declines that too. The uneasiness in Rafael's stomach grows.

At dinner, Miranda makes up for Irina's silence. She asks Rafael lots of questions about his trip and what he found and where he stopped. Irina takes a long time moving the playpen back to the guest house and putting Matteo to bed.

After Rafael helps Miranda get ready for bed, Irina still hasn't returned. He's certain now that he's done something wrong, though his exact sin is unclear to him. He's familiar with this dynamic from his marriage.

He starts a fire on the front patio and gets two glasses and a bottle of wine. He fills his own glass and leaves hers on the table beside her usual seat. The fire crackles against the evening chill. The stars and moon appear above him. The night wind whispers through the high grass. His apprehension grows.

Finally, she appears and sits in her usual chair.

"Is something wrong?" he asks, fearing that even that approach is incorrect. Perhaps she expects him to guess what's bothering her.

Irina pours herself a glass of wine. "Miranda had a nightmare the first night that you were gone." His stomach drops. He knows now what this is.

"Who is the mountain man?" Irina asks.

He takes several long sips of his wine, gathering his thoughts; then he tells her about the darkest day of his Pandemic experience.

"The November after the Pandemic started, a man showed up at our cabin. He looked sick."

The man had been dirty and emaciated, with questionable stains on his shirt. His beard had been flecked with something? Vomit? Or just dirt? Rafael couldn't tell from fifty feet away.

"He was coming toward our front door through the yard, telling me that I had to help him. I told him to back off a bunch of times, but he kept getting closer and closer. I fired a warning shot, but he didn't stop."

He recalls the man's staggering toward him and Miranda across the yard of the cabin, the feeling of his heart pounding in his ears, the weight of the gun in his hand, the knowledge that Miranda was standing just a few feet back in the living room, the overriding desire to protect her.

Irina watches him intently in the firelight. Rafael takes a deep breath, and he continues, "I was terrified that he was going to get Miranda and me sick. The Virus was so contagious; anything he touched could be deadly to us. If he coughed, the droplets could infect us."

The man had stumbled slightly but continued advancing toward the door of the cabin, ignoring Rafael's commands— then pleas—to turn around. "I panicked . . . , and I shot him." The scarlet stain spread across the man's midsection, he staggered forward . . . .

Rafael tries unsuccessfully to keep his voice steady and his emotions in check. "In the movies, people always die immediately when they get shot, but he didn't. He was on the ground, screaming. I kept trying to finish him off but missing him or hitting his arms and legs."

Of course Rafael had been unable to finish the job. He was, as his friend had once said, "insufficiently committed to killing." Instead he'd fled in disgust and terror, chased by the agonizing cries of the man he'd shot.

"I took Miranda and left. We camped in the woods overnight, and when we came back, he was dead."

It had only been Miranda's navigation skills that had allowed them to find their way back to the cabin. Rafael had been too blinded by panic and horror to pay attention to their surroundings as they hurried away from the cabin through the rainy woods.

"I managed to lasso his foot and drag him into the woods down the road so we didn't have to see the body, but Miranda saw everything else. She's had nightmares ever since."

He takes a deep breath. "I shouldn't have shot him." Irina hears his voice break slightly.

"I'm not sure what else you could have done," she says. "It almost sounds like he wanted you to shoot him. He probably was sick."

Rafael puts his head in his hands. "I still killed a person. I should have been able to find another solution, but I panicked."

"I don't think there was another, better solution. You had to protect Miranda and yourself. I would have done the same thing. I probably wouldn't even have given him as many warnings as you gave him."

Rafael sighs. "I'm sorry I didn't tell you. At first it seemed like you weren't sure if you wanted to stay here, and I didn't want you to leave. Then once you decided to stay, I really didn't want you to leave."

"I wouldn't have left because of this, but I really wish you had told me earlier." She pauses. "Is there anything else I should know about? If we're going to live here together, we have to trust each other."

It's a test. Did he see the occupied house that she'd noticed in Eureka on her way here?

"There's someone living up toward Eureka, I think," he replies. "I saw a house with smoke and some livestock. I remembered our agreement, so I didn't get anywhere near it, but it was overlooking the highway, so it's possible they saw me."

"Thank you for being cautious. Is there anyone else you've seen around here?"

"No one closer than the Brothers at the Monastery and the Sisters at the Convent nearby, but there are bound to be at least a few other people still left."

Irina thinks for a moment. "Have you ever talked to Miranda about what happened?"

"I tried a few times, after she started having nightmares, but it didn't seem to help. I don't know where she came up with the name 'mountain man.' I guess it was a character in a book or movie. She's had nightmares about him once or twice a month ever since. I really fucked up when I let her see that."

He looks up at the sky, "In case it isn't already really apparent, I have no idea what the hell I'm doing."

"With parenting, you mean?"

He scoffs. "With anything."

Irina knows how he feels. "I think you're doing as good a job with Miranda as anyone could do under the circumstances. She's fed, loved, and pretty happy."

"I was actually really struggling before you arrived," he replies.

Irina wants to reach out and take his hand, but she's pretty sure they have an unspoken rule not to touch each other, so she keeps her hand to herself. Rafael offers her a second glass of wine, but she declines.

"So how was your trip?" Irina asks, realizing that they hadn't gotten to talk about it at all. Only Miranda had asked him about it, and her questions weren't exactly focused on the important survival-related aspects.

"I found books on food preservation, horse training, first aid, and basic survival. Some of the sections of the library were a little thin, though, so I guess that whoever's living in Eureka checked out a bunch of books," he says. "I also found a store with some solar panels, which could be useful, but we'll have to wait until we can bring them here in the horse cart."

"There was another museum there with a bunch of steam-powered equipment," Rafael says, with excitement in his voice. "We can't really do steam power because we don't have coal, and I think it would require a lot of firewood, but it got me thinking—maybe I could figure out how to generate wind or hydroelectric power. The solar panels will give us some power, but there aren't many of them; they'll eventually wear out, and in the winter we may not have enough sun to run large appliances. So I picked up a couple of books about wind and hydroelectric power generation from the library."

He seems energized by his time spent alone, and she likes seeing this side of him. They talk for a while longer before saying goodnight. The last thought both of them have before falling asleep is relief that the conversation went better than expected.

+++

Irina spends the next few evenings reading the horse-training books, while Rafael lounges on the couch in his reading glasses, perusing the books on electricity. When they return to town again, Irina finds a functional-looking horse harness in the museum. She also gets a few ropes and a tarp from the warehouse.

On a clear, breezy morning, she takes Lily to a pasture down the road. Rafael, Miranda, and Matteo watch from outside the fence as she puts the harness on Lily and adjusts it to fit. It's old, but the leather still seems sturdy. Lily steps sideways, uncertain of her new attire. Irina gives her some time to get used to it. Then, as the book instructed, she attaches a rope to either side of the harness and coaches Lily to walk in circles, working on stop and walk commands. When the horse seems comfortable with that, Irina tries to acclimate her to having a possibly-frightening object behind her. She brings out the tarp and attaches it to a long rope tied to Lily's harness.

She commands Lily to walk, and the horse does, turning to warily eye the tarp behind her. Irina watches with satisfaction from a few feet away.

A sudden wind whips the tarp up off the ground, making it snap loudly. Lily's eyes widen, and she bolts in terror, followed by the tarp, which flaps and flutters in the wind with greater intensity as Lily picks up speed. The lead rope that Irina had carelessly looped around her wrist yanks Irina forward violently. She screams as she lands hard on her left arm and is dragged by her right arm across the rough ground until she manages to twist her hand out of the loop. Lily gallops to the other end of the pasture and stops as suddenly as she had started.

The pain in Irina's arm is blinding. Rafael is over the fence and next to her immediately, shouting back at Miranda to hold onto Matteo.

"Fucking amateur," Irina curses herself, "like I've never been around a fucking horse before. Goddammit!"

Rafael has never heard her curse like this, and now he's certain of the gravity of the situation. He tries unsuccessfully to remain calm. He offers a hand to help her up, but she waves him off and tries to pull herself up out of the grass on her own. She stops and curses again. "Fuck. My shoulder is dislocated."

She lets out a long, angry cry of frustration as tears stream down her face.

"Please let me help you," Rafael says, feeling physical discomfort at the sight of her pain.

He takes her working arm and gently lifts her up to assess her. Her face and arms are abraded and bleeding from being pulled over the ground. Her left arm hangs useless at her side.

"I can't believe I was that fucking stupid," she sobs, then winces. "And I think I cracked a rib."

"Can you walk?" he asks her gently. She nods through her tears. He leads her through the field to the gate.

"We have to take the line with the tarp off her," she says, sniffling.

"You're worried about the horse right now!?" Rafael exclaims. He's uncomfortable approaching Lily, but his desire to keep Irina from trying to do it herself wins out. He approaches Lily slowly. The horse watches him with wide, nervous eyes as he carefully unknots the rope tied to the tarp and cautiously pulls the tarp away. He folds it, then jogs back and hands it to Miranda, realizing that she, too, is crying.

"Irina is going to be okay," he tells her, even though he's not entirely sure about that. He has no idea how to put a shoulder back in place. His best hope is that it's covered in one of the medical books he picked up in Eureka. Rafael sweeps Matteo up into his arms, and they all walk slowly back up the hill to the house. A half mile feels like ten miles. At home, Rafael puts Matteo down for a nap and asks Miranda to go play in the yard for a little while. He doesn't need an audience to add to his nervousness.

He gets the First Aid Kit from the master bathroom cabinet and the medical books from the shelf. Irina stands in the light by the window.

"What hurts?" He asks the same question he's asked Miranda dozens of times.

"My shoulder, my side, my arms, my face, my knees. And my pride." She starts crying again.

"You haven't been around horses for a long time," he says. "It's understandable to make a mistake."

He takes out some gauze and alcohol and begins to clean the wounds on her face and arms. It burns, but she doesn't complain.

"Do you know how to fix a dislocated shoulder?" she asks, as he finishes dabbing slightly expired antibiotic ointment on her wounds.

"I don't. I'm sorry. Do you?"

"I've dislocated it before, but it was years ago, and I looked away so I couldn't see what they were doing."

"We've got the books, then."

She nods. He pages through the first book with shaking hands, fearing he won't find what he's looking for and dreading what will follow if he does. He sees nothing, so he picks up the second book. He finds the topic in the index and turns to the relevant page, but the pictures seem to blur before his eyes, and he can barely comprehend the words.

"I'm sorry," he apologizes again. "I think we've firmly established that I'm not good in a crisis."

"You can do it," she tells him. "I trust you."

"In this instance, you really shouldn't."

He takes a deep breath, willing himself to set his anxiety aside for her sake. "Okay, you need to lie on your back."

He helps her lower herself onto the floor, gingerly.

"Brace yourself on the door frame and hold your arm out at a 90-degree angle. I'm going to pull on it, ok?"

She nods, and he pulls on her arm gently. It doesn't work, and he's forced to try again, more firmly. She screams as her shoulder pops back into its socket. He helps her onto the couch, then gets ibuprofen and a glass of water. He crouches down in front of her, as she'd seen him do with Miranda when the little girl fell and scraped her knees. He puts the pills in Irina's uninjured hand. She reflexively reaches for the glass with the other but winces and sets her arm back down.

She pops the pills in her mouth, and he hands her the glass. "How bad is it?" he asks her.

"Not as bad as it was. Thank you."

He leaves and comes back a few minutes later with a piece of a bedsheet. He slips it under her injured arm, then ties it above her uninjured shoulder. "I'll get a real sling when I'm in town. I'm sorry, but I don't think I can do anything about your rib. I wish we had some ice and a doctor."

"I'll be alright," she says.

"Just rest for a little while. I can get Matteo when he wakes up. Maybe you two should stay in the guest room for a couple of days. You're going to need help."

She nods and walks carefully up the stairs and into the guest room. She lies down gingerly on the bed. When she realizes how long her arm will be useless, she starts to cry again. She won't be able to help with anything. She may not even be able to dress herself. She's grateful that she can at least ask Miranda's assistance with that; the idea of having to ask Rafael makes her burn with embarrassment. She chastises herself again for her carelessness. Eventually, the ibuprofen does its job, and she falls into restless sleep.

When Irina wakes later in the afternoon, everything hurts. She tries to help with Matteo, but she can't even lift him, so she's relegated to sitting at the table on the patio, watching as Rafael cooks dinner.

After Rafael has moved Matteo's playpen into the guest bedroom and put both children to bed, Irina sits on the patio, watching the fire and trying to ignore the pain that radiates through her body. Rafael brings more ibuprofen and a glass of water, then pours a cup of peppermint tea for each of them.

"I think we need to try again to invite more people to come to Ferndale," Rafael says.

"I don't know . . . ," Irina replies.

"What if you'd broken your arm or gotten some kind of internal injury? What if it had been Miranda or Matteo who got hurt?"

"I like what we have here, though. Every additional person we have to live with complicates things."

"I understand that, but this isn't sustainable. How much longer do you think we can keep living this way? Another year? Another ten years? Right now we can still eat nonperishable food if we get hungry, but that will run out eventually. And the antibiotics? They're expired already or will soon. The bicycle parts? The windows? The ammunition? The clothing?" As he lists the items, the dam of calm he's held in place all day bursts, and all of Rafael's worries stream out as his voice raises. "And what happens when the resources run out? When what's left of humanity is competing for scraps? Then this becomes the other kind of apocalypse. Then it's 'Mad Max' or 'The Road' or whatever post-apocalyptic thriller you want to name. That's what happens in ten or twenty years."

Irina is surprised by how upset he is. She rubs her temples and sighs. "Look, I really can't talk about this right now. My arm hurts, my face hurts, everything fucking hurts. Why are you pushing me?"

"Because when I saw you on the ground today, it terrified me!" he exclaims, more angry than she's ever heard him. "Because I have no idea what I would have done if you'd been seriously hurt! Because I'm afraid for us! I'm afraid for Miranda and Matteo. I'm terrified that we'll go hungry or have some kind of medical emergency or that they'll just miss out on life. I want them to have full lives or at least as full as a person's life can be now. I want them to do something meaningful, to explore, to fall in love. I want them to be happy, and I don't think they can be, if we stay alone here."

Irina doesn't respond, and Rafael sighs and takes a different direction, "What made you decide to ride four hundred miles to Ferndale?"

Irina recounts the story of Matteo's head injury.

He grimaces. "You had to do the stitches yourself? That's awful."

"It was, and my trip to get here was also really difficult, because of other people."

"I know," he says. "But what were you hoping to find here? I know you were hoping for more than just me and Miranda."

"I was hoping to find a town with some teachers, a doctor, law enforcement, farming," she replies.

"We could still build that."

"I don't know. Even if we agreed to invite other people here, there's no guarantee anyone would come. You tried before. Why would this time be different?"

"I think I was too early," he says. "No one was ready to move yet, and I didn't have anything to offer at that point. If we can offer people something worthwhile, maybe they'd make the trip."

"And what are we going to offer them?"

Rafael didn't want to get her hopes up and then disappoint her, so he hasn't told her what he's been tinkering with in the basement rec room while she's been training Lily, "Electricity. We have the solar panels, and . . . I think I have a working prototype for hydroelectric power."

"That's fantastic!"

"I'll still need to scale the prototype, though, and even if I can generate hydroelectric power and I get all the solar panels working, it will still probably only be enough for lights, refrigeration, and some battery-operated tools."

"Still, that would be incredible! I bet that would be enticing enough to get people to travel here. But what would we do when they arrive?"

"That's why I cleared out the houses."

"That's not enough. It's a lot of work to actually build a new society from the foundations. You'd have to set up some kind of political system, economic system, criminal justice system."

"That's your piece. You were a lawyer, right?"

"I'm hardly qualified to write a constitution or think about currency or property ownership," Irina argues.

"But you're smart," he replies. "You could figure it out. Write a first draft of the world you want to live in, and when people get here, they can help you edit it."

"I don't know . . . ."

"Just think about it, alright?"

"Alright," she concedes.

+++

Irina spends the next two days struggling to accept her temporary uselessness, as Rafael struggles to care for the children while doing all the chores. He doesn't complain, but Irina can sense his stress in his short responses to her and his impatience with Miranda.

Rafael is especially bothered that he isn't able to fulfill his obligation to check the library for new arrivals, so on Sunday evening, after putting Matteo to bed, Rafael uses the last of the daylight to bike to Ferndale and change the library sign, while Irina oversees Miranda's bedtime rituals.

Rafael arrives back home after dark and finds Irina on the front patio. "You're right," she says as he steps up onto the patio.

He smiles, "I do love to hear those words, but it would help to have some context."

"We should bring more people here. I have conditions, though."

He nods and sits down.

"First, we don't invite anyone until the spring," she says. "We can't have a bunch of other people showing up and expecting us to feed them this winter. In the spring, if things go well, we'll have a wheat crop that will help. But right now we're just a little too close to the edge."

"That makes sense."

"Second, you aren't going to like this, but I have to keep training Lily."

"You could have been killed, Irina!" he exclaims.

"If we're planting wheat this fall, we need her to plow," Irina points out.

"I can work on the electricity," he says. "Maybe we can charge one of those battery-powered rototillers."

"By October we need to have wheat fields ready to be planted, and there's no way we can do that amount of plowing by hand. Unless you're absolutely certain you'll be able to get a rototiller working within a couple of months, I need to continue training her. Are you certain?" She looks at him intently.

When Rafael flashes back to the image of her on the ground in the pasture, he's tempted to lie, but then he recalls their conversations about honesty. Reluctantly, he admits that he isn't sure.

"I made a stupid mistake," Irina says. "I'll be more careful, I promise."

He sighs. "Fine."

"How do you plan to reach people? Fliers again?"

"I have a better idea," he smiles. "I'll show you next time we're in town."

+++

On Wednesday, Irina is able to take off the sling. After days of idleness, she's desperate to begin working again. With a little caution, she's able to do a few basic tasks, which allows Rafael to make his usual Thursday trip to Ferndale with Miranda. While they're gone and Matteo is napping, she walks down to visit Lily and Sunshine. She feeds Lily handfuls of hay and nuzzles her neck, whispering, "I know it's not your fault."

That evening, Rafael invites her, Miranda, and Matteo into the basement for a demonstration of his electricity-generating prototype. He pumps water over a small water wheel he's fashioned from pieces of scrap metal, and they watch as a small light turns on. Miranda, who barely remembers a time when there was electricity, is mystified. Matteo reaches out to try to grab the lightbulb. Irina feels both pride and trepidation that their plan is moving forward.

+++

Irina's shoulder and rib improve every day. The abrasions on her arms and face heal. One evening after dinner, Miranda emerges from the kitchen carrying an apple cobbler with a birthday candle in it. Irina had stopped marking her phone calendar a month ago and had forgotten her own fortieth birthday, but Miranda had remembered the date that Irina had mentioned to her in passing. Miranda holds the dessert with the candle far enough away that Matteo can't grab it, while she and Rafael sing a somewhat off-key happy birthday.

"Are you crying because you're sad?" Miranda asks Irina, after she blows out the candle. "No. I'm crying because I'm happy," Irina says. Her emotions feel jumbled, though. She's touched that they remembered, but it also feels strange to sit here on a momentous birthday with these people who feel like family but aren't actually her family, while at the same time missing her actual family.

Rafael nudges Miranda, and she runs inside and returns with a messily-wrapped gift. Irina starts crying in earnest as she unwraps oil paints and canvas notebook.

"I saw an arts and crafts store in Eureka," Rafael says, "and I thought of you."

Irina swipes away her tears. "Thank you."

She reaches out her arms and pulls Miranda into a hug, squeezing Miranda and Matteo tightly against herself. Matteo, as always, tries to wriggle free. Rafael watches, longing to join them but fearing that it would be inappropriate.

Later, after Miranda and Matteo are asleep, Irina and Rafael sit on the patio by the fire.

"Thank you again," Irina says.

"You're welcome," he replies. They sit in silence for several moments, watching the fire and listening to the night insects.

"I don't think my hydroelectricity plan is going to work," Rafael says. Irina can hear the disappointment in his voice.

"What do you mean?"

"When I was in town last week, I surveyed the river. The water volume is too low for the system I've been planning."

"And it's too wide to build a dam?"

"Correct. So I'm out of luck on the hydropower plan for now. I'm going to investigate the possibility of wind power, but that might take a while to scale. For now, we'll have to rely mostly on solar panels and hope we get enough sun during the winter. When do you think Lily will be ready to help us get the panels from Eureka?"

"In a month or two. I'm coming with you this time, though," she says. He starts to object, but she continues, "You don't like Lily, and you'll need help loading everything into the cart.

He wants to argue with her that this is impractical, but it seems unfair and a bit old-fashioned that she would stay home with the children and animals, especially since if they run into trouble, she's a far better shot than he. He knows that if they were ever threatened and Irina had to defend them, she wouldn't fail.

"The solar panels still aren't a long-term solution, though," he says. "They wear out over time, and they rely on batteries that may wear out even sooner. This buys us twenty years at most."

Irina watches him in the firelight, feeling a renewed appreciation for his long-term thinking. She envies his ability to envision something larger, even though she sometimes feels a bit inadequate in the face of it. She tries to remind herself that they have complementary skills, that they're working together as a team.

"How's your constitution coming along?" he asks.

"Oh, don't call it that! That's way too much pressure." She sighs. "I haven't made much progress. I've got a few ideas, but it's hard to articulate them."

"Well, if you ever want to bounce your ideas off of someone, I'm happy to listen."

"I might take you up on that," she replies, feeling a bit self-conscious. Her thoughts about this are still too half-formed to stand up to any amount of scrutiny. She changes the subject to ask a question that's long been on her mind.

"Why did you pick Ferndale, really?" Irina asks. "It's not for the fertile soil, because you were close to Hood River, where any seed you drop in the ground sprouts pretty much instantly. And it's definitely not for the weather."

"The weather is great!"

"A balmy 70 degrees in late August. And if you wanted moderate weather, you could have stayed in Oregon. Why come all this way?"

"Other than the cows?" he asks.

"Surely you didn't travel five hundred miles for the possibility of cows. I bet there were some cows between here and there."

He sighs, watching the dark ocean. "I came here because I remembered being happy here. When Helena and I were here for Christmas, things were better than they'd ever been between us. Miranda is actually named after a little town south of here where we went for a really nice hike in the redwoods on our drive up from Sonoma."

Rafael doesn't share the fact that Miranda was conceived on that trip to Ferndale. Despite their marital difficulties, Helena was set on having a baby. Though she swore to him that she was on birth control at the time, he's always suspected it was a lie. Still, he's glad for the result.

"I also came here because I loved this town," he continues. "And I knew that the people here were resourceful. There were farms and cows and a blacksmith shop and even a boat builder. The town was isolated enough that I hoped that the people here might have survived."

He recalls all the bodies he's cleared out of the houses, and sadness pierces him. "That Christmas that I visited, I was walking down the street, and I heard someone playing carols on a trumpet. I walked around the block, and there were two men standing on a front stoop, playing songs together, while their neighbors sat in lawn chairs in the yard. Someone had set out a folding table with a bottle of wine and some homemade Christmas cookies. It felt like something out of a movie."

Rafael's mother had been a big fan of the kind of American movies that featured wholesome love stories, hometown heroes, quirky local businesses, and neighbors who all knew each other. As a child, he would often sit on their worn-down couch watching them with her.

"Then one of the people in the audience got up and invited me to sit down and watch the 'concert.' I was just a stranger, standing on the sidewalk, and they welcomed me into their little impromptu party and it just felt . . . magical. Like the archetype of what a town should be. The people here were so happy and welcoming. It felt like this wasn't just a place where people lived; . . . it was a community."

During his darkest days in the cabin, he'd held onto this fantasy tightly. That—and Miranda—were the only things that had kept him going.

"I know those people are gone now," he says sadly. "But that's what I want to rebuild here: a community of people working together. I don't think it's enough just to survive. We have to rebuild something that's worth surviving for."

He pauses for a moment, "Even before the end of the world, this town was kind of at the end of the world or at least at the end of the continent. Doesn't something about this place feel magical to you?"

Irina looks out at the hills to the east and the ocean to the west, and she can't help agreeing.

+++

The next afternoon, in the warehouse, Rafael shows Irina what looks like a walkie-talkie. "This is what I'm hoping will help us bring more people to Ferndale," he says. "A ham radio."

Irina is skeptical. The device has nothing but a tiny two-inch antenna. "You think that will broadcast far enough to reach anyone else?"

"It didn't when I found it last spring, but if I recall correctly from a class I took a decade and a half ago, this might broadcast far enough if we have repeaters and if there's nothing in the way."

"We're surrounded by mountains," she observes.

"We'll climb to the top of the highest mountain," he replies.

"And what makes you think that other people will have radios?" Irina asks.

"There are ham radios all over the place," he replies. "A lot of them run on batteries, which are still good. And some people might have power, too. There was a big push for solar panels in California over the past two decades."

Irina shrugs skeptically. "If it actually works, it beats having to ride around on bicycles and hang up fliers."

+++

They fall into a comfortable rhythm of tasks over the next few weeks. Irina resumes training Lily, and she and Rafael spend evenings working on their separate projects—Irina on her government plan and Rafael on wind power. Irina realizes one night that they haven't had a real conversation in days, so she gets two glasses and a bottle of wine and invites him onto the patio with her. She starts a fire as he pours the wine.

"How are your experiments going?" she asks, seating herself in her usual chair.

"I think I'm close to a prototype. How's your writing going?" He hands her a glass of wine.

"Slowly," she says, taking a sip. "I keep bumping up against the same problem."

"What's that?"

"If we invite other people here, we'll have to give up some of our own self-determination."

"Isn't that the usual cost for living in a society?" he asks, as he sips his wine and watches the last vestiges of the sunset over the Pacific.

"I guess so. I'm just trying to accept that if we build a real democracy, we won't be leading it for long."

"You aren't designing a system in which we'll be benevolent dictators for life?"

"That seems unlikely to entice more occupants." She takes another sip of her wine and feeds a log into the fire, shivering against the chilly night air. "Do you think we'll ever be able to get back to the way things were?"

"Good god, I hope not. Can I be honest with you about something that's kind of messed up?"

Her curiosity is piqued. "Sure."

"I'm happier now. Maybe it's just the change in perspective, or maybe it's that I'm doing things that feel very immediately meaningful. So much of happiness is having a sense of purpose. I didn't really have that before, and I think a lot of other people didn't either. We lived in an unsustainable world. Didn't you feel it during the past twenty years? Everything always seemed to be on a knife's edge. So I don't think we should go back to the way things were. We had to pay a terrible price to start over, so we should build something better."

He's an idealist, Irina realizes belatedly. She'd never had the chance to be one, given her childhood, but she'd known plenty of idealists over the course of her work. It's probably why he was depressed before. Idealists are always disappointed. She asks, "But what does that even look like? What is 'something better?'"

"Less misery. Less inequality. More collaboration."

"Concretely, though. This community you want to build, ... how do we create that? What political system am I supposed to put together?"

126

He shrugs. "I was never very interested in politics. If you come from a place like Venezuela, it's a waste of time to take an interest, because the outcome is predetermined. So I'll build the physical infrastructure and trust you for the philosophical parts."

"What if the people we bring here hate my system?"

"Then you'll have to convince them."

Chapter Seven

As October approaches, they spend their days harvesting and preserving fall crops. The weather grows colder, and Irina and Rafael agree that it would be more efficient for her and Matteo to stay in the main house for the winter so they don't have to heat the guest house.

Though Irina tries to ignore the imminent anniversary of Clara's death, her body seems to know. As the date approaches, she often wakes at 3:00 a.m. and can't fall back asleep. Her thoughts and her stomach churn with the memory of the worst days of her life. She forces herself to breathe and read by candlelight. Sometimes she gets up and paces the moonlit living room.

In the mornings, her exhaustion hangs below her eyes. Rafael, and even Miranda, notice that she's withdrawn. Miranda makes increasingly demanding bids for Irina's attention and is hurt when she gets little response. In the evenings, Irina often excuses herself to her room after putting Matteo to bed, leaving Rafael to do reading lessons with Miranda, who takes her disappointment at Irina's rejection out on him. Rafael wants to talk to Irina about it, but she seems to be avoiding him as much as possible, so he has little opportunity. One evening, as he sits at the kitchen table with Miranda and the reading workbook, his patience breaks just as Irina is coming up from the basement with a bucket of water.

"Miranda! Sit still and finish the damn page!" He exclaims. Miranda hurls the book onto the ground and storms off to her room. Rafael sighs, rubbing his forehead with his hand. He picks up the book and places it on the bookshelf.

"You should be more patient with her," Irina says, setting the full bucket on the floor by the staircase.

"That's easy for you to say. She behaves better with you," he replies testily. He also hasn't been sleeping well. Several nights that week he'd awoken to the sounds of Irina pacing the living room like a caged animal.

"Children die, Rafael."

He's taken aback. "What?"

Irina looks up at the ceiling. "You never know when you'll lose someone. Any interaction can be your last. It's important to be patient."

Rafael considers this; then he has a sudden realization. "You said Clara died in autumn?"

"October 8th. Or at least that's the date I count. The day she lost consciousness."

Tomorrow, Rafael notes. He chastises himself for not getting up in the middle of the night to talk to her.

"I wasn't patient with Clara, and I regret it," Irina says. She sits down on the couch and looks out the window into the darkness instead of facing him. She's only told this story to one person, and he's dead. Sam had exonerated her, but she's always been sure that he was wrong.

The quote about how "grief doesn't change you, it merely reveals what you always were" has seemed trite and judgmental to Irina in the wake of Clara's death. Anyone who says that has obviously never had to stand in the firebombed ruins of their own life, after watching their child breathe her last breath. Grief doesn't reveal you, Irina thinks; it deconstructs you, dissociating every molecule of you to its component atoms. If you're very fortunate, you may one day rebuild something of yourself, but it won't be the same. It's impossible to return those pieces to their previous configuration. Only the luckiest people will find themselves transformed, like the Phoenix, into something more beautiful. The rest will struggle always with the bone-on-bone friction between who they were and who they are.

"Clara's death was my fault," Irina says quietly. Rafael stands by the bookshelf and doesn't move. "On the day of the accident, we were arguing. Clara was upset because Sam was out of town visiting his mother, so she didn't want to go to school that morning. She fought every step, and I was tired and stressed and impatient with her. I was driving her to school, and we stopped at a light, and we were still arguing. She took her shoe off and threw it, and I turned around to yell at her. I saw the light change to green and I . . . ." Her voice catches on her tears. "I pulled forward without looking and this fucking pickup truck t-boned us on Clara's side."

Rafael crosses the room to her and kneels down in front of her, as he had when she'd been injured. "Irina, that wasn't your fault. It was the other driver's fault."

"It was both of our faults!" She exclaims, the dam of guilt and sadness breaking. "In law two parties can be responsible if both of their actions were necessary for the event to occur. Sine qua non—'without which, not'—a condition that's essential in order for another event to occur.

"Two conditions can both be essential. My carelessness was an essential condition. If I had been paying attention, if I hadn't been arguing with her, I would have seen that truck; I would have stopped short, and she would be alive!"

They're both quiet for a moment; then Irina says, "Or she would have died anyway with everyone else. But at least it wouldn't have been my fault, and I wouldn't have gotten pregnant again, and I could have joined her and Sam."

Rafael gets up and sits next to her on the couch. He breaks his rule and wraps his arms around her.

Irina needs to share at least part of this with someone. "I remember seeing the ambulance pull away with her in it, and I just lost it. They had to sedate me."

She's never been sure if the blurriness of these memories is because of the sedatives or the trauma.

"Sam flew home from California and met us at the hospital. Clara was still alive, but she was in a coma. After two days, they told us that she had no brain activity, and she wouldn't recover."

Irina has one clear memory from that day: the conversation they had with the social worker. Irina, in denial, had argued with the social worker about the brain-death diagnosis, saying that it couldn't be right; Clara was supposed to grow up and climb mountains with her and Sam. The woman had taken Irina's hand and said, gently but firmly, "Even if she lives, she won't be climbing any mountains."

It had felt devastating and cruel, which is probably why it still stands out clearly in Irina's otherwise hazy memory. It had been necessary, though.

"We decided to disconnect life support and donate whatever organs we could."

Actually, Irina had decided and convinced Sam. It's a decision that still weighs heavily on her. She'll always wonder if she acted too early, if she was selfish, just wanting to arrive at the devastating end, instead of lingering in miserable ambiguity. That night, under the dim hospital room lights, Irina crawled into the bed and wrapped herself around the empty vessel of Clara's body, now free of the tangle of wires that had surrounded her. With Sam's hand stroking Irina's hair, they had listened as Clara breathed her last breath. Irina could have sworn that she heard singing, a wordless and beautiful harmony, and then there was profound silence, broken only by the sound of Sam's sobs.

Afterward, they drove home in Sam's car with an empty car seat behind them. Irina vividly recalls opening the door to their silent house. For weeks they slept on the guest room bed in an awful liminal state, unable to bear even returning to their own bedroom. Irina remembers lying beside Sam, facing him in the dim evening light, both crying in silence, wordlessly staring into each other's eyes. She remembers the mass of cards and slowly dying flowers that arrived in her living room. She remembers sitting across the desk from the funeral home director, choosing options numbly. She remembers the memorial service, though she doesn't remember what she or Sam said there. There is still a small urn—impossibly small, how can it contain all that Clara was?—on her nightstand. Irina carried it with her for all those miles.

She isn't sure she can share these details with Rafael. They aren't the kind of memories that can easily be conveyed to another person. Only Sam was there, and only he could ever understand. And yet, it's too heavy to carry alone anymore. Rafael wraps his arms around her, and she sobs out the broken, ugly memories against his chest as the room grows dark around them. His tears fall into her messy braid, and hers soak his t-shirt.

Irina grows quiet and still against him, and Rafael thinks that perhaps she has fallen asleep. He looks up to see Miranda standing at the stairs, and he's unsure how long she's been there or how much she's heard, but he can see the tear tracks on her cheeks. He mouths, "I'm sorry," to her, and she turns and tiptoes back up the stairs.

Irina sniffles against him and pulls back, looking at him for a long moment, her reddened eyes meeting his. She swipes away her tears and says, "Sometimes I feel fine. Content even. Then sometimes I feel like this, and I'm not sure when it will ever end. When does it fucking end?"

"I'm not sure that it does," Rafael replies, thinking of the moments when he still remembers his mother, his friends, even Helena. "Maybe the proportions just change over time. You still feel just as sad but less often."

"It has been better these past few months," Irina agrees. She moves away from him, and cool air slips between them. "Thank you. I'm sorry."

"Please don't apologize," he says gently.

She shivers. He gets up and gets her a blanket, then restarts the fire. He returns to the couch, wrapping his arms around her again. She leans against him, exhausted. Her eyes slip closed, and Rafael lowers her gently onto the couch and covers her with the blanket. He takes Buddy out, then calls the dog to follow as he ascends the stairs to Miranda's room. She's lying in her bed, staring at the ceiling, eyes open, tears on her cheeks. Buddy jumps onto the bed and settles himself beside her. Miranda wraps her arms around him.

"Irina was Clara's mommy," she says. "And Clara died."

Rafael nods and slips into the bed beside her. He wraps his arms around her tightly, just as she does with Buddy.

"My friends died too, didn't they?" Miranda asks, as though this is a sudden revelation, as though, despite everything, it still has never occurred to her that another child could die. Rafael realizes that he's never really told her what happened to everyone else she cared about. Perhaps he's worked too hard to protect her from the worst realities of the Pandemic. He longs to lie, but he senses that it's time for honesty.

"Yes, honey, they probably did. I'm so sorry."

Miranda cries quietly into Buddy's fur, until she, too, falls asleep.

Rafael lies awake for hours, turning Irina's story over in his mind; remembering the suicide family in the craftsman house, the mountain man, Helena and his mother and his friends; feeling anger and despair like he hasn't felt in years. It's almost dawn when he recalls Irina's theory about shared grief, and an idea occurs to him. As the sun rises, he closes his eyes and falls into restless sleep.

+++

The following week, Irina and Lily spend an exhausting day plowing a new field. She rides Lily back through the hills as the sun sets over the Pacific. Then she, Rafael, and Miranda plant the wheat that will help to ensure their continued survival and the survival of anyone else who chooses to come here.

Life, Irina thinks, is moving forward. She's the only one who's standing still.

Chapter Eight

The winter rains start in earnest. The skies grow cloudy, and the days grow shorter. Irina and Rafael decide that it would be better to stay in Ferndale once or twice per week, so they maximize the time they have to clear out the houses and minimize the amount of time they spend biking in the rain.

On the second Monday in November, Rafael and Irina stand on the porch of the yellow-and-peach bed and breakfast Irina had spotted on her first day in town. Rafael had cleared the partial corpse from the porch earlier that morning, while Irina and Miranda worked on sorting items at the warehouse.

Irina has bundled Matteo up and put him in the playpen on the covered porch. She eyes him with concern as he tries to pull himself up and over the playpen rail. Miranda agrees to keep a close eye on him. Rafael picks the lock on the door and lets himself and Irina inside.

They find another gruesome scene—scratch marks on the door, the skeleton of a large dog, and the partially dismantled skeletal body of a human on the floor of the kitchen. Irina grimaces. She and Rafael gather the pieces of the human corpse and pick up the body of the dog, setting them on a tarp in the middle of the kitchen.

"This never gets easier," Rafael says, and Irina agrees. They carry the tarp out the back door and place it in the cart there. Rafael rolls the cart away, and Irina returns inside to clean the floor. After mopping, she walks around, surveying the space, considering the possibilities. There's a spacious, comfortably-furnished sitting room with a large fireplace surrounded by several Victorian-style wingback chairs and a small sofa. Down the hallway is a dining room large enough for several tables and a generous kitchen with a modest walk-in refrigerator. She explores the rooms upstairs, bracing herself for more unpleasant discoveries, but the rooms are empty of occupants and look to be in good order, furnished with careful attention to detail.

"This is the place," she tells Rafael when he returns. He looks at her quizzically. She explains, "You said that I should create a draft, and when people arrive, they can help me edit it. I want this to be the place we meet."

"You don't want to do that at the town hall?"

Irina makes a face and shakes her head. "That building is uninspiring and too formal. This is just right. I don't want Independence Hall. I want an informal conversation between friends. There are lots of rooms upstairs too, and most of them have fireplaces, so people can stay overnight if they like."

"How many people will be in this conversation?" he says, looking around at the sitting room.

"Five. We'll work on formalizing a governing system when five people arrive, including us. More people than that seems unmanageable."

He nods. "Interesting. We'll leave this space as is, then."

He walks into a small office and begins searching through the drawers there. He pulls out several pieces of mail and notes the names in the book he always carries. Then he and Irina clear out the food from the kitchen pantry and take the unexpired items to the warehouse.

Rafael leaves to go and hunt for some things he needs for a wind turbine.

As Irina and Miranda inventory items in the warehouse, Irina's mind turns to the spring. She knows the days of her steady, predictable existence with Rafael in the House by the Sea are drawing down. She wonders who will join them here, if anyone does. She's close to a completed draft of the criminal code for their society. She suspects this will be the easiest part. The economic and governmental models will be more challenging. It's hard to imagine something outside the system she'd grown up in, but she senses that she has to, for both practical reasons and the reasons Rafael had expressed.

+++

The week before Thanksgiving, Rafael sets up his wind-turbine prototype on the top of the hill near the house. As he hammers stakes into the ground to tether it, he explains proudly that he's constructed it from a modified building exhaust fan he'd found in one of the industrial buildings in town. It begins to spin in the coastal wind, and he plugs in a string of LED Christmas lights to a battery and outlet he's affixed to it. They glow in the dim light of the rainy season's afternoon, and everyone claps. Rafael runs an extension cord down the hill, and they spend their evenings lit by the warm glow.

On a blustery, misty morning a week after Thanksgiving, they set off toward Eureka. Irina and Miranda ride in the horse-drawn cart. Rafael follows on the bike with Matteo in the child seat and Buddy in the trailer. The rolling hills along the highway have turned emerald green in the winter rain. Beyond them, the coastal mountains are shrouded in mist. Irina enjoys the scenery and the steady rhythm of Lily's hooves. She thinks of the document she's working on. She's started to formulate what she hopes will be a good idea for a government.

A few miles south of Eureka, the bay appears along the highway, and they pass by the occupied house they'd both seen before. Several cattle graze on the hillside beside a small blue house surrounded by gardens. As they pass, Irina has the strange intuition that they're being watched.

By late afternoon, they arrive in front of the library, where Irina hopes to get some books on political systems, and Rafael hopes to find more information about ham radios. Miranda peruses the children's section. Irina is proud that Miranda is now adept at sounding words and seems to have taken a real interest in reading. Matteo, however, just likes to tear the books up, so they keep a close eye on him.

"I was thinking," Rafael says as they eat lunch in the library, "maybe we should introduce ourselves to whoever's living on that farm."

Irina considers this, as she slices another piece of soft farmer's cheese that she'd made herself. "Are you sure that's safe?"

"No. But it's efficient. If they don't have a radio, we'll have to come all the way back to invite them to Ferndale."

Irina is instinctively reluctant to risk interacting with other people, but she remembers her agreement with Rafael, so she concedes, and they decide that Rafael will visit the house, while she waits nearby with the children—and a rifle. After stopping at the solar panel store and loading up the cart with as many panels as they can fit, they take their caravan back down the highway toward Ferndale.

A quarter of a mile north of the house, they tie Buddy to one tree and Lily to another nearby. Irina tucks Matteo into the backpack, and they hike up the road toward the farm. A dozen sheep are grazing in the pasture behind the cows. A small stream winds down through the verdant grass, and a column of smoke rises from the chimney of the small blue cottage next to the pastures. The cottage is surrounded by well-tended raised-bed gardens and fruit trees. Irina and the children duck into the bushes, and Rafael continues to the house.

He knocks on the door and hears several different barks from inside, then a male voice, slightly accented, telling the dogs to get back.

A man in his early fifties, with ebony skin and graying hair, opens the door. Despite the circumstances, he's dressed in a crisp button-down shirt and trousers. He smiles broadly at Rafael.

"I hoped you'd come back!" He says. His cheerfulness feels like a relic. "Come in, come in."

He shoos the dogs away again and gestures for Rafael to follow him into the bright living room. A large window overlooks the highway. In the corner is a wood stove with a stack of freshly cut firewood beside it.

"You were here in Eureka a couple of months ago, right?" the man asks. Rafael nods. "I've forgotten my manners!" the man exclaims. "Dr. Ifeanyi Igwe."

He sticks out his hand with vigor, and Rafael shakes it uncertainly. "Rafael Delgado."

"Tea?" Dr. Igwe asks him.

Rafael nods, and Dr. Igwe gestures for him to sit down on a worn sofa nearby. Six dogs assemble themselves around Rafael. The largest mutt leans against Rafael, pressing himself into Rafael's thigh. Several cats lounge in the windowsills and on cushions by the fire. From a perch by the window, an African Grey parrot greets Rafael continually with "hello, hello, hello."

Through the window, Rafael can see the surprisingly large waves of Humboldt Bay and the ocean beyond.

"Are you a medical doctor, Dr. Igwe?" Rafael asks, hopefully.

"Much to my parents' disappointment, I am not," Dr. Igwe replies from the kitchen on the other side of the doorway. "They were both medical doctors, and I'm fairly certain they had my medical school picked out for me even before I was born. But I preferred animals."

Rafael looks around at the assortment of pets. A veterinarian, then. Still, a useful skill, and close enough to a doctor that he may be able to extrapolate some medical solutions for humans.

"You can just call me Ify." Ify returns with two cups of tea. He hands one to Rafael. "Would your companions like to join us?"

Rafael notices a pair of binoculars on a table by the living room window.

"There isn't much to do around here but watch what's left of the world," Ify explains.

"I'll get the others," Rafael says. He returns a few minutes later with Irina—without her rifle but, he's certain, with her handgun—and the children. Ify has already prepared a few more cups of tea. They do introductions and assemble themselves in the living room chairs. Miranda is entranced by the variety of animals. She stands under the parrot, staring at it.

"That's Beatrice," says Ify, "I rescued her from the Sequoia Park Zoo. She's been my only conversation partner for the past year."

"There's no one else here in Eureka then?" Irina asks.

Ify shakes his head. "Not since last Christmas. Delia Parker was my closest neighbor, but she took her own life."

Rafael looks around the room, taking in the well-worn decor and the walls crowded with family photos. A blonde woman and three children at various stages of growth. Ify sees him looking. "Shanna, my wife, and our boys: Nnaemeka, Chibuzor, and Nkem. All gone that September. But death didn't want me."

"I'm sorry about your family," Irina says gently.

"We'll be reunited one day," Ify answers softly. For several moments, there's only the sound of a dog's tail thumping as Miranda pets him.

"What brings you to Eureka?" Ify asks. "Do you live nearby?"

"We live in Ferndale," Irina replies. "We came to get books and solar panels."

"I had seen the solar panel store in my wanderings," Ify says, "but I have no way to get them here."

"We could bring them," Rafael offers. "Or, if you want, you could come to Ferndale with us, and we could get you set up with some there."

"We want to rebuild the town," Irina says. "With electricity, a government, an economy."

Rafael looks around, "You're probably comfortable here, but if you'd consider relocating, we'd be happy to have you in Ferndale."

"How large is your community?" Ify asks.

"Only us for now. But we plan to invite others," Irina says. "And you could be a part of that."

"Can I bring my companions?" Ify asks, gesturing to the menagerie of animals.

"Yes. We'll help you move them," Irina offers.

Ify considers, looking around at the frames on the wall. "It's hard to live with ghosts."

Irina nods, remembering her impulsive flight from Salem.

"I'll join you in the spring," Ify says finally. He invites them to stay at his home for the night. Rafael and Irina retrieve Lily, Buddy, and the bike. Ify, Irina, and Rafael stay up late, talking about the Pandemic, their plans for the town, and their Before lives. Like Rafael, Ify had immigrated to the U.S., though he had been much younger when he arrived with his parents from Nigeria. He'd grown up in Atlanta and had moved with his wife, also a veterinarian, so they could be close to her family in Eureka after they had children. He confesses that he's always missed Atlanta.

"It never really gets warm here!" he tells them, and Irina looks at Rafael smugly.

The next morning Rafael and Irina agree to return to Eureka on March 20th to help Ify move his things and his animals to Ferndale; then they depart down the road toward Ferndale.

+++

Two weeks before Christmas, they trek into the forest near the house to find a suitable tree. They cut down a small Sitka Spruce, and Rafael and Irina carry it home and adorn it with the string of LED lights. It adds a bit of festivity to the living room during the dark, rainy days.

They celebrate on Christmas Eve in keeping with the Venezuelan tradition. At Miranda's request, they all dress up. Rafael is trying to revive the living room fire, when he hears Irina and the children descending the stairs. He looks up and immediately averts his eyes. This was a terrible idea, he realizes, with a stab of anxiety. If he had hoped to quell his attraction to Irina, he really should have avoided this scenario—though he's not sure how he might have, given Miranda's insistence.

His disobedient eyes flick back up to Irina as she approaches him. Her auburn hair falls in soft, touchable waves, and she wears a figure-hugging vintage-style green dress that calls attention to all of the parts of her he works hard to ignore. Her lipstick is the perfect pinup red of his adolescent fantasies.

But there is also something else, something intangible, that really captures his attention. She carries herself just slightly more upright as though her shoulders bear a little less weight than usual. There's a sparkle in her eyes that might be the makeup, or it might be something approaching happiness.

Irina seems to sense his looking at her, and her eyes meet his, widening slightly—at his own formal attire or at the inappropriateness of his gaze, he cannot tell.

Irina feels suddenly flushed and nervous. It's strange to see him outside of the context of their precarious and challenging existence and in attire that is comparatively form-fitting.

Rafael's suit highlights his broad shoulders and lean, muscular body in a way that's difficult for her to ignore.

He is attractive, she admits to herself, but that's irrelevant. They have to continue to live here together sustainably—as he likes to put it. Dressing up and gazing at each other promises to undercut that goal. Also, there is Sam. And Helena. And all of Irina's long-standing issues and problems.

It's too late to turn back, though. They both look away from each other as Rafael turns his attention to the fire.

After dinner, they exchange gifts. The smell of pine, the firelight, candles, and twinkling LED lights, and the drizzly rain outside infuse the air with a slightly magical feeling. As they all depart for their beds, though, Irina is touched with melancholy, remembering past Christmases with Sam and Clara. That night she dreams with both of them, but when she wakes, she remembers no details, only the hazy certainty of their presence.

On December 28th, for Miranda's birthday, they camp on the beach. They sit on blankets in the sand, in the cold, clear evening, watching the early sunset. As the sun nears the horizon, it catches behind a bank of towering cumulonimbus thunder clouds far out at sea, outlining them in brilliant glowing light. Lightning arcs from the distant clouds to the Pacific. Then the sun lowers, and a waterfall of heavenly light pours from the clouds, reflecting in the sea like liquid fire. Even Matteo stills and stares at it. Miranda snuggles against Irina under the blanket.

Irina has seen many beautiful things in her life but few as breathtaking as this. She wishes she could paint it, though she's certain that no likeness could do it justice. She burns the moment into her memory. She's never felt the presence of a god, but she's fairly certain that this is how an encounter with the numinous and infinite would feel.

The light fades into darkness, and the stolid stars come out, innumerable in the vast sky above them. Matteo falls asleep in Irina's arms, and she tucks him into his sleeping bag in the tent.

Miranda asks for Irina to read her bedtime story. Rafael tries not to let the rejection sting, but it does a little.

Miranda wiggles into the sleeping bag in her tent and leans back against Irina as Irina reads the next chapter of Harry Potter by flashlight. When she sees Miranda starting to doze off, Irina settles the little girl down on the ground and leans and kisses her forehead. The move feels familiar, despite her never having done it to Miranda before.

"I love you," Miranda says softly.

Irina's eyes blur with tears. "I love you too."

She kisses Miranda once more on the forehead lightly, then leaves before her tears spill over. Outside Irina sniffles and wipes her eyes but not before Rafael has seen her. She's certain he's heard their exchange. He feeds another piece of driftwood to the fire, and Irina sits down a few feet from him, facing the ocean. They're both silent, listening to the restless waves against the sand.

"I think you gave Miranda the best birthday gift she could ever hope for," Rafael says to Irina finally, his voice heavy with emotion. "Thank you for . . . ," he can't quite find the words to express what he wishes he could, ". . . everything. I know it's difficult sometimes, filling that role in Miranda's life when you're missing Clara."

Irina sniffles again. She never used to cry much. It's just another way these years have changed her, another subtle transmutation of the woman she used to be.

"Thank you," she says to him through her tears, "for giving me and Matteo a future."

"You would have found a way to do that yourself," he replies. "And anyway, none of this would have been possible without you. I was just as stuck as you were."

"You just had a hot shower and a seaside dream house," Irina laughs through her tears.

Rafael wishes he could express to her how grateful he is for her friendship, for her love of Miranda, for her knowledge and determination and resilience, but words feel inadequate, so they sit in companionable silence until Irina breaks it.

"Matteo is more like Sam every day," she says.

"How so? What was Sam like?" Rafael asks. He's formed a composite sketch of Sam in his mind based on Irina's passing comments, but he's never heard her talk about Sam at length, other than in the context of his death. Still, Rafael senses that Sam is always there, a ghost that lingers in the corner of every room Irina occupies.

"He was brilliantly smart, but never arrogant. He got into Stanford for biology. He could have worked anywhere, but he chose to teach. Everyone always wanted to be around him. He had a way of drawing people out, even people like me who aren't easily drawn out. He was kind and patient. He would never have fought with Clara like I did, which is probably why he was always her favorite. And he fucking loved me. Even when I didn't love myself, even when I was disintegrating after Clara died, he stood there with me in the flames."

She takes a deep breath. "I could never figure out why he picked me, you know?"

Especially now, when she doesn't recognize her own face, body, or mind; when she still carries the guilt of Clara and Sam's deaths weighing down her shoulders; when she still vacillates between being mostly content and feeling soul-deep ennui.

"Matteo is like him. He's gregarious and funny. He wasn't that way before we came here, though, before he met Miranda . . . and you."

Her words linger in the air, and Rafael feels the warmth of them, their mutual appreciation and friendship, born of interdependence and cooperation and just a little desperation. They sit for a while longer, watching the stars rise over the sea.

+++

The following week, Irina and Rafael mount the solar panels on the roof of the yellow-and-peach bed and breakfast. Rafael peers at the instructions through rain-spattered reading glasses as he connects the panel to the battery and necessary hardware, then to the electrical system of the house. Miranda throws the light switch in the sitting room, and, for the first time in more than two years, there is overhead light.

They all shout and dance with excitement and relief. There's a refrigerator, freezer, and heating system, though Rafael isn't confident that they have enough electricity to heat the house or use the stove or water heater, so he proposes they still default to the fire for heat and cooking.

That night by the sitting room fire with the lamp alight beside her, Irina finishes the first draft of her governmental system. She consults her book and footnotes her writing. Rafael joins her after putting Miranda to bed and taking a bath. His hair is still wet, and a droplet of water slides down the side of his neck. Irina has a strange, sudden urge to put her lips there and kiss it away. Without her permission, her mind conjures an image of him in the bath. These thoughts surprise and alarm her. Rafael hands her a glass of wine, breaking her reverie.

She tries to calm her racing heartbeat as she raises her glass to his, clinking it lightly. "Great work today."

"Thank you. How's your draft coming?"

"I've finished two of the three parts. Do you want to see?"

"I'd love to." She hands him the papers, and he puts on his glasses and sips his wine as he skims them.

"This is fascinating. Not what I expected. I've never really been a fan of elections, to be honest. I think this could work. It might be a tough sell to other people, though."

She nods, "I've been thinking the same. I need to have my best arguments ready."

"Try them out on me."

She sips her wine and rehearses. Maybe it's the wine, or maybe it's Irina's persuasive ability, but Rafael is fairly convinced of the governmental system she's created.

Chapter Nine

The days of winter are dwindling now, Irina knows. They celebrate Matteo's birthday in the bed and breakfast. Then January has passed into February and another day of dread is approaching.

Irina decides it's only fair to warn Rafael that she's approaching a bad anniversary. He's already been calculating around Matteo's birth, though, based on the story she'd told him. On the day before the anniversary of Sam's death, Rafael proposes that they stay in the bed and breakfast. It's not difficult to convince Irina, given the prospect of a refrigerator of already butchered rabbit meat.

That night, Irina soaks in one of the Victorian claw-footed tubs in blissfully warm water heated over the fire, trying to banish the memory of the tent in the yard, the sound of Sam's shovel hitting dirt and stone.

The next morning, there's no sunrise, just the cloudy, sputtering sky. Rafael makes breakfast and invites them for a walk. They walk down the cobblestone path in the small park where Irina had sat with Matteo on the first day they'd arrived in Ferndale. At the far end of the park, Rafael leads them inside a small, circular grove of rain-soaked, bare pine tree stumps, each about six feet tall, obviously uprooted from its original location and anchored here in the ground with metal stakes. In each tree trunk, names are carved. Irina recognizes "Rosa Lopez Delgado" and "Dolores Hernandez Delgado." Dozens of others she doesn't recognize. She realizes that they are probably the former inhabitants of Ferndale—the notes Rafael always takes when they clear a new house.

"I remembered what you said about collective grief," Rafael says. "And I think you're right. Some of these people didn't even have graves, and probably no one left alive remembers them, but they deserve to be remembered."

He hands her a box cutter, then takes out another and begins carefully helping Miranda carve Helena's name into the soft wood of one of the stumps.

Irina stands in the drizzly rain with Matteo in the backpack and carves Sam's and Clara's names, then Kylee's name, the names of her neighbors and other friends, the name of a former president, her favorite musician, the Supreme Court Justice she'd always admired. It feels strangely cathartic. Afterward, they all stand and read the names aloud like a prayer.

+++

In the last week of February, Rafael tells Irina that for his birthday he wants to climb King Peak, the highest mountain in the King Mountain Range that surrounds them. He tells her that he's set up a ham-radio repeater on an old radio tower atop a nearby mountain, but he'll need to add another repeater at a higher altitude to reach beyond the mountains.

When she imagines others arriving in Ferndale, Irina feels a stab of panic. She still hasn't finished the economic plan. She's less certain of this part of her work than any of the others. It's complex and entirely outside of her realm of expertise. She pulls every remotely relevant book out of the Ferndale library and stays up late, working beside the string of LED lights in the living room of the House by the Sea, scratching pages, then throwing them into the fire.

Four days before they depart for King Peak, Rafael decides that they need a break, and they take a cloudy, drizzly afternoon hike down to the beach. The rain clears just as they arrive at the sand, and the sun hangs dimly in the afternoon sky. Irina sits on the blanket in her raincoat, watching Rafael hoist Matteo up to see Buddy's and Miranda's game of tag. The toddler shrieks with joy as Rafael pretends to toss him up into the air, never really letting go.

Irina's eyes rest on Rafael. He's not perfect. She can see that. Yet, the overall picture of him is very appealing—his hazel eyes, long lashes, defined cheekbones, the lean muscles of his body that are apparent through his clothes. She likes looking at him. She likes looking at him even more because she knows him to be kind, funny, insightful, intelligent, and an exceptionally good friend and survival partner.

She realizes suddenly that most people don't expect perfection as a prerequisite for attraction. She hadn't required it with Sam—she had desired him, even as his once-firm abs had melted into soft middle age. And Sam had seemed to desire her, even when she was hugely pregnant.

Is it possible that Rafael could also see the sum of her and judge her to be desirable, admirable, even lovable? Better yet, is it possible that she could view herself that way, even absent his—or anyone's else's—positive assessment?

It pains her that she has to ask herself these questions, that birthing two children, losing one child, and reaching middle age have destabilized her so profoundly. She'll have to rebuild her foundation block by block.

She realizes that she hasn't taken her eyes off him during these ruminations, and he's now looking back at her with a puzzled expression. She looks away, embarrassed.

+++

The next morning, Irina stands in front of the mirror of the beauty salon, holding a ponytail of her long auburn hair out in front of her like a unicorn horn, as Miranda watches with rapt attention.

Irina takes the scissors and cuts the end of the ponytail, as she'd learned to do at the beginning of the Covid pandemic. She releases her hair and lets it fall in soft waves around her shoulders, then touches up a few places where the layers don't look quite right.

"Do mine!" Miranda insists. She climbs up into the salon chair. Irina drapes a cape over Miranda, then gathers the little girl's soft dark hair into a ponytail on the front of her head and cuts it at an angle. She releases the ponytail and touches up the uneven ends, then trims Miranda's bangs, just as she'd done for Clara. Miranda grins into the mirror as Rafael steps into the salon, his hair and raincoat dripping from the drizzle outside.

"Do Daddy's hair!" Miranda commands.

"That's fine, you really don't have to," Rafael says.

"You look messy, Daddy. And you said that people will be coming here. You should let Irina cut your hair," Miranda insists.

Rafael looks at Irina, trying to judge whether she is amenable to this. She shrugs, "I used to cut Sam's hair during Covid. I think I still remember how. But no promises."

"I'm sure that anything you do will be better than what I could accomplish on my own. I trust you."

"In this instance," Irina says, smiling, "you really shouldn't."

"I'll take that risk," he replies, sitting down in the chair in front of her. She shakes out a black salon cape and wraps it around him, her body startlingly close to his face, her waves of auburn hair near enough that he can smell her shampoo. Then she begins trimming.

The feeling of her fingers in his hair is so pleasurable that Rafael has to close his eyes for a moment to try to keep his body from reacting. When he opens them, she's looking at him in the mirror. When he looks into her eyes in reflection, though, he's surprised to find his own desire mirrored back at him.

He feels a flutter of anxiety and looks away, quickly. She continues to run her hands through his hair, separating sections and trimming. Finally she concludes, and he stands, shaking the cape off, trying not to look at her. That moment of eye contact was so fleeting that he can almost convince himself that he imagined it. Still, that night in bed, as he struggles to fall asleep, he wonders if she could desire him too. He dreams of her with her legs wrapped around him, green dress hiked up above her hips. He wakes covered in sweat and filled with guilt.

He needs to hold the line on this, he reminds himself as he dresses the next morning. Their survival is still precarious. They can't afford to introduce unnecessary and distracting complications, and he can't afford to lose her help. She's also clearly grieving Sam and not ready to start anything new. And initiating any physical intimacy with her would feel unethical, given their living arrangement. He is resolved. He makes breakfast , and they navigate their day, moving like a planet and moon in tight orbit around each other, trying to pretend that there's no gravity between them.

+++

"It's sixty miles?!" Irina exclaims as she and Rafael look at a map in a book of hiking trails. "We couldn't pick a closer peak?!"

"Sixty miles of riding. But only 4.8 miles of hiking!"

"Not better," she replies. "What will we do about the chickens? It'll take two days to ride, another day to do the hike, and two days to get back. This isn't a feasible plan."

"I bet you could ride there in a single day."

"No. I can't. I did forty miles per day, max, when I rode here. Sixty miles is impossible with Matteo, Buddy, and the gear."

"I'll take Matteo, Buddy, and the gear. You take my bike and ride with Miranda. This is the highest peak," he persists; "It ensures the greatest range. Also . . . didn't you tell me you liked climbing mountains?"

"When I was young. I'm not young anymore."

"You don't want to bag the highest peak in the King Range?" he asks. "Did I say that right? I think that's the word they use in the book."

She sighs. "Fine. But you'll see what I mean."

+++

She's right, he realizes midway through the next morning. It had been easy to switch bikes since there's only a few inches of height difference between them, but that's been the only easy part. The road to Highway 101 had washed out in a few places, and they had to stop twice to clear trees from it. The highway is beautiful, winding through verdant green hills and rich pine forests, but it's consistently hilly. As his legs burn from climbing yet another hill, he sees exactly what she meant.

"You . . . were . . . right," he pants, when they pause for a water break. She smirks at him. "Do you want to switch places?" she asks.

Out of masculine pride, he instinctively wants to say no, but he's exhausted. "Yes."

Miranda protests the change in co-pilot, but Rafael overrules her. "Only another . . . twenty miles or so!" he says to Irina hopefully.

The last portion of the ride, once they leave the highway to get on local roads, is the most difficult, and by late afternoon, Irina is exhausted. She refuses Rafael's offer to switch places again. Rafael knows better than to argue with her when she declares, "We camp here tonight, then ride the rest of the way in the morning and, hopefully, start the hike before noon."

+++

The next morning they wake at sunrise and continue into the mountains with Rafael hauling Matteo and the trailer. The scenery is beautiful, but the road is unpaved and filled with potholes. Several times, the bike pitches wildly with Matteo in the front seat as Irina watches from behind. They have to walk the bikes when the road gets rougher still. The morning mist clears, and the sun comes out.

It's past 1:00 p.m. when they arrive at the trailhead. Irina purses her lips and gives Rafael a look as he packs the repeater components and camping gear into his and Miranda's backpacks. She doesn't say anything, but Rafael hears the unspoken, "I told you so."

Despite the chill, Rafael, Irina, and Miranda soon have to strip off several layers. The hike is strenuous, ascending almost 2,000 feet in the first two miles. They have to stop frequently for water breaks and to catch their breath. Miranda drags her feet and whines until they reach the first place where the trees open up and the vista stretches out before them. She stands in shocked silence, gazing out at the seemingly endless green rolling mountains.

Buddy bounds in front of them as Irina lets Matteo hike a little bit of the path, holding his hand and bolstering him when he loses his footing on stones or roots. She returns him to the pack and continues upward through the forest, catching occasional glimpses of the mountains that surround them. Late in the day, the trail opens up, and they're surrounded by mountains on all sides, marching to the horizon in ever hazier shades of blue. Suddenly, the sea peeks out from the mountains to the west. Irina lets Matteo walk the final stretch of the path to the place where Rafael's map marks the high point. The sun sinks toward the horizon, bleeding pink light into the sky and ocean.

Irina and Miranda set up the tents, make a fire, and cook dinner, while Rafael gets out the solar-powered repeater components and assembles them. He climbs a nearby tree, and Irina hoists the pieces up to him with a rope so he can mount them high in the branches. Then he climbs down, turns on the radio and begins speaking, introducing himself and announcing their location on the Lost Coast. At first there's silence. He switches the frequency a dozen times, praying that they haven't come all this way for nothing. Then . . . .

"Hello Rafael Delgado, this is Frank Hunt from Sacramento."

"Sacramento?!" Irina exclaims.

Frank and Rafael talk for several minutes. Rafael is just telling him about Ferndale when a third voice breaks in: Shantal from Yuba City, who seems very interested in coming to Ferndale with her son. Irina leaves to put Matteo to sleep in the tent, and when she returns, Rafael is talking to two more people, Scott from Santa Rosa and Shasta from Geyserville. As the conversation winds down, Rafael invites them to tell others about Ferndale. He switches frequencies again and begins a conversation in Spanish with Julián from Whiskeytown. Rafael is surprised at how easily the Spanish words flow from him. Irina watches him, drawn by the excited energy he exudes as his plan comes to fruition.

Irina feels a strange sort of melancholy as she kisses Miranda goodnight. Things will change now. It will no longer be just she and Rafael and the children in Ferndale. There's comfort in that but also a prospective nostalgia for what she knows they're about to lose.

It's late when Rafael wraps up his tenth conversation. Irina sits with her back to the fire, looking out at the stars. Rafael sits down a few feet away.

"You were right," Irina says.

"Oooh, say it again," he says, laughing.

She's serious, though, "You had a plan, and you implemented it flawlessly. How do you feel?"

"Relieved. Excited. I think a few of them might actually come to Ferndale this summer."

"It sounded promising," she agrees.

"Now that we've got repeaters set up, I'll be able to communicate from Ferndale." Above them the Milky Way stretches out.

"Do you know the constellations?" Irina asks.

"None except the Big Dipper," he replies.

"Do you want to learn?"

"Sure. If you want to teach me."

They both lie down on their backs, a few feet from each other. Irina points to the brightest star. "That's Sirius, the dog star." She traces a path through several nearby stars. "And that's Canis Major—the Big Dog. See? It kind of looks like a dog."

Rafael doesn't see. Irina moves closer, figuring that might make it easier for him to see what she's pointing at. Their shoulders and arms are just touching, and every part of Rafael's body is aware of it. She points to a group of stars shaped like an imperfect pentagon. "That's Auriga."

Rafael is barely tracking what she's saying. She's too close to him, and he recalls the look in her eyes in the mirror of the hair salon. He tries to banish the memory, but it lingers.

She points to another constellation. "Orion, the hunter."

When her arm moves away from his, goosebumps rise on his skin, and he shivers—from the chill of the night or the nearness of her, he isn't sure.

"Are you cold?" she asks.

"Yes," he says, his voice sounding loud to his own ears. She gets up and pulls a blanket from one of the bags. She kneels back down beside him and lays it over his body without touching him. She's so close. He can see the shadows of her lashes in the flickering firelight, and his heart races. He wills himself not to reach out. Her eyes meet his, and he sees the same look there again. He could swear it's desire. He freezes as she looks down at him, her face inches from his.

He knows he should move or at least pull his eyes away from hers, but he can't. He wants this to happen, and he's terrified of it. He's completely still as she leans down and brushes her lips lightly against his. She pulls away, and he sees her vulnerability as their eyes meet.

"I'm sorry," she says. "Did I misread this? Did I just mess everything up?"

Rafael reaches up, bringing her back to him and kissing her with an intensity she wouldn't have thought he possessed. His tongue sweeps her lips, and she opens her mouth to his, letting out a surprising little moan of pleasure that reverberates through his body.

She pulls back and traces a line of kisses down his neck, enjoying his sharp inhalation of breath and the feeling of his pulse racing beneath her lips. His hands tangle in her hair, loosening her braid until her soft auburn waves fall around his face, and he's enveloped in the scent of her shampoo.

He's surprised when she shifts position so she's on top of him, her thigh between his thighs, her body against his. It takes all of his self-control to keep from pressing his hips insistently into her. He's wanted this for so long and denied it for so long. It's surreal to finally have her in his arms, to feel her lips on his, matching his hunger and urgency.

They kiss until her arms ache from holding herself up over him; then they both roll to the side, facing each other, so close it's hard to focus on each other's eyes. As he brings her hand to his lips and kisses each of her knuckles, the metal of her wedding ring glints in the firelight. She feels a momentary stab of guilt, but her desire for him overrides it. She pulls him to her and presses her lips to his again, their tongues meeting, his beard rough against her skin. They kiss until the fire dies, and Rafael gets up to add more firewood. She watches him, appreciating his silhouette against the light.

He sits back down behind her and pulls her to him so her back is against his chest as his lips wander down her neck. She lets out a little sigh and leans her head back against his shoulder so he can explore more of her bare skin. His desire is obvious, but he's careful not to let his hands wander too far. She wants more too, but already feels trepidation about that.

His lips meet hers again, though, and for many long minutes her doubts disappear.

Finally, he pulls back and exhales raggedly against her hair. For a few moments, they're silent, trying to catch their breath, as they listen to the pop of the fire and the sound of the wind sweeping through the trees.

Then he says, "You're going to have to be the one to initiate any next steps here."

Rafael is acutely aware of the power dynamic between them. Kissing her is foolish enough. Initiating anything more would be almost coercive, given their context.

"You don't mind taking things slow?" she asks.

"I haven't been with anyone for almost four years, so I figure I'll survive a bit longer."

Irina does the math. "But you said Helena left you in the cabin that June. Almost three years ago."

"That's what happened. We just hadn't been together for a while before that. I was depressed, and our marriage was awful," he pauses, gathering courage, "and she cheated on me."

"What? With who?"

"With one of the doctors she worked with at the hospital. This guy who'd been at our house for dinner a bunch of times. Someone who had friendly conversations with me in my own home, then slept with my wife."

"That's awful. I'm sorry."

"The thing is, I don't really blame her. I was a terrible husband. Our marriage had been bad for years. We weren't sleeping together—and that was my choice, not hers."

He can see the confusion on Irina's face. He feels a strange need to share the ugly truth. What is it that makes him want to lay himself bare before her?

"The last time we tried to sleep together, I couldn't do it. It was after I found out about the affair. I think she was trying to reconcile with me, but I just couldn't do it."

"You mean you didn't want to?"

He rubs his forehead and closes his eyes. "No. I couldn't. It didn't work."

"Oh." Irina remembers the picture of Helena and her confusion grows. "You weren't attracted to her?"

"It wasn't that simple." He remembers his confusion when Helena had stood naked before him and his body had refused to respond. It had infuriated her as though he was still obligated to react to her hard-won physical perfection, even after everything that had happened. "I think most women think that men are simple, but it's more complicated than that. It's hard to sleep with someone who seems to dislike everything about you. Helena was a good mother and a good person, but she and I were awful together."

"But you never cheated on her?"

He shakes his head. "Never. I never wanted to be like my father."

Rafael still remembers the day his mother arrived at his apartment in Caracas for their monthly visit and found the third new woman in a row. Dolores had calmly asked him to join her at a cafe down the street. She hadn't berated him. She'd simply said, between sips of coffee, "I hoped that you'd be better than your father." Her few words, delivered without malice or anger, had found their mark. He hadn't slept with anyone else until the following summer, when he met Helena. Eduardo was a man who slept with his children's nanny, his receptionist, and any other attractive woman who crossed his path. Rafael had seen the damage that caused.

Irina nods, and they sit in silence for several seconds. Rafael feels that gnawing tension that always comes with thinking he's overshared.

Finally, Irina offers him a bit of her own vulnerability. "I haven't been with anyone since before Matteo was born, and his birth was pretty awful, so I don't know how it would even go."

He'd guessed this, based on when Sam died. "Everything is on your timetable here," he says. "You shouldn't take my decision not to initiate as a sign of disinterest, though. I'm just trying to be mindful of our situation."

"I appreciate that."

"I don't deserve a medal for trying to do the right thing," he says. "I told you when you arrived that I don't expect anything from you, other than for you to contribute in whatever way you can. I don't ever want you to feel obligated to do anything you don't want to do."

She kisses him again and continues until she's too tired to keep her eyes open. She leaves for her tent, and Rafael remains by the dying fire, turning the day's events over in his mind, trying to quiet his doubts about his plan to bring people to Ferndale and about kissing Irina. When he finally drifts off to sleep that night, his dreams of her are so vivid that when he wakes he reaches for her, expecting to find her there beside him.

+++

Irina wakes the next morning in the grip of anxiety. She recalls the prior night with trepidation. People will arrive in Ferndale within months, and she hasn't finished the last prong of her plan.

Also, she'd kissed Rafael—at length and with enthusiasm. She swears that she can still smell the faint scent of him on her clothing. Her chin feels raw from his beard. Her hair is knotted from his hands tangling in it. She recalls the feeling of his body against hers, and she touches her wedding ring, trying unsuccessfully to banish her guilt. She isn't ready for this, even though she does want him. She does her breathing exercises and tries to slow her heart rate.

Finally she drags herself out of her tent and finds Rafael making oatmeal over the fire. He's been awake for hours already, replaying every detail of the prior evening. He wants to pull her to him again, to feel her warm lips against his own.

For a moment they consider each other wordlessly. He remembers his promise to let her take the lead, though, so he holds himself back and simply says, "I made tea if you want some."

She nods. As she takes the cup, she's careful not to brush his fingers, fearing that if she touches him, her resolve will fail and she'll pull him quickly back into her arms. She moves several feet away from him, consciously seating herself on the opposite side of the fire.

Awkward silence settles over them.

"Oatmeal?" he asks, offering her a bowl.

"Thank you."

Rafael isn't sure what to make of her distance, so he defaults to their usual morning planning conversation. "So I guess we should leave right after breakfast?"

"Yeah, but I still don't think we'll be able to get home today," she says, following his lead and deciding to stick with normality, wondering if he's as confused by the previous night as she is. Kissing him was probably a mistake . . . but it's one she'd like to make again.

"Maybe it will be faster since we're going downhill," he replies. Should he have greeted her with a kiss? Said something to show her that he was happy that she had kissed him? He fears that he's missed the opportunity.

Conversation ceases as they eat their breakfast. Irina tries to contain her anxiety enough to appreciate the beauty of the foggy sunrise from this lonely peak, the warmth of her tea against the morning chill, the promise of the future before them.

+++

The descent is hardly faster than the ascent. Irina's knees protest with every downward step past the first mile. She finds a few sticks to use as hiking poles, but by the time they reach the bikes, sharp pains are shooting through her knees at regular intervals. They ride cautiously down the pockmarked mountain road slick with morning rain.

They get as far as they can—about forty miles—before setting up camp for the night. Irina wants to pull Rafael to her and lose another evening in his arms, but she stops herself, knowing that she's not in a place to offer him anything beyond that. Instead, she pulls out her notebook, pen, and lantern and makes up a convenient excuse to avoid him. "I guess I really should wrap the economic plan up as soon as possible."

"It would probably be best if we had a completed document before too many people arrive," he agrees. Irina begins scrawling notes in her notebook.

He says nothing about the night before and her apparent avoidance of him. Instead he retires early to his tent, where he doesn't sleep.

+++

They arrive back at the House by the Sea just before lunchtime, and Rafael and Miranda immediately go to take care of the chickens. Irina unloads their things, puts Matteo down for a nap, and sits at the kitchen table to write, but no words come. She stares out the window at the gray sky and the slate-colored sea and feels a bit forlorn. She isn't sure what to do about Rafael. He hasn't acknowledged what happened that night, but neither has she. She remembers his words—that she shouldn't interpret his failure to initiate as a lack of interest. That salves her feeling of rejection a little. And yet . . . she would be wrong to feel rejected in any case. She still feels married. She still wears her ring. She still hasn't finished her conversation with Sam.

She forces herself to return to her writing. As she scribbles the words, her ideas become clearer. She reads back over what she has written with satisfaction. This might just work. For two hours, she barely lifts her eyes from the notebook, until she hears Matteo wake and is forced to set her writing aside and go upstairs.

Chapter Ten

The next morning Irina takes the children to the warehouse to store the camping gear, and Rafael goes to check the library. He's startled to find a man standing inside. The man is probably about the same height as Rafael, with darker, caramel-colored skin and black hair, roughly cropped. Beside him is a bicycle with a very full trailer.

For a moment, they both stare at each other. Rafael is unarmed, and he's relieved to see that the man is too. After another moment of hesitation, the man smiles a broad smile and offers Rafael his hand.

"Julián Pérez Martínez. Rafael Delgado?"

Rafael switches to Spanish. "That's me. It's a pleasure to meet you. We talked on the radio, right?"

Julián nods. "I've been living on a lake near the edge of the valley, but I've been alone all this time, so when I heard your broadcast, I packed up and biked straight here. One hundred sixty miles in two days."

"I hope it will be worth it," Rafael says, impressed. "You're the first to arrive, and we're still working on figuring out what we're doing with the town.

Julián shrugs, "I'll just be happy to be out of the Sacramento Valley this summer. It's too hot there."

Rafael's cracks a smile, "I agree."

As Rafael picks out a few new books, he and Julián talk. Julián tells Rafael that he worked a variety of jobs in the Sacramento Valley—picking produce, doing home repairs, landscaping, and construction—whatever he needed to do to send some money home.

"Those will all be useful skills," Rafael says, as he drops a book into his tote bag. "Where's home?"

"El Salvador," Julián answers. "My wife and kids were still there. But they passed that first August. May they rest in peace."

He crosses himself, and Rafael joins him reflexively.

"Do you want to meet my . . . ," Rafael isn't sure how to describe his companions in relation to himself, ". . . the other people who live here? Then I can show you around?"

Julián nods and follows Rafael out into the misty morning. As they walk to the warehouse, Rafael explains to Julián about the houses he's cleared, the ham radio and repeaters, the grave and the memorial, the solar panels he's set up, his inventory system, and the pieces he's still working out—running water and wind power. As they open the door to the warehouse, Miranda looks up from one of the pews inside.

"My daughter, Miranda," Rafael tells Julián in Spanish. Matteo walks toward Rafael but freezes when he sees Julián, and Irina turns the corner, following him and stopping short. Rafael can see the surprise and fear on her face. He gives her a subtle thumbs up and a nod to try to communicate that Julián isn't a threat; then he continues the introductions. "Matteo," he says, gesturing to the toddler. "And Irina."

Irina is unnerved that she's left her gun on the other side of the warehouse. She scans the stranger and is relieved to see that he appears to be unarmed.

Rafael translates as Julián introduces himself and says he's pleased to meet them.

"Welcome to Ferndale," Irina says. Rafael translates her words but not the wariness in her voice.

Rafael steps back outside with Julián for a tour of the town, but Irina asks him to come back inside the warehouse to help her with something.

"How do you know he's not a threat?" Irina asks Rafael as they stand inside. "That he won't hurt us or steal from us?"

Rafael shrugs, "I don't know that. I can't exactly run a background check. We knew that was the risk we were taking inviting people here."

She sighs, and he thinks for a moment, then says, "If we want to move forward, we're going to have to trust the people who come here."

"It's too late to turn back now anyway," Irina replies, sensing this is true about both the radio broadcast and the other things that had happened that night. They'd made choices, and now there would be consequences.

"I think it will be alright," Rafael says. "Keep your gun close, just in case." He leaves her standing there with her uncertainty.

"You've done a lot of work," Julián tells Rafael as they walk around town looking at the houses Rafael had cleared. Rafael appreciates his praise. It's amazing to him, though, how much work it has taken to make so little progress.

Julián picks a house close to the library. Rafael leaves him to get settled in with a promise to help him find anything he needs in the warehouse.

Rafael finds Irina in the bed and breakfast, braiding her newly washed hair, as Matteo naps and Miranda colors. He tries not to watch her with too much attention, but he's perplexed and hurt by her cool distance from him after their night on King Peak.

"When we move Ify here in two weeks, we'll have four people," Irina says. "One more, and we can start discussing the plan I've written up. It's not ready, though."

"What I saw looked pretty close to being ready," Rafael answers. "Why not start with that part? I've got a laptop you can use if you want to start transcribing it so you can print it out for people when they get here."

"That's a good idea," she agrees. "I didn't think anyone would show up so soon."

"Me either." For a moment they both stand awkwardly, recalling the night of the radio broadcast. Finally, Irina excuses herself to check on Miranda.

Julián joins them for dinner, after Rafael helps him pick out some supplies from the warehouse. Irina can't tell if Julián's quietness is because he's been alone for so long, because of the language barrier, or because of pre-existing introversion. He asks polite questions—translated through Rafael—and replies to Irina's own questions, but the conversation slips into several long lulls. He departs early for bed after thanking them for dinner.

Irina, Rafael, Miranda, and Matteo depart after dinner with a promise to Julián that they'll return in two days. As they ride past the Fern Cottage in the setting sun, Irina can see that the wheat is beginning to sprout in the field she'd tilled.

When they return to Ferndale two days later, it's clear that Julián has been busy. He's already half done clearing out another house. He's also spent some time surveying the stream, and over lunch he proposes some possible options to divert it for irrigation. Irina listens to Julián's and Rafael's speaking and resolves to learn Spanish. It seems not only practical, but also like it would be a good way to honor Abuela Mariana. She stops by the library to get some books that afternoon.

The following Thursday, they open the door to the bed and breakfast and hear voices. Julián is speaking to a woman who replies back in halting Spanish. In the living room, two women sit on the couch together, and a young girl sits in one of the arm chairs off to the side.

Rafael tries to puzzle out their relation to one another. The two women look to be in their mid-twenties. One has long blonde hair and blue eyes, the other has cappuccino-colored skin and close-cropped, tightly-coiled hair. The young girl looks East Asian and a few years older than Miranda.

The three of them assess Rafael, Irina, Matteo, and Miranda, obviously trying to puzzle out their relationship as well.

So am I, Rafael thinks.

The blonde woman stands and offers him her hand. "I'm Emma Jones-Macy, and this is my wife Justina Jones-Macy and . . . ."

"Our daughter," Justina inserts. "Jing Lee."

Jing and Miranda watch each other with interest.

Justina stands and offers her hand to Irina, then Rafael. "Justina. Or Just Tina."

She grins at her own joke. Irina smiles weakly but is a bit troubled by the fact that this woman, unlike Julián, is heavily armed. She wears two pistols and a bowie knife in holsters on her waist and an assault rifle strapped across her back. Her wife, however, appears to be entirely unarmed. Irina recovers her manners enough to introduce herself, Rafael, and the children.

"Julián was telling us that you're the one who left the fliers," Tina says to Rafael. "We found the one you left in Hood River. He also said you've got solar power up and running. Nice."

"We both did that," Rafael says, gesturing to Irina, not wanting to take credit for her work. Tina scrutinizes them for a moment.

"Are you still looking for people to move here?" Emma asks.

"Yes," Rafael answers. "We've cleared out a bunch of houses. You can take your pick."

"I can show you around, if you want," Irina says, feeling uneasy but trying to remember what Rafael had said about trust. Tina, Emma, and Jing walk their bikes beside Irina as she shows them the town and tells them about the things she and Rafael have been working on. They walk past the memorial, and she stops to explain it. Irina notices a fresh set of names carved there and guesses they are Julián's family.

Tina looks around. "This is beautiful. Your husband did a good job."

"He's not my husband," Irina says reflexively, realizing that the assumption is fair, given that she's still wearing her wedding ring. "But yes, he did a good job."

Tina raises her eyebrow but says nothing else.

Irina shows them a few houses, and they pick a small tan-and-cream Victorian that's close to the library. They all agree to meet at the warehouse later that afternoon once they've had time to rest and assess what they need. Irina returns to the bed and breakfast, where Rafael is feeding the children lunch.

"That's six," Irina says. He looks up, puzzled.

"Once Ify gets here, we have six adults. I don't see how I can tell anyone they can't participate in the process I'm planning."

"I can sit it out," Rafael offers.

"No way!" Irina replies. "This whole thing was your idea. You deserve to have a say in what we end up doing here."

He shrugs. "You could just be my representative."

"No."

Rafael suspects that she would be unhappy to hear that even after he became a citizen, he rarely voted. He hadn't been exaggerating when he'd told her that he was jaded about elections.

"Can you make it work with six?" he asks.

"I guess so, but I was planning on having things be decided by majority vote. If we have an even number of participants, everything will have to be decided with a two-thirds vote, which is more challenging."

"I'm sure you'll make it work," he says. "And now it's time for this little guy to take a nap."

He lifts Matteo out of the high chair and hoists him up into the air, tossing him upward but holding his waist. Then Rafael lowers him down and blows raspberries on his belly as Matteo giggles.

"Let's go, buddy," he says, switching the toddler to a football hold and carrying him off to the bedroom. Irina watches them with a strange longing.

+++

Later, after Tina, Emma, and Jing have taken what they needed from the warehouse, all of them meet up for dinner at the bed and breakfast. Rafael tells them about Ify, and Irina summarizes the process she wants to embark on to decide the future of Ferndale. Rafael translates to Julián in fast Spanish. They agree that once Ify arrives, they will meet to discuss the Charter in the evenings from Monday to Thursday. Everyone can stay overnight in the bed and breakfast so the children can sleep in the upstairs rooms while the parents discuss the future downstairs.

They'll eat dinner together, rotating the responsibility for cooking to two different people every night.

Irina stays up late that night transcribing the government plan and criminal code with the laptop. She sends them to the printer Rafael had connected for her, and she watches with satisfaction as it spits out six copies of each. She collates and staples them, then slips them into folders labeled with each person's name. Her nervousness hasn't abated, but the activity helps to calm her. Soon she'll know whether these ideas are workable or not.

+++

Rafael had almost begun to believe that he'd only dreamed that Irina had kissed him, until she does it again. The night before Ify's move, Rafael and Irina are alone in the lantern-lit warehouse gathering supplies. He turns to hand her a bag of rice, and his hand brushes hers. Her eyes widen, as they did that first night in the House by the Sea. She drops the bag and it breaks, scattering rice across the classroom floor. They both crouch to sweep it up with their hands at the same time, and their faces are inches from each other. She pulls him to her firmly, and he loses his footing, tumbling down on top of her on the floor. Irina can feel the grains of rice digging into her back as he presses his body against hers, and they kiss hungrily, her lips opening to his. Her hands drag through his hair, then slip lower, tracing the muscles of his back and pulling his hips against hers as she lets out a little moan of pleasure that he knows will be replayed endlessly in his dreams.

Finally, one or the other of them—neither would ever be really sure which—remembers themself. He helps her up off the floor, and they stand, staring at each other. He reaches to brush a grain of rice from her hair; then he captures her hand and kisses her knuckles, skipping her ring finger, unable to ignore the ring she still wears. They both pull back guiltily.

"Irina . . . ," he starts to say.

"I have to go," she says, fleeing abruptly out the door into the night. He stares after her, confused and disoriented.

+++

After another restless night, Rafael wakes at dawn the next morning and packs up the last items into the cart. He's expecting Irina, but it's Tina who comes out to meet him instead.

"I'm afraid you're stuck with me," Tina says. "But I'm pretty sure that I can lift a lot more than Irina." She flexes her impressive biceps with a grin.

"Miranda was upset and wanted Irina to stay, so I volunteered," she explains. Rafael is relieved that this isn't just Irina avoiding him. Or is it?

"Irina said you don't like the horse, but she's confident you and Lily can work it out."

Tina gives Lily a gentle pat then hops onto her bicycle and rides beside the cart, as Rafael gives Lily the signal to get moving.

"Were you here during the Pandemic?" Tina asks, raising her voice a little so he can hear her over the sounds of the cart's wheels and Lily's hoofbeats.

"No. I was at a cabin near Gifford Pinchot National Forest in Washington."

"We were south of there, near Hood River," Tina replies.

"That's a good location," he says.

"I did my research. I figured we could live off the orchards and berry farms."

They talk for a while, and Rafael learns that Emma and Tina had been friends since they were in elementary school, but hadn't started dating until a few months before Tina shipped out for the Marines. Tina had been to a couple of places while she was in the military, most of which Rafael had heard about on the news. Rafael finds her to be an easy conversationalist. She has plenty of stories to tell about her time in the Marine Corps and her life growing up outside of Sacramento. She also recounts several hilarious misadventures she'd had while she was working in private security in Portland before the Pandemic. The conversation is entertaining enough to distract him from his concerns about Irina for a little while.

They arrive at Ify's house in the midafternoon. Ify doesn't have many possessions that he wants to bring along with him.

"Just my friends," he says, gesturing to the animals.

They spend the night at his house and depart early the next morning after loading his crated pets and three boxes in the cart. Rafael counts the parrot plus six cats and eight dogs, including two herding dogs that pace around the sheep, nipping at their heels. Ify spends a few minutes inside, saying goodbye to the house where he had raised his children. When he joins them, his eyes are red, and he seems somber.

Ify ties the cattle together in a long chain, leading the first one himself. He lets two dogs herd the sheep as he walks beside them in his button down shirt and trousers. Tina draws him into conversation, and Rafael is glad to sit in the cart, listening to them talk without feeling obligated to participate. From behind him comes the occasional whimper or yowl.

At midmorning, they take a long break by a stream so the animals can drink; then Rafael and Ify switch places. Tina asks Ify how he ended up with so many pets.

"I was with my wife and two younger sons when they got sick. I kept waiting to get sick, but I never did. I figured that if death was going to pass me over, I may as well do something useful with myself, so I rescued my neighbors' pets, whatever livestock were nearby, and the African Grey Parrot from the Sequoia Park Zoo. I hated the idea of them dying, starving and lonely."

Ify wipes a tear from the corner of his eye. Tina nods sympathetically. Ify takes a breath to calm himself; then he starts asking them more about Ferndale and the other people there. Rafael and Tina tell him about Emma, Julián, and the children and their plan to discuss Irina's drafts. Ify seems very interested in that idea.

"I haven't had a proper intellectual conversation since Shanna got sick," he tells them. "She was brilliant. She even did a TED Talk once on animal rights. If I had the internet, I would show you."

They stop in the late afternoon and set up camp there. The last thing Rafael thinks about before falling asleep is Irina. He tries to untangle the knot between them. It's clear that she's still grieving Sam. It's strange to feel envy for a dead man, but everything he's gathered about Sam only heightens Rafael's sense of inadequacy. Rafael reminds himself, though, that he was the idiot who'd kissed her or let her kiss him, knowing that she wasn't really in a place to get involved with him.

+++

In the House by the Sea, Irina, too, lies awake trying to decipher her own mind. She gets up and lights a candle, then takes out her favorite book. She runs her finger over the envelope tucked between its pages, considering it. Then she sets the worn envelope aside and rereads her favorite passage in the book.

Sam and Clara's birthdays are both approaching, just three days from each other. Two days ago she realized that a full day had passed since she had thought of either of them. Maybe Rafael's memorial had freed something in her, but it felt like a betrayal. She wonders what obligation the living owe the dead. She will always be Clara's mother, but will she always be Sam's wife?

She falls asleep with the book in her hand and dreams that she is in her house in Salem, waiting for someone who will never arrive.

Chapter Eleven

A week later, Irina stands before the mirror in her room in the bed and breakfast, assessing herself. She's put on the green dress and let her hair air-dry in gentle waves down her back. She applies her red lipstick. She thinks she looks a little less tired than she used to, a little less drawn, and her curves fill in the dress better. She feels almost pretty. She slips her feet into low, practical heels. Five days before, she'd finished her economic treatise and added it to the folders, then distributed them to everyone. She tries to remember herself as she was: the lawyer, the advocate, the expert. There's a knock at the door.

"Everyone's about ready," Rafael says as she opens the door. Then, when he sees her, "I'm afraid I'm underdressed. You look . . . ," he wants to say 'beautiful,' but he catches himself, ". . . prepared."

Irina feels a twinge of self-consciousness.

"I can change, if you want," he offers, sensing that he's made her feel uncertain. "I've got time to run over to the warehouse and grab something."

"No, it's fine. I just feel like I need to be in character for this. I have no idea how it's going to go, and I thought it might be better if I was my old self."

Rafael understands exactly what she means.

"I'll see you in a few," he says, walking off down the hallway.

Irina steps outside, feeling as though she's about to do something that may either be monumental or inconsequential. She squares her shoulders. This will go well or badly. Either way, in a few hours she can return to her room and pour herself a glass of wine by the fireplace.

In the sitting room, Ify is talking with Tina in front of a roaring fire. They both turn as Irina enters. Ify, at least, is in his usual inexplicably crisp button-down. Tina wears her typical uniform of army-surplus cargo pants and a thermal shirt.

"Well shit," Tina says. "I didn't know we were dressing up."

Emma enters from the kitchen, "You don't even have dress clothes!"

"I have a cleaner shirt!" Tina replies.

Ify and Irina laugh. Emma takes Tina's hand.

"We're just waiting for Julián and Rafael," Emma says, looking around. "They were both here a minute ago."

"Drink?" Tina offers Irina a decanter of whiskey.

"I probably shouldn't," Irina replies.

"You look a little tightly wound," Tina observes. "It might help."

"It's alright. I'm used to being tightly wound."

"I got that," Tina says with a smile. She lifts the water pitcher. "Water then?"

Irina nods. The clock on the wall ticks. Irina perspires in her dress as she absently bends the corner of her folder back and forth. This feels like an unnerving dream of the world's weirdest dinner party: a small group of random strangers discussing political theory in a hundred-and-thirty-year-old house—an island of light in a dead town, a dead world.

The front door opens, and Julián steps inside, wearing a slightly wrinkled button-down shirt and black slacks with his usual work boots. Rafael follows him in a polo shirt and khaki pants and a pair of loafers. Irina feels a surge of gratitude to Rafael for trying to make her feel a little more comfortable. They all assemble around the fireplace, pulling the furniture forward across the ornate area rug so they can be a bit closer to each other.

"So, to review: in order for a measure to be adopted as part of the Charter or the Code, four of us need to vote in favor of it. Of course, a unanimous vote is preferable, but I don't think we'll always be able to achieve consensus. Anyone can suggest changes to what I've drafted, and anyone can call the vote on a topic," Irina says. "Ideally, we'll have a finalized document before more people get here."

The others look skeptical. Irina takes out her folder, "I thought we could start with the governmental system."

"I'd like to start with the economic system," Tina says.

"Um, okay," Irina replies, leafing through her papers with shaking hands.

"Looks a lot like socialism to me," Tina says. "Rafael, you grew up in a socialist country. What do you think?"

"Nominally socialist," he replies. "More of a kleptocracy, really . . . ."

Rafael translates for Julián; then he and Tina spend a while discussing whether or not Venezuela was really ever a socialist country. Irina tries to bring the discussion back to the Charter.

"Do we want to look at the economic system first?" she asks the group. "Those in favor, raise your hands."

Tina, Emma, and Ify raise their hands. Rafael translates to Julián, who then also raises his hand. Rafael shrugs at Irina. Tina narrows her eyes at him.

"The economic system then," Irina says. "Starting with . . . ."

She leafs through her stapled papers and drops them. Rafael retrieves them and hands them to her, whispering, "You've got this," with an encouraging smile. Irina takes a deep breath and decides to start with what she expects will be the least objectionable part of this plan. "Starting with professions. I've outlined an initial list of professions. At a later date, the council can add new positions as needed. Positions will be assigned by the Council based on pre-existing skillsets and need."

"So someone could be forced to do a job they don't like?" Emma asks. Julián raises a hand to pause the conversation as Rafael translates for him.

Rafael translates Julián's reply, "Most people throughout history have had to do work that they didn't want to do. That's how we survive."

"He's right," Ify agrees, "The luxury of choosing whatever profession you desire is a very modern one, and it didn't even work very well in the modern world, judging by the number of unemployed humanities graduates."

Irina says. "Everyone can do what they want in their free time, but as a compensated profession, there are certain roles that must be filled in order for this town to function. Most people will have to work in agriculture, hunting, lumber production, and maintenance. We'll also need to provide basic services: education, electricity, medical care, childcare, criminal justice, inventory management, sanitation, administration, and law enforcement."

"But do you really think that people will be okay with just taking whatever role we assign them?" Emma asks.

"I think it has to be a prerequisite to joining us here," Irina says. "And if people don't like the role they're assigned, they can apply for another role, as discussed later in the Charter. But, ultimately, because we have to prioritize survival, roles will need to be assigned by the Council."

Emma is unconvinced, and Irina and Julián spend an hour trying to convince her that this loss of freedom is justified by their precarious circumstances. Eventually, Emma concedes the point, and Irina calls a vote.

"If we vote 'yes,' can we still add more professions tomorrow?" Tina asks. Irina nods.

"And if we agree to this, we're not necessarily agreeing to the rest of this economic system?" Tina asks.

"No, only this, paired with whatever economic system we all agree on later," Irina replies. Tina shrugs. Irina calls the vote again.

Rafael, Julián, Ify, Emma, and Irina raise their hands. Tina raises hers reluctantly.

Irina feels a swell of relief and pride that they've accomplished something, and she wants to ease everyone into these discussions, so they agree to break for the night.

"I need a drink," Irina says. Rafael follows her into the kitchen and searches through the drawers for a corkscrew, then uncorks a bottle of wine as she takes down two glasses.

"You did great," he tells her.

"This is already off script, and it's only been one night," Irina replies.

Rafael pours himself a generous glass of wine, then pours one for her. "Tell me when." She lets him pour on and on.

"When?" he asks, as the wine approaches the top of the glass.

"When."

They clink their glasses together.

"To democracy," Irina says, rolling her eyes, then gulping her wine.

"Hey, you had the option to create a benevolent dictatorship in which you and I would rule jointly for the rest of our days."

"I regret missing that opportunity," Irina replies. They stand in the kitchen, considering each other, until Emma comes in and pours herself a glass of wine.

"I saw that 'teacher' is one of the professions on your list," Emma says. "And there are provisions for a school. Have you thought about what that will look like?"

"That's well outside of my area of expertise," Irina replies. "But then . . . so is most of what we're doing here. Were you a teacher?"

"I was hoping to be. I was waitressing for a few years, waiting for Tina to come back from the Marine Corps. I'd just gotten into Portland State University when everything shut down. I've done a lot of reading, though. I really like the forest-school model."

"What's that?" Irina asks.

Emma spends the next twenty minutes or so talking about various educational models. Despite her exhaustion, Irina finds the conversation fascinating. It's almost midnight by the time Irina and Rafael open the door to Miranda and Matteo's room to check on them before going to sleep.

They both step back out into the darkness of the hallway.

Their eyes meet, and Rafael is almost ready to say something to her about the night in the warehouse, but he remembers his promise not to initiate things, and he looks away.

"Tomorrow is Sam's birthday," Irina says quietly. "And Friday is Clara's."

"I'm sorry," Rafael replies. "Anything I can do?"

"No. If I'm out of sorts, I just wanted you to know why," she says, turning toward her door. "Goodnight."

+++

The next morning, Rafael and Julián mow a few more acres of land near the Fern Cottage, using the manual mower. At the warehouse, Irina struggles to load the cumbersome battery-powered rototiller into the horse cart.

"Want a hand?" Tina asks, appearing behind her.

"Yeah, thanks," Irina says. Tina grabs the heavier end and lifts it with little effort. They slide it into the cart.

"You get the horse; I'll get the tiller," Tina says, "We can knock this out before dinner." She gets into the seat beside Irina. "You trained this horse yourself?"

"I've got the shoulder injury to prove it," Irina answers. It still aches sometimes; she's just learned to live with it.

"Did you work with horses before the Pandemic?" Tina asks.

"I spent my teenage years on my grandparents' ranch in Utah." Irina tells Tina about the canyons, the cattle drives, and the horses.

"Your grandparents raised you?" Tina asks.

"After my mom died, yeah."

"My aunt raised me."

"Did you like living with your aunt?" Irina asks. What she really wants to ask is if her teacher's—Ms. Keller's—statement about life's getting better was true for Tina, too.

Tina considers for a moment. "I think that even if you have a shitty childhood, having one loving adult who actually shows up can save you. My aunt was that person for me."

"Mine, too," Irina says. "I was actually lucky to have a lot of caring adults once I moved to my grandparents ranch."

"I want to be that person for Jing," Tina says.

"What's her story? Pandemic orphan?"

Tina nods, "Yep. She showed up on the road outside our cabin in Hood River that Christmas Eve. Her whole family got sick. She survived. They didn't."

"She just showed up, and you let her in!?" Irina remembers the mountain man.

"Hell no, I didn't. You think I'm an idiot?! There was an empty cabin down the road. I stayed a safe distance away and told her to go there. Then I dropped off food nearby for three weeks. After the contagious period was over, Emma and I invited her to stay with us."

Irina is glad Rafael probably hasn't heard this story. She's sure it would make him second guess himself about the mountain man again, despite the fact that Jing's situation was clearly different.

"We're all she's got now. And she's all we've got. My aunt didn't listen to me when I warned her in the beginning. She thought I was crazy, and I am, just not about that. I was prepping before the Pandemic, and I guess she just figured this was another false alarm," Tina says. "Your son was born during the Pandemic, right?"

"That January. I got pregnant right after the Pandemic started. Stupid, I know, but I also thought it was a false alarm. My husband, Sam, knew it was serious, though, which is why Matteo and I survived . . . , even though he didn't . . . . Today would have been his birthday." Irina knows she's oversharing, like she often does when she feels this emotional. She congratulates herself, at least, on not crying in front of this relative stranger.

"That sucks. I'm sorry."

Irina nods. She realizes that though she's felt melancholy, it seems to be noticeably easier to bear this year. She runs her thumb over her palm and touches her ring, reflexively, feeling guilty about not being as sad as she thinks she ought to be.

Tina watches her. "You're allowed to be happy again, you know? We all are. I hope that's what we're building here—a place where people can find a second chance to be happy."

Irina nods. Rationally, she believes Tina's words, but part of her still can't accept them.

Rafael arrives with lunch, and Irina suspects that he really came because of Sam's birthday. He asks her how she's doing, and she says she's okay. She's surprised to find that it's mostly true.

+++

That evening they gather in the sitting room again. Ify revives the fire, while Tina pours herself a tumbler of whiskey, and Irina, in a dead woman's dress slacks and a silky shirt, shuffles nervously through her papers. Finally, Irina summons the courage to ask everyone to sit down so they can get started.

"I think this plan is missing something important," Tina says. "A military."

"As a full time position?" Irina asks.

"One person in a full time position but everyone else in part time positions. I don't see anything in any of these plans about defense."

"You think we need a standing army?" Ify asks skeptically.

"We sure as hell do!" Tina replies. "Look, right now we've still got plenty of resources. There were 8 billion people on this planet, and, conservatively estimating, 7.9 billion of them died. So there's not a lot to fight over now. But there will be. If we build something worth having, someone will try to take it. Guaranteed."

"I'm inclined to agree," Rafael says.

"Me too," Irina says. She's surprised she overlooked this, given how skeptical she was about bringing others to Ferndale. "What do you have in mind?"

"Something like the Israel Defense Forces. Everyone serves," Tina replies.

"Some of us don't even have a gun," Ify says.

"You didn't bring a gun to an apocalypse, man?!" Tina is incredulous. "How the hell did you hunt?"

"I'm a vegetarian," Ify proclaims proudly. "And I think it's unlikely that anyone is going to come all this way to steal from us. We're more than a hundred miles from anywhere."

"It's true that our isolated location is our best defense," Tina agrees, "But if we have resources, people might think it's worth the effort to steal them."

There's a pause long enough for Rafael to translate for Julián.

"I propose we have mandatory military service. For everyone," Tina says. "If you don't know how to shoot, I'll teach you."

Rafael decides to take her up on that. Tina calls the vote on her proposal. Only Ify votes nay. Irina makes a note on her pages, and something occurs to her.

"We need a legislative history," she says. Everyone looks at her blankly. She clarifies. "We need to take notes on our discussions here. What things we agreed to and why. It will be helpful for future decision-makers to have that context."

"I'll do it," Emma volunteers.

"Julián has a suggestion," Rafael says as he hands Emma a pen and notebook from the nearby desk. "He proposes that jobs that are physically demanding or undesirable should be shared. Everyone should participate in harvesting, food service, and sanitation."

"So, mandatory public service?" Irina asks. Rafael translates and Julián nods.

"I like it," Ify says. "One of the challenges of the system you've written here, Irina, is that it's quite different from what we're used to. It requires a culture of collaboration and collective responsibility that wasn't common in the Western world, especially in the United States. We're going to have to reprogram people, to an extent. If you want people to think collectively, it makes sense to have them regularly engaged in service that benefits the community as a whole."

Julián and Rafael have a brief exchange in Spanish, and Rafael translates, "Julián says that this will keep us from having an underclass of people, who do essential things but are looked down on by everyone else."

Irina takes a vote. Everyone agrees. Emma scratches down fast notes in her notebook; then she pauses to raise her hand. "What about parents? It seems like in this system everyone would have an assigned role, but what if they have children?"

"People with children will have to assume a role just like everyone else," Irina replies.

"But what if they want to stay at home and raise their children instead?" Emma asks.

"We're too resource-and-service poor to have a system where anyone doesn't contribute," Irina replies.

"Parenthood is a contribution," Emma says.

"I know that," Irina says. "I have . . . had . . . two children. But the idea that anyone could simply raise children and do nothing else is a very modern one, and even in modern times, most people couldn't afford to do that. I couldn't afford that."

Emma thinks for a moment. "Someone has to take care of the children. What if anyone who wanted to opt out of other work to take care of their own children was allowed to do that if they agreed to take care of other people's children as well?"

"I guess that could work, provided that there are other children who need care," Irina says, remembering the crushing guilt about not spending more time with Clara. "Also, one of the problems of modernity was that kids and adults were separated all day long. That doesn't work for a parent who wants to spend time with their child, and it doesn't work for a child who needs to learn to become an adult. So maybe we make it explicit that so long as it's safe, people can bring children along with them while they're working. Or they can use childcare if that's easier for them. And we give everyone breaks and a long lunch and flexible hours. We want people to have children; it's essential for our survival. So we should try to make a system that accommodates that or even encourages it."

Rafael watches her. She seems more confident tonight, and it looks good on her. He's glimpsed it before, but now he can clearly see the person she used to be. He finds that he likes both versions of her. He has sometimes wondered if they would have even spoken to each other, let alone been friends, if they'd met Before. He knows now that if he had been free and unencumbered by his bad marriage, he would have been drawn to Irina immediately. If he had been married to Helena, he would have avoided Irina entirely, sensing it would be difficult not to fall for her.

He spent his youth thinking that love was a roller coaster of highs and lows—the ecstasy of sexual connection and the agony of separation. He never had a good model for love in his family, and books and movies were rubbish, perpetuating the myths he once believed. He'd declared his love for Helena within a month of their meeting, without ever truly understanding what he was claiming. He'd boasted of visiting a land he'd only ever glimpsed from offshore.

Rafael thinks of the way that Irina has accepted him, while, at the same time, sometimes gently pushing him to improve. He recalls all the things they've confessed to each other, trusting, somehow, that they would offer each other grace. Love is the small acts of consideration and kindness they practice every day, the ways they notice each other, the quality of attention they grant to each other. It's physical desire too—he hopes to one day share with Irina the vivid, sensual dreams he's had about her. Desire is part of it but not the sum of it. Desire, like a fire kindled with paper, burns off. If there isn't a more substantive fuel to feed it, the flame will die.

He loves her, and he's fairly certain he's loved her for a while, without ever naming that feeling. He suspects that she loves him too, though she feels conflicted about it. This revelation on her dead husband's birthday, no less, is terribly timed. There's nothing he can do but wait.

He returns to awareness of the room around him to find everyone looking at him expectantly.

"Rafael? Are you going to translate for Julián so we can take the vote on Emma's proposal?" Irina asks.

Rafael translates the portion of the conversation he was paying attention to.

"You forgot what Emma said at the end," Tina tells him. He looks at her blankly, and she explains, "About holidays?" Seeing his still confused expression, she clarifies, "that we should create some public holidays to give people shared rituals to look forward to? She said we should consider what holidays are important to each of us and talk about it next week?"

Rafael translates to Julián, who nods in enthusiastic assent. They take a vote. Unanimous agreement for Emma and Irina's ideas about childcare and parents. Emma writes this down in her notebook. Irina makes a checkmark on her printed page. Tina pours herself another drink and offers one to Ify, who declines as always. Julián reaches for the glass instead, and Tina converses with him in halting and imperfect Spanish. Irina feels a deep satisfaction. It mutes the unavoidable pain of Sam's birthday. The last thought she has before she falls asleep is that her plan is actually coming together.

+++

"We haven't addressed the core problem here," Tina says as they all sit together the following night. "You've set up a socialist system, and I just don't think that works."

"Some of the most successful countries in the world are— were—social democracies," Irina replies, a bit flustered,

187

because this wasn't on the agenda for the evening. She flips through her papers to where she'd laid out the backbone of her economic system: a centralized government, which would control all of the community's resources and redistribute them evenly.

"Those were hybrid models—a mix of capitalism and socialism," Rafael points out. "There are far more examples of places where socialism really went awry. Latin American history is filled with them."

Tina looks satisfied. Irina feels stricken.

He continues, "The model you've created relies too much on centralized government control. That might work if you have good, selfless people in leadership roles, but many people aren't good or selfless, and when a system like this goes bad, it's a disaster. My country had some of the richest oil reserves in the world, yet children literally starved to death."

"People went hungry here, too!" Irina exclaims. "And you said, yourself, that Venezuela wasn't really a socialist country."

"True, but my point remains—it's risky for people to be dependent on their government for everything. It gives bad leaders too much leverage over their people, and the fallout is more severe when leaders make mistakes. The centralization of power in Venezuela is part of what allowed the system to collapse so completely," Rafael argues.

"The bigger problem, though," Tina inserts, "is that people get lazy."

"The free rider problem," Rafael agrees.

"That's just a political talking point!" Irina argues.

They debate this for more than an hour. Irina has known Rafael for almost a year, lived with him, had innumerable conversations with him, yet she's never realized that their beliefs are so different. It's disorienting.

It grows late and Rafael says, "I think we need to re-envision the economic aspect of this system, pull back some of the governmental control."

Irina could call a vote. She knows Emma and Ify agree with her. It's hard to gauge where Julián stands—he's been quiet all evening. She struggles to remember the history of El Salvador.

Might Julián's experience have been similar to Rafael's? The vote might be 2:4. Or it might be 3:3.

"Julián," she asks, "What do you think about this?"

As Rafael translates, it occurs to Irina how problematic it is that he's Julián's only means of receiving and transmitting information in this discussion. How can she be sure that Rafael isn't coloring his translation with his own opinions?

Rafael translates Julián's response, "He'll have to think about it. He's seen the ways that government power can be used to solve problems and to create them."

"I think we should call it a night," Ify says.

As they break, Irina asks Rafael to help her with something at the warehouse. He follows her outside, feeling trepidation. Her irritation with him is obvious.

"I can't believe you did that!" she exclaims as soon as the front door of the bed and breakfast closes behind them. "You knew I wasn't ready for that conversation!"

"I'm confused," Rafael replies, "You insisted that I join you in this exercise, and now you're mad because I have an opinion?"

"You said you'd have my back."

He motions for her to follow him farther away from the house so others don't hear their argument. "I always have your back."

"You didn't seem to today."

He sighs. "I think you need to decide if you really want feedback here, Irina. Do you want a system that takes other people's perspectives into account? Or not?"

"I do."

"But you're mad at me for having a perspective that's different from yours?"

"I don't know. I put a lot of work into this, and I guess it just . . . bothers me that you don't think my ideas are good."

He looks at her so intently that she has to look away. "I think your ideas are brilliant, Irina. Truly. But even brilliant ideas need some refining."

They're both silent for a beat; then he says, "Tell me again why you think this is the best system."

+++

The next morning, Tina joins Rafael to clear another house, as she's done twice that week. It seems to Rafael that she's taken a particular liking to him, though he's not sure why. They remove three bodies from the house, then cart them to the grave where Ify and Julián cover them with soil.

As they clear the kitchen pantry and cabinets, Tina asks his advice on how to bond with Jing. Rafael outlines several ideas. He's moved by the memory of overhearing Miranda tell Irina that she loved her for the first time.

"You might want to ask Irina's opinion on this," Rafael tells Tina. "She had a little girl, and she's done a great job bonding with Miranda."

"They do seem close," Tina agrees. "You and Irina lived here alone for almost a year?"

"With the children, yes," Rafael says, sensing that she's digging for information, trying to parse out the nature of his relationship with Irina. He has no answers for himself, though, so he can't offer her any further clarity, and it's also not in his nature to discuss romantic matters. So he changes the subject, asking her about her thoughts on how much land they should farm that fall and what crops they should grow.

+++

That evening when they gather in the sitting room, Irina wastes no time reopening the previous night's discussion.

"I know not everyone agrees with the system I've laid out," she says, "but I want to explain why I set things up that way."

No one interrupts, not even Tina. Irina continues, "The world we lived in was broken. There were people starving, people dying from despair, while others had mega yachts and five houses. I think we need to imagine something different, something that flattens the inequalities that we'd gotten used to living with, maximizes the contributions everyone can offer, and ensures that everyone's needs are met.

"Your points, Rafael and Tina, are well taken. Maybe the kind of system I've envisioned hasn't been proven to work on a larger scale. Maybe in the future we'll have to change it if it can't grow with the society we end up creating. But right now, we're starting small, and, as I see it, our primary priorities are minimizing concrete threats, like starvation and more abstract threats like social unrest. I think this system does that. It ensures that everyone receives an equal amount of resources—we all contribute, and we all benefit—and no one hoards food or supplies. Everyone is compensated equally, which honors the fact that all of us are essential to the survival of our society, and minimizes the social discord that comes from some people being treated like their work is more valuable."

Rafael watches Irina, realizing that she had used their conversation the night before to hone her arguments. She must have been a formidable attorney.

She pauses to let Rafael translate for Julián; then she asks, "Is there anyone here who really thought the old system was working for them? Were your needs met? Did you feel like things were distributed in a way that was even remotely fair? Did you think that everyone really had an equal shot at success? Raise your hand."

No one does.

"We don't have to replicate the mistakes of the past," she concludes. "I think we can build something better."

Everyone is silent after she finishes speaking. Finally, Ify speaks, "I have an idea for a compromise."

All eyes turn to him, and he continues, "We leave Irina's system in place, but we add bulwarks against the problems that Tina and Rafael identified."

Emma scratches notes quickly as he goes on, "The first problem, which Rafael aptly noted, is the problem of self-interested leadership and corruption. That kind of corruption and systemic failure was the reason my parents left Nigeria. We need to address that, and I don't see anything about it in your criminal code. The penalty has to be severe."

"Exile?" Irina asks.

"Or death," Tina replies.

"That seems excessive and would have been an outlier in modern times," Ify says. "Let's stick with exile."

"I like that, but it still doesn't reach the larger problem of government power," Rafael says.

"I think Irina's Declaration of Rights does address part of that, but perhaps it could stand to be expanded," Ify says. Rafael considers it.

"You haven't addressed the free rider problem," Tina says to Irina. "If someone even suspects that another person is free-riding, that's going to kill your goal of avoiding social conflict. For people to buy into this system, they have to know that everyone else is working just as hard."

They argue for a while about how prevalent such behavior is. Finally Irina concedes that even the perception of someone's free-riding would be a problem, "Okay. How can we fix that?"

"Not contributing would be a crime," Tina says, "Depending on the severity, the penalty would be extra labor or exile. But I'm still not buying into your larger idea here, because I don't think a society can function without robust property rights."

Ify agrees. "I think the prospect of obtaining non-essential but desirable items motivates people to work harder and produce things in their free time."

"But we're trying to encourage people to think of the community, not of themselves," Irina replies.

"We're all self-interested actors, Irina," Ify says, "We have to align our system with people's instinctive inclinations. No one needs to get rich, but there has to be some incentive for creative projects or personal endeavors."

"What you're proposing requires some kind of currency, and we don't have the expertise for that," Irina says.

"While I would advocate for currency, I don't think that's necessary," Ify answers, "People can barter and trade. Plenty of societies have existed that way."

"Just to be clear," Irina says, "Most things will still be community property, right? The crops, the animals, any items we need for survival?"

"That was how I was envisioning it," Ify replies. "Everyone would have their basic needs provided for and would also be paid a modest additional wage in goods that they could trade. People would be assigned jobs by the Council, but in their free time they could take up whatever endeavors they wanted, including doing things or making things that they can barter with."

"Over time and generations, though," Rafael translates for Julián, "small inequalities of property become larger inequalities."

"The intergenerational transfer of wealth is a problem," Ify agrees. "What solution would you propose, Julián?"

Everyone turns to Julián as he and Rafael speak back and forth in Spanish. Rafael translates Julián's words, "There should be no inheritance. When we die, our property, except anything that's purely sentimental, reverts to the collective. Homes are reassigned by lottery."

"So," Irina says, "To review . . . what are we voting on here?"

Emma looks at her notes. "Most assets would be community-owned, but residents would receive a small wage of goods that can be used to barter, stiff penalties for corruption and slacking, checks on government power . . . ."

"Which hasn't really been addressed," Rafael interrupts.

". . . limited property ownership without inheritance rights," Emma concludes.

"It's getting late," Irina says, "Can we table the conversation about checks on government power and just vote on the rest?"

"You promise to address that later?" Rafael asks. Irina nods and calls the vote. Everyone but Tina votes in favor.

Tina corners Rafael in the kitchen afterward.

"I hope you didn't just decide the future of our society based on who you're sleeping with," she says.

"I did not," Rafael replies. Despite their growing friendship, he feels no particular need to disabuse Tina of her assumptions about him and Irina. Tina's eyes widen.

"Oh fuck, it's even worse than that!" she says, seeming to read his mind. "You just decided the future of our society based on who you're hoping to sleep with! Jesus Christ!"

Rafael lets out a long-suffering sigh, which only seems to confirm Tina's assumption. "I thought the compromises were sufficient and Irina made her case."

"Sure you did." Tina rolls her eyes and leaves him alone in the kitchen. Rafael rubs his forehead. He's not sure why Tina has singled him out for both friendship and opprobrium. He decides to take a walk, thinking again that he should have resisted Irina's insistence that he join these conversations. He could be off designing more efficient wind turbines or irrigation systems or doing anything he's better at than dealing with other humans. People may be systems, he thinks, but he clearly still has no idea how they work—even Irina, whom he thought he understood.

He walks until the town is at his back. It's growing dark, and the stars have started to come out. He looks up at the constellations and remembers the night on King Peak with both fondness and regret.

When he returns, Tina is sitting on the porch in a rocking chair with a tumbler of whiskey in her hand.

"I'm sorry," she says as he comes up the steps. "What I said was shitty. It's just that the decisions we're making here are really important. They seem theoretical right now, but they could impact a lot of lives."

"I meant what I said," Rafael replies. "Irina made her case. I think that with the modifications we discussed, her system makes sense in this context."

Tina nods. "If you really think so, then fine." He reaches for the doorknob.

"One more thing," Tina says. "I've been where you are, man, and I wish I hadn't wasted so much time. Life is so fucking short, you know?"

Rafael nods, though he's unsure of what to do with that advice. They say goodnight, and he goes inside, leaving Tina to her thoughts and her whiskey.

Chapter Twelve

The next morning, after they bike back to the House by the Sea, Rafael offers to watch the children so Irina can take some time to herself on Clara's birthday. Irina gathers her painting supplies and leaves for the beach.

She sets up her portable easel in the sand and tries to paint the bluffs to her south, but verisimilitude evades her. She sighs in frustration and pulls out another piece of canvas. She begins to paint Clara's face from memory, quickly realizing that the details are starting to slip from her.

'Why does grief go on and on?' she wonders. It's so redundant, so endless, just the same feeling over and over again.

And yet . . . she has felt something shifting in her over time, a glacier receding and revealing reshaped ground. She's made progress over the past year. There are still these miserable moments, especially on anniversaries, but there have also been moments of joy—her birthday, Miranda's "I love you," the moment the four of them reached the summit of King Peak, and dozens of other, smaller moments on average days.

That evening, Irina and Rafael sit by the fire on the patio drinking wine. It's strange to be alone with him, after spending four nights in town with everyone else. Something has changed between them. She shouldn't have kissed him, even though she really wanted to. She'd been impulsive and changed their friendship.

She wants something more than friendship from him, though. Kissing him hadn't been spontaneous. She'd entertained many vivid fantasies about him. She was surprised to find that she even had the capacity to desire anyone that way. She'd been pretty sure that any sexual or romantic part of her had died with Sam.

She remembers her kiss with Rafael on the warehouse floor. What if they'd let that play out to its conclusion? Her body reacts noticeably when she imagines that.

It's not really Rafael, she tries to tell herself. She recalls reading an article about how, with the right set of questions, you could fall in love with anyone. It's just the intimacy of their circumstances muddling her feelings for him, and she's dragged him into that confusion.

"Are you alright?" he asks her, assuming that her silence is because of the anniversary of Sam's and Clara's birthdays.

Can she talk to him about this strangeness between them? It seems too fraught, so she just says she's fine.

"We need to talk about what we're going to do," he says, and for a moment she panics. "Since we abolished most property rights today, we should probably honor that by moving our livestock into town."

Irina rolls her eyes and scoffs, "You and Tina."

A question has been nagging at her since Tina arrived with her guns and strong opinions. "Do you think she's going to be a problem?"

"I think she's strident but . . . ," he trails off and Irina looks at him pointedly, ". . . you're also strident."

He can see that she's annoyed, but he continues anyway. "This is too important to avoid scrutiny. It's better to stress-test your ideas now than to see problems play out in real life and create a crisis. Don't think of her as a nemesis. Think of her as a partner, an editor. You set up a process that includes input from others. That was a good intuition, but I know it's difficult to actually live it. You were a lawyer, though, and you've been married before, so you should be used to dealing with some constructive disagreement."

"Sam and I never really disagreed much."

"Well, that's . . . unusual. But you were still a lawyer in an adversarial process, right? Did you ever argue against people in court and have drinks with them afterward, or does that only happen on television?"

She smiles, "I did. When I was prosecuting cases, one of the defense attorneys was a good friend of mine."

"So think of this process that way. An adversarial process where all ideas are thoroughly vetted results in a better outcome, right?"

"Theoretically, at least."

+++

They spend the weekend working on ordinary tasks, but Irina has a premonition that things are ending. Rafael hasn't brought up the idea of moving to town, but that would be the practical thing to do and will probably be expected by everyone else. If they do move to town, will they still live together? The thought of living apart fills Irina with melancholy, which follows her like a shadow for the entire weekend.

On Sunday evening, they prepare to leave for the week in town. Irina's sense of anticipated loss over their home and companionship intertwines with memories of the other losses in her life, and she finds herself spiraling into deeper sadness and anxiety. She fills her wineglass a bit too full and sips it steadily as she packs her things. The wine barely turns down the volume of her feelings, though, so she refills the glass and finishes it as she stuffs the last items of clothing into her duffel bag. She struggles clumsily with the zipper of the bag, finally pulling it tight and hefting the bag over her shoulder. Her balance wavers just a bit, but she rights herself and walks across the living room. She forgets, though, that there's a step down into the garage. For a moment, her foot searches for the ground; then she pitches forward and lands on her knees.

Rafael is next to her a moment later, asking if she's alright. He helps her up, his hands on her elbows to steady her. He's

198

so close that she can see the flecks in his hazel eyes, but she wants him closer.

Then her lips are pressed to his, and her hands are roaming his body, but her kisses are sloppy with drunkenness and urgency, and he can taste the wine on her lips. When he pulls back, he sees tears on her cheeks and the glint of her wedding ring in the dim light.

"Wait," he says, summoning all his willpower. "Please, wait." She looks stunned as though he's pulled her from a dream. "What is this? What are we doing?" he asks.

She moves away from him to the other side of the doorway.

"I can't keep living in this in-between place where you kiss me, then pretend it didn't happen," Rafael says.

He pauses for a moment; then his insecurities and doubts spill out. "I can't be him, Irina. I can't be Sam."

Irina is earnestly surprised by his words. "I don't expect you to be."

"I honestly don't know what you expect!" he exclaims, then takes a deep breath, trying to calm himself. "You kiss me, then pretend it never happened. You get upset with me for arguing with you, then tell me Sam never argued. You seem to want me, but then it seems like you really want someone else entirely."

She stares at him with wide, tear-filled eyes, and she can see the tears in his eyes reflecting the lantern light.

"I'm not as good of a man as he was. I'm not as patient or as good of a dad or as likable or easygoing. Hell, I've killed a man. I doubt that Sam would do that. The way you talk about him . . . he sounds perfect, and it seems like you had a perfect marriage. It's impossible to live up to that."

Irina doesn't know what to say. He continues without needing a response, "I love you enough that if I could bring him back, I would, even if it meant you and I could never be together. But I can't do that.

"I don't think you're ready to start something new," Rafael says. "We should go back to the way things were before."

"We can't do that," Irina protests.

"We're not in high school, Irina. We're adults capable of maintaining a friendship after ending . . . ," he struggles to even name what is between them, "whatever this is."

"No, I mean; I don't want that."

He sighs in frustration. "Then I don't know what you want." She stares at him, unsure of what to say or do.

"Let me know when you figure it out," he says. "I'm going to bed."

It's only after he's left that she realizes that he'd told her that he loves her. She finds that she isn't surprised by it. He's shown her that he loves her plenty of times, without ever actually saying it.

Rafael lies in bed, agonizing over their conversation. Maybe he shouldn't have said anything. It was better to have some of her than none of her. Now their friendship may be irrevocably broken.

He regrets telling her that he loved her, especially in the same breath as breaking things off with her. He'd wanted to find some way to tell her that would convey the gravity of the words, and now he's lost that opportunity.

At dawn, he pulls himself out of his exhausted self-doubt to make breakfast. Irina emerges from her room, looking every bit as miserable as he. He isn't sure what to say, so he simply says, "Good morning."

They sit in silence as he prepares breakfast. Finally, as he sets the bowl of oatmeal in front of her, she says, "I'm going to leave for town as soon as Matteo wakes up."

He isn't sure if she's saying that she's just leaving for the day or if she's signaling a more serious, lasting separation. He nods in assent, feeling he has little choice in either scenario.

+++

That evening they sit across from each other, pretending that nothing has happened. Rafael is cordial, but he looks drawn, and the warmth between them has disappeared. Irina has put on her green dress and admonished herself to stay in character. There are more important things to deal with than her personal drama.

"So, let's talk about holidays," she says with false cheerfulness and confidence.

She begins the discussion with an idea inspired by Sam's recent birthday: a memorial holiday for those who died in the Pandemic. Rafael is grateful for the concentration required to do simultaneous translation for Julián.

The conversation takes a turn when Emma suggests adding several Christian holidays to the calendar. Had Irina not been distracted by her personal troubles, she would have anticipated this and had a plan to manage it. Instead, she says, "Wait . . . you're religious?"

Tina raises an eyebrow, and Emma narrows her eyes and says, "I don't know why you would assume that I'm not."

Irina stumbles, "I just thought that the Christian church wasn't very accepting . . . ."

Tina scoffs, "Our church has had the rainbow flag on the flagpole since 2003."

Irina catches herself. "I'm sorry. I shouldn't have assumed."

The awkwardness of her fumble, combined with the headache she's had all day and the sting of Rafael's cool distance makes tears rise in her eyes.

"It's . . . fine," Emma says, looking at her with concern. Rafael stops his translation to Julián to stare at Irina.

Get your shit together, Irina thinks to herself. She takes a deep breath. "I hadn't been planning on having religion be a part of this."

"See!" Tina exclaims, "I told you this was socialism. Limited property rights, government control, a ban on religion."

"I didn't suggest banning religion. I just don't think we should make religious holidays part of our official, governmental calendar," Irina replies. "That implies that we're endorsing a particular religion, that this is a religious society."

"If you're worried about endorsing the Christian religion, then why not just leave open the possibility of adding holidays from other religions, as well, if believers show up?" Emma asks.

"That's still an endorsement of religion, as an idea, and I think we want to avoid that here," Irina answers. "Religion separates people. It creates factions."

Julián, through Rafael, speaks up, "Religion gives people comfort and a sense of purpose. And it gives them moral rules. We need that right now."

The conversation grows more contentious as Irina argues futilely that religion is another thing that shouldn't be carried over into their new society. Tina, Emma, and Julián argue passionately against her. Ify tries to mediate, and Rafael is silent, except for his translations. At 10:00 p.m. they still haven't agreed on anything other than a public memorial holiday. The night is unsalvageable. Irina wraps up the conversation, and everyone goes to bed without talking.

Irina lies awake in tortured self-doubt. Who is she to draw up a new society? There's nothing in her background that qualifies her for this kind of responsibility. It may also be pointless anyway, if no one else shows up here in Ferndale. When the swirl of anxiety starts, she reaches for her favorite book, but realizes that she's left it in the House by the Sea. She tries counting and breathing, but that doesn't work, so she gets up to look for something to read in the sitting room.

"Shit," she says, when she sees Rafael seated in front of the dying fire, glasses on, reading a book.

"I can leave if you want," he offers.

"No, you were here first," she replies. "I'll get a book and go."

"I'm sorry about last night," he says as she begins to peruse the bookshelf. "I was upset and harsher than I should have been."

She turns to look at him. "I'm sorry, too. I was sad and confused, and I pulled you into it."

"If you want to kiss me when you're sober and you know what you want, I'd like that. If you want to be friends, that'll work too. It just has to be one or the other."

She nods, and he continues, "Just to be clear, I'm not saying you have to be completely done grieving. You can still be sad sometimes. I'm still sad sometimes about Helena, and our marriage was terrible. I'm just asking you to know what you want, to be consistent with me."

"Okay."

They're both quiet for a beat; then he says, "So . . . democracy is fun, isn't it?"

Irina smiles and shakes her head. "I really fucked up today."

"I think the group will forgive you. Everyone here is struggling a little. We have to give each other grace. You might not see it, but they've put a lot of trust in you. Most of them are buying your overall framework, even if there's dissent around the edges. Just keep going."

She nods. Her exhaustion, the stress of the day, and the headache that still hasn't eased are making her feel emotional.

"I'm going to bed. The room is all yours," he says, taking off his glasses and getting up. She wants to hug him or kiss him or thank him or all of those things, but instead she just says "goodnight."

+++

The next morning, Irina walks into the kitchen of the bed and breakfast with a peace offering: a bin of butchered venison from the morning's successful hunt. She's relieved to find that no one treats her any differently than usual.

"Nice work," Tina says as Irina cleans up at the sink. "Venison stew tonight?"

"Unfortunately, it has to age for a few days. It should be ready by Wednesday or Thursday."

"I'm looking forward to it," Tina says. An olive branch, despite their many differences.

+++

That evening they meet again in the sitting room. Irina still feels melancholy, but it seems more manageable after her conversation with Rafael the prior night. She proposes that they stick to the model most of them had grown up in: free exercise of religion without state endorsement or interference. They compromise to include Christmas and Good Friday as official holidays, along with a Day of Remembrance, Thanksgiving, and holidays that correspond to each of the equinoxes and solstices. Everyone agrees that Halloween is too fun to eliminate. They leave open the option of adding more holidays if believers from other faiths show up. Julián proposes a Founders Day to commemorate the drafting of the Charter, but Irina balks at the idea.

"I don't want us to be venerated," she says.

"People need heroes," Rafael translates Julián's response.

"I'm nobody's hero," Irina replies. "And no one should be valued above anyone else in this society."

"I think that Julián is right," Ify says. "If you want to build a culture, you have to have a mythology that inspires people."

"It's inevitable, anyway," Rafael remarks. "If we build something and people actually do come here, we will be capital 'F' Founders. People will look at us as authority figures and examples. That's why you asked Emma to take notes, right? Because you know the conversations we have here will be the basis of decisions in the future."

"They'll write songs and poems about us!" Emma jokes. Irina makes a face of disgust.

"And they can even be paid minimally with goods and services for those songs and poems!" Tina laughs.

Irina concedes, and Emma reads off a list of holidays, and Irina calls the vote. Unanimous.

"We've skipped around a bit." Irina pages through her printed notes. "Let's go back to apprenticeships. To review, the process is that for each profession, the Council will appoint a professional—or more depending on the circumstances—and apprentices. When a professional retires or moves on to a new position, the apprentice moves up to replace them. People apply for apprenticeships through an exam designed by the professional. The top scorer becomes the apprentice."

"I don't like exams," Rafael says. "They only measure one kind of aptitude, and that doesn't necessarily indicate who would best fill the role."

Irina is disappointed in herself for not considering his past when she drafted this. She asks, "Do you have an alternate proposal?"

"Actually, I do," Rafael answers. He's spent some time considering this after reviewing her draft, "Interested applicants register for a lottery. For each apprenticeship, two candidates are selected by lottery and intern for three months. After that, the professional picks her apprentice. The other returns to their prior position."

"What if the professional thinks that neither of the candidates is qualified?" Irina asks.

"Then both candidates are returned to their old positions, and the process begins again," Rafael replies.

That seems inefficient to Irina, but she recalls his history and softens.

"But we really need the smartest applicants for some positions," Ify says. "For instance, a person shouldn't become a doctor by chance."

"Exams don't measure intelligence," Rafael replies. "They just measure someone's test-taking skills."

"And they tend to be culturally biased," Emma points out.

Irina counts opposition and support. "Julián?" she says, "What do you think?"

Rafael translates for him, "I think Rafael's suggestion is more well-rounded. Let the professional take the time to decide on the candidates. That's better than an exam."

"All in favor of Rafael's proposal, then?" Irina asks. Everyone but Ify agrees. They spend the next two hours discussing what to do about people who are physically unable to work, deciding that nearly anyone can contribute something and that roles can be tailored to that; then they break for the night.

+++

The next day, Rafael and Julián demonstrate their new wind-turbine system for the group.

They've connected a house's electrical system to a bank of car batteries powered by roof-mounted windmills. Julián flicks on the light switch and smiles.

"It's not enough power for heating but should be adequate for lights and a mini fridge," Rafael says.

"Refrigeration alone is life-changing!" Irina exclaims, recalling how much time they used to spend preserving and preparing food.

Rafael thanks Julián for his idea of linking the car batteries.

"We can use this to supplement the solar panels. The batteries will die in another couple of years, but this buys us time to develop something else," Rafael explains. Irina watches him with admiration. He sees her looking and smiles, but it doesn't quite reach his eyes.

+++

They spend the next few nights discussing minutia of the economic plan—what the expected work hours are, how much leave people will get, how they'll set up the work week. They leave open the question of currency for the following week.

Melancholy and anxiety follow Irina, joining her at the gardens while she weeds and waters, at the barn outside of town where she helps Ify clear out dead livestock to make space for new livestock, in the fields where she hunts rabbits, in the kitchen while she makes venison stew with Tina on Thursday. The others seem to notice her and Rafael's withdrawn moods, but no one says anything. They've become accustomed to each other's ebbs and flows. Irina has found Ify crying while doing various tasks; she's seen Emma carving a long list of names in the memorial grove, and she's noticed that sometimes Tina or Julián drink to excess. Rafael was right about everyone struggling together. Irina feels some relieved solidarity in that.

As she packs her things on Thursday evening, she thinks again of the worn envelope. She wakes early the next morning to walk to the memorial grove. There are a lot of new names there, including "MM" in clumsy letters—Rafael's attempt to help Miranda come to terms with the mountain man. Irina runs her fingers over Sam's and Clara's names. She can feel something shifting in her.

"Ready to go?" Rafael asks from behind her. Matteo holds Rafael's and Miranda's hands. Matteo still mistakenly calls Rafael 'dada,' and Irina has given up correcting him. Rafael has earned that title. Miranda also calls Matteo her brother, though she's never called Irina 'mommy.' Irina senses that will require a formal invitation. The three of them have formed a family on their own. It's only Irina who has held herself apart.

She feels a pang of guilt when she looks at Matteo. She's spent so little time with him these past weeks. "Let's go to the beach today," she says. She has an appointment with the unopened envelope, but she wants to wait a bit longer.

They spend the morning on the foggy beach. Irina and Miranda peer at the seabirds through the binoculars, and Miranda reads their names from her book. Matteo chases Irina around with handfuls of sand until she collapses on the beach, laughing. Irina watches Rafael playing with the children. She considers where she was a year before, and she traces her path to this moment.

"We're going to have to move into town, aren't we?" Irina asks.

"I think so," Rafael replies sadly. "But for now, let's enjoy this."

"You were right," she says, "This place is magical."

Chapter Thirteen

The next day after putting Matteo down for his nap, Irina tucks the envelope into the pocket of her hoodie, feeling a flutter of anxiety as she does, wondering what's inside. She's waited too long for this, yet some part of her still doesn't feel ready.

"I need a little time to myself today," Irina says to Rafael. "Can you watch the kids?"

He looks at her, sensing that something has changed. He's spent all week hoping and trying not to hope. "Sure."

She departs for the beach, tracing the familiar path through the early spring wildflowers.

She sits down in the sand before the endless Pacific. For a while, she watches the waves and the seagulls that soar above them. In the largest tree on the cliff to her right, a bald eagle perches. She wishes that Miranda were here to see him. She wishes that Sam and Clara were too. She reaches into her pocket and pulls out the worn envelope. It's time to read the last words of her conversation with Sam. With shaking hands, she carefully opens it and unfolds the letter, holding it out so that her tears don't fall on his words.

My love,

I'm so sorry that I have to leave. There's nothing that I want more than to stay here with you both, to watch Matteo grow and try to rebuild our life together. I don't know what will be left in this world, but I wish I could have been there to face it with you.

Do you remember the day we went to Depoe Bay with Clara and watched the whales? That was one of the best days of my life. Loving you and our children has been the most important and best part of my life. Even if I'd known the ending, I would still have picked us.

You're so resilient. It's one of the things that I love most about you, and it's the thing that gives me comfort now: I'm certain that you're strong enough to make a life for yourself and Matteo. I hope, though, that you'll find a way to do something more than survive. I hope that whatever is left is enough for you both to find some happiness. Whatever you find that brings you joy, I want you to grab it with both hands. I hope that you find a place that moves you, a person that loves you and Matteo, something to do that gives you a sense of purpose. You deserve that.

My life ends here, but your life and Matteo's life don't have to. Please remember that. If you have any doubts about what I would want for you, imagine that I was the one left behind—what would you want for me?

If there's an afterlife, Clara and I will see you there. If there's reincarnation, I'll come back to look after you some other way. And if there truly is nothing after death, then know that you've given the collection of cells that is me the best possible experience of consciousness.

All my love, Sam

Irina doesn't check the tears that run down her face and fall into her lap. She reads his letter several times over. She memorizes his words. She sits for a long time as the sun moves through the sky.

She remembers the day in Depoe Bay but in a hazy way. It had been a good day, but for her it had been an ordinary good day, one of what she thought would be an endless collection of good days spread out over their long lives together. She wonders what it was about that day, in particular, that was so moving for Sam. Sam loved whales, but he'd seen them many times before.

Then she realizes what it must have been about that day that was special. Sam had seen whales before, but the day in Depoe Bay was the first time that he and Clara had seen the whales together. Irina remembers the joy and curiosity on Clara's face as they watched one of the whales breach the surface, its white belly shining in the sunlight against the blue Pacific.

That was one of the best days of Sam's life because that was the day he got to share something he loved with someone he loved.

She recalls the day that Matteo said his first word and the day that he took his first step; how much she longed to share those moments with someone else. She recollects the evening she, Rafael, Miranda, and Matteo had watched the sun set over the ocean. That moment had felt transcendent because she'd shared it with them.

She's certain that she loves Rafael. She remembers his reassurance when she dropped her papers in that first group meeting, his smile as she unwrapped the oil paints, his laughter with Matteo. She thinks about the little ways that he pays attention, his small considerate acts—starting the fire when he wakes up so she and the children won't be cold, doing the chores that he knows she hates, making everyone's breakfast every morning. Warmth spreads through her chest and radiates out.

Why was it so easy for her to reply to Miranda's "I love you" but so hard to say it to Rafael? Why is it so easy to accept that loving other children doesn't take away from her love for Clara, while it's impossible to contemplate the same about her love for Rafael and Sam?

She's told herself that her feelings for Rafael mean less because they never truly chose each other; they simply ended up here together at the end of the world. It isn't love, really; it's necessity. Would they have picked each other if they had a world of options? That's impossible to know.

It doesn't matter, though. Plenty of arranged marriages have resulted in love, and plenty of love marriages have been illusory. She didn't pick many of the people she's loved most deeply. Her children, her grandparents, her aunt, her cousins—they had all simply arrived in her life, fully-formed with all their perfections and imperfections. She hadn't chosen Miranda either, yet it was easy for her to admit to herself that she loves Miranda.

And in a way, she and Rafael have chosen each other, with every small act of kindness and consideration, every risk and vulnerability, every act of trust and confession; they've grown love over time.

She had imagined that she was honoring Sam by trying to stifle her love for Rafael, but Sam would never have expected that. *Imagine that our roles were reversed and I was the one left behind—what would you want for me?*

She would have wanted him to be happy, to lean into love. When she thinks of him raising Matteo alone, she feels deeply sad for both him and Matteo. If she had died instead, she would have wanted Matteo to have another mother, a woman who loved him the way that she loves Miranda now, the way Rafael loves Matteo.

The idea of Sam loving another woman still stirs jealousy in her, but the idea of his spending the rest of his life without that emotional and physical intimacy makes her feel unbearably sad. To wish that for him would be an act of incredible selfishness, anathema to the love they shared.

The sun is sinking toward the horizon, painting the sea with tones of peach and pink. A flock of gulls passes overhead, and she watches them until they disappear to the south. She looks up at the house. Rafael is choosing to give her this time and space—an act of love and understanding; she sees now. One of many.

She rereads Sam's letter one final time in the dying light; then she folds it neatly and slips it back into the envelope, along with her wedding ring. Then she puts the envelope in the front pocket of her hoodie.

When the stars emerge, she lies down in the sand and looks up at them, tracing the constellations that Sam had taught her and Clara. As the moon rises, she pages through what she would consider her best days with Sam. She imagines what she would say to him if she'd had a chance to properly end the too-short conversation that was their marriage. She would have thanked him for being patient with her and teaching her how to love another person in a healthy way. She would have listed all of the things she loved about him—his kindness, his smile, his curiosity about the world, his enthusiasm for life, his warmth. She would have apologized for how hard things were after Clara died. She would have agreed that even if she had known their ending, she would still have chosen him.

She whispers a goodbye into the wind and the waves, and she thanks him for loving her enough to give her permission to love another. She looks up at the house, bathed in silvery moonlight, and sees the fire Rafael has lit on the front patio.

Then she slowly picks her way up the trail under the nearly full moon, following Rafael's beacon home.

Rafael is watching her from one of the chairs as she steps onto the front patio. The crackle of the fire is the only sound as she approaches him. She can see the uncertainty in his eyes. She leans down and answers his unspoken question with a gentle brush of her lips on his. She pulls back, leaning over him, her hands on the arms of the patio chair, her legs flush against his, their faces inches from each other. For a moment, Rafael doesn't breathe.

"I love you," she says softly.

"I love you too." She leans in and presses her lips hard against his, their tongues tangling. She straightens and takes both of his hands, bringing him with her so they're standing together on the patio. He brushes her fingers with his thumb and realizes that her ring is missing. He pulls her tightly against him and kisses her deeply. She steps back and leads him into the house, closing and locking his bedroom door behind them.

For a few moments, they both stand several inches from each other, uncertain, in the semi-darkness of the room. Rafael moves to light the candles.

"Don't," Irina says, thinking of every flaw she's ever noticed in the mirror.

"Please," he says, "it's been so long."

She realizes that she wants to find out if she can be imperfect and still be desired by him. She takes the match from him and lights three candles herself. By flickering candlelight, with shaking hands, he reaches for her and carefully undoes the hair-tie that holds her long auburn braid, then runs his hands through her hair, unbraiding it as he's longed to do since the first time he'd seen it falling in waves around her shoulders. She pulls his shirt over his head, and his hands grasp the bottom hem of her hoodie. He feels the envelope inside her pocket, confirming what he already suspected. He takes off her hoodie; then she helps him take off her tank top and bra. He steps back.

They stand in the candlelight, considering each other. Irina has the strong desire to wrap her arms around her uncovered breasts or to close the distance between them so he can't see her. She resists it, turning her attention from herself to the man standing before her, the lean muscles of his arms as he reaches out his hand to brush the tattoo over her heart. She realizes that she's forgotten to take a breath, and she does, finally, her breast rising to meet his fingers. She shivers.

Rafael desperately wants to touch every part of her, his body urges him to rush this to its completion. He does his best, though, to quell that desire. He runs his hand over her breast and down her waist. "Beautiful," he whispers.

She reaches for the button of his pants, and he feels momentarily vulnerable, remembering the last time he'd tried to do this. It seems to take forever for her to undo the button and gently slide his pants and boxers to the floor. This time, at least, his body is responding. The flutter of anxiety stills in his chest. He kisses her as he fumbles with the button on her pants, finally sliding them down her legs along with her underwear. He pulls her toward him, skin on skin, puzzle pieces interlocking. For a while they kiss, the lengths of their bodies touching, their hands exploring. Then she leads him to the bed.

He lies down beside her, sliding his hand up her thigh and between her legs. He's glad to find that she wants him as much as he wants her, and his desire increases in kind. After nearly four years, though, he's uncertain of how to touch her, and his fingers are awkward at first, until finally he gives up and asks her to tell him what she likes. After a moment of hesitation, she obliges, finding that after so long she's a little uncertain herself. His hesitation falls away, and she realizes that she's forgotten that anything could feel this good. Her body arches to meet his hand, and she cries out his name, her muscles tightening around his fingers. He leans in and kisses her hungrily, his lips rough against hers.

She reaches down to touch him, but he takes her hand away, certain that he won't last long. She pulls him over her, and he struggles to clear his mind enough to remember how to do this responsibly.

"I was tested after Helena, and I'm clean. But I don't have a condom," he says.

"I don't care. They're probably all expired by now anyway. Just, um . . . pull out, I guess?"

"Got it."

He kisses her lips, her face, her neck, her breasts. She tugs his hair with one hand and pulls his body toward her with her other hand.

"Are you sure?" he asks.

"Yes. Please . . . ."

He's gentle with her, remembering that she hasn't been with anyone since she gave birth. Still, he sees a pained look on her face as he slides inside her, and he pauses.

"Don't stop," she says, pulling him in further. So he continues, the pleasure of her surrounding him is nearly overwhelming. They're both out of practice and unfamiliar with each other's body, and it takes a moment for them to find a satisfactory rhythm, but as with so many aspects of their life together, they slip wordlessly into a mutual accord. He loves the way her body rises up to meet his, the flush that spreads across her breasts and collarbone, the urgency of her kisses, the things she whispers to him as they move together. He tries to hold himself back but finds that he can't, and he lets out a strangled moan and pulls away from her at the last moment, finishing in his hand.

He collapses beside her, fighting the urge to apologize for the fast ending. She seems satisfied, though, and he comforts himself with the hope that there will be another opportunity. He brushes a kiss against her temple, whispering, "I love you."

"I love you too," she says, tilting her head up to look into his eyes as she does.

He cleans up in the bathroom, then blows out the candles as he crosses the room. He pauses beside the bed, taking her in. Her eyes are closed, and at first he thinks she is sleeping; then she opens them and looks at him, her gaze sweeping the length of his body as he stands by the bed, bathed in moonlight. He feels his old insecurities: that he isn't tall enough, muscular enough, bold enough. But desire is plain in her expression. She reaches out a hand and runs it up his thigh, over his stomach, then takes his hand and tugs him back down into bed beside her. He pulls her against him under the sheets, running his hands over her body as they both fall asleep.

Rafael wakes in the middle of the night, his arm pins-and-needles beneath her. He shifts carefully, trying not to wake her, but her eyelids flutter, and she looks up at him. She moves on top of him, straddling him, and slides down, taking him into her with a sigh of pleasure. She looks him in the eyes as she does, and the intimacy of it is nearly overwhelming. He closes his eyes, willing himself to move slowly, to follow her lead. He uses what he's already learned about her body, his fingers now more practiced as he touches her while she moves over him. This time he feels her tighten and release around him before he finishes. Afterward he trails kisses over her forehead and hair, repeating again that he loves her, hearing her say it back, certain that he could never hear it too many times. She gets up, gathers her clothes, and slips out to her own bedroom, leaving him with a last kiss and the lingering scent of her in his sheets.

+++

Rafael wakes the next morning feeling more relaxed and happier than he can remember feeling. He recalls the night before and has to take a deep breath and deliberately think about something else to stifle his body's reaction.

As he dresses and brushes his teeth, he tries not to second guess himself, not to question if he was good enough, not to worry about whether she will regret this.

He lights the living room and back-patio fires, then gathers his fishing gear and sets off for the beach. Fog still hangs over the valley. As he walks down the driveway, the last of the stars are fading as the sunrise spreads across the sky. The grass along the path glows in the morning light. When he reaches the sand, he walks south toward the bluffs. He baits his line and casts into the water.

217

Sea birds call to each other. The ocean breathes against the shore. Stillness settles over him. He wonders what was in Sam's letter, but he knows that he has no right to eavesdrop on Irina's final conversation with her deceased husband. Whatever Sam said, it was sufficient to free Irina, and Rafael is grateful for that.

After almost an hour, he still hasn't gotten any bites, so he begins the trek back home in the evanescing fog, feeling a little wary of how Irina will react when she sees him. Will she pretend that last night didn't happen, as she had after they kissed? Or will they move forward together?

Irina has already set the kettle over the fireplace and two mugs on the table, but he doesn't see her outside. He leans his fishing pole against the house and turns to go in the back door, just as she walks out. She smiles at him a bit shyly, looking into his eyes before looking down at the ground. He pauses, unsure of how to react to her. She raises her eyes back to his, and he chooses to take a risk and closes the distance between them. He pulls her into his arms and presses his lips to hers. She wraps her arms around him and kisses him back.

"What do we do now?" She asks him as they both pull back, a bit breathless.

"We've done everything out of order," he says. "So I have no idea what the next move is."

She leaves him to pull the kettle off the fire and pour the steaming water into the French press. They sit down across from each other at the table. He takes her hand, brushing his fingertips over her upturned wrist. She closes her eyes and tries to remember what she'd been thinking about. "If I'm going to sleep over in your bedroom, I guess we should say something to Miranda?"

"She doesn't wake up until 8:00 anyway, so as long as we get up before her, I don't think we need to say anything, right?"

"So we never say anything to her, and one day she just kind of figures it out on her own?"

"Hey, you're the self-proclaimed expert on the birds and the bees; . . . maybe you should explain it to her."

"Touché."

"I'm just saying, we already live together. She's seen that, and she seems fine with it. She loves you, actually. I don't think we need to explain the finer points of this to her."

They both sit in silence for a moment, watching the fire. Irina pushes down the plunger on the French press and pours them each a mug of stale coffee.

"So you want to sleep over in my room, huh?" He jokes, feeling a rush of relief at her assumption, at the way they easily slip back into their rapport.

"I don't know about sleeping . . . ." She smiles suggestively at him and sips her coffee.

"We do need to talk about something, though," she says after a moment. Rafael feels a twinge of anxiety. "We probably should have talked about this last night."

"You seemed pretty goal-oriented when you got back from the beach." Rafael sticks with humor to try to quell his rising tension about where this conversation might go.

"And you were generous enough not to get in the way of that goal," Irina smirks at him.

"There was no way I was going to slow you down with questions."

"I'm glad you didn't," Irina says. "But I do need to talk to you about this now."

"Ok." She hears his hesitation.

"You said that you can't live up to Sam because he was perfect and we had a 'perfect marriage.'"

Rafael nods. Hearing his own insecurities repeated back to him is excruciating.

"Sam wasn't perfect, Rafael, and neither was our marriage. That marriage book you have? I recognized it, because he and I read it in marriage counseling. It took us years to work through our issues."

Rafael's brow furrows. She pauses and takes a breath, fighting the guilt she feels about saying this. "You were right that Sam wouldn't have shot the mountain man. That's not necessarily a good thing, though. You did what you had to do to protect yourself and Miranda. I would have done the same, but Sam wouldn't have. He was never very good at laying down boundaries. He would never have confronted me like you did last week. But I'm glad you did. We needed to talk about this.

"Sam was a wonderful person, but he was also kind of a pushover. The only time he ever really confronted me was to demand marriage counseling, and I'm pretty sure he did that because he was being pushed by the only woman who was more strong-willed than I am: my mother-in-law. His unwillingness to stand up for himself caused a lot of problems raising Clara. It was impossible for him to really enforce rules or expectations with her. So I was always the bad guy, and he was always her favorite."

Rafael reaches for her hand, but he doesn't say anything, sensing that she has more to say. "It would have fallen to me to deal with the mountain man, and I would have done it. But that's so much pressure! It's exhausting to be the one who fights every battle. After the accident, when Clara was in the hospital, even though I was still recovering, I was the one who had to push them to test her one last time for brain activity. I was the one who had to decide to disconnect life support. It was always, always me.

"And yes, everyone loved Sam. He was a charismatic people pleaser, but sometimes that was hard too. Sometimes it was difficult to be the less popular one, to be the one who was overlooked. I'm not the most likable person, and sometimes it wasn't fun to stand next to him and feel that contrast."

"I've never thought you were unlikeable," Rafael interrupts.

"I'm argumentative."

"You were paid to argue!"

"Pushy. Opinionated."

"Okay, I guess that's true."

"You didn't have to agree so quickly!" she says.

"I like pushy and opinionated. It keeps me from getting bored." He smiles.

"You like it now, but let's check in on that in twenty years."

"I like that you're implying that I'll have twenty years to evaluate this," he replies.

She rolls her eyes at him. "Anyway, my point is Sam was a good person, and our marriage was a good marriage. But he wasn't perfect, and I'm not perfect, and I don't expect you to be perfect either. Every person and every relationship has issues. And if I led you to believe anything else, I'm sorry. That was wrong of me."

He squeezes her hand. "Thank you."

+++

That night the door to Rafael's bedroom is barely closed behind them before he has her pinned against it. This is crazy, Irina knows. They're much too old for this. It's undignified and irrational and not at all what she would have expected from herself, let alone Rafael. It's strange to suddenly see this other side of him after nearly a year of living together. It has the disorienting, dreamlike feeling of finding a hidden room in a house she's lived in all her life.

221

No words pass between them, until afterward when they lie facing each other on a blanket in front of the fire, as they had the first time she kissed him. His fingers brush her tattoo again.

"Memento Mori," he reads. After seeing the tattoo peeking out from beneath her comparatively low-cut green dress, he'd translated the words in the library: "*Remember death*. Why?"

It seems crazy now, she knows. They're always remembering death. There is no way to forget it. Death surrounds them. "I got it after Clara died, to help me remember that every interaction I have with someone I love could be my last," she says softly.

He considers this. He's rarely seen Irina get angry with Matteo, even when he does difficult toddler things. Still, he imagines this awareness is a heavy thing to bear.

"And sometimes it was comforting to think that one day I won't have to be separated from her anymore," Irina says. "When I was really despondent, it helped to know that at least there was still death, the end of suffering."

She closes her eyes for a moment, thinking. "Now it means something else—a sense of urgency. I spent two years being stuck. I don't want to waste any more time. I don't want to be saved from something; I want to be saved *for* something."

Chapter Fourteen

Monday morning arrives, pulling them from their strange, dream-like refuge. As Rafael loads the crated chickens into Lily's cart, Irina feels a stab of sadness. These are the first, small steps; they will be moving imminently. She and Rafael had made choices that led to this, without truly considering the implications. She looks back at the house sadly as they depart.

At the bed and breakfast, Irina and Rafael unload their things into separate rooms out of habit and propriety. They steal a moment in Irina's room, kissing and laughing at their own foolishness.

Irina and Ify spend the morning settling the chickens and the horses. After lunch, she takes Ify out to see Blaze, the stallion. They contemplate moving him, but neither of them has enough expertise to be comfortable trying. They resolve to build a small open stable for him and to breed him and Lily again that summer. Another horse will be useful, even if it means that Lily can't work for a while.

At the Fern Cottage, Rafael and Julián use a solar water pump that Julián had found to pump water from a nearby stream into an irrigation system they'd salvaged. As the water trickles out onto the fields of sprouted wheat, they toast their victory with flasks of whiskey. Rafael's thoughts turn to Irina for the hundredth time.

+++

That evening Irina brings an unusual amount of energy and enthusiasm to the discussions. Rafael sits in the chair nearest the fire, trying without success to keep his eyes off of her and his concentration on what Ify is saying. Something about currency again. Rafael can't follow, and several times, Julián has to remind him to translate. His translations come out garbled and incomplete though, and Tina breaks in to supplement them in imperfect Spanish.

Rafael's mind keeps summoning vivid recollections of the past few nights, flashes of skin and sensation. It's frustrating and intoxicating to find himself in this state of distraction. He knows this is just infatuation, a chemical and hormonal reaction. And yet, it's undergirded by more substantial things: love and friendship. He'll have to ride it out, enjoying the more pleasurable parts and trying not to humiliate himself in the less dignified parts. He feels sudden solidarity with the mostly useless stallion. The thought makes him smile. His eyes flick to Irina and she blushes and gives him a knowing look.

He glances at Tina and finds her watching him with a smirk.

They end the evening without resolving the currency question, deciding to wait for Ify and Irina to research the topic with whatever books they can find in the Ferndale Library.

"You seem distracted," Tina says to Rafael afterward as she hands him the decanter of whiskey.

"I didn't sleep well last night," he replies.

Tina chuckles, "I bet you didn't."

Then she turns back to her conversation with Ify. Irina and Rafael slip out to "check on the children."

As soon as they reach the hallway upstairs, he pulls her to him and kisses her hungrily, his hands wandering down her body. Irina pulls back when she sees Tina rounding the corner from the stairs.

Tina shakes her head, "I would suggest that you get a room, but you've already got two. So maybe just consolidate?"

She chuckles to herself as she walks away down the hall.

"Maybe we should tell her that the comedian position in Ferndale was already filled?" Irina suggests. Rafael laughs as he pulls her into his room.

+++

The next evening, they finally discuss the portion of the plan that Irina had intended to start with two weeks before. Her brain is a bit foggy from sleep deprivation, but she's propelled by the manic energy of infatuation.

"So," she begins, "As you've seen in the folder, the basic government structure would be a council of five, selected by lottery of all interested adults in the community. The six of us will run the council for the first four years. In year four, two of us rotate out and are replaced by one lottery pick, after that, one rotates out each year and is replaced by an annual lottery. From then on, Councilmembers will serve staggered five year terms. When the population reaches five hundred adults, we'll add two new Council seats."

She pages through the notes she'd prepared for this meeting, "The council has the power to create or eliminate professional positions, to appoint the inaugural round of professionals, to allocate resources, to remove professionals who aren't performing well, and to pass new laws. Amendments to the Charter are the only thing requiring a public vote; they have to be approved by two thirds of the public."

"This doesn't look like any democracy I've ever seen," Tina says.

"It's the original European democracy," Ify replies. "Athenian government by sortition. I understand what you're going for, Irina, but I think this system has a serious problem: there's no consideration for expertise here. You'd have an entirely unqualified group of people running the government."

"An entirely unqualified group of people . . . like us?" Irina asks, raising her eyebrow.

"I wouldn't say you're unqualified," Rafael says to Irina. Tina rolls her eyes at his obvious pandering. "But we were essentially selected by chance."

"That's not true," Ify says. "We self-selected. We chose to come here."

"Fair," Rafael replies. "But so will anyone else who joins us. And Irina's point stands—none of us, except maybe her—are qualified to form a government, yet here we are. We chose to come to Ferndale, but we survived by chance."

"I'm decidedly unqualified," Irina says, both charmed and a little annoyed at his flattery. "But thank you. And actually, anyone who's survived this long didn't do so just by chance. They had to be resourceful and intelligent."

"And it's not like the supposedly qualified people did such a great job, anyway," Tina remarks. "Just look at Covid. Or this Pandemic."

"The real failures in both pandemics were because people didn't listen to experts," Ify says. Irina senses that old and useless political grievances are going to be relitigated. She's about to intervene when Rafael begins to translate Julián's words.

"Elections don't select the qualified. They select the popular and the power-hungry. We can all think of examples of terrible politicians who won elections."

"And some who didn't but became President anyway," Emma jokes.

Irina tries to steer the conversation back to her notes. She glances at her talking points and says, "This system would eliminate parties, factions, demagogues, and power-hungry politicians. We've all lived with the consequences of a two-party, election-based system. To Julián's point, there was a reason that people frequently rated 'politicians' as the least

trustworthy profession in public opinion polls: in order to get elected, a person generally had to be self-interested, arrogant, and Machiavelian. Elected officials were usually rich, well-connected, white, and male. They bore little resemblance to the people they claimed to serve."

"I'm all for getting rid of the two party system," Tina says. "I'm a goddamn unicorn. I've never fit in either party."

"And yet," Emma replies, "You and I usually ended up voting for the same party, despite our very different beliefs. The two-party system flattened everything to a binary choice, it put you in one of two camps then taught you to hate everyone on the other side."

"But if you're concerned about the failures of the American two-party system, why not just create a multiparty system?" Ify asks.

"A multiparty system would still divide people and foster demagogues—some of the worst leaders in history have emerged from multiparty elections. We need something different, a system that will be more representative and will encourage social cohesion," Irina says.

"What about a direct democratic model where everyone votes on referendums?" Ify asks.

"Well, technically, this is that," Irina says, "Something just has to elevate to the level of a Charter change to trigger that vote. More frequent referendums would create factions and would require people to pay more attention to their government than most people have the time or energy for. This system requires that only a few people focus on governing at a given time."

They debate this for more than an hour. Finally Ify reluctantly agrees. Just when Irina is about to call the vote, Emma asks, "What about lobbying? That pretty much wrecked the American system."

Irina considers this, but Ify answers before she can. "We have to allow people to advocate for themselves and their interests before the Council, especially if we're going to have an unelected, unscreened council."

"But no money, no gifts," Irina says.

"Or they get exiled," Tina adds.

"Irina, can you write up some ethics rules for the Council?" Ify says. Irina nods then calls the vote. Unanimous.

Everyone pours their drink of choice. They're all feeling a little elated at what they've accomplished. Irina is desperate to take Rafael to bed, but she knows they need to maintain some moderation. Finally, after a half hour of conversation with the rest of the group, she excuses herself. Rafael is left in the kitchen, washing glasses hastily.

"I can't decide if you were worse when you were trying to get laid or now that you have!" Tina teases him.

The glass slips out of Rafael's slightly flustered grasp. Thankfully it doesn't break.

"I'm just fucking with you, man," Tina says. "I'm happy for you. I love a good love story! I'll even have Emma make a note about it in our legislative history so everyone knows why you voted the way you did!"

"I didn't ask to be here," Rafael replies, rolling his eyes and smiling a crooked smile as she places her whiskey tumbler in the sink for him to clean. "I don't even like politics!"

Tina laughs and walks back to the living room, pulling Emma into a slightly sloppy kiss as they depart. Rafael looks after her, deciding that her teasing is a sign of affection. He finishes the dishes as quickly as he can, then hurries to the room where Irina awaits him.

+++

Their good humor is ruined the following evening when Irina introduces the Declaration of Rights. They agree on nothing. During a tangential conversation arguing for border security, Tina accidentally insults Julián by assuming that he'd been in the country illegally. He quickly and angrily corrects her, through Rafael, telling her that he was here legally on an H-2A visa. Julián also spars at length with Irina over the unlimited abortion rights she'd included in the declaration. Rafael, exhausted with translating their increasingly passionate arguments and remembering Tina's admonition to take this seriously, proposes a compromise that he's sure he'll pay for later when he and Irina are alone.

"There's no compromise on this," Irina argues. "Frankly, I don't think that men should even get a say."

"Well, by that standard, I guess Emma and I don't get a vote either, since we don't have sex with men and don't have to worry about getting pregnant," Tina says. Irina sees a flicker of sadness cross Emma's face. For the rest of the evening, Emma says nothing.

"I'd just like to remind everyone that this conversation is purely academic," Ify says. "I have no qualifications to perform this procedure, and we're unlikely to find anyone who will."

"It's the principle of the thing. This would have been in the original constitution if women had been included in that conversation," Irina responds.

"Irina, none of us would have been included in that conversation," Rafael points out. "And we're all included now, so maybe we should compromise."

"Abortion without time limits would be outlier in the modern world," Ify says.

Irina purses her lips in irritation. She'd been counting on Ify, Tina, and Emma to back her. Emma remains morose. Tina shrugs, "I think Ify makes a good point. It's probably not a good idea for our unity town to be founded with such a controversial provision . . . . "

Irina starts to interrupt her, but Tina shoots her a look and continues, "I don't agree with Julián about the whole 'life begins at conception' thing. But I also think that at some point it's more than a blob of cells. And most people agree."

Irina argues that women, and not governments, are in the best position to determine when a pregnancy should be terminated. They all regurgitate political talking points as the night grows late.

"Fine," Irina says reluctantly at 10:00PM, conceding to a vote on Rafael's compromise proposal.

Julián still votes no. "Twenty weeks or fifteen weeks or six weeks, it doesn't make a difference," he says. "A life is a life, and I'm not going to vote for murder."

They also disagree strongly over speech and assembly rights. Irina had assumed some greater limits on these things, given their exigent circumstances and the need for unity, but Tina, Rafael, and Emma argue with her stridently about their importance. Ify backs Irina, suggesting that the limited definition of hate speech in pre-Pandemic America had resulted in a lot of harm and that they should follow European models—or perhaps even consider the racial harmony laws in Singapore. Julián, still angry from their prior conversation, sits rigidly in his chair. Irina and Ify are outvoted, and she's pretty sure Julián voted against her purely out of spite.

This, Irina thinks, is where things fall apart. They can do their best not to import old political grievances into their new society, but the differences of race, religion, sex, and background will always be there. Their prior disagreements had been more distant from the politics they had all simmered in before the Pandemic. This conversation, though, is viscerally political.

By the end of the evening, everyone is exhausted and irritated. They haven't had such a bad session since Irina had faceplanted on the issue of religion.

"I think you should stay in the other room tonight," Irina tells Rafael.

"No. You told me that I'm entitled to my opinion. You can't punish me!"

"I'm not punishing you," she says, glaring at him. "I'm protecting you from being smothered by me in your sleep."

+++

The next evening they all gather for dinner. Irina is still irritated with Rafael, but Tina, veteran of many relationship political disagreements, had told him that afternoon as they cleared another house that "she'll get over it."

Nonetheless, when Rafael walks through the door a few minutes late, he's carrying a bouquet of flowers that Miranda had helped him pick. He figures Irina isn't going to like him any better after tonight's discussion, so he'd better try to earn back some credit while he can.

She accepts his peace offering with an eyebrow raise. Miranda tells Rafael about her day while Matteo steals the food from Rafael's plate. Irina watches him as she fills a jar with water and arranges the flowers. Her annoyance wanes.

Julián looks surprised when Irina sits down next to him and hands him a book she'd found about distilling. He'd mentioned an interest in it the other night as he and Tina sipped whiskey by the fire.

"I'm sorry for last night," Irina says in imperfect—wrong actually—Spanish. But Julián seems to understand.

"Me too," he replies in English. They eat together, conversing in a mix of broken Spanish and English.

The parents put their children to bed and everyone assumes their usual places in the sitting room. Rafael speaks first, "I hate to rush everyone, but we need to finalize this. I've been on the radio every day and a lot of people are hoping to come here soon. It'll be easier if we already have a system in place when people arrive."

Everyone nods and he continues, "I think the rest of the Declaration of Rights is pretty unobjectionable."

"I based it on the U.S. Bill of Rights," Irina says. "We can even import the U.S. legal precedents on things like search and seizure."

"There's no Right to Bear Arms," Tina points out.

"We're going to be living in a small town full of traumatized people," Ify says. "We have to be able to keep dangerous people from having guns."

"But we're creating a very powerful government," Tina argues, "Gun ownership is a tool against tyranny."

Tina and Ify debate this for a while, reciting pre-Pandemic arguments that everyone has heard before, until Rafael steps in and points out that with mandatory military service, everyone will have guns anyway, then he calls the vote. Everyone agrees to the remainder of the Declaration of Rights, with the exception of Tina, who disagrees on the gun ownership point.

There's a lull in the discussion as Rafael pulls out six stapled packets of paper from his folder. "We agreed to discuss some measures that would help protect against government abuses. These are my proposals."

Irina is shocked. She has no idea when he's had time to draft this. Any free time they've had in the past week has been spent in bed together. She looks over his draft as he explains, "I've put in a mechanism for recalling a Councilmember—a two thirds vote initiated by a member of the public. This is important because there has to be a way for people to remove someone who's plainly incompetent or ill-intentioned. I've also added a provision that triggers the creation of a currency after one hundred people arrive. Everyone would be paid the same amount in currency for their work. People have to be free to buy what they want, instead of being paid in goods that they may not want or need. Essentials like food, shelter, and medical care will still be provided. Most property will still be communally-owned. Irina and Ify, this will give you enough time to research how currency would work."

"You're reopening the economic discussion?" Irina asks.

"I voted in favor based on the understanding that we would formulate some checks on power," he replies. "The system we've put in place here is pretty extreme. Some of us have only agreed to it because we're in equally extreme circumstances now and survival is paramount. But even in the Soviet Union there was currency."

Irina stares at him. Tina raises an eyebrow. Everyone is silent for a beat. "I'm happy to have the time to work out the currency question," Ify says.

"Okay," Irina agrees finally—perhaps because Rafael's argument is compelling, or perhaps because she's in love with him and had missed sharing a bed with him the night before. Rafael looks and feels greatly relieved. Everyone else agrees, apparently happy to avoid the discomfort of witnessing another lovers' quarrel.

"Also our deliberations and decisions have to be open and documented," Rafael says, "If this is going to work, people have to trust us."

Irina agrees, then rattles off the basic elements of most pre-Pandemic open meetings laws as Emma scratches down fast notes.

"One last thing," Rafael says, "I think what we've created here could work on a small scale, and the tradeoffs we've agreed to are justified in our current context. I'm not confident, though, that this system can scale or that it will be as relevant fifty years from now. We should be clear that this document is meant to evolve and change with the circumstances."

He calls the vote on his proposals and everyone agrees. They have an hour to consider the criminal code.

"The criminal code isn't meant to be a part of the actual Charter like the other documents are," Irina says, "So the Council can change it more easily."

Rafael skims the page, "There are a lot of exilable offenses here."

"Not nearly enough, in my opinion," Tina says.

"And you've included a death penalty for some sex offenses?" Ify asks, a bit incredulous. "That would be an outlier in the modern world."

"We aren't in the modern world. It makes sense in context. We can't support a prison right now, and letting sexual predators back into the world endangers everyone," Irina replies. Ify still looks unconvinced.

They talk through the various punishments—extra labor, exile, and execution. They're mostly in agreement. Irina calls the vote and is pleased that it's unanimous.

There's little discussion about the ethics rules Irina hands out next—prohibitions against a Councilmember using their position or the community's resources to benefit themselves, prohibitions on soliciting or accepting gifts related to Council business, and a list of other typical pre-Pandemic rules. After a unanimous vote, Irina shuffles through her documents.

"I think we're. . . done," she says tentatively.

"We should celebrate!" Tina exclaims. They pour their drinks and raise their glasses.

"To Ferndale," Rafael says. The clink of glass, then a moment of silence while they take a sip.

"I'm so glad you're all here," Irina says, feeling a bit emotional. "I think we've created something promising, and it's better because of your contributions."

"Thank you and Rafael for getting things started here," Ify replies. "And for inviting us. It's good to have a fresh start."

"That was mostly Rafael," Irina says, feeling a renewed surge of desire and affection as she meets Rafael's hazel eyes. "He was the one with this vision for Ferndale: the town at the end of the world."

"Oh, I like that," Emma says. "We should put it on the town sign!"

They sip their drinks and make plans for the week ahead. Between them is the unspoken question of whether anyone will accept their invitation.

+++

Later, Rafael trails kisses back up Irina's stomach after fulfilling one of their mutual fantasies. She sighs in pleased relaxation as he rests his head on the pillow next to hers.

"So I'm not going to be smothered in my sleep tonight?" He asks her.

"You've served your purpose, now I can dispose of you."

"But then you'd never get to hear about all of the other things I've dreamed about doing with you."

"Tell me another," Irina is surprised to find that she likes this. She and Sam had never really spoken openly about such things.

Rafael, however, is surprisingly brazen, and, in keeping with his literary interests, exceptionally good at vivid descriptions, and they lose another half hour of sleep after she puts on her green dress and makes his dream into reality. Afterward, she lays in his arms feeling both tired and strangely giddy.

"I think we should pick out a house together," Rafael says.

"So soon!?" Irina jokes. "But we've barely started. . . . I don't even know what to call this." Rafael makes a few graphic suggestions. She swats him.

"I guess you're right," she says. "We should pick a house and start moving our things there. It just makes me sad. It feels like the end of something."

"But the beginning of something else."

+++

They decide on the sage green Victorian next to Emma and Tina's house, close to the library, and just around the block from Ify's modest house with its fully fenced yard. This was the first property that Rafael had cleared when he'd arrived here. He doesn't tell Irina that he found the bodies of an elderly couple in this home.

As he walks through the front door with Irina, Miranda, and Matteo, Rafael keenly recalls the loneliness and the hope he'd felt a year ago. He'd left the fliers as an act of desperation after he realized how truly empty the world was. He'd stood outside the front door of this house, uncertain that anyone would ever join him here. He'd almost fled when he found the corpses in their bed. Until then, except for the mountain man, he'd mostly avoided the more gruesome aspects of the Pandemic. He stood there in the bedroom, looking at the bodies for a long time, wondering how the modern world had made it so easy to avoid the reality of death. Then he'd decided that if he ever wanted to build a town worthy of new inhabitants, he'd need to get to work.

Now he stands in the doorway of the earth tone living room and watches as his family explores their new home.

+++

That Saturday, Emma babysits while Rafael and Irina move things out of the House by the Sea and into their new home. When Irina and Rafael return late in the afternoon with the final cart load of items, Emma offers to watch the children and Buddy so Irina and Rafael can spend a final night at the House by the Sea.

Rafael and Irina return to their old home, both feeling a bit melancholy. It occurs to Rafael that it's been a while since they actually talked. They've spent lots of time together over the past few weeks, but it was usually in the company of others or in bed together. He hasn't been this infatuated with anyone since high school, but he reminds himself that he's older now and knows that they need to balance this.

So he opens a bottle of wine and invites her to join him on the patio, where they take their usual places overlooking the sunset. Rafael breathes in the beauty of this remote, rugged piece of the otherwise previously crowded California coast.

"Do you think it will work?" Irina asks him, bringing him back to himself.

"Only time will tell," he says. "But we've got a pretty good runway until we have to turn the Council over to whoever else shows up here—if anyone else shows up."

"Do you think seven years is enough time to get things going before that transition? To create a stable, sustainable town?"

He shrugs. "I think so, but a lot will depend on the people who choose to come here. We've done what we can to optimize for a good outcome. There are no guarantees, but I'd like to think that we can learn from the lessons of the past and guard against any Animal Farm-type shenanigans. We'll have to be diligent, though, and so will everyone who comes after us. The problem in human systems is almost always the humans themselves."

"Good governments, like good marriages, require constant maintenance."

"I don't have much experience with either of those things," Rafael says, "so I'll have to take your word for it."

For a moment, both of them wonder separately if the other would ever consider remarrying. Then he says, "You should be proud of what you've built. Inertia is easy—we could have just fallen right back into the way things were before the Pandemic. You gave us an option for something different."

"I wouldn't have done it without you," she reaches to take his hand. For several moments, they're both silent.

"This isn't the apocalypse I was expecting," Irina says, taking a sip of her wine. "There are far more planning meetings, and far fewer zombies and cannibals."

"I've always wondered why the cannibals didn't just take up agriculture or fishing," Rafael says. "Cannibalism seems both morally fraught and fairly inefficient."

"It's because they didn't plan ahead, obviously. They weren't thinking of making something sustainable." She smiles.

They talk for a while longer before retiring to Rafael's bed in the House by the Sea one final time.

+++

There's an air of excitement the next afternoon as the group gathers for a picnic at the park on the outskirts of town and discusses their plans for the week. Tina plans to organize an armory.

Julián and Irina will plow and plant more fields. Emma will work on lessons with the children. Rafael and Ify will return to Eureka to bring more solar panels back to Ferndale. With a few more panels, Rafael thinks they should be able to charge an electric car, which will open up lots of new possibilities.

"We really should make communal meals a part of Ferndale's culture," Ify says. "This helps build camaraderie and it makes the logistics of providing people with food much easier."

"That's a great idea!" Irina agrees, in part because she hates cooking.

"Let's add 'cook' to our list of professions, then?" Emma asks. The group is happy to take its first official Council vote on this measure.

After dinner, Irina pushes Matteo on the swing. She feels a swell of pride as she watches Miranda identify birds for Jing. Irina wants to find some way to invite Miranda to be her daughter, for the four of them to be a true family, though she still isn't sure how to do that. It seems at once belated and too fast.

She still sometimes feels pangs of guilt about Sam. Occasionally, it feels like betrayal when Rafael touches her. Every so often, her mind summons memories of Sam at inopportune moments. It will take time, she knows.

Chapter Fifteen

A week later, Rafael arrives late to dinner. Irina notices immediately that he seems out of sorts. He's quiet for the entire meal as the conversation swirls around him. Eventually Ify and Julián get up to do the dishes. Emma and Tina take the kids outside to the yard, and Irina and Rafael are left alone.

"Do you want to take a quick walk?" she asks. He nods. The sun is setting as the day cools, and a light fog gathers at the foothills of the mountains. They stroll toward Main Street in the pinkish light.

"What's wrong?" she asks.

"The car battery still isn't fully charged," Rafael says. "Four days of solar power monopolized for a single vehicle isn't a problem now, but it will be when we have more people who need power."

"We'll get more solar panels."

"There aren't that many left nearby. And anyway, this isn't exactly a prime location for solar power. We're going to have serious power problems in the winter, when there's even less sunlight."

"We can't fall back on the wind turbines?"

He sighs. "My wind turbines can't power anything but modest lighting and small refrigerators. I don't have a solution to these problems because I'm entirely unqualified to be doing this."

"You're not. You've done a lot in just a year."

"No, I really haven't made much progress."

She takes his hand and stops him so he's facing her. "We'll figure it out. Other people will join us and help us figure it out."

"Where are they!?" he asks, his voice raised just slightly. She looks a little hurt, and he catches himself. "I'm sorry. I'm just stressed. Everyone is counting on me to improve things, and I'm stuck."

"If you have the solar panels, that buys you a little time to find a solution. You'll work something out," Irina replies. It's strange to find herself playing the optimist.

He sighs. "I'm really not that smart, Irina. I've been cast in the role of engineer, when I'm not even qualified to be the understudy."

"We all feel that way about our roles. No one expects you to perform miracles; just do the best you can."

"What if the best I can ever do is just some strings of lights, refrigeration, and a single operating vehicle that's often not charged?"

"I'll take it. We'll take it. I bet a lot of people would take it." She pulls him to her and wraps her arms around him. He sighs and reciprocates.

"We'll see," he says.

+++

Irina and Ify are clearing out the other bed and breakfast a week later, when a stranger rides into town on his horse with a cart and several goats in a rope-line behind him. The man sees them and walks his horse—a gelding, Irina is disappointed to note—toward them.

"I'm looking for Rafael," the man says. He's in his mid-forties, Irina guesses, with brown hair and dark eyes. He looks a bit on the thin side but otherwise well-kempt.

Irina leaves to find Rafael, while Ify engages the man in conversation. Irina hears the man introduce himself as Brady Calhoun.

Rafael follows her back to the library, where Ify is deep in conversation with Brady. After introductions, Brady tells them that he'd ridden up from Los Molinos after hearing Rafael on the radio. Rafael invites him to meet the others at lunch. In the dining room of the bed and breakfast, Julián has already set out a tenth bowl. Emma arrives with the children in tow. They hesitate at the door when they see the stranger, but Emma ushers them inside.

Brady joins the adults at their table. "Are there more of you?" Brady asks.

"Only us so far," Tina replies.

"But you have power?" Brady says.

"Enough for refrigeration and lights," Rafael answers.

Brady nods. "Refrigeration would be an improvement."

Brady recounts his survival story. Like Tina, he'd been prepping for a long time before the "shit hit the fan," as he puts it. Everyone else offers their own story of how they had survived the Pandemic.

The children grow restless, so Emma lets them out into the yard. She sits by the window, watching them and listening to the conversation. Irina starts to tell Brady about their vision for the town and the Charter they drafted.

"Wait," Brady says. "You're telling me that I'll have to surrender my livestock? And just do whatever you tell me?"

Tina meets Irina's eyes. Irina does a momentary 'I told you so' there, but Tina is actually the first to answer Brady's question. "You'll have to surrender your livestock, and, like us, you'll take a role that's suited to your skillset. In exchange, you'll get electricity, a share of what Ferndale's livestock and fields produce, shelter, protection, and our fine company."

"Your company is fine." His eyes fall on Emma, and Tina's eyes narrow. "But I don't think I'm made for group living, and I'm not into communism."

Irina purses her lips. Under the table, Rafael puts his hand on her knee and squeezes lightly.

"You're welcome to find yourself a house on the other side of the river in Fortuna. We'd be happy to trade with you," Rafael offers.

"I guess that's it, then," Brady concludes, getting up, "It's a shame to come all this way and leave, but I'm no commie. You all should probably tell people about the whole communism thing in your radio talks, you know?"

"We'll . . . do that from now on," Irina says, trying her best to keep an even tone. They offer him a room in the bed and breakfast for the night, but Brady declines, seeming uncertain about whether the group can be trusted.

"I'll be on my way, then," he says. "The trading does sound good, though. So I'll probably be back for that if I need anything. And maybe I'll be back for your fine company."

He smiles at Emma. Tina rolls her eyes. Rafael walks him to the door and watches as he rides back toward Main Street. The group sits in disappointed silence for several moments before Ify speaks. "That, my friends, was self-selection. This may seem disappointing, but this is actually what it looks like when our system works. We don't want lone wolves or sovereign citizens. We want people who share our vision. Not everyone does, and that's fine. It's a big world with a lot of empty space for people to choose their own adventure. We've chosen ours, and others will join us. I'm sure of it."

Irina is always impressed by Ify's optimism.

"Brady's right about the radio, though," Irina concedes. "We should do regular broadcasts that describe what Ferndale is and what's in our Charter."

"One thing, though, as your Head of Security," Tina says. "If you're going to advertise where we are and what we have, could you please also advertise that we're armed and trained to defend ourselves?"

That evening, Rafael and Ify meet at the town's old radio station, where Rafael had recently hooked up a bank of solar panels in the parking lot. Rafael turns on the radio and switches to several frequencies he's used previously, announcing in English and Spanish that the leaders of Ferndale will be hosting a question-and-answer session about the town on another frequency at 8:30 p.m. After putting the children to bed, Irina joins them, and Rafael hands her the radio. She presses the button to speak. "Is anyone here?"

Several people greet her, and Irina starts by telling people about the town and its benefits: the soil, the mild climate, the proximity to the mountains for timber and the coast for fishing. She summarizes the Charter, emphasizing the communal nature of Ferndale and its unique form of government by lottery. Several people ask questions, and Ify is happy to jump in from the standpoint of a former skeptic and give them the answers that he'd come to believe. Rafael breaks in occasionally to translate the important parts to Spanish.

"This is Mark Petrov from Fort Bragg," a man says. "My only question is: do you have childcare?"

"We do! We have a teacher who's working with the kids on reading and survival skills. She uses holistic education models." Irina hopes that she's correctly represented Emma's work.

"I'll be there tomorrow!" Mark says, laughing.

"How old is your child?" Irina asks.

"I've got three kids I've been taking care of on my own since my wife died. Three, four, and seven years old."

Irina takes her finger off the speaking button and turns to Rafael. "How the hell did he survive?"

"Right?! Can you imagine?" Rafael replies.

"This is Yumiko Hirano at Stanford University," a woman's voice comes through. "Is your community religious?"

'Stanford?!' Irina mouths to Rafael in disbelief. That's several hundred miles away.

"Some members of our community are religious, but many aren't. Our charter guarantees the free exercise of religion," Ify replies.

"And what if I come to Ferndale, and I don't like it there?" Yumiko asks.

"You can leave anytime," Irina replies. "We want people who want to live in this kind of society. We're not interested in forcing anyone to be here."

"If I leave, do I get to take the things I brought with me?"

Irina has to improvise, because the group has never discussed this topic. "If you bring a horse you can leave with your horse." She hopes that the others will be okay with this. "But, if, for example, that house has a foal, the foal stays with Ferndale."

"What if we have nothing to offer?" another voice chimes in.

"If you've survived this long, I'm confident that you have something to offer," Ify replies. "Hunting, cooking, farming, fishing, mechanical knowledge—all of these skills will be useful here."

Yumiko speaks again, "Excuse my skepticism, but this sounds a bit utopian."

"It is a bit utopian," Rafael replies, "but it's also pragmatic. We have a criminal code with strict penalties, mechanisms for removing bad leaders, and security forces to protect us. We aren't assuming that everyone is altruistic, hardworking, or well-intentioned, but we're assuming that many people are. If you are, you're welcome here."

"We're just supposed to trust that we'll come there, surrender our property and weapons, and you won't force us into labor or worse?" Yumiko says.

"First," Irina says, "you don't have to surrender your weapons. Everyone has to serve in the security force, so everyone will have a weapon. But you're right, you can't exactly run background checks on us. At some point, it's an act of trust."

She looks at Rafael as she continues. "When I found Rafael's flier for Ferndale, I was living alone with my baby. When my son got hurt, I knew that I had to take a risk to try to make a better life for him. So I rode my bike four hundred miles to Ferndale, and I've built a life here that's better than I ever would have expected."

"I lost my wife and three children in the Pandemic," Ify says. "I came here because I was tired of being alone. It was a huge risk, but I've found a community here."

Rafael looks at Irina as he takes the radio and speaks, "I invited people to come to Ferndale because I believe that we need to build something sustainable, and that requires cooperation. If we don't take the time and trust to do this now, things will become worse over time as resources become more scarce. Inviting others to join me here was a risk, but it paid off with love, friendship, family, and hope. Any act of community, any human relationship, is a risk. I'm very glad I've taken this one."

He lets go of the microphone button, and they wait. There's silence for a moment, then several people start talking. The group answers questions until 11:00 p.m. By the end of the conversation, Mark, Yumiko, and five others are making plans to come to Ferndale.

Rafael reminds everyone to share the information about Ferndale with anyone else they meet. When Rafael finally turns off the radio, the three of them are exhausted but hopeful.

+++

A week later, two young men arrive on bicycles with heavy-laden trailers. Both are in their late twenties and have dark hair and blue eyes and strikingly handsome faces. The shorter of the two offers his hand to Irina and introduces himself as

François. Irina thinks she detects the hint of a French accent, perhaps Québécois. The taller man introduces himself as Benoit.

"We heard about you from someone who heard you on the radio," François says. "You're ham-radio famous!"

Irina invites them to dinner and learns that Benoit had been a minor actor in Hollywood before the Pandemic. When he'd heard about the Virus, he'd spent his savings stocking up on supplies and buying a cabin near Mt. Shasta. He'd begged his brother, François, a middle-school teacher, to join him there. When François's husband contracted the Virus and died while on a business trip to New York, François realized the severity of the situation and left his home in Sacramento to meet Benoit at the cabin.

"I'm really not sure that you have much use for a B-list actor here in Ferndale," Benoit says. "But I'm a pretty good gardener now, and I've gotten very good at improvising recipes, so I'd be happy to cook."

"And we did bring an offering," François says. "A couple of jugs of oil from one of the only olive farms left in the state of California."

"Also a few bottles of the last Sonoma Valley Chardonnay that will be produced for a long time!" Benoit adds.

"We may yet need actors in Ferndale," Irina says, thinking of one of her favorite novels, a book that featured a post-apocalyptic Shakespearean acting troupe. "People need entertainment and art."

"Let's put one of those bottles of chardonnay in the refrigerator and toast to your arrival later tonight," Emma suggests. Benoit and François are happy to agree.

+++

Irina is clearing out another house four days later when a man rides into town with three children on bicycles behind him.

247

He's very thin, looks to be in his mid-thirties, and has a close blonde crew cut. The three children look neat, if a bit skinny to Irina's eye.

"Are you Mark?" Irina asks, offering him her hand, after taking off her rubber gloves.

He gives her a firm handshake. "Sure am. You must be Irina. I'm real pleased to meet you."

Mark joins everyone at dinner, and Irina notices that both he and his children eat Benoit's latest culinary creation with a lot of enthusiasm as though it's been a while since they've had a real meal. Irina feels for him, imagining how difficult it must be to watch your children go hungry. She asks him how he's managed.

"Just barely. It's hard to get anything done while taking care of young kids, but you probably know that." He looks at Miranda and Matteo. "We'd been relying a lot on rice and dried beans, but those ran out last month. Your broadcast was like a miracle. I don't have much to offer to you, though."

"What are you good at? What did you do before the Pandemic?"

"I was an auto mechanic."

"Maybe you can help me solve a problem I've been working on," Rafael says, thinking of Irina's comment about letting others help him figure things out.

"What's that?" Mark asks.

"Car batteries," Rafael says. "I've got an electric vehicle, and I've got enough solar power to charge it . . . slowly. The car runs on a lithium battery, but still needs a 12-volt lead-acid battery to start . . . and the lead-acid batteries will all die in another year or two, right? Most of the ones I've found are already pretty low."

Mark smiles. "You need an EV with a lithium 12-volt battery. Those will last twenty years, if you believe our former tech overlords. I know about only one brand with lithium 12-volts." Mark names the brand. Rafael had always wanted one, but Helena would never allow it, given his limited contribution to their household income. "They're on the higher end, cost-wise," Mark continues, "so they're not that common, but this was a pretty environmentally-conscious place, so we may find a few."

"There's at least one in Eureka," Ify says. "My wife, Shanna's. You're welcome to it."

Rafael thinks for a moment. "There are still some solar panels left in Eureka. We could hook them up to Shanna's car and power it up enough to drive it here. Then we'd have two EVs, until the battery dies on the other one."

+++

Rafael, Mark, and Julián leave a few days later with Lily and the cart to retrieve Shanna's car and more solar panels. Everyone else spends their days tilling and planting fields. Emma and François are even able to enlist the older children in agricultural tasks. Irina carries Matteo in the backpack, narrating her actions as she goes about her chores.

Even with the horse and the electric rototillers, plowing is exhausting. Irina comforts herself with the knowledge that fields are easier to maintain than to create.

On the afternoon of the third day, Irina is on her way to lunch, when she looks up and sees a blue car coming down the road. Rafael pulls up beside her and leans over to open the passenger door. She slips inside and seats herself, reflexively putting on her seatbelt. The seats are plush leather, and the display on the dashboard still tracks them with perfect GPS accuracy.

"This is very weird," Irina says.

"It is," he agrees.

As they pull up to the bed and breakfast, they notice an unfamiliar bicycle. An East Asian woman in her mid-thirties crouches next to the bike's trailer, checking on the three chickens inside. She stands and stares at the car.

"You didn't mention that on the radio," she says as Irina and Rafael step out.

"This is a new development," Rafael replies.

"Yumiko Hirano," the woman introduces herself without offering her hand, "but just call me Yumi."

Irina and Rafael introduce themselves and invite Yumi inside for lunch. Over bowls of rabbit stew, they do the usual background and introduction talks. Before, Yumi had been a professor in Stanford's Microbiology and Immunology Department, studying virology.

"I'm not sure how helpful a virologist will be to you now, though," Yumi says, "since most of the viruses are dead."

"What do you mean?" Irina asks.

"Viruses need human hosts to spread. Most of the humans have died or live in isolated pockets. At this point, I wouldn't expect there are many communicable diseases left," Yumi answers. "The GII.4X Virus killed the other viruses."

"Well, that's the only good news coming out of the Pandemic," Irina replies.

"In that way, we're better off than our ancestors," Yumi says. "Many of the things that used to kill humans quickly— like cholera, typhus, or Covid — are probably eradicated. Of course, animal-borne viruses and viruses that live in the human body for a long time without killing their hosts — like herpes or HIV — probably still exist, and bacterial infections, like syphilis, are still a threat."

"Do you think the Virus was engineered?" Tina asks.

"Some people in my department thought GII.4X was human-made and escaped from a lab," Yumi says. "Most of the riskier gain-of-function research was shut down after Covid, but there were probably governments that did it anyway. I don't think we'll ever know for sure."

It's strange, Irina thinks, to be so profoundly affected by something you'll never understand even the most basic aspects of. The Virus had disappeared, taking nearly all of humanity with it, yet they still know nothing about its origins or why an extraordinarily small percentage of people—like Ify or Julián— had survived, and almost no one else had. And they probably never will.

Chapter Sixteen

By late June, their community has grown to forty-three people, but Julián thinks they have a problem. He and Rafael converse in Spanish as they stand in the newly plowed and planted fields near the Fern Cottage.

"Most people aren't bringing anything with them but their appetites," Julián says as he squints into the afternoon sun, surveying the sprouting vegetables.

"And hard work," Rafael points out. "Everyone did a great job on the wheat harvest last month."

The harvesting, threshing, and grinding of the wheat had been exhausting, even though they had almost thirty adults sharing the work.

"A lot of the people are coming with young children," Julián says. Almost a third of their new arrivals have been children ten or younger. Childcare seems to be Ferndale's most enticing feature. "I know we planned for everyone to have a profession, but right now, everyone has to be in agriculture, hunting, or fishing. Emma's going to hate to hear it, but older kids need to be doing more labor and fewer reading lessons. We need to store supplies for the winter months. We have a lot of extra people and very little extra livestock. We're out of pre-Pandemic food. If we don't make some adjustments, we're going to have a problem."

Julián pauses for a moment, before delivering more bad news. "Also, is it usually this dry this time of year? It hasn't rained since May."

"I honestly wouldn't know. I've only been here a little over a year myself. It wouldn't surprise me, though, if we're in a drought."

"We need to start tracking the weather," Julián says, "and we might want to put a pause on inviting new people to join us."

Rafael nods. He suspects that Julián is right. If they expand too quickly, they'll collapse. But he's certain that the other Councilmembers won't like to hear this.

Regardless, they all celebrate the summer solstice with an afternoon at Centerville Beach, followed with a wild-boar roast in the park. The night is clear and starry, and Emma and the children have strung solar LED fairy lights that twinkle against the darkness. Benoit sets up a record player he'd found in the warehouse and plays whatever records he could find there—a strange mix of the Beatles, Taylor Swift's Covid-era records, Pink Floyd, the Jackson Five, Bon Iver, Queen, Marvin Gaye, and Simon and Garfunkel. Everyone dances and laughs and compliments Benoit on his culinary skills. They have way too much wine and stay up way too late.

Rafael and Irina don't stumble into bed together until after midnight, barely waiting until the door is locked before stripping off each other's clothes. Things have fallen into a regular rhythm between them, and the initial infatuation has burned off a bit, but this night feels especially magical.

Despite Julián's warnings, Rafael can't help feeling optimistic. They're all building something here together.

+++

The Council begins holding regular meetings in the old Town Hall, a nondescript building on the same block as the library. The Council chambers are small, only large enough to fit a maximum of one hundred fifty very crowded chairs with a raised stage at the front where the council sits and large windows that look out over the park and Victorian homes beyond it.

The subject of the Council's July 7th meeting is intake forms. Ify and Shantal Johnson—a former receptionist at a Dermatology office who is now their Head of Administration—discuss what information to collect from new arrivals. Rafael sits in his seat, interminably bored and feeling a bit rundown.

He ruefully recalls Irina's comment about their apocalypse having far more planning meetings than expected.

"I think," Rafael says, "that we need to delegate."

Everyone turns to him. It's unusual for him to say much in these meetings, unless they're discussing an engineering-specific question. His disinterest in politics hasn't changed. Out of the corner of his eye, Rafael notices one of the audience members abruptly departing. Had he insulted her somehow?

Rafael continues, "We should agree, as a Council, that we need an intake form, then leave it up to Shantal to devise one. Our time is limited, and this isn't the best way to spend it."

Rafael feels oddly sweaty all of a sudden, and his stomach churns. Nerves? He wonders. He hates public speaking. As he translates for Julián, he feels increasingly unwell. He excuses himself abruptly. By the time he makes it home, he's gripped with anxiety and almost doubled over in pain with waves of stomach cramps. He staggers into the house, locking the front door behind him, then stumbling over to lock the back door, before rushing into the bathroom.

He's still in the bathroom when he hears Irina banging on the front door a half hour later.

"Rafael!? What is going on!?" she shouts. She's understandably confused and angry, because no one in Ferndale locks their doors, so neither of them carry a key.

"Stay out, I'm sick," he shouts. ". . . I think I have the Virus."

It's too late, both of them know. A person is contagious for at least five days before the symptoms appear. He's touched her and everything around them. It will only be a matter of time before the Virus spreads through the town. How did it get here? How could it possibly have survived this long after killing everyone off?

On the other side of the door, Irina is silent for a moment; then she replies in a shaking voice, "I'll get Ify."

Rafael is asleep on the bathroom floor when he hears the banging resume on the front door. He rouses himself, uncertain of how much time has passed.

"Rafael, open the door," Ify says.

"I don't want to get you sick," Rafael answers.

"It would be far too late for that if this was GII.4X, but I don't think it is," Ify says.

Rafael drags himself up and shambles to the front door to unlock it. He lets Ify in, but commands Irina to stay outside. He feels terribly lightheaded, and he collapses on the couch.

"Symptoms?" Ify asks, sitting down on a chair nearby.

"Cramps, diarrhea, dizziness."

"You haven't had a high fever? Chills? Uncontrollable vomiting?"

Rafael shakes his head, grateful to have avoided those things, and Ify continues, "Neither has anyone else. I don't think this is GII.4X. The symptoms and progression are all wrong. GII.4X always started with two days of high fever, then progressed to vomiting."

Ify digs into a cloth tote bag he's carrying and hands Rafael a bottle of boiled water. As Rafael drinks it, Ify tells him that a dozen other people are sick, and none of them have the trademark symptoms of GII.4X. Ify says, "I think this might be some kind of food poisoning, but I'll consult with Yumi."

"Thank you," Rafael says. "But tell Irina to stay away in case it's something communicable. I don't want her or the kids to get sick."

Ify departs, giving Rafael another bottle of water and instructing him to stay hydrated. Rafael hurries back to the bathroom. Irina, apprised by Ify of Rafael's wish to be left alone, utterly disregards that and knocks on the bathroom door, insisting to be let in. She starts to open the door, but he blocks it. Even if this isn't contagious, he's not ready for that level of intimacy.

It gets far worse before it gets better. Rafael spends a miserable night sleeping on the bathroom floor, waking every hour or so when his body decides to relaunch its attack against the contents of his digestive system. Irina checks on him occasionally, but he refuses to open the door.

Eventually she falls into a restless sleep and wakes at 5:00 a.m. with stomach cramps. She's in the second bathroom when she hears Miranda start crying about her tummy hurting. Within an hour, Matteo, too, is sick. When Irina opens his diaper and finds bloody diarrhea, she's filled with panic that twists her guts even more than the illness. Matteo is still so small, and he seems to have gotten the worst of it. She begins to spiral into anxiety, wondering if she's about to lose another child.

When Ify knocks on the door to deliver more water at noon, Rafael is sitting in the bathroom with Miranda, while Irina is trying to force Matteo to drink more water.

"Yumi is sick too," Ify says to them. "Along with about half the town. But she is confident that this isn't GII.4X, so at least there's that silver lining."

"Matteo doesn't look well," Irina says, taking Ify to see him. Matteo lies in his bed listless and pale. Looking at him, Irina feels another wave of anxiety and nausea. She sees her own fear mirrored in Rafael's eyes. "Can you give him a saline drip or something?"

"The saline solution is long expired by now," Ify says. "I could try to use it, but it's a big risk. I wouldn't take it, unless I absolutely had to."

Two days later, Ify has to take that risk. Mark's youngest daughter, Kasey, has gotten progressively sicker. Her eyes are sunken, and her skin is pale. Ify tries to get her to drink with a syringe, but she keeps losing fluids. He's forced to use an expired pouch of saline fluid and an unused IV line he'd found at a veterinary office in Fortuna. Her veins are so dehydrated that it takes him three tries to find one. By the time he does, both she and he are crying. He recounts this afterward to Irina as they sit in her living room. Irina, Rafael, and their children still have no appetite, but they're feeling a little better.

Once Kasey and most of the town have started to recover, the Council convenes to discuss the illness.

"My guess is that it's E. coli," Yumi says from the stage. "Without laboratory tests, I can't confirm that, but it fits the symptoms we've experienced. I suspect it came from something we all ate together, since so many of us got sick."

"How did it get into our food?" Irina asks.

Yumi shrugs. "There are a few possibilities. First, our livestock are upstream from where we draw our irrigation water. Second, while we're all boiling our drinking water, we haven't taken the same precautions with the water we use to wash our food and our hands."

"What can we do?" Rafael asks.

"We can start by moving the livestock," Yumi replies. "The larger project, though, is creating a water purification system."

Rafael had researched this before. "Most municipal water sanitation requires chemicals, right?"

"Right, and those are expired, and we probably don't want to risk putting expired chemicals in our drinking water," Yumi says. "But some municipalities were switching to UV-C light. That would require power, though."

"I think that's worth spending some solar cells on," Rafael says. "But where would we find the lights?"

Yumi thinks for a moment, then asks, "Have you checked the local water processing plants?"

Rafael nods. He'd been to a few. "They all have nothing but expired chemicals."

"Is there a hospital around here?"

"In Eureka," Ify replies.

"After Covid, a lot of hospitals started using UV room disinfection machines or air purifiers," Yumi says. "We may be able to repurpose those lights."

"Let's take a trip to Eureka," Rafael replies.

+++

Rafael, Yumi, and Ify step out of the car in front of the St. Joseph Hospital in Eureka. To get to the entrance, they have to step over the pieces of scavenged skeletal corpses strewn on the sidewalk outside the hospital doors. Yumi frowns, but Ify and Rafael have cleared enough houses to be able to do this without flinching.

Ify pauses at the threshold and says quietly, "This is where my wife died."

"Are you sure you want to go inside?" Rafael asks, wondering why Ify had been so insistent about joining them on this miserable field trip.

"I feel like I need to see the last thing she saw," Ify replies.

They step through the empty door frames and into a large open lobby filled with more mostly skeletal corpses, many of which have also been dismembered by scavengers. Even two years later, the stench of death hangs heavy, making Rafael's still weak stomach churn.

"Best guess which way we should go?" Rafael asks.

Yumi shrugs. "The surgical rooms or the NICU, if there is one. Those are probably the places with the highest need for disinfection."

"There's a NICU here," Ify says, "my oldest son spent a week there."

Rafael steps over several corpses to get to the information desk, where he finds a map. "Surgical rooms first, because I can't handle the NICU right now."

They take the stairwell up to the second floor, where they find a dark windowless hallway crowded with bodies on stretchers. This, Rafael thinks, is the kind of place where Helena spent her final days. The thought lances him. Even in the end, when it cost her her life, she was committed to her patients. He wishes again that they had loved each other better.

For an hour they search for portable UV disinfection devices in storage closets and operating rooms crowded with bodies. Ify cries silently. Yumi hands him her clean handkerchief and touches his arm gently. In the fifth operating room, Yumi looks up at the ceiling for the first time.

"There," she says, "I think those are what we need. We've been right under them. We should check the air filters too. Each of these rooms should have an individual filter.

Rafael retrieves a ladder from a storage closet, then climbs up and begins to unscrew one of the large light bulbs. Yumi looks at the back and confirms that it's a UV-C bulb. Rafael removes them one by one; then he unscrews the vent on the wall. He disassembles the filter and finds a long bulb inside. He extracts it carefully and hands it to Yumi, who confirms that it's UV-C and wraps it in a clean hospital sheet.

They move from room to room, repeating this.

"Is that enough?" Ify asks, when they've cleared the operating rooms.

"More is better," Yumi says.

"To the NICU then," Rafael says reluctantly. They retrace their path back to the information desk, then navigate to the doors of the NICU. Ify hesitates as Rafael pushes the doors. Surprisingly, they're unsecured. Inside are three glass-walled rooms with rows of tiny plastic baby bassinets. Most are empty, but a few are still inhabited by the shells of their former occupants. Rafael feels the bile rise in his throat. He wants to run. He swallows down his nausea and tries to stay focused. Yumi is crying too now. Ify touches her shoulder lightly. She pulls a second handkerchief out of her pocket and blows her nose as she walks around the room.

"I don't think these are UV lights," she says, looking at the ceiling. Rafael gets a ladder and checks anyway to confirm that. Yumi picks up a one-foot-by-one-foot metal box. "This is UV-C. I remember something like this being used to disinfect visitors' phones and tablets when I visited my niece in the NICU."

She opens it and inspects the lights inside. She tucks it in a tote bag she'd brought; then she checks each of the other pods and returns with two more similar devices.

"Why don't we ever talk about all of this?" Ify asks no one in particular as he stares at one of the tiny corpses. "We talk about how we survived, but we never talk about all of the people who didn't."

Rafael remembers thinking the same thing after the Covid pandemic. The whole world had experienced a strange, life-changing phenomenon; then it seemed like everyone just moved on and never spoke of it again. He and Irina have touched on their Pandemic trauma with the stories they'd told each other, but not everyone in Ferndale has a friend like that. He resolves to ask Ify more questions, to share more with him.

"We should talk about it," Rafael says as he begins to disassemble the air vent. He extracts a light tube from it, then moves to the other rooms and does the same.

"Is it possible that there are UV disinfection systems in all the patient rooms?" he asks Yumi.

"Possible, but not probable in a small hospital like this one. We can check, though."

They take a random sample of several patient rooms and find none. Yumi suggests that they check the cancer ward. That suggestion pays off with a few more boxes of lights.

On the way out, Ify stops in the hospital pharmacy. It's pretty empty, but he does find a few useful medications.

"Aren't those all expired by now?" Rafael asks.

"Officially, they are, but studies have shown that many medications are good for several years after the official expiration dates," Ify replies.

Emotionally exhausted and fearing that they won't be able to fit much more in their vehicle, they depart.

As Rafael drives home, he thinks again of Helena, of the horrors she must have seen in her final weeks. He knows now why she didn't stay at the cabin: she wasn't good for him, but she was a good person. She'd wanted to help.

He arrives back in Ferndale and goes to find Miranda and Matteo in the children's garden that Emma had created to teach them about agriculture. Rafael wraps them in a tight hug, then takes them to a nearby playground and plays with them until dinnertime.

When Irina returns from plowing another field with Lily, she lightly brushes her lips to his, but he still feels melancholy.

"How was Eureka?" she asks him.

"Awful," he answers. She watches him, detecting his sad mood, hoping that he'll tell her his thoughts, but not pushing him. Neither of them eat much that evening. That night he isn't in the mood to make love. Instead, they lie in bed as he tearfully recounts what they'd found in the hospital, the brutal particulars of the Pandemic, which never seem to get easier, no matter how much time passes.

+++

Over the next few weeks, Rafael and Yumi take field trips to two nearby water processing plants, taking detailed notes and making diagrams of their designs. They construct a smaller-scale system that directs water through several small concrete pools to filter out sediment, then into a large aquarium surrounded by UV-C lights. Julián and Tina dam the little stream that runs through town and divert it to the water processing system.

Rafael and Yumi test out various lengths of time to leave the water under the lights. She grows cultures in small, sanitized dishes. When she's satisfied that the bacteria in the water haven't produced a culture, they set a battery-operated hose timer so it releases the sanitized water into a large tank with a spigot.

They all toast to the completed system, but Irina doesn't drink her wine. When she tells Rafael that they need to talk, he senses already what she's going to say. He prays that he's wrong.

While François watches Miranda and Matteo, Irina and Rafael walk down the block toward Main Street. They make it half a block before she blurts out, "I'm pregnant."

"It was the damn summer solstice party, wasn't it?" he asks. He'd been careless that night, not pulling out or bothering with a condom, lulled into a false sense of security by the wine and her age.

She thinks for a moment. "Probably."

"Fuck." He's quiet for a few seconds; then he asks, "Are you sure?"

"I took every pregnancy test in the warehouse. They were all expired, but five out of seven gave me positive results."

"It could be a false positive."

"Unlikely. I've been pregnant before. I know how it feels."

He stops and takes several deep breaths. "I'm so sorry. I should have been more careful. We can fix this. We included the right to terminate in our charter, and Ify said a lot of medications should still be good. You can use that pill that everyone was fighting about a decade ago."

She takes his hand, "I don't want to."

He stares at her, incredulous. "Are you crazy?! We have no medical doctor, no hospitals, no pain relief, questionably effective antibiotics. And we already have two children."

"Two living children."

"Is that what this is about? Irina, Miranda is your daughter as much as any other child could be. She loves you, and she needs you. I love you, and I need you. We can't afford to take this kind of risk."

"I think abortion is wrong, Rafael, for me, personally."

He tries to contain his frustration. "I don't understand. You fought to include the most extreme version of this in the Charter."

"It's a matter of principle. Women should get to choose. Choice implies that there are options. One option is to have a baby. I want that."

"Please, please reconsider. It's too dangerous."

"I hoped you'd be happy about this!" He hears the tears in her voice.

"I need to take a walk," he says, knowing that he's nearing his emotional limit. "I'll see you at home later."

He walks the streets of Ferndale in the gathering darkness for a long time, past the lit windows of the families who live there because of his and Irina's collaboration. He thinks of everything he has, and everything he has to lose.

He doesn't return to the house until Irina is kissing Miranda goodnight. She joins him in the living room.

"You have to understand," he says. "I can't lose you. I don't know how I would survive it. That day when you got injured and I saw you on the ground, I could barely breathe. And I loved you a lot less then than I do now."

"It'll be fine. Women gave birth for almost all of human history without modern medicine. I've done it before myself."

"But you got an infection! You could have died!" he exclaims.

"There are still antibiotics," she replies. "And Ify can help me."

They're both silent for a minute; then he says, "Please, Irina, don't do this. We have a good life. Please don't risk that."

There's nothing left to say to each other, and they both go to bed anxious and sad.

Irina wakes in the middle of the night. Buddy follows her and climbs onto the living room couch beside her. She wraps her arms around him and cries into his fur, trying to convince herself that things will be alright.

She looks up and sees Rafael standing in the doorway, watching her. He joins her on the couch.

"Why is this important to you?" he asks, trying to remember that marriage book he'd read three years before.

"I love the idea of a person who's a little of both of us, who'll live on after we're gone, like Sam lives on in Matteo. I want to know that person."

Despite his misgivings, he's touched that she wants to have his child. He sighs and wraps his arms around her. It isn't his choice anyway, and standing between Irina and what she wants seems more dangerous even than a post-apocalyptic pregnancy. He understands now why Sam had yielded.

Besides, even if she wanted to terminate the pregnancy, the medicine might be too old. They're strapped into the roller coaster seat and halfway up the first hill. There's no getting off this ride. He should have been more careful.

"At least promise me that you'll talk to Ify soon so he can be as prepared as possible," Rafael says.

"I'll talk with him tomorrow," she agrees.

+++

The next morning as they walk to breakfast, Irina prevails upon Rafael to do a public demonstration of the new water sanitation system.

"We messed up," she says. "And people got sick. We have to show them that we're going to fix it. We need some kind of ribbon-cutting ceremony."

"You think they doubt us?" he asks.

"I think we need to earn their trust. We still need 'the consent of the governed.' There are a lot more of them than us, and this system only works when everyone is invested in it."

So later that day, Rafael and Yumi stand before the assembled residents of Ferndale. They turn on the spigot of the water sanitation system, fill their glasses, clink them together in a toast, then take a sip. The crowd applauds. Irina and Ify give short speeches about the importance of cooperation and hard work. Rafael and Yumi answer questions about the system, and the residents line up to fill their water bottles.

Chapter Seventeen

The first Monday in August, Irina watches through the window of her living room as a man and woman dismount from horses in front of the house that Shantal has repurposed as the Ferndale Administration Building.

They both have dark hair and caramel skin, and Irina guesses they might be Native American. She's heard from a few new residents that several of the tribes in the coastal mountains had survived. She walks outside and crosses the street to the Administration Building, where she overhears the woman telling Shantal that they'd like to meet with Ferndale's Councilmembers.

"I'm one of the Councilmembers," Irina says. The woman introduces herself as Gail Simpson. She looks to be about the same age as Irina, and her raven hair is in a similarly practical French braid. Her handshake is firm. Irina likes her immediately. The man, who is a decade or so younger, shakes Irina's hand and introduces himself as Rick Smith.

Irina thanks Shantal and invites Gail and Rick to her office across the street. When they're seated and she's poured glasses of purified water for them and a cup of ginger tea to try to combat her own morning sickness, Irina asks, "How can I help you?"

"We represent the Six Rivers Tribe," Gail says. "We'd like to establish trade agreements with Ferndale."

"What were you hoping to trade?" Irina asks.

"We'd like to exchange goods and knowledge," Gail says. "We know this land better than anyone—what plants are edible and medicinal, how to run fish hatcheries, and what agricultural methods are best suited to this soil and climate."

"You seem much better prepared for survival here than us," Irina observes. "I'm not sure what we can offer you."

"Many of our young professionals left for the big cities, and we've struggled to fill those gaps," Gail says. "We lost our doctors in the Pandemic. Our veterinarian passed away last year. Our only engineer is long retired. We'd like to apprentice some of our people with your professionals. And we'd like to improve our power generation systems."

"We'd love to trade with you, but I'm afraid we're not as advanced as you think. Our doctor was trained as a veterinarian," Irina replies, "and our veterinarian was a vet tech. I'm not sure our power situation is much better than yours."

She hates to say that because it feels as if she's betraying Rafael.

"We do have one thing," Irina says. "We've set up a UV water purification system. It's not a permanent solution, but it helps for now."

"A water purification system would be very useful," Gail tells her. "We saw that you've also got wind power. We're relying on solar cells, but we'd like to find a longer-term solution. There was supposed to be an offshore wind project moving forward just before the Pandemic—we actually commented on the environmental impact of the plans several times. If the wind turbines were already installed and hooked up, we may be able to connect to that system. We'd need to work together to find the system and get it running again.

"And we've heard that you have a stallion," Gail continues. The Brothers from the monastery must have told her. They'd brought several of their mares to Ferndale in late July for breeding. Blaze had been thrilled. "We've also got one, but we'd like to diversify our next generation of horses. We could do an exchange."

"That would be very helpful. How many people are in your Tribe?" Irina asks her.

"One hundred sixteen. We pulled out of the world early in the Pandemic but not early enough to save all our people," Gail says sadly.

They talk for a while about their communities' respective structures, the obstacles they've faced and the solutions they've found. Irina isn't surprised to learn that Gail is the tribe's attorney. Like Irina, she's also a mother. As they discuss post-apocalyptic motherhood, they almost forget Rick's silent presence in the room.

It's almost lunchtime when Irina suggests that they walk over to the bed and breakfast to find rooms for Gail and Rick. She invites them to get lunch, once they're settled, and to meet her for dinner that evening so they can prepare to present at the Council meeting.

+++

When she arrives for lunch, Irina sees Rafael and the children already sitting with Jing, Emma, and Tina. When fifty people had joined the community, they'd moved community meals to the Ferndale High School cafeteria, which has ample seating and a commercial kitchen. Because of their power constraints, Benoit and his assistants are still forced to cook outside over several recently-constructed fireplaces, but he's glad for the extra prep space.

In the cafeteria line today's rotation of food service workers are spooning helpings of wild-boar stew and roasted squash. Irina feels a swell of satisfaction as she watches members of her community eat and converse around her.

Rafael greets her with a soft kiss, but she can still sense that things are off between them. She can feel his enthusiasm, though, when she tells him about her conversation with Gail.

On her walk to lunch, she'd turned that conversation over in her mind, wondering if maybe they could dream bigger. The month before, a woman had told the Council the story of how her old neighbors had died from botulism. Surely there would be value in some larger exchange of survival-related information. Irina turns this idea over in her mind.

Gail's presentation is met with enthusiasm by the Council. Ify says that he would be happy to train a few Tribal members with whatever limited medical knowledge he has and to train several in veterinary medicine as well. Julián is keenly interested in learning about the Tribe's agricultural methods. Several of their crops have been faltering, and he's been unable to identify the cause. They vote unanimously in favor of the trade agreement, and Irina senses that it's time to bring up her more ambitious idea.

"Maybe we could also have a regular exchange of knowledge and trade goods that's open to the larger community," Irina says. "If we give people the tools to provide for themselves, they're less likely to be a threat to us."

"I think that could be helpful, and I'd be happy to co-organize it with you," Gail replies. She pauses, thinking, "We could invite the Brothers and their Sister Convent, the eastern Mennonites, and all of the smaller communities. Maybe we could even get the Sacramento Valley farmers to travel north to trade."

"I've been in touch with some of them on the radio," Rafael says. "We could also use the radio to publicize the event and to broadcast whatever trainings we give."

"In English and Spanish," Julián says, in English.

"Do you think we could organize it by spring?" Irina asks Gail.

"That seems reasonable," Gail replies. Irina is pleased when the Council backs the idea unanimously.

The next morning, Irina and Gail draw up the trade agreement. Gail jokes that they shouldn't call it a treaty, and Irina feels a pang of guilt about her Utah ancestors' history. Irina starts to make an awkward apology. "I understand why you might not trust us . . . ."

Gail waves her off, "With respect, I'm not sure that anyone else could ever really understand. But I appreciate the sentiment. We've all lost a lot. Let's just focus on the future. It seems like you're trying to hit the reset button on historical mistakes here in Ferndale. Learn the lessons; leave behind the baggage. I'd like to do the same. We both benefit if we trust each other."

"I like what you're doing here," Gail continues. "I like that you've eliminated historic wealth disparities and set everyone up as equals. I hope it works."

"I hope so, too," Irina says, though she's constantly plagued with doubt.

+++

The following week Irina takes Miranda and Matteo to the playground after dinner, as she often does. She pushes them both on the swings as the sun sets over the town, bathing them in golden hour light. As they walk home, Matteo holds Irina's one hand, and Miranda holds her other.

"Jing says that her mommies are going to do an adoption party with her," Miranda says. "Like a wedding. They're going to get dressed up and recite promises to each other."

"That sounds beautiful," Irina replies, "Would you like to do something like that?"

"Then you'll be my mommy?" Miranda stops and looks up at Irina earnestly.

"I'm already your mommy, if you want me to be."

"I do! But can we have a party? Maybe Daddy can adopt Matteo too!"

"I think that's a great idea. I'll talk to him tonight."

After Matteo and Miranda are asleep, Irina asks Emma and Tina, who are on the front porch next door, to keep an eye on them; then she and Rafael take a walk down Main Street. They pass the dark storefronts, then a church where a few members of the community are hosting an evening candlelight service. They're both proud to see how many of the houses around Main Street are occupied.

"Miranda asked me to do an adoption ceremony with her," Irina says.

"She told me. I like her idea of doing one for Matteo too." He stops and takes her hand so she faces him. "I was actually thinking maybe we could do it as a family—that you and I could do a ceremony too."

Irina raises her eyebrow. "Is that a proposal?"

"If you'd like something more romantic, I'd be happy to oblige—a proper proposal on one knee with a ring and everything," he offers, fearing that he's disappointed her.

"I've already had several proper proposals. I'm more interested in the marriage than the archaic chivalries."

"Nonetheless," he says, kneeling down on the street before her, "I'd love it if you'd marry me."

Irina is amused. She pulls him back up in front of her. "Are you only asking me because I'm pregnant?"

"Hell no. I've wanted to ask you since April. Probably before that, even. I just wasn't sure if you would think it was too soon."

She shrugs. "We've both been married before. We've been living together and raising each other's children for more than a year. I think the usual social norms around timing don't apply. If you'd asked me in April, I would have given you an enthusiastic yes."

"And now? Is your yes still enthusiastic after last week?"

"Of course it is!"

Irina pulls him tightly against her and kisses him deeply. Above them the summer moon rises.

+++

After announcing their impending family commitment ceremony at breakfast two weeks later, Irina and Rafael drive with Ify to Eureka. Rafael brings along a small battery-powered generator he'd charged with solar panels, hoping that it will be sufficient to run an ultrasound machine.

They park next to the obstetrician's office that Ify's wife had used.

"Just to be clear," Ify says as Rafael plugs the ultrasound machine into the generator, "I'm going to be guessing about this, so don't get your hopes up."

Irina says that she understands; then she lies back on the table and lifts her shirt up. Ify squeezes a little bit of cool gel on her skin and begins to move the wand around over her belly.

"Further down, I think," Irina says, moving the wand down below her belly button, trying to summon the memory of her prenatal appointments during her pregnancy with Clara. The memory and her hormones make her feel weepy. She moves the wand around her stomach until she sees something she recognizes on the screen. A small, bean-shaped thing inside a large black circle.

"That's it!" Irina exclaims. She grips Rafael's hand tightly. He smiles a tight smile, trying to summon some emotion other than anxiety.

Ify picks up a small device that Irina recognizes as a Doppler and holds it to her belly. Thankfully the batteries still work, and she can hear the sound of her own heartbeat and another faster one alongside it. She smiles up at Rafael, and he can see the joy in her eyes, and he feels all the more wretched about his own discomfort with this.

Irina looks at Ify as she wipes the gel off her stomach, and he tucks the Doppler and a few other supplies into a tote bag. "Is it hard for you to be here?"

272

"It's hard for me to be anywhere," he replies. She nods knowingly, and he continues, "But everything has been better for me since I moved to Ferndale."

"Me too," she says.

+++

The residents of Ferndale gather around Irina, Rafael, Matteo, and Miranda as they stand on the beach reciting handwritten vows to each other. Rafael's hands shake as he reads the words aloud. He's certain that he wants this, but he isn't certain he'll be able to succeed at it. He feels as unqualified to be a good husband as he is to be the community's engineer, but he hopes he'll be able to figure both out. He comforts himself that at least he and Irina will have her prior marital experience to guide them.

Later, Jing, Tina, and Emma follow with their adoption vows. Everyone eats dinner together and dances to the same old songs on the record player.

Irina slips out to take a walk down the street to the memorial garden. She stands in the grove of stumps and reaches her hand out to trace the letters of Sam's and Clara's names, remembering Sam's words: *I hope that whatever is left is enough for you both to find some happiness*.

She's shocked to realize that she's happy. She'd assumed that she'd received a life sentence with Sam's and Clara's deaths. She's surprised to find that it has now been commuted.

+++

When Rick and two women from the Six Rivers Tribe arrive with mares for breeding a few days later, Irina prepares rooms for them at the bed and breakfast, figuring that they'll need to stay for a couple of weeks to maximize the chances of impregnating the mares. Ify had just confirmed two days before that Lily was pregnant. Irina loves the idea that she and Lily will be pregnant at the same time.

273

At the next Council meeting, Julián reminds them again that they need to focus on food.

"We have no idea how many people will arrive this winter or next spring," he says. "We really need to focus on plowing and planting as many fall crops as possible."

"None of that will matter if people show up and steal our crops or livestock," Tina replies. Rafael starts to translate, but Julián waves him away. "We need to start dedicating more resources to defense."

"We're a hundred miles from anywhere," Julián argues in English. "No one will come this far to steal."

"We're out of pre-Pandemic food, right?" Tina asks him. Julián nods, and she continues, "So is everyone else. We've been actively advertising our location and resources on the radio . . . ."

Irina starts to interrupt, but Tina shoots her a look and continues, ". . . which we agreed is necessary to expand the town. But it's also a huge security problem. We need to train people and station them in strategic locations—keeping watch over the livestock and the town at night, keeping watch over the fields and the bridge over the Eel River—though the river is so low now that anyone could just walk across. . . ."

Julián and Rafael had just discussed this the previous day. Rafael is certain that the river is lower now than the prior August.

". . . . When resources get scarce, that's when we'll have problems with theft and aggression. Our best security asset is our isolated location, but we still have to be diligent," Tina concludes.

They discuss this until it grows late, finally agreeing to divide the town up into five groups, one of which will be trained by Tina each afternoon of the workweek.

"We also need to start creating an armory," Tina says. "Anyone with access to a goddamn Walmart Supercenter is going to be better armed than us, if we don't get moving. We've got vehicles now, so we should also be clearing every gun store, Walmart, sporting goods store, National Guard Armory, and Coast Guard station within a hundred miles of here."

"Is that really necessary?" Julián asks. "That will take a lot of time."

"And a lot of electric power for the vehicles," Rafael points out.

"It's absolutely necessary," Tina replies. "Look, . . . we can't produce ammunition, and as far as we know, no one else can either. Eventually all the ammunition left in the world is going to run out. We want ours to run out last."

Ify frowns at that statement. "I think that's excessive."

Tina sighs with frustration. "It's really not. It's realistic."

She considers for a moment, then tries a different line of argument. "Every weapon we have is a weapon someone else doesn't have."

Ify still doesn't look convinced.

"Not everyone in the world is well-intentioned," Tina says, looking at the rest of the Councilmembers around her and still seeing skeptical faces. "It's our job to protect the people in this town. We promised security in our radio addresses."

That's convincing enough for Irina, who then takes up the mantle of convincing the rest of the Council. After a half hour of discussion, Ify still isn't convinced and votes against the rest of the Council.

Tina shrugs at him apologetically, then looks to the audience and calls for volunteers to begin scavenging for weapons. Mark and two others quickly offer to go to Eureka with the electric cars to gather all available weapons and ammunition. Irina suspects that they just want the opportunity to drive around in the electric cars.

After Irina talks him into it, Ify reluctantly agrees to go with them to show them where the gun stores are.

Tina concludes, "And we should look into archery too, for when we run out of bullets."

It's 11:05 p.m. when they finally wrap up the meeting. Irina and Rafael retrieve their children from the bed and breakfast, where François has been watching them. They carry them home through the uncertain night.

+++

Irina wakes the next morning with painful cramps and a sense of dread. In the bathroom, she's distressed to find that she's bleeding. She sits on the toilet for a long time, trying to deny the stark red reality before her. She finally stands up when she hears Matteo rousing in his room. She puts on one of the pairs of period underwear she's been using for the past few years.

Rafael had already left for his regular Friday morning food-service shift, so she gets the children dressed and walks them to breakfast.

In the high school bathroom, she can tell that the bleeding has increased. She returns to the cafeteria and pulls Ify aside in a nearby hallway. "I need to borrow the Doppler."

He scrutinizes her. "Why?"

"I think . . . ," she takes a deep breath and tries to push her emotions back, "I think I've lost the pregnancy."

"I assume you want your husband to join us for this conversation?" Ify says. Irina nods tearfully, and Ify goes back inside to get Rafael from the kitchen. The moment Rafael looks at Irina, he knows. He takes her hand, and they walk back to the store that Ify has turned into his office. Irina spends twenty minutes searching for that fast little heartbeat in vain. She hands the Doppler back to Ify and says she's going home. Rafael stays behind.

"Will she be alright?" he asks Ify.

"Physically? Probably. Emotionally? That will take a while. Miscarriages are terrible, but they're very common. My wife had three of them," Ify says. "Do you want my advice?"

Rafael nods, and Ify continues, "Don't try to fix it. Just let her have her feelings. Sit with her in her grief. Be patient. This is different for her than it is for you. It was a part of her. Next month, you can try again."

Rafael doesn't tell Ify that he has no intention of trying again, that they hadn't even been trying this time. He returns home to a silent house. Upstairs, he finds Irina in bed with Buddy. He lies down beside her and wraps his arms around her. She cries silently next to him, and he's ashamed to admit to himself that his feelings are a muddled mix of sadness for her and relief that the pregnancy is over and she's safe. He'll never tell her this. Instead, he just holds her and kisses her hair.

+++

Days pass but Irina's sorrow doesn't diminish. She's withdrawn from everyone but Matteo, Miranda, Buddy, and Lily, whom she holds closer than ever. Rafael is stunned to find himself on the outside.

A week after the miscarriage, Irina broaches the subject of trying again. Rafael demurs, saying it's too soon. He knows, though, he's just postponing the inevitable argument.

The visitors from the Tribe depart, hopeful that their horses are now pregnant. The harvest begins. The days grow shorter. Irina hunts most mornings while the others gather at breakfast. She avoids everyone, always arriving at the very end of the meal period, eating little, and departing quickly. She usually comes to bed long after Rafael is asleep. Rafael tries to remember Ify's advice to be patient, but her distance stings.

In a moment of desperation and mild intoxication, while Irina is on an overnight trip hunting for weapons and ammunition, Rafael confesses his situation to Emma and Tina as they sit on the back patio after the children are asleep.

"I'm going to lose her," Rafael concludes. "Because I can't agree to try again."

Emma, who had listened empathetically to his story, says, "You have to try again. Even if you don't want to."

"I can't take that risk," Rafael replies, "It was bad enough when it was an accident. If I choose this and anything happens to Irina, it's my fault."

"It's her choice, too!" Emma says emphatically. Emma seems surprisingly emotional about this discussion, and Rafael notices a peculiar, pinched look on Tina's face.

"It's a totally unnecessary risk," Tina replies to Emma.

"Having a baby is worth the risk!" Emma exclaims at Tina, and Rafael senses that perhaps he and Irina aren't the only ones whose marriage is being challenged by this question. "If you don't give her this, she may resent you forever. Sometimes being in a relationship means that you have to accept the risks the other person wants to take."

Emma looks at Tina pointedly. There's a long, uncomfortable pause, during which Tina refills Rafael's whiskey. Finally, Tina sighs and says, "Emma wasn't super happy about my plan to join the Marines. She told me all the reasons it was a bad idea, especially from a safety standpoint. I wanted to do it anyway, and despite her reservations, she agreed to be in a relationship with me while I was off chasing that dangerous dream."

Tina looks at Emma, not Rafael, as she speaks. "She was right, of course, but that's a different story. She supported me anyway, because she knew I had to do this, and if she didn't support it, it could poison the relationship slowly."

She turns her gaze back to Rafael and says sadly, "Sometimes that's just the price of admission."

Tina and Emma's eyes meet again, and Rafael sees the wordless exchange of communication there, the near telepathy of two people who've known each other for a decade and a half: a flicker of triumph in Emma's eyes and concession in Tina's.

The three of them talk for a while longer. Eventually Rafael retires to his bed with only his turbulent thoughts for company. He runs his fingers longingly over the indentation in Irina's pillow. He reminds himself that he had fallen in love with Irina, in part, because of her strength and resolute nature. Those are the very traits that had allowed her to survive a terrible childhood, the death of her own child, and a world-ending pandemic. Her headstrong nature had carried her to him through four hundred desolate, dangerous miles. Those same traits, though, have now put them at odds with each other. Her mind is made up about this, and if he doesn't yield, his refusal to give her what she longs for will likely play out in their marriage for years. He'll have to agree to move forward and try again, or his marriage will be deeply—possibly irreparably—damaged.

A hundred miles away, Irina is also awake, staring at the ceiling of her tent in the darkness. She's bewildered and frustrated by Rafael's apparent indifference to their loss. She suspects that he's a bit relieved that she won't face the perils of pregnancy, and she's almost positive that he won't agree to try again.

She feels angry, despite knowing that the odds were always stacked toward this. She's forty-one years old. It was unlikely that she would get pregnant and not guaranteed that she would carry to term. It's confusing to mourn the loss of a pregnancy she hadn't anticipated or tried for, but she'd fallen in love with the idea of having Rafael's child. She also believes that she's paid her dues to grief already, that the loss of Clara and Sam should have somehow guaranteed her safe harbor from future tragedies. Rationally, she knows this isn't how life works—she need only look as far as Ify, who lost all three children and his wife—yet she still rages against the injustice of it. The upcoming anniversary of Clara's death only amplifies her sorrow and anger.

The next morning, she and Mark finish their search for weapons and return to Ferndale with two cars loaded with guns and ammunition. Irina is grateful that she can at least contribute something, despite her sorrow. She senses that things are precarious with Rafael, but she's unsure of how to fix that, so she avoids anywhere she thinks that he will be.

She checks Miranda and Matteo out of school and takes them to visit the horses, then to the playground in Firemen's Park on the outskirts of town. As she pushes them on the swings, she tries to find some peace, but it eludes her. The afternoon grows late, and she reluctantly returns to town with them. Rafael is already sitting beside Julián in the cafeteria when she arrives.

Rafael's eyes meet hers, and she can see the hurt there. He knows she's been avoiding him.

"Tina said you did a good job," he says as she sits down without getting a plate of food. The implication of his statement is clear: he should have heard about this from Irina, not another person. After dinner, they walk home with the children, saying little to each other. After the children are in bed, he joins her in the bedroom with trepidation. She's lying curled up in the bed with her back to him. He's familiar enough with her body language that he can guess that she's crying. He feels a swell of empathy for her and disappointment in himself for reducing this conflict to a battle of wills, without realizing how viscerally emotional this must be for her, especially given the prior loss of her daughter. He lies down next to her and wraps his arms around her from behind.

"Are you sure that you want to get pregnant?" he asks her. "Even though it's risky?"

"Yes."

She's already dismissed his arguments. There's no point in reiterating them. Rafael sighs, "Alright, I guess."

Rafael spends the next few weeks constructing a peace offering, which he presents to Irina on the anniversary of Clara's death. He invites her to walk with him to Firemen's Park, where he's built a bench with Clara and Sam's names carved into it. She cries as she sits down and traces her fingers over the carvings there.

"Thank you," she says softly.

"I thought maybe we could come here for anniversaries and birthdays, that maybe you and Miranda could plant flowers together here for Clara," he replies. He wants to say much more to her, to try to close this distance between them, but he can't seem to find the words, and he has little experience with successful marriage repair attempts, anyway. He'll have to wait and hope.

Chapter Eighteen

After the last of the fall crops are harvested, the summer wheat is ground into flour, and the winter wheat is planted, Rick and the Tribal apprentices arrive.

At the Council meeting, Rick shows a printout of a plan for a wind farm twenty miles offshore from Eureka.

"This was an incredibly ambitious project," Rick says, "It was supposed to supply 25 gigawatts of power to millions of homes."

"But it's unlikely that it was ever completed," Ify remarks.

"Why not?" Rafael asks.

"Ballooning construction costs and a hostile presidential administration that inherited this project then tried to shut it down," Rick replies.

"And, of course, California's notoriously onerous permitting system," Ify says.

Rick shrugs, "For decades, we used the environmental laws to fight back against fossil fuel projects and environmental hazards, but the same laws could also be used as a tool to slow renewable energy."

"As I recall," Ify says, looking at Rick pointedly, "there were a lot of stakeholders around the Lost Coast who weighed in against the wind turbines."

"We were one of them," Rick admits. "We're usually strongly in favor of renewable energy, but this project had a lot of potential negative impacts, and we were trying to reduce them, to make sure that it was done the right way."

There's a flicker of annoyance on Ify's face, and Irina senses there is some old political disagreement underlying this exchange. She doesn't want Ferndale to be at odds with the Tribe, so she tries to direct the conversation back to tangible goals.

"Do we have any idea how we could find out what ended up happening with the project?" she asks.

"There was supposed to be a wind turbine construction site on the other side of Humboldt Bay," Rick says. "We should start there."

The following week, Rafael, Rick, Mark, and the two engineering apprentices leave for Eureka in EVs, pulling a modified trailer behind them. As they drive out of town, Rafael notes that the road along the river has started to wash out. He adds 'decaying infrastructure' to his list of worries.

Things have at least stabilized between him and Irina. Because Miranda hadn't been planned—at least on Rafael's end—Rafael had never experienced the process of actively trying to conceive. He's a bit mystified by it, especially after Irina tries to explain the subtle body signals that tell her it's time to try. He's not going to complain, though, about her sexual interest, even if he does sometimes start to feel that he, like Blaze, has only one purpose.

They drive across the bridge from Eureka to the peninsula on the other side of the bay and, after checking several side streets, find a large construction site. Two motionless wind turbines, about eight stories tall, stand sentry over a collection of wind turbine components and construction equipment.

"I think these are electric," Rick observes, standing next to a bulldozer. Rafael walks around a small skid steer, inspecting it. "You're right."

If they can get this to Ferndale, it could be useful. They break down the door of a small, locked shed and find the keys. The machine doesn't start, of course, but Rafael figures that if they bring some solar panels and charge it, a skid steer could probably make the journey to Ferndale.

Nearby they find a massive, shipping-container-sized backup battery, designed to provide power during low-wind periods, and a small building. They crowbar open the building door.

"This control system was probably powered by the wind turbines themselves, but the battery is dead now. We'll need to power the computers and access this system to turn the turbines back on. Your tribe doesn't happen to have a computer expert, do they?" Rafael asks Rick. He can't recall anyone at Ferndale's having computer expertise.

"We do, actually," Rick says. "Amy is very good."

"Any chance she could help?" Rafael asks.

"She loves a challenge," Rick replies. "I'll ask her on the radio."

Rafael thanks him, and they get back in the car. In Eureka, they load up several solar panels and return to the construction site. They spend the afternoon hooking the panels up to the skid steer, then depart for Ferndale.

That evening, Rafael reports their findings to the Council.

"We have no idea how many wind turbines there are or whether they're still in working condition," he says. "But it's worth investigating."

He looks at Julián, who seems to be following. "We have to remember that everything we do, though, is at the expense of anything else we might do, so we still need to focus primarily on food, firewood, and irrigation."

The river is very low, and the autumn rains haven't arrived. Julián worries about it constantly and never lets the Council forget the precarity of their situation.

"We may also be able to salvage the electric motor systems from the construction equipment and use that to power our farming equipment. But it will take time to do the retrofitting and a lot of power to run that equipment." He'd talked to Mark at length about this. Mark seemed confident that they could figure it out. "We'll have to divert all solar power resources to those things during relevant agricultural periods."

By the end of the meeting, Rafael is exhausted. He longs for the simpler days, when he and Irina completed their work by dinnertime and spent evenings on the patio with a bottle of wine. At home, she reminds him that it's time to make good on his promise to try again, and, despite his fatigue, he manages to rally enough to do this final thing before falling asleep.

Amy Yates arrives four days later, cantering into town on a dappled horse with a huge smile on her face. She dismounts with a flourish and kisses Rick deeply in the middle of the street. He blushes, and she laughs.

Over lunch, she talks excitedly about the power station control system. She's young, but Rafael can tell that she's both clever and experienced. That afternoon, they leave for Eureka.

Rafael is pleased that the skid steer starts. He diverts the power from the solar panels to the computer control system, and Amy powers the system on and says, "It looks like the system was controlled by a PIV card, but I think I can get around that."

She plugs in a USB passcode cracker, and they wait. A little while later, she's able to access the system, and they see that only two wind turbines are connected to it. Amy turns them on through the computer, but it doesn't generate any power. They spend several hours troubleshooting the system without results.

They return to town that afternoon, with Rick arriving several hours later on the electric skid steer. Amy is characteristically cheerful, having bested the power control system.

Rafael feels defeated. That night he summarizes for the Council. "No sign of a functional offshore wind system. There are two small industrial wind turbines, but neither is operational. These were probably designed to generate the power needed to run the construction site. There's a backup battery that would ensure continuous power if we can get the turbines running, but even if we do that, we'll need to run twenty miles of power lines to get power to Ferndale."

"Can't we disassemble the wind turbines and bring the components here to reassemble them?" Ify asks.

"The turbines are eighty feet tall. Any one component would be too heavy for Lily or the towing capacity of our EVs—which weren't meant to tow anything at all, technically. Reassembling them would require cranes and a lot of other equipment," Rafael replies. "If—and that's a big if—we can get one or both of the turbines working again, we may be able to use that site to charge electric vehicles and batteries, which we can then transport back to Ferndale. That will free up our solar panels here."

The Council agrees to put Mark, who's been appointed Head of Mechanical, in charge of retrofitting the farming equipment with salvaged electric engines, and to approve Rafael, Mark, and the two engineering apprentices to work on the turbines.

At home, Rafael's work isn't finished. Irina gets annoyed with him because he's too tired to provide her with the genetic material she requires.

"You wouldn't be so tired if you didn't work so much," she remarks as he pulls back from her in bed with an embarrassed apology.

"Everyone is counting on me," he replies, trying to keep his voice even, not wanting to argue with her.

"I'm counting on you too," she remarks. "But I'm farther down the priority list than pretty much everyone else."

He sighs and runs a hand through his hair in frustration. "If I can't fix our electrical problems, then our refrigerators will fail, and people might literally starve, so, yes, that's a bit higher up the priorities list than pretty much everything else."

He's right, factually, but it still stings to hear him say it. She knows she's being unreasonable, but she can't seem to talk herself out of this feeling of desperate sadness about the miscarriage and irrational desire for another baby, and she's too proud to apologize for her own unreasonable emotionality, so she rolls over without replying.

Exhausted but unable to sleep, he lies awake, while she sleeps beside him. He feels his old melancholy tugging on him. A future and relationship that had seemed so promising now seem fraught. Irina's grief had lessened when they started to try for a baby, but still, something has shifted between them. Sex has started to feel transactional, and they're both so wrapped up in their work, parenting, and the Council that they rarely have time for meaningful conversation. Even if they did have time to talk, he isn't sure what they would say to each other. His mind is entirely occupied with their power problems, and hers seems entirely occupied with fertility. He still doesn't understand her fixation on having a baby, and his inability to share her enthusiasm for it has only worsened the rift between them.

His work, once seeming to promise a forward trajectory, also seems mired in failures and setbacks. He tries to recall the way he felt on King Peak at the top of the world, that sense of inevitable progress and hope. Recalling that now only makes him feel sorrow. He closes his eyes and tries to sleep.

Chapter Nineteen

The winter rains arrive, and the days turn dreary. The solar panels barely generate enough to power the refrigerators and freezers. Amy leaves for the Tribal lands. Rafael spends most days in Eureka, trying to figure out what's wrong with the wind turbines. Some days, Mark or Rick join him. They conclude that because the machines weren't properly shut down during the Pandemic, after several years without maintenance, they overheated, causing damage to the generators. The northern turbine also has signs of fire damage, which Mark speculates may be from overheating or could have been from a power surge caused by lightning. Rafael recalls sitting on the beach with Irina and watching the lightning storm over the ocean the prior winter. The disparity between that moment and this one weighs on him for the rest of the day.

A steady stream of half-starved new residents arrive. In a heated December Council meeting, several early-arriving members of the community suggest that they should close the doors to new arrivals during the winter months.

"I agree," Julián says, his English growing better every day. "We have eighty-four residents, and our supplies are limited."

He calls the Inventory Manager, Shasta Danvers, up onto the stage. She gives the Council a full accounting of what supplies are left, then says, "If we're not careful, or if something goes wrong—if our food stores get mold or the freezers fail— we may have to start rationing later this winter."

It's a sobering update, but Ify and Emma still refuse to turn people away. Emma says, "That's not in the spirit of Ferndale. People will literally starve."

The fact that several recent arrivals are in the audience only makes the situation more awkward. Emma calls an older African American woman up to the stage and asks her to introduce herself.

"My name is Khadija Brown, and I work in animal husbandry. My six-year-old granddaughter and I arrived here two weeks ago," the woman says. Her uneasiness with speaking in front of this room full of people is obvious.

"Where did you travel from?" Emma asks.

"From Sacramento. I was an accountant there."

"Can you tell the Council the story you told me when you brought your granddaughter, Zekia, to school for the first time?" Emma asks, trying to draw her out.

Khadija sighs and looks down at her hands. "My daughter and son died in the Pandemic, but Zekia and I survived. For two years, we scavenged houses and lived off a small garden and a few chickens. One day four men with guns came and took our chickens and everything in our garden. They said that was their territory now and we had to leave, so we started moving from place to place, trying to scavenge from houses, but we could never find enough food."

Her voice wavers slightly. "Every night we went to bed hungry. There were people going around scavenging houses, hoarding food and supplies, taking anything they could find."

She pauses and looks at the Founders. "When we heard about Ferndale from a flier someone posted on a storefront, it felt like an answer to our prayers."

This piques Rafael's interest. He'd never traveled that far south. Others must be posting fliers after hearing about Ferndale on the radio.

Khadija looks at Julián. "I'm certain that Ferndale saved our lives and many other people's lives. If you close the doors to this place, people will starve."

Julián says nothing, but he appears to be contemplating Khadija's words as Emma thanks her and she gets up and departs for her seat.

"There are also practical reasons not to turn people away," Tina argues. "Anyone we turn away could return as a threat."

"Generosity is insurance against theft," Ify agrees.

Rafael is silent, as he's usually been in recent meetings. Julián drops the proposal to stop taking new residents, and everyone agrees to allay Julián's concerns by training every new resident immediately in hunting, fishing, or agriculture.

Another month passes without Irina's getting pregnant, and her ennui increases. The loss of the miscarriage amplifies, and her feeling of alienation from Rafael continues. She remains troubled that he doesn't seem to share her grief or disappointment. Her age makes every month seem high stakes, and she grows frustrated anytime he's too tired or busy to try. Many days they barely speak, both busy with Council business, work, and childrearing until they collapse into bed for sleep or goal-oriented sex.

After a long string of cloudy days, Rafael's fears are realized when the solar panel backup batteries fail to produce even enough power for the small walk-in refrigerator and chest freezers Ferndale has been using. Two freezers are emptied, and all electric resources are diverted to food preservation and water sanitation. The two electric cars are put away in garages until sunnier weather reappears, and the work on the Eureka wind turbines is indefinitely delayed.

Rafael sinks further into despair.

Still, Irina provides the community with an elk for Christmas dinner. They bring out the record player and dance in the high school auditorium until late that night.

While everyone else is ringing in the New Year together with an outdoor party on Main Street, Julián, Shasta, and Danielle Schmidt, Ferndale's veterinarian, are guarding the livestock in one of the barns. The three of them sit in silence, bundled in blankets and lit only by a dim LED lantern, with

Julián in the loft and the two women on the main floor with the animals.

Julián hears the faint sound of footsteps on the gravel outside. He's aware of every creaking board of the hundred-year-old barn as he moves carefully to the loft door where Tina had drilled a few small, vent-like slits in the wood so the guards can see outside discreetly. The night is very foggy, but in the dim light of the LED Christmas lights Tina had strung, Julián sees two shadows crouching by the barn door, whispering to each other. The festive lights glint dimly on the handle of a weapon in the taller man's holster.

Julián waves to his two fellow guards. They rouse quickly and quietly from their positions, using hand signals to communicate with each other as Tina taught them. Julián and Shasta stand against the wall on either side of the door where the two men are crouching; Danielle huddles behind a stall door near the back entrance to the barn. For several tense moments they wait, unmoving in the cold silence of the night.

The barn door opens with a muffled creak, and the dim light filters inside. The two men are backlit, their raised weapons gleaming. One of the cows, surprised by the sudden light, lets out a soft moo.

Julián makes eye contact with Shasta and nods. For a moment they both hesitate. The taller stranger steps forward into the barn, and Julián raises his weapon and aims. The man looks at him. Julián recognizes his familiar face just before he pulls the trigger. His aim is true, and the man staggers back and drops to his knees as a bloodstain blossoms on his chest.

When the other man takes aim at Julián, Shasta fires three fast shots immediately. The first shot goes wide into the field behind the man, but the other two hit him in the gut and shoulder, throwing him back onto the ground.

The first man is cursing and trying to level his weapon at them from where he kneels on the ground. Julián panics and shoots him four more times, until the man's arm falls down to his side and he stops moving. On trembling legs, Julián steps over to the man and kicks his gun away.

The first man is silent, but the second man is moaning in pain. Danielle kicks his gun away, then picks it up with shaking hands, replaces the safety, and tucks it into her own waistband. The livestock make frightened, anxious noises. In the distance, the faint sounds of the ongoing New Year's party carry across the fields. Julián and Shasta stare at each other for a long moment.

"Mierda," he says, his voice wavering. "We need to get Irina and Tina."

He sends Danielle to get them. Shasta sits down heavily on the dirty, straw-covered floor. She begins to cry. He sits beside her, uncertain of what to do, and ends up just patting her shoulder lightly and offering her water.

Irina and Tina arrive twenty minutes later. Irina is still incongruously dressed in a red sequin dress and gold high heels that stick in the mud of the field as she gets out of the car.

"We know this guy," Tina says, peering down at the taller of the two men as she takes his pulse and confirms that he's dead.

"Brady Calhoun," Julián says. He explains to Shasta, "He was the first person to come here after the six of us, but he left immediately."

"He's not a commie," Irina recalls.

"He's a thief," Tina replies.

The other man lets out a loud howl of pain, then drifts out of consciousness. When he wakes again a few minutes later, Tina tries to question him, but he seems barely cognizant of his surroundings.

"What does the Declaration of Rights say about criminal trials for outsiders?" Tina asks Irina.

"It doesn't say anything," Irina says. "The Charter is about what the government owes to its own people, not to outsiders."

Tina shrugs. "Should I finish him off then?"

Irina is horrified, but then she remembers the mountain man's long, painful death. "That would be kinder than letting him suffer."

Tina chooses her smaller pistol. "You probably don't want to watch this," she says to everyone else. Then she fires once into the man's head at close range. Irina recoils when a large drop of blood lands on her gold party shoes.

"I don't get it," Julián says, looking at Brady. "He had goats and plenty of time to grow his own food. If he wanted something, he could have traded with us."

Tina shrugs. "Maybe something went wrong on his farm, or maybe this other guy convinced him that stealing was better. I'm sure livestock are really valuable. He could have stolen our cattle and horses, then gone back to the Valley and traded for whatever he wanted."

"Do we have any idea where he lived?" Irina asks.

"I saw his horse in a pasture over in Fortuna when I was scavenging for fertilizer there a month or two ago," Julián replies.

"Let's check out his farm tomorrow, then," Irina says. "Maybe we can figure out what happened, and we can get the goats and horse if they're still there."

The next day, during a break in the rain, Irina and Tina ride their bikes to Fortuna. They follow Julián's directions and find Brady's horse grazing beside a large farmhouse. In the backyard, they see his goats, also well and healthy. Beside the house is a sizable garden, with a decent supply of winter crops.

When Tina kicks in the locked front door so they can investigate the house, she hears muffled shouts and banging from the other side of a door in the kitchen. She and Irina pause, momentarily uncertain of what to do. Irina shrugs. Tina takes out her gun as Irina undoes the three bolt locks and throws the door open.

On the other side stands a woman in dirty clothing with long, disheveled black hair. Tear tracks cut lines down her dirty cheeks. Behind her, at the bottom of the stairs, is another woman with a short, roughly cut bob. She stands defiantly upright with dark, angry eyes, looking like she's ready to fight them with her bare hands if she needs to.

Tina lowers her gun, and they all stare at each other for a long moment; then Irina steps back and says, "You're safe now. You can come out."

The woman at the top of the stairs rushes out the door, through the kitchen, and into the yard. The other woman peers at them suspiciously, then steps carefully up the stairs, never turning her back to them as she follows them outside into the muted daylight.

"Do you want some water?" Irina offers them her water bottle. The woman with the short hair lets the other woman drink first, then takes the bottle.

"Who are you?" the woman with the shorter hair asks, after she finishes the bottle of water. Irina and Tina introduce themselves.

"We came from Ferndale," Irina says. "We were investigating two men who tried to steal our livestock."

"Are they dead?" the same woman asks.

"Yes," Tina replies.

"Good fucking riddance," the woman says.

There are several beats of silence, then the long-haired woman, who looks a few years younger, offers Tina, then Irina, her hand. "I'm Aditi Patel, and this is my sister Jaya. We were trying to get to Ferndale when two men held us up at gunpoint, tied us up, blindfolded us, and brought us here. We don't even know where we are."

"You're in Fortuna," Irina says. "Just across the river from Ferndale."

"Do you know why they were in Ferndale?" Tina asks.

"They were going to take your horses and cattle, drive them up the riverbed, and hide them in the mountains, then eventually take the livestock—and us—through the mountains and back down to the valley," Jaya replies. "Wynn had a place there."

"Do you know how they met?" Irina says, "Brady was alone when he came to Ferndale last summer."

"It didn't seem like they'd known each other for long," Aditi answers. "Brady goes on the radio sometimes, so maybe they met there."

"How long have you been here?" Tina asks them.

"Only about a month," Aditi says, beginning to cry again. "An awful month."

"You can come with us to Ferndale," Irina says. "Things are going to get better."

+++

That evening, Irina and Tina debrief the Council and the public about the attempted theft and the women they had freed. Julián is quiet during the meeting, speaking only when he's called on.

Rafael senses that he's troubled by having killed the thieves, so when the meeting finally ends, Rafael gets a bottle of whiskey and knocks on Julián's door. When Julián answers, he's already a bit drunk. As Rafael gets two glasses from the kitchen and sits down on the couch, Julián tells him that Tina had just left.

"How are you doing?" Rafael asks him in Spanish. Despite Julián's fluency in English, they still tend to default to Spanish with each other, both preferring the comfort of their mother tongue.

Julián shrugs.

"You haven't had to shoot anyone before?" Rafael asks as he pours them each two fingers of whiskey and hands a glass to Julián.

"I've never had a reason to," Julián replies. "I avoided the gangs when I was a kid, and after I recovered from the Virus, I went far enough away that I didn't see anyone until I came here."

"I think you did what you had to do, shooting the thieves," Rafael says. "Brady could have traded with us. He chose to steal instead. They were armed. They could have shot you, Danielle, Shasta, or the livestock."

"That's what Tina said: we aren't obligated to risk our lives to try to protect dangerous people who come here to steal from us."

Rafael had heard this argument when a security trainee had questioned Tina's 'shoot first and ask questions later' policy. He hadn't been comfortable with it then, and he's not much more comfortable with it now, but he knows this isn't the moment to introduce moral ambiguity into the conversation.

"That's true, but I know it's hard to accept," Rafael says. He finishes his whiskey and sets the glass down, sensing that a bit of candor about his own history might help Julián. "I know it's hard to accept because I've been there."

"You shot someone?" Julián doesn't bother to hide his surprise.

"I did." Rafael recounts what happened with the mountain man. He doesn't withhold the gruesome details, sensing that

Julián needs the solidarity of knowing that someone else had witnessed such things.

"Does it still bother you?" Julián asks, when Rafael finishes his story.

"Sometimes." Rafael and Miranda both still occasionally have nightmares about it. "But if I hadn't shot him, he might have gotten Miranda sick. I don't think I had a better option. Neither did you."

"I could have told them to put their weapons down."

"That would have increased the risk to you, Danielle, and Shasta." It's true, but it doesn't feel sufficient to Rafael, even as he says it.

"This is exactly what we were trying to prevent when we founded this place," Julián says.

"And we've done a pretty good job of accomplishing that," Rafael replies. He parrots what Tina has told the Council several times. "But there will always be dangerous people in the world."

They talk for a while longer as the night grows late. As Rafael walks back up the street, disquiet follows him. He'd recited the rational justifications to Julián, without truly believing them himself. He understands, intellectually, why they have to make moral compromises, but he's still uncomfortable with it. He can't help feeling as if these compromises are only necessary because Ferndale is still fighting for survival, and they're in that position, in part, because he's not doing a good enough job of finding solutions.

In the bedroom, Irina is asleep. He wishes he could talk to her about these doubts he's having—she's the only person he would have felt comfortable talking to about this—but he senses that she'll be annoyed if he wakes her, so he climbs quietly into bed. She's only a foot from him, but she may as well be miles away. There's a distance between them now, born of her grief, his uncertainty about having a baby, and the grind of their daily lives. He reaches out and touches his fingers to her cheek, trying to reassure himself. In her sleep, she rolls over, away from him.

+++

The whole town is on edge after the incident, and soon nearly everyone has sunk into an anxious malaise. Council meetings become more contentious as people disagree about how to allocate time and resources. Tina wants to double the guards and increase the security training time. Julián argues that they should be devoting time and power to developing indoor growing systems. Emma and several members of the community complain that children are being pulled into labor tasks instead of being educated.

When Irina gets her period again, she pours her glasses of wine with a heavy hand for the entire week. Rafael's well-intended efforts to comfort her only result in arguments and distance, so he ceases to try.

One morning, when they finish with another round of rushed and exhausted—but well-timed—sex, he stands up from the bed, pulling his boxers back on. As he buttons his pants, he turns to where she lies in the dim winter light and says, "I'm not even sure it's me you're interested in anymore. I'm just a means to an end."

Before she can muster a reply, he leaves for work.

The day after Matteo's third birthday, when Irina has informed Rafael that her fertile window for the month is probably over, he announces that he's going to leave to spend a week in Eureka, working on the wind turbines. Rafael's depression hasn't escaped Irina's notice. He's withdrawn and irritable with everyone, preferring to spend his days working on electricity generation and solving mechanical problems. She watches him bike away with concern. She knows his history. She's pretty sure he's not that depressed, but she recalls reading that it's often difficult to tell with men.

298

She thinks of him constantly after he leaves. While she's starting to train Sunshine with the harness, she reflects on how frightened he was when she got injured and how gentle he was afterward. When she plows another field with Lily, she recollects the day they found the horses, how often they used to laugh together.

When she opens up her favorite book, the folded flier for Ferndale falls out. She vividly recalls their first meeting, how kind he'd been to her then and every day after. She remembers his sense of duty and dedication to the town, his hard work to improve everyone's lives. She touches the tattoo above her heart.

She suddenly realizes what she's done. He's put her happiness first so many times—waiting until she was comfortable before inviting others to the town, waiting patiently for her to decide that she loved him back, backing her proposals when it really mattered, agreeing to try again for a baby. She's put so much pressure on him to deliver her from her unhappiness after the miscarriage. She's certain that he's interpreted his inability to do that as his failure, in the same way that he's interpreted the electricity limitations as his failure. She needs to find a way to fix this, though she knows it will take time.

It begins with giving up this desperation to have another baby. Rafael had been right when he'd tried to remind her that they already have a family. She's been resentful of him for not being as dedicated to this goal, without realizing that it was his indifference about having another child that had allowed him to form a union with a woman who was very likely too old to give him one.

Her goal-oriented obsession with this has leached all the joy and spontaneity out of their sex life, monopolized their conversations, and increased the distance between them. She'd thought that it was of paramount importance that they create an amalgamation of both of them, but what good does that do if she loses him in the process?

She also realizes that they've already created something meaningful and beautiful together—an entire town, a community of people who are surviving together, a place that was born of their mutual effort and vision.

For a long time, she sits in the living room formulating a plan. A grand romantic gesture is a start, but they'll need consistency and hard work to get this back on track. She's done it before with Sam, so she knows it's possible. She takes a midnight trip to the library to find the marriage book she'd read with Sam; then she packs an overnight bag with supplies.

At breakfast the next day, she asks Ify for recommendations for a romantic bed and breakfast in Eureka. He raises an eyebrow but offers her a few options with a hand-drawn map. She asks Mark to draw her a map to the wind turbines. Then she asks Tina and Emma to watch the kids overnight, and tells Shantal that she's taking the afternoon off.

She's halfway to Eureka when it occurs to her that Rafael may not be interested in her romantic gesture. Then she thinks back to their recent interactions, to the hurt in his eyes when he'd accused her of not wanting him. Clearly he still loves her.

She stops at the bed and breakfast closest to the bridge to the power plant. She finds the keys inside the office and unlocks the door to one of the rental cottages. She checks to make sure there are no decaying former occupants; then she sets out candles and exchanges the dusty bedding with the clean sheets she'd brought. She finds some firewood at a gas station nearby and starts a fire in the fireplace. Then she rides over the bridge.

It's almost sunset when she arrives at the wind turbines. The evening light slants over the hulking construction vehicles and the bay beyond them. The door to the control building is slightly ajar. She calls out his name as she steps inside, and he turns, startled, to face her. He wears his dark-rimmed reading glasses, and his face shows obvious exhaustion.

"What are you doing here?" he asks. "Are the kids okay?"

"Everything is fine," she says, crossing the room to him. She stands in front of him, and they look at each other for a moment. "I wanted to see you. I miss you. Can we talk?"

He follows her outside and down to the small strip of beach across the road from the building site.

"What's going on?" He asks her as they sit down. For a moment, he thinks that she's come to tell him that she's pregnant, but the timing would be off.

She sits in the sand facing him with the ocean sunset to their sides. She takes his hands, and a look of confusion crosses his face. "I'm so sorry, Rafael. I'm sorry that I demanded that you give me something that neither of us has control over. I'm sorry if I made you feel like you've failed me. I'm sorry we haven't talked in so long. I'm sorry . . . ," her voice cracks, "I'm sorry if I've broken this."

He's a bit stunned, and for a moment he says nothing. Then, finally, "You haven't broken it, but I think I have. I'm sorry I wasn't there for you the way you needed me to be after you— we—lost the pregnancy. I'm sorry I'm always so stuck in my own head that we barely talk. I'm so sorry."

She runs her fingers over the inside of his forearm, as she often used to do, and she hears his breath catch. His eyes close, and she leans forward and gently takes his glasses off, then presses her lips to his. He stills for a moment, then reaches for her, pulling her down on top of him in the sand. They kiss with an intensity they haven't had since the previous summer, with little moans and wandering hands. She wants him, but she wants them to take their time, so she doesn't reach to take their clothes off. Instead, she slows down, kissing him with increasing gentleness until their lips are just barely brushing. She pulls back and looks into his hazel eyes. She hasn't seen that kind of desire in months.

"I love you. I'll do anything to fix this," she says. "Please fix it with me."

"I love you too. I want to fix this. I just don't really know how," he confesses. She stands and offers him her hand, pulling him up to stand against her.

"Come with me," she says, getting on her bike. He follows across the bridge in the fading light to the door of the cottage. She opens it, and he steps inside and watches as she rekindles the fire and lights the candles. She turns to face him in the flickering light.

"We don't need to have another baby," she says softly, her eyes meeting his.

"You can be happy with the family we have?" he asks, searching her face and noting the tears in her eyes.

"Yes. If I have you, I can be happy," she replies, looking at him earnestly. "Our marriage is more important to me than having another baby is."

He's quiet as he considers that. Then she draws him to her and kisses him as she undresses him slowly in the candlelight. He moves to take her clothes off, but she takes his hand away, leads him to the bed, and tells him to sit. Rafael's heart races. It's been a long time since she's been this way with him. He's missed it desperately. She stands in front of him, just out of reach, and undresses with agonizing slowness, taking her time with each piece of clothing as he watches with wide eyes from the edge of the bed. She's long since shed her insecurities. He's always made her feel beautiful.

She walks over, stands between his thighs and kisses him slowly. "I want you."

"I want you too."

She leaves a trail of kisses down his neck and chest as she sinks to her knees in front of him and traces kisses up the inside of his thigh. At first he's unsure; then she makes her intentions clear as she takes him in her mouth. For a moment his mind goes blank in ecstasy. It's been months since they did anything sexual just for the pleasure and intimacy of it. He closes his eyes and just lets himself feel her.

Afterward, after enthusiastic reciprocity, after exchanging "I love you's," when the candles have started to burn down, he holds her to him.

She runs her fingers lightly over his stomach, making him shiver. "I'm worried that you're depressed."

"I have been."

"Because of our marriage?"

He sighs, "That's a big part of it. But it's also the power setbacks and the reality of how much work we both have to do, the constant maintenance it takes to keep things going. I wanted a community, but I didn't stop to think about what that requires. I feel like everyone is looking for me to lead, and I'm just not made for that."

Irina feels the scrutiny too. Despite their intentions, they're set apart. People watch them, their marriage, their parenting. "Sometimes I miss when it was just us. It was simpler."

"I miss it too," he says. "I miss you. Tell me how to fix this."

She'd spent the entire bike ride considering this after rereading several chapters of the marriage book. She outlines her plan for purposeful time together, for evening conversations, intimacy, shared activities, small acts. "I know it sounds forced," she says, "but we have two kids and more than full time jobs, and this is the only way that we aren't going to fall between the cracks."

Rafael agrees. He has no experience building a happy marriage, so he figures he'll have to trust her.

She pauses, trying to phrase her next request in the least critical way possible. "Would you consider cutting back your hours a little bit? Spending more time at home? I know you're worried about the power problems, but I miss having that time with you."

"Yes," he says, grateful that she'd recognized his concerns about their infrastructure and moved by the fact that she'd missed spending time with him. "I'll ask the Council for another junior engineer."

She adds two more logs to the fire, and they lie on their backs in bed talking for hours about their childhoods, their hopes for the town, Rafael's disquiet after the episode with the thieves, Irina's lingering grief about Clara and the miscarriage. When the fire has died down to embers and the moonlight casts shadows around the room, she falls asleep with her head against his chest.

He breathes in the familiar scent of her hair and appreciates the comfort of her body against his. He's certain that by giving up the possibility of having another baby, she'd just surrendered something that is deeply important to her. He wonders if he should really accept that sacrifice, though. It loosens something in him to know that she's chosen him and their marriage, over something she longs for.

He contemplates the strange trajectory of their relationship. Nearly a year as friends, then suddenly lovers, then just as suddenly "companions in a shipwreck," as he recalls J.R.R. Tolkien had once aptly described spouses. He prays to the Catholic god that he'd lost touch with decades ago, desperately hoping that he and Irina will survive this first shipwreck in their marriage.

+++

Early the next morning they bike back to the wind turbine construction site. She follows him through a door at the base of one of the turbines. Before them is a long ladder, scaling the

304

eighty-foot-high, ten-foot-wide enclosed steel tower. Just looking at it makes Irina feel dizzy.

"This is where you've been going every day?! It looks dangerous!" she exclaims.

"There are safety harnesses," he replies with a shrug. "Do you want to check it out?"

Irina really doesn't, but it seems as though he wants to show her, so she reluctantly agrees. He reaches around to help her put on her safety harness, and he's so close to her that she can't help reaching out and pulling him against her, pressing her lips to his. The harness falls to the ground as she walks him back until he's pressed against the cool steel wall of the windmill.

"You're just trying to distract me because you really don't want to climb that ladder," he laughs. She silences him with a kiss. She reaches for the button of his pants, and for a moment he nearly stops her, uncertain about her choice of venue, but then decides to follow her lead in the name of romance and spontaneity.

They hastily strip off each other's pants and underwear, leaving their jackets and shirts to ward off the winter chill, and he flips their position so her back is pressed against the wall as he kisses her neck and slides his hand under her shirt to cup her breast. She sighs with pleasure and pulls his hips against hers insistently, but he resists, wanting to draw this out, to hear her beg for him, to know that it's him that she wants after so many months of uncertainty and ambivalence.

"Please, Rafael," she says, "I need you. Now."

He loves the sound of his name on her lips. "You have me. Always."

He lifts her, her hips pinned against the wall, her thighs wrapped around his hips as she takes him into her. Their sounds of desire echo off the hard surfaces of the wind turbine tower. She grasps his back, her fingers slipping under his shirt and digging into the muscles of his shoulder blades as he moves in her. Her lips glide over his face and neck, grazing his skin with her teeth as he leans his head back and closes his eyes with ragged intake of breath. Waves of pleasure ripple through her, but her hips ache from the position, so she says, simply "floor," and he gently slips away from her and lowers her onto the rough, rubberized ground, kneeling above her and returning to her. He moves slowly over her, his lips not leaving hers, her hands roaming his arms, his back, his thighs. They move with increasing intensity, and he pulls back and looks into her eyes as she calls out his name and her body tenses around him. In that moment, he makes a choice, more instinct than conscious thought, and he follows her into momentary oblivion, not bothering to leave her body before he does.

He collapses beside her and wraps his arms around her, and they're both still for a moment, recognizing the significance of what had just happened. Irina realizes that he's chosen to give her the possibility of another baby, even though she'd freed him of that obligation. Her eyes tear up at the knowledge that he loves her enough to meet her surrender with his own.

"I love you," he says, looking at her earnestly—a ritual that he never skipped, even at the moments when sex felt entirely transactional.

"I love you too," she says. It's strange how categorically different this act feels from the obligatory intimacy they've had over the past few months.

The floor grows cold and uncomfortable, and they reluctantly stand to put their clothing back on.

"Sometimes you're not at all what I expected," he says with a smile as he picks up her pants from the floor and hands them to her.

"What did you expect?" she replies.

He laughs. "You seemed very straight-laced. I'm pretty sure I never even saw your ankles until you wore that green dress for Christmas."

"I was trying not to be tempting," she smirks, relieved that they can be lighthearted with each other again after months of seriousness.

"It clearly didn't work."

"You didn't seem tempted."

"I was always tempted," he says. "I was pretty self-disciplined about not fantasizing about you during the day . . . , but my subconscious was just not on board with that plan at night."

"I wasn't so self-disciplined," she laughs. "I had many vivid daytime fantasies about you . . . ."

"You never told me that!"

"I didn't want you to feel objectified," she chuckles.

"I don't mind being objectified by you . . . . Tell me one."

She smiles. "I had one where you left the curtains in your room open while you were undressing—you were always so careful not to do that in real life." He had been. He hadn't ever wanted to make her uncomfortable. "And you looked up and saw me watching you from outside, and our eyes met, and you could tell that I wanted you. Then you invited me into your bedroom . . . ."

He inhales a ragged breath. "I like that one. Tell me another."

She laughs. "I had another where we got caught in the rain and ended up under the pavilion at the park, and we made love on the picnic table."

"It's a real shame we didn't fulfill that fantasy before people got here, . . . though there is a pretty nice park over in Fortuna that no one ever goes to. I think they have picnic pavilions . . . ."

"It's too cold here during the rainy season to make that one into reality," Irina replies. "We'd get hypothermia for sure!"

"We could just get in the car and turn the heat up afterward!" He smiles.

She laughs again. "I really admire your commitment to problem solving."

He draws her to him and kisses her.

As he helps her put the safety harness on, he remarks, "Now every time I'm here, I'll think of you."

"That may have been my plan," she smiles.

He snaps their harnesses to a safety wire; then they begin the long climb up the tower. Irina tries her best not to look down. At the top, they step into a small room, just barely high enough for them both to stand without hitting their heads. There are a variety of gears, wiring, and large machinery.

"This is the damaged generator," Rafael says, showing her a huge machine that is almost as tall as he is. "Mark and I may be able to repair it, but we'll need replacement components, and I don't think we can salvage them from the other, burnt-out turbine."

"There aren't any generators in the construction site?"

"I think this site was just to assemble the external portions of the turbines, and anyway, the offshore turbines are ten times bigger, so the components would be far too large."

"What about another power plant? I saw one on the ride up to Eureka."

He'd seen it before but discounted it because it was powered by natural gas; still, it seems worth checking out. "Maybe. We can stop on our way home."

He sighs and runs his hand through his hair before continuing. "Even if we can fix the turbines, though, we have bigger problems. The solar panels and the wind turbines both rely on lithium or nickel-cadmium battery backups for low-energy-generation periods, and those batteries will wear out within a decade. It's the same problem with everything—the medications, the batteries, the building components—everything decays over time, and we don't have the people, the materials, or the supply chains to make more. I'm worried that we've brought people here and built this town just to watch our technology slowly degrade around us."

She takes his hand. "We'll figure it out. You don't have to manage this on your own, you know?"

"I know," he says without sounding convinced.

They carefully descend the ladder and get back on their bikes. They take a detour to the natural-gas power plant and find ten huge cylindrical engines surrounded by walkways.

"We might be able to work with this," Rafael says, peering at the machinery around him. "I'll bring Mark by so he can check it out."

They get back on their bikes, pedaling for home.

"Even if I can't get the wind turbine generator running," Rafael says as they ride, "this won't be a total loss. I think I can use this system as a model for something on a smaller scale. We need to figure out how to manufacture components, though."

"Are we now in need of blacksmithing? Maybe it's time to look at that exhibit in the museum?" Irina smiles.

"It may be."

As they ride south, the morning fog starts to lift, and the winter sun comes out. It barely heats the day, but the scenery is lovely.

Irina asks, "Do you think that we can spare enough power to run a projector and a couple of speakers once per week?"

"That seems like a negligible amount of power. I'm sure it can be arranged. What do you have in mind?"

"In the spirit of our conversation about working on our marriage and spending time doing fun activities together, I was thinking that maybe Ferndale as a community could stand to have a little more fun. We all eat together; we work together; but aside from the holidays, we don't really have fun together. People are on edge. Every Council meeting seems like more bad news. I think we need something to lighten the mood. Movie nights, dances, board games, maybe an evening with childcare so parents can have some time alone. "

He nods along. "I like that. We have been very focused on survival, and like you said, we need to aim for something more than survival."

When they return to Ferndale, Rafael visits the children in school and thanks Emma for watching them. Irina goes to the Administration Building to talk to Shantal about an idea that had struck her as she'd considered Rafael's depression and their marital struggles.

"Do we have any former mental health counselors here?" Irina asks Shantal.

Shantal thinks for a moment. "Charlotte Gregory. Licensed Mental Health Counselor, fifty-five years old, came here from Ashland, Oregon, in September. Currently works in animal husbandry."

"You have everyone memorized?" Irina says, impressed.

"That's my job," Shantal shrugs.

+++

"I'd like to create a new professional role," Irina announces at the next Council meeting. Everyone turns to her. "I think we need a community mental health counselor."

"Right now we need to focus on food production," Julián replies.

310

"I think a counselor is a good idea," Ify says. "I'd like to hear more."

Irina invites Charlotte to the stage. Together, they explain the program they've planned for individuals, couples, and group therapies. Irina had been pleased that Charlotte had been enthusiastic about the possibility of working as a counselor again and had been trained in Cognitive Behavioral Therapy, the same model that had been helpful to Irina in the past.

"That's a little higher up Maslow's hierarchy of needs than we are right now," Tina remarks. "We don't have time for long discussions about our feelings. We have to focus on security"—she looks at Julián—"and food."

"Therapy is a luxury," Julián agrees.

"We can spare one person to do mental health counseling," Rafael says. "It saves lives." He meets Irina's eyes, "It saved mine."

"A lot of the kids in the school are really struggling," Emma says. "I think this could be helpful for them."

"We have to acknowledge that we're all grieving and this is a stressful situation," Irina argues. "Like Rafael said, the right kind of therapy can be life-changing. This won't just be 'long discussions about our feelings.' Charlotte will use evidence-based models that have been studied and proven to be effective. This does require an investment of time and resources, but if we want our community to thrive, we need to invest in this."

"I agree," Ify says. "It would also be wise for us to have someone on staff who can provide marital counseling. If we want a stable community, that starts with stable families. Studies have shown that a happy marriage can actually give people longer, healthier lives."

"But does marriage counseling actually work?" Julián asks skeptically.

"In my personal experience, yes," Irina replies. "And Charlotte reports that she's had great success with evidence-based methods. This is worth the investment."

Julián doesn't look convinced, but Irina decides to press forward with the other part of her plan anyway.

"We also need to invest some resources in things that are just joyful. Things that make survival worthwhile," she continues. She lays out her proposal for weekly social events for the community, calling Benoit up to the stage to talk about the plan they'd made.

"I like it," Ify says. "We knew when we put together the Charter that one of our challenges would be teaching people to think communally. This will build community and create a shared culture."

"Are you asking for another full-time staff position for this?" Julián asks.

"Head of Post-Apocalyptic Social Events!" Tina jokes.

Irina smiles. "Weekly social events will be staffed by volunteers. In their free time. This is a very low-cost proposal, and it will build camaraderie and, as Ify said, a shared culture."

They debate for a while longer before Irina calls the vote. Even Tina and Julián reluctantly agree.

Nearly everyone attends the first movie night. Benoit and the volunteer kitchen crew hand out big bowls of popcorn, and the community watches a DVD of a 1990s comedy that reminds them of all the things they don't miss about the pre-Pandemic workplace. Several residents stop to thank Irina and Benoit on their way out. Their gratitude and the sense of community she's fostered helps take the sting out of the upcoming anniversary of Sam's death.

Charlotte's counseling services are also very popular. Irina checks in with Aditi and Jaya to make sure that they're getting the counseling they need and are adjusting to the community.

She often sees Tina stopping by their house as well. Rafael and Irina spend an hour every other week with Charlotte, sorting through their more pedestrian marital problems as well as the more complex issues around the miscarriage. At Charlotte's recommendation, they try to recreate the best parts of their time at the House by the Sea by spending one or two evenings a week reconnecting as they sit together and ask each other questions and really listen to the answers. Most weekends they exchange a few hours of babysitting with Tina and Emma so they can bike to the beach or go for a hike nearby. Over the course of the next few months, they're happy to find that things are improving between them, incrementally but steadily.

Rafael honors his agreement with Irina to spend more time at home with his family. He tries to remind himself that it's not his sole responsibility to figure out all of Ferndale's various infrastructure-related problems. He struggles, though, to quiet his worries at the end of the day.

Rafael's stress lifts a little when he, Mark, and their apprentices finally make progress on the wind turbine generator with parts salvaged from the other power plant. The blades spin, and the turbine generates more power than they've seen in years. They find some containers of coolant but have to use oil from an auto supply store to lubricate the system. Rafael and Mark both know it's a temporary solution, but for now they're able to power the EVs, some battery generators, the skid steer, and the rototillers. They find several more EVs in one of Eureka's wealthier neighborhoods and add those to their fleet.

Mark also makes progress on retrofitting a combine he found in a barn outside of town. He extracts the engine from the electric bulldozer and, with some modifications and a handmade hoist, is able to fit it in the combine. They charge the battery at the Eureka wind turbine, place it in the combine, and are thrilled when the front of the machine begins to rotate.

Chapter Twenty

The town spends April preparing for the trade conference. Irina, Ify, and Rafael make radio announcements, inviting their listeners to share the details with other survivors. Julián sets aside jars of seeds, and he and Shasta make an inventory of the extra crops and materials they can afford to trade. Irina, Ify, and Rafael work on their training presentations.

On April fourteenth, they celebrate the first Founders Day. Everyone is relieved that they've made it through the first winter. Julián presents the community with a batch of moonshine he'd made from corn he'd grown in his backyard and distilling equipment he'd salvaged from a distillery in Fortuna. It isn't the best thing they've ever tasted, but it does get them drunk.

Irina tries to keep herself from feeling envious when Emma and Tina invite the other Councilmembers for drinks in their backyard and announce that Emma is pregnant. Irina smiles as she sips her wine but cries alone in the bathroom at home, until Rafael knocks insistently on the door and demands to be let in. He's learned not to try to fix this, so he just wraps his arms around her and kisses her forehead gently.

Emma and Tina stubbornly refuse to reveal who the father is, which touches off endless speculation between Irina and Rafael. Artificial insemination is easy enough but still requires male genetic material. Because of the close friendship among the Founders, Rafael's top suspects are Ify and Julián. Irina, however, bets on François, because he and Emma are good friends, he loves kids, and, given that he isn't attracted to women, he might welcome this non-traditional opportunity for fatherhood.

The day before the trade conference, Emma assures them that everything will be fine as Irina and Rafael kiss their children goodbye at the door of the school, then ride their bikes to Fortuna, where three EVs have been charging. They split up, with Rafael and Irina leading, Julián and Shasta following behind, and Tina and Mark in the final car.

They've parked the cars in Fortuna and topped them off with the solar panels for the last two days, but Rafael is still anxious about their range, especially because the cars are weighed down with items to trade. He frets about it as Irina drives, reminding her that it's more efficient to ride inertia down the hills and drive at a slower speed.

"If you keep driving this way, we're going to be walking home," he remarks as she accelerates around a bend.

"Alright, grandpa." She rolls her eyes and smiles. Since the wind turbine breakthrough, Rafael has been a little more relaxed. Still, she sometimes senses his underlying tension. He often points out that everything around them is decaying and that they need to plan for that. Two weeks before, he'd forced the Council to take a full accounting of all the things that they'd need to manufacture to replace pre-Pandemic items—clothing, batteries, shoes, lumber, machine parts, medications, household items—and the timeline by which they must do so. It was a staggering and sobering list. He'd emphasized that they're in a race against time and that some things—like lithium batteries, car tires, and medications—will be impossible to reproduce in the foreseeable future, so they need to develop low-tech alternatives. That night he'd gotten drunk and confessed to Irina a laundry list of worries about Ferndale and humanity's future, the sustainability of the society they have created, and her health if she got pregnant.

Which is why Irina hasn't told him that her period is four days late. She keeps that hope—and concern—to herself as they pass through California's scenic coastal mountains. Several times, they have to stop to clear fallen trees from the road and once to carefully drive over a section that has washed out. Rafael adds 'roads' to the list in his notebook. He launches into another conversation about batteries, and Irina tries to listen with interest, despite the fact that a large percentage of their recent conversations have been on this same topic.

Memento Mori, she reminds herself again, recalling her regret over the conversations with Sam for which she'd been only half-present.

Rafael tries again to set his worries aside. They're on a trip, and for three days they'll have no childcare responsibilities; they'll get to stay in a new place, meet people, and share ideas. They connect Irina's old smartphone to the car's Bluetooth and listen to the albums she'd downloaded before the internet died. She tears up when she hears the live album she always used to listen to at night. She tells him a little more about what her life was like when she was alone with Matteo in Bend, and he talks about his time in the cabin. Two hours pass quickly; then they're in the green foothills and, finally, an hour later, outside of Red Bluff. They follow Gail's directions to the fairgrounds, where a crowd is already gathering. Gail and Rick stand near a small paddock of horses.

"Nice ride," Gail says as Irina pulls up.

"Thanks to Rick and Amy," Irina says. Rafael has been working with Dana and Alice, the tribal apprentices, to figure out the blacksmith forge and begin using recycled metal to create smaller-scale windmills modeled after the industrial ones in Eureka. He hopes to visit the tribe and build wind turbines with them once he has a good prototype.

"Looks like we'll have a good turnout," Gail says, looking at the other people milling around the fairground.

"Have you had a chance to talk to anyone yet?" Irina asks.

"A few people. We've got some olive growers, a vintner from Sonoma, a couple of citrus growers from down near Sacramento, and I've heard a rumor that there's even someone here who has tea plants."

"That would be lovely," Irina says. Herbal teas just aren't the same as the real thing. "What about coffee?"

"Not that I've heard about, unfortunately. I'd probably trade my horse for a bag of fresh coffee at this point . . . ."

Mark and Shasta begin handing out fliers they'd printed with the program for the next two days of training. The medic from the Monastery will do a demonstration on first aid, Irina will discuss horse training, a member of the Six Rivers Tribe will do a demonstration on manufacturing traditional bows and arrows and leather goods, Rafael will discuss the basics of electricity generation, Tina will talk about self-defense methods and weapons maintenance, the Brothers will give a training on beekeeping, members of Six Rivers Tribe will discuss regional edible and medicinal plants, Mark will demonstrate engine and motor maintenance, a member of the Mennonites will talk about traditional harvesting methods and wheat production, Shasta will present on food preservation methods, a farmer from the north central valley will cover year-round growing strategies, and the Sisters will discuss textile production, soap making, and candle making. They've left several "open mic" slots for anyone who wants to give a demonstration on a useful skill.

Gail takes Irina to a small amphitheater, where they'll do the training. Rick produces an aging karaoke machine connected to a small solar cell.

"Good thinking," Irina says. She hadn't anticipated that they would have a large enough crowd to warrant sound amplification. She feels a buzz of nervous energy as she looks out at the rows of empty seats. She turns to Gail, "Thank you for organizing this with me."

"Happy to do it. We should do one in the fall too."

Irina nods. She and the residents of Ferndale leave to set up their tents on the outskirts of the fairgrounds. For the first time, Irina and Rafael will be sharing a tent. She remembers the times they'd slept in separate tents the year before, with just layers of fabric and a few feet separating them. She used to lie in her tent, trying not to think of him sleeping so closeby.

They all eat dinner together around a campfire, talking excitedly about the next day. Tina schedules everyone for a few hours of night watch. The night passes uneventfully, though, except for a nearby group of campers who get loudly drunk.

"I hope they save some of that to trade with us," Tina says as she hands the watch off to Irina.

They all wake at dawn and begin setting out their trade goods at a table inside a large open-air building. Irina confers with Shasta and Julián about their top priorities. They haven't brought everything the Council had approved for trade, because they're planning on setting a date in the future to drive to meet trade partners and exchange larger or bulk items, so Shasta sets up a sign at their table with a list of additional available trade goods, including stud services by their male livestock.

By 8:00 a.m. more than one hundred people have gathered. Many have set up tables, others are just perusing the offerings. Julián mans the table, while Irina and Shasta haggle for the items they need, even procuring four tiny tea plants. They confer regularly with Rafael, who is bargaining uncomfortably in Spanish, after reminding Irina that this is really outside of his skillset. They quickly have a long list of reservations for livestock stud services.

At 11:00 a.m. the training presentations begin. Rafael turns on the ham radio; then he, Irina, and Gail stand on the stage together to welcome the audience. Irina looks out over the crowd and counts at least one hundred forty people. When Rafael smiles at her, though, the flutter of anxiety in her stomach calms.

"Thank you all for being here," Irina says. "And thank you to the Six Rivers Tribe for co-hosting this event. We hope to make this a regular meeting—the second weekends of May and October."

Gail says, "Please invite others. The more people participate, the more useful this will be. If you have suggestions for trainings you'd like to see or give, please let us know."

They go over logistical details for the event, including telling everyone that it will be live broadcast, and it feels very pre-Pandemic, until they have to remind everyone to station night watches and alert others if they see anything suspicious.

Rafael translates everything in Spanish; then the Monastery's medic takes the stage for his presentation.

Irina is anxious to hear anything about first aid. As the medic covers shoulder relocation, she meets Rafael's eyes, where he stands beside the stage, translating into Spanish for the ham radio audience. People eat lunch in their seats as Irina prepares for her presentation on training working horses. She stands before the audience, recounting how she'd trained Lily with the cart and plow. She answers several questions, then her forty-five minutes are up, and she sighs in relief.

As she walks back to the trading building to check in with Mark, a man calls out her name. She turns to find a clean-shaven stranger in a worn polo shirt and jeans.

"Can I help you?" she asks him.

"I wanted to apologize to you," he says.

Irina is confused. "For what?"

"You stopped on my farm two years ago," he says. Irina feels a rush of shame and trepidation as she places his face. There are plenty of people around, and she's armed, she reassures herself.

"I was distraught, and I threatened you, and I'm sorry," he says.

She doesn't know what to say, but he continues, "I'm living by the Monastery now, but when I saw you up there, I recognized you, and I wanted to say how sorry I am."

"Thank you," she manages to reply finally. He turns and walks away, leaving her to consider the vast distance she's traveled since that day. She walks out to the far end of the fairgrounds, where the open land fades into a residential neighborhood. She is, at the same time, the person she's always been but also not. She considers that terrified, grief-stricken woman who stood beside her bicycle, retching into the woods after her encounter outside of Grants Pass two years before, and she feels both shame and pride at the same time. She hates that she was so weak, so devastated, but she's proud to have come so far. She's carved out a life and a love for herself. She's created a future for her son and has adopted a daughter. She, Rafael, and the other founders have built something that may last. She's found contentment, even joy, on the other side of devastation.

She turns and walks back to the amphitheater, not wanting to miss Rafael's presentation. He's handed off translation responsibilities to Julián, and he's now sitting in the audience with Tina and Shasta. Irina sits down beside him and takes his hand.

"I can't believe you got me to agree to give a public presentation," he whispers to her. "I've never spoken in front of this many people!"

"Just imagine them all in their underwear."

He winks at her. "I'll imagine you in your underwear."

"You can imagine my rolling my eyes," Tina remarks. Rafael gets up and takes the stage.

Irina watches him with pride as he describes the basic principles of electricity, options for hydropower and wind power, configurations of solar panels, and the problem of batteries. He's brought a few small prototypes, and he demonstrates them while discussing places where key components might be salvaged. He doesn't ever look fully comfortable on the stage, but he does a good job anyway.

+++

The next morning Rafael translates into the ham radio, while Irina takes extensive notes. She listens with fascination to the Tribe members discussing edible and medicinal plants. She's pleased to see that several attendees have signed up for the "open mic" slots, including presentations on meat preservation, fishing techniques, and organic pest-control and fertilization methods. They wrap up the final training late in the afternoon, and groups of people congregate around fires, eating, drinking, and laughing. Several people congratulate Irina and Gail on the success of the conference.

Rafael watches as Irina passes when Tina offers her the bottle of wine. She stays up late again, answering questions about Ferndale from two men from San Francisco, who are interested in joining the town.

When she opens the flap to the tent, Rafael is lying on his back in the dim light, staring at the lantern hanging from the top of the tent.

"You're late," he says.

"Not that late. It's barely past eleven."

"No . . . ," he says, sitting up and looking at her, "you're late, and you passed on the wine."

Rafael had started keeping track of dates in his notebook in December, figuring that he could do a better job of being supportive if he could anticipate when she'll be upset about another unsuccessful month.

They stare at each other for a few moments, until he asks, "Why didn't you tell me?"

"I wasn't sure how you'd feel about it, and I'm not sure it's anything. There are variabilities."

He opens up his arms, and she goes to him. He resolves not to bungle things this time, and he sets aside his fears and ambivalence to say what he knows she longs to hear. "I hope it's something."

They talk for a while about ideas for the fall conference. Finally he turns out the lantern. She falls asleep quickly beside him, but he lies awake for a long time in the company of familiar worries.

Hours later, someone wakes Irina from a dead sleep. She opens her eyes in the darkness to see a figure looming above her; she wants to scream, thinking of the man from outside Grants Pass, but a hand covers her mouth. Despite the self-defense training she's received while in Ferndale, Irina's body freezes in familiar terror.

"Shhh!" a voice hisses above her.

Slowly, Irina's eyes adjust to the darkness, and she realizes that it's Tina looming over her. Tina releases her with a finger to her lips in the semidarkness.

"Thieves outside," Tina whispers. "Get your gun." Irina nods and inclines her head toward Rafael. Tina shakes her head no.

Irina stumbles through the darkness and searches blindly for the gun she'd tucked carelessly into her bag. This day had seemed ordinary enough that it hadn't occurred to her that she might have to use her gun.

Irina and Tina slink out of the tent and into the chilly night, crouching low to the ground. Irina surmises that it must be a few hours before dawn, because everyone has settled into their tents, and the campfires have died down to embers. The campground is illuminated only by the half moon. Irina hears nothing but the night insects, a faint scuffling near Ferndale's EVs, and her own heartbeat in her ears.

Ferndale's five tents are arranged in a semicircle, with an extinguished fire pit in the middle. Nearby, Six Rivers Tribe's eight tents are in a loose cluster around the dying embers of a larger fire. Beyond them are Ferndale's three EVs, which gleam dimly in the moonlight.

Irina follows Tina between the shadows of the tents, trying to step as lightly as possible. They join Mark behind one of the cars. Tina signals toward the other car about twenty feet away, where two shadows are having a whispered argument about how to open the embedded door handles. Irina's gun feels slippery in her sweaty palm. She's never shot at another person. She's never had to.

Looking at the scene before them, she's fairly certain that she's going to have to shoot quickly if these men—she's assuming they're men—try to fire. There are lots of tents around that could get hit by stray bullets if they get into a prolonged gunfight. She does mental calculations of trajectories in her head. She'll need to keep her shots angled as low as possible to minimize the chance of hitting any of the tents beyond the vehicles. She hopes that Mark and Tina are making similar calculations, but there's no way for her to confirm that, without risking the thieves' hearing their conversation.

"Step away from the car," Tina says loudly. "Put your hands up."

One of them reaches toward his waistband. Tina doesn't hesitate before shooting, hitting the man and shattering the car window behind him. The other shadow lifts a gun, and Mark fires off two quick shots. The man's body jerks backward against the car. A third shadow appears from behind a bush. Irina aims and fires, just before Tina gets off a shot. That man staggers, then falls to the ground with a loud cry. The entire exchange takes only seconds.

Irina can hear the other campers waking up. There are exclamations of panic and confusion from the tents around her. On the ground, the thieves writhe and scream in pain. The car alarm shrieks belatedly. Somewhere, Rafael calls out her name. Her ears ring from the gunshots. Her wrist aches from the recoil.

"Irina!" Rafael exclaims, pulling her to him. She feels disoriented. He leads her back to a spot by the dying campfire. Her legs shake, so he helps her sit down on the dusty ground. She trembles as the cold night air seeps in under her thin pajamas, and panic fills her. Her stomach churns, and for a moment she's sure she's going to throw up. She struggles to recall the words of her favorite book. She regrets leaving it at home.

She hears three more shots; then the thieves' cries stop. She tries hard not to think too much about what that means.

"I think I shot him," she says. "Them. Someone."

Rafael brings her water, then says he'll be back in a minute. She can hear him arguing with Tina in hushed tones.

Irina's mind goes to work justifying her actions. She recalls the glint of the weapons in the dull moonlight, the shadow appearing from behind the bush. She thinks about all the other people in the tents nearby. She recalls Tina's admonition that they aren't obligated to put themselves at risk to save people who would steal from them.

Tina sits down next to her, with Rafael on her other side.

"You missed him," Tina says. "You need to work on your aim. I got him, though."

Others have gathered. The two men Irina had been talking to earlier that evening drag the bodies away. Irina takes short, choppy breaths. She recalls her possible pregnancy. Will she miscarry again from this stress? Rafael crowds her, and Tina tells him to give Irina some space. She crouches down a few feet in front of Irina, her dark brown eyes meeting Irina's. "Breathe. Count."

'How does she know this?' Irina wonders. She breathes. She counts. The world begins to reassemble in front of her. Her heart rate slows, and she feels suddenly exhausted. She stands up and walks wordlessly back to the tent. She hears Rafael speak in a sharp tone to Tina as he follows Irina. They lie down in their zipped-together sleeping bags, and he wraps himself around her. Then the darkness finds her.

+++

A morning search of nearby buildings reveals that the thieves had struck several other campsites and stashed things there. The owners of the items reclaim them. Tina speculates that the thieves were hoping to hotwire the cars to carry away the rest of what they'd stolen. Irina overhears several people saying that the thieves got what they had coming to them, but she also hears a rumor that the Mennonites, unhappy with the violence, have promised not to return.

Mark seems a bit withdrawn, but Irina sees Julián and Tina speaking with him several times as they pack that morning. Irina senses that Rafael is watching her closely, trying to gauge how upset she is.

"This was an inauspicious end to our first trade conference," Irina says to Gail as Rafael finishes packing up the car. "Do you think people will still come back in the fall?"

Gail shrugs, "I think a lot of them will. We'll just need to work on security next time. Other than the thieves, I think this went really well. Lots of people have told me so."

Irina is unconvinced, but she says goodbye to Gail and Rick and gets into the passenger seat of the blue car. She's quiet as Rafael navigates out of Red Bluff toward home.

"Are you alright?" he asks.

"I think I'm fine," she says, uncertainly. "I don't think we had a choice."

"It's still a really hard thing to have to do," Rafael says. Irina senses that they are different in some essential way. She strongly suspects that her shot was true and Tina had lied to her. Yet she doesn't feel as tortured about this as she knows Rafael feels about the mountain man.

325

Should she feel worse? Is something wrong with her? She longs to discuss this with Rafael but worries that if she admits to feeling comparatively untroubled, he may think less of her, so she changes the subject and puts on some music, and they recall the concerts they used to go to Before and the things they miss about modernity. The hours pass, and before they know it they're back in Ferndale. They decide to take the afternoon off to take the kids and Buddy to Centerville Beach.

Irina sits in the shadow of the large white cement cross that adorns the dunes and watches Matteo playing, marveling at how much he's grown. He looks more like Sam every day—his hair has even begun to stick out awkwardly at the sides, just as his father's did. A few months before his third birthday, he suddenly began speaking in full sentences. Irina is grateful that he's still little enough, though, to come into Irina's bedroom many mornings and curl up in bed with her for snuggles.

Miranda minds Matteo, ensuring that he stays a safe distance from the surf as they pick up stones, and when she sees shorebirds, she points them out to him. A bald eagle flies overhead, and Irina gets out the binoculars so the children can get a closer look. The day is beautiful and ordinary, and it sets Irina's mind at ease.

+++

Rafael is pretty sure Tina can tell that he's been avoiding her, which is why he isn't surprised when she corners him in one of the warehouse classrooms two days after they return.

"You're still mad about Red Bluff," she says.

He sighs and turns to face her from where he's been searching for a new pair of boots. "Yes. I'm unhappy that you pulled Irina into that. You could have woken me instead."

"You would have hesitated. And in that situation, your hesitation could have caused you—or someone else—to get hurt," Tina says, sitting down in one of the chairs. "In a crowded place with a bunch of tents, I needed a small number of people with good aim who wouldn't hesitate."

Rafael purses his lips in frustration, and Tina continues, "I'm not insulting you or your masculinity or whatever."

"It kind of feels like you are," he says, turning back to his task.

"We're friends in part because you're the kind of guy who hesitates, who thinks about things, who tries to avoid hurting anyone," Tina says. "But Irina's a survivor. She doesn't hesitate."

"She's survived enough," he replies, his back still to her. "Even before the Pandemic, she'd lost her mother and daughter. She doesn't need any more trauma."

"That's not how it works," Tina says. "The universe doesn't dish out misfortunes fairly."

"This wasn't the universe!" Rafael exclaims, turning to her. "It was you, your choice to involve her instead of picking Julián or Shasta."

"Julián and Shasta just shot two men a few months ago. I was not going to involve them!"

He sighs in exasperation. "Just don't ask Irina to do something like that again, I don't want her having to deal with killing a person."

"She didn't kill anyone, though; she missed, remember?" Tina says, raising her eyebrows meaningfully. He realizes belatedly that it had been a lie, concocted for Irina's benefit.

He recalls all the losses in Irina's life. "Please, Tina. Irina isn't as tough as she looks. I don't want her to carry that kind of guilt."

Tina sighs. "Fine. I'll try to avoid it next time. But she'd be pissed if she knew we were having this conversation."

"I know," he concedes, "which is why I'm trusting you not to tell her."

"I won't tell her," Tina assures him. "But you should remember that this isn't the modern world. Other people aren't playing by modern world rules, and we can't afford to either. Sooner or later, everyone will have to make moral compromises."

"Would you put Emma in that position?" he asks her.

"Emma's like you. She would have hesitated. So no; she wouldn't be my first pick." Tina considers for a moment, then says, "But one day it might be unavoidable."

"I hope not," he says, frowning. He looks at her keenly. "Does it ever bother you?"

"Having to shoot someone?" she asks. He nods, and she continues. "Not really, to be honest. It's my job to protect the people of Ferndale. If I fail at that, every person I care about could be at risk. I won't torment myself over shooting someone who threatens me or people I love."

"Some of these situations could be avoided, though," he replies.

"How? I told them to drop their weapons. They decided not to, so I had no choice. There's no room for hesitation in that moment. Hesitation costs lives. Weakness costs lives."

She sighs. "Look, I know you don't see the world this way, but I need you to believe me when I say that there are a lot of dangerous people out there. If we don't project strength, if we don't stand up for ourselves, if we don't neutralize threats . . . , they will overpower us. We—I—have an obligation to this town to prevent that from happening."

"I know there are dangerous people out there," he says with irritation. "I'm not naive. But I also think it's our obligation to react to that in a way that upholds our own principles. Otherwise we're no different from the people you say we need to neutralize."

She scoffs. "Trust me, Rafael; we are very different from the kind of people I'm talking about. And our survival depends on our being strong enough to effectively defend ourselves. Your job is wind turbines. Mine is security. I need you to respect my decisions here."

There's a long moment of silence. Finally, he says, "Fine. But next time, keep Irina out of it."

Chapter Twenty-One

They try out Mark's electric combine for the wheat harvest the following week. Mark and Rafael are disappointed to find that the batteries don't last as long as they'd hoped, but still, it eliminates a few fields' worth of hard labor. When the wheat is harvested and processed, they celebrate long into the night. Irina, having confirmed her pregnancy with several tests from a Fortuna pharmacy, confides her condition to Emma as they sip mint tea together. They compare due dates and are thrilled to realize that they're only seven weeks apart.

Still, most of the time, Irina and Rafael have an unspoken superstitious agreement not to mention the pregnancy. Irina does her best to conceal her morning sickness, and they tell no one but the other founders.

The town struggles to clear out houses and plant new fields fast enough to accommodate the steady stream of new arrivals. Visitors also arrive regularly to make use of Ferndale's livestock stud services. Several times, Julián, Danielle, Oliver O'Donnell—one of the men who had joined Ferndale after talking to Irina at the trade conference—transport Ferndale's female livestock to other communities for breeding. Irina oversees the town's first criminal trial—for two men accused of fist fighting over a woman. She sentences them to extra labor.

The night before the Summer Solstice, Ify brings Yumi with him to the founders' evening gathering in Julián's backyard, and they announce that they'll be getting married the following weekend. Rafael isn't surprised. He'd seen Yumi leaving Ify's house several mornings when he'd woken early to go fishing. Still, he's a bit concerned about their sixteen-year age difference. Irina, though, is happy that Ify has found someone who could potentially have children with him. She's often wondered how he survived after losing all of his children and not having another.

The wedding is a small gathering on Centerville Beach on a clear afternoon with a sapphire sky and a strong breeze. Ify looks happier than Irina has ever seen him.

When their ninety-eighth resident arrives during the final week of June, Shantal confirms that there still isn't anyone in the community with an economics background, so Ify and Irina do their best to formulate a currency plan on their own. They begin using the blacksmith forge to melt down pre-Pandemic coins and mint new ones.

All members of the community are required to attend the next Council meeting so that Ify and Irina can explain their currency system.

"Everyone will be issued equal quarterly payments in currency," Ify tells them. "Food, medical care, childcare, housing, and other necessities will continue to be provided universally, without a fee. Community-owned items—like household goods, additional clothing, or specialty food items—will be available for purchase at stores downtown. You can also buy privately-produced items from other members of the community."

"My moonshine is available!" Julián says with a smile.

"We'd also like to remind everyone that materials salvaged within Ferndale or on official work time are community property and must be surrendered to our Inventory Manager, Shasta. If, in your free time, you want to salvage materials from Fortuna or other communities, you can keep or sell those," Irina tells the crowd.

"We'll periodically assess supply-and-demand levels and inflation and make adjustments to currency disbursements," Ify concludes.

There are many questions, but the community seems mostly to accept the change.

Two weeks later, Rafael and his apprentices depart on bicycles for a month of wind turbine and water treatment construction for the Six Rivers Tribe. He's apprehensive about leaving Irina while she's pregnant, but she assures him that she'll be fine and they need to honor their agreements. Though they talk on the ham radio several times per week, she misses him terribly.

As she stands before the mirror each morning, surveying the ways her body is changing, she feels renewed gratitude for Rafael's choice to give her this gift, despite his reservations. She touches the tattoo over her heart and vows to be a better partner, to find more small ways to express her love, to do more to make him happy.

With that vow in mind, Irina buys some extra corn from the town's store and works with Benoit to try to make arepa flour. It's been more than a year since they'd used the last of the pre-Pandemic arepa flour, yet they haven't found the correct preparation to reproduce it. Benoit has a breakthrough, though, when Irina shows him an empty bag she's pulled from their landfill in Fortuna.

"Pre-cooked," he reads. "That's an important detail."

While Rafael is away, Irina also spends many hours with Emma, who's happy to receive any pregnancy advice and information Irina provides. The Saturday before Rafael is scheduled to return, Emma and Irina rent one of the electric cars and drive down to the Eel River. It's an especially warm day for Ferndale, and Emma is in her sixth month of pregnancy and feeling increasingly uncomfortable. They pull down the gravel drive to access the river, then they carefully pick their way down the path to the water. The water level looks lower than Irina remembers its being, but there are still a few places where it's deep enough to swim. They both wade in, laughing, and float on their backs with their bellies sticking up out of the water.

"This is much better," Emma says. She closes her eyes in the sunlight and touches her stomach when she feels a kick. "No one told me that pregnancy was so uncomfortable."

"I'm sure they did," Irina laughs, knowing that it will only get worse. "You just didn't want to hear it."

"Well, they didn't tell me the specifics! Just that it wasn't pleasant," Emma replies with a smile. "You're probably right, though, I didn't want to hear it. I've always wanted to have babies. Tina and I were actually planning on trying with artificial insemination when she got back from the Marines. Then the Pandemic happened."

"How's Tina doing with this?" Irina asks.

"She's worried. She wasn't entirely on board with the idea, given our situation, but I've waited years, and I didn't want to wait anymore. I want to have a big family, three or four kids, so we needed to get moving." Emma reaches down to press lightly where she feels another kick. "What about Rafael?"

"I think he's pretty worried, but he won't tell me so," Irina says. He's been more irritable than usual since she's been pregnant, and before he left, she'd woken in the middle of the night several times to find him gone from their bed, reading in the living room. She wonders if he regrets their decision. Still, he'd joined her for several ultrasounds at Ify's office in May and June, and he helped to plan the joint baby shower for her and Emma that Yumi will be hosting when he returns. Apparently he'd told Gail about the baby, because she'd joined him on the radio one night to congratulate Irina.

As usual, Emma peppers Irina with questions about sleep training, feeding schedules, baby sign language, and a number of other related topics. Irina recounts how she'd managed these things with Clara and Matteo.

"But every baby is different," Irina emphasizes. "What worked for Matteo might not work for your baby. A lot of it is random chance."

"I know," Emma says, "but I want to give her the best foundation possible. If I have the right routines and the right food and the right habits, she'll have the best start possible and the best chance for a good life."

Irina recalls her early conversation with Rafael about trying to affect outcomes in parenthood, and she feels a stab of longing for him. She maintains the belief that much of parenting—and marriage and most human endeavors—is a matter of luck, but she doesn't want to disabuse Emma of her dreams, so she listens as Emma details the reading she's been doing on disciplinary methods, language acquisition, co-regulation, and social and emotional learning. Irina does, however, feel the need to try to keep Emma from falling into the perfectionism trap that many mothers end up in.

"You don't have to be perfect to be a good mother," Irina says. "It's really hard to maintain all of those 'best practices' when you're sleep deprived, stressed, and full of postpartum hormones. You'll have to cut yourself a little slack."

But Emma resists this idea, as Irina had when people had tried to tell her the same thing. "I think I can do it, though. I'll have Tina and François's help. And I'm properly motivated . . . ; after all, what could possibly be more important than this? I've wanted a child my entire life. Even when I was a little girl, I knew I wanted to be a mother."

Irina thinks but doesn't say that romantic notions of motherhood don't hold up well in the face of motherhood's uglier, harsher realities: mastitis, shirts stained with breastmilk, the constant smell of baby spit-up, weeks of alarming postpartum bleeding, and months of sleepless nights that make it hard to string together a coherent sentence, let alone perfect emotional co-regulation. Images of the Madonna and child leave out the stretch marks, incontinence, flattened breasts, and loose skin of the postpartum body. Irina knows that the postpartum glow isn't so much beneficence and joy as it is the oily sheen of a perpetually unwashed face.

Emma asks about Matteo's birth, and Irina tells her the story of that snowy day. She doesn't cut the story off where she should, though, and it strays into her infection and Sam's death, and then she's crying unexpectedly, hot tears rolling down her cheeks and into the cool water of the Eel River. Emma listens sympathetically, crying with her. Out of some misplaced sense of loyalty to Rafael, Irina has never really spoken much about Sam to anyone other than Rafael. It feels strange but cathartic to tell another person about Sam.

The day grows late, and they return to the car, relaxed and just a little bit sunburned.

+++

Rafael feels a rush of relief when he arrives back in Ferndale, and he wraps his arms around his family in the late afternoon light on their front porch. He longs to get Irina alone, but knows there are several hours between now and his first opportunity for that. It's shocking to him that he survived literally years of abstinence, given that a month now seems nearly unbearable.

After several days on the road, he's also exceedingly grateful for the dinner Benoit has prepared. He eats enthusiastically, while recounting the details of his trip to Mark and Julián. Irina sits beside him, running her hand teasingly up his thigh under the table. He's glad for the distraction of the conversation, which keeps his body from reacting too enthusiastically to her touch.

They join Emma and Tina to take the children to the playground as the sun sinks toward the western horizon. Rafael and Tina play tag with the children until sunset; then they all walk back home. Rafael looks fondly at the town as they stroll down Main Street with the children running in front of them. The summer evening is lit pink, with towering cumulus clouds hanging over the forested foothills to the south and east.

Irina and Rafael sit in Miranda's bed while she reads a bedtime story to Matteo. Then finally Rafael and Irina are alone in their own bedroom. He lights a fire in the woodburning stove he'd installed there the prior winter. He stands, and for a moment they look at each other with uncertainty and a little shyness. Irina feels a stab of self-consciousness about her pregnant body. Then he crosses the room and pulls her into his arms, their shadows merging on the wall.

He undresses her with reverence, surprised by how much her body has changed in the month that he's been gone. He appreciates the new fullness of her breasts, the glow of her skin, the places where her curves have softened. She takes off his clothing, and he sees her desire as her eyes sweep over his bare skin.

"I missed you," he says. "I dreamed about you all the time."

She smiles. "What was your favorite dream?"

"I'll show you," he replies, leading her over to the bed and lying down with her. His lips trace a path down her neck, her breasts, and the swell of her belly as he kneels between her open thighs. He plants teasing kisses on her hip bones and thighs before finally giving in to her increasingly fervent pleas. He loves the taste of her and the sounds she makes. She's taken the time to teach him, and he's made an effort to listen, so he knows what she likes. She isn't sure if it's the pregnancy or the fact that he's been gone for a month, but she feels every sensation more acutely. She begs him not to stop. His lips are on her, and his name is on her lips as the wave of pleasure overwhelms her. She pulls back, unable to bear the sensation of even one more touch. He kisses his way back up her body slowly, allowing her to recover, before he aligns his hips with hers.

She pulls him toward her, but he's a bit tentative because of the pregnancy. "Tell me if I hurt you."

"You won't," she says, her voice breathy with desire. "Just do what you usually do. I love what you usually do."

He smiles. "Yes, ma'am. The usual, then."

She laughs against his lips as she kisses him and pulls him into her. He stills for a moment, looking into her eyes; he traces the line of her cheek with his fingers gently.

"I love you."

"And I love you."

After a month apart and a half hour together in bed, his body is sensitive to her every move. She rocks her hips against him, touches his chest, bites his neck gently the way she knows he likes. She reaches to touch her own body, and they're both surprised when she finishes with him as he buries himself deep inside her and cries out.

They lie beside each other, skin on skin. "I missed this," she says.

"You missed me or you missed sex?" He laughs.

"Sex, childcare, house cleaning, the way you can still make a perfect cup of tea from long-expired tea leaves. All the services you provide . . . ."

"I'm glad to be so indispensable," he jokes, kissing her neck as she sighs happily.

She turns toward him, suddenly serious. "And I missed talking to you. You're my best friend."

"And you're mine."

"Really? Not Tina or Ify or Julián?"

"There's no one else I trust like I trust you."

She's surprisingly moved by this. For a long time they talk, catching each other up on the updates they couldn't give on the radio.

The next morning, Rafael skips his usual fishing trip to stay in bed with his wife. After making love again, she slips out from under the sheets enigmatically, wrapping a robe around herself and telling him to wait there. A half hour later, she reappears with the first arepa he's seen in a year. It's rich with melted butter and farmers cheese and fresh eggs. He almost cries from the thoughtfulness of the gesture and the nostalgia it inspires.

+++

Rafael and Tina sit on the porch of the bed and breakfast with their tumblers of whiskey, watching the people gathered in the street and on the lawn for the Autumn Equinox party. Emma and Irina, both obviously pregnant, are laughing as they hand out slices of honey cake.

Rafael's initial relief at Irina's finally getting—and staying—pregnant has ebbed as his anxiety over the particulars of childbirth without modern medicine has increased. He's fallen back to his childhood Catholicism and has begun praying and even occasionally attending services at Julián's church, hoping that Irina won't find out.

Lately, Rafael hardly sleeps. He often wakes at 3:00 a.m. and lies in bed, watching Irina breathe, filled with existential terror and a certainty that he will lose her. He doesn't tell her this, of course. He knows that if he did she would only tell him that she's done this before, that most women throughout history have done this. He remembers, though, the infection that she'd gotten after Matteo's birth, and the fear of that constantly follows him.

"Are you as worried about the risks of childbirth as I am?" Rafael asks Tina as they watch their wives.

"Hell yeah, I'm worried," she says. "This was a terrible idea."

"It really was. We already have two kids," Rafael replies. "I don't understand why Irina was so set on having another baby."

"Maybe she just really wanted to have your baby," Tina says. Rafael can hear something he's pretty sure is sadness in her voice. He imagines what it would be like to be in Tina's place, knowing that she and her wife can never have a child that is biologically both of theirs. It makes him deeply melancholy. These days, he finds that the lack of sleep and the ambient level of anxiety in his life bring all of his emotions—sadness, frustration, irritation—close to the surface.

The idea that Irina would have so desperately wanted to have his child—that she loves him that much, that she sees something extraordinary enough in him to want to have a child that shares his genes—tips him right over into embarrassing emotionality. His eyes betray him with tearfulness.

Tina looks over at him, and her sadness snaps back so immediately that Rafael knows that her humor is a coping mechanism born of great adversity.

"What's the matter, man," she says; "pregnancy hormones getting to you? You need a tissue?" She chuckles.

"Smartass," Rafael responds, shaking his head with a wry smile.

"Emma keeps telling me that everything will be alright. Birth is natural," Tina says.

Death is also natural, Rafael knows. To point this out would probably only increase Tina's anxiety, though, so he keeps that thought to himself.

He watches Irina. She looks happy. The woman that he knew—the advocate, the comedian, the friend, the lover, the mother—has returned. Rafael's depression has eased. And yet . . . his anxiety has created a new distance between them. He knows he can't burden her with his worries, so he keeps these thoughts to himself, which means that he sometimes feels lonely in her presence. He hopes that this will pass, that their marriage will shift again like a kaleidoscope. They've only known each other for two and a half years, he reminds himself, and in that time so much has happened. He'll wait, as he had during that first year when they were friends, that March when she had kissed him and the prior year when they had struggled to conceive.

Irina looks up at him, and their eyes meet, and she smiles as the sight of him brings her joy. His worries ease a little.

"I heard our hundred thirtieth resident arrived yesterday," Tina remarks. "We're going to need to open up some more professional slots. I was thinking 'brewer-distiller.'"

"Of course you were," Rafael says. "I was thinking of another junior engineer. We need more wind turbines."

"We also need to enjoy our lives," Tina replies.

"Julián told me that we could use some more agricultural positions too. We really need to be plowing and planting even more land. Last winter was too tight."

Mark had rigged up a plow on the skid steer, which had helped, but, like the combine, the batteries seemed to have suffered from sitting outdoors for several years without use. The way things were trending, the horses were looking more and more important. Brady's gelding had proven useful for hauling and plowing, especially when Lily had to take time off after foaling. Irina had also successfully trained Sunshine to haul and plow, which gave them a two-horse team for heavier tasks.

Rafael's new wind turbines, which they had erected along the coast near the House by the Sea, are far better generators of electricity than their predecessors, but even the coastal wind isn't enough for consistent wind power. The lead-acid car batteries have mostly ceased to function, so they've started cannibalizing whatever lithium batteries and extra solar panel batteries they can find to fill the gaps. Rafael never forgets that any progress they make is temporary. Every piece of technology has a deadline.

Chapter Twenty-Two

Two nights later, Irina awakens to someone's knocking softly on her bedroom door. She gets up, thinking it must be Miranda with one of the nightmares that she still occasionally has. When she opens the door, she's surprised to find Yumi on the other side.

Still half asleep, she somewhat irritably asks Yumi what she's doing in her house in the middle of the night.

"Emma is in labor."

"No. She's got almost two months left."

"She's in labor. She's asking for you."

A lead weight settles in Irina's stomach. It's far too early for Emma to have the baby. She wakes Rafael, and they dress. They pass Jing sleeping on the couch in their living room on their way out. They leave Yumi with the children and walk with trepidation to Emma and Tina's front door, then follow the sound of voices upstairs. Rafael hangs back for the sake of Emma's privacy, while Irina steps into Tina and Emma's bedroom. Emma is pacing awkwardly, her blonde hair matted to her forehead. Tina holds her hand. Infrequently, Emma groans in pain. Beside the bed is Ify's ultrasound machine. Irina takes Ify outside into the hall, where Rafael lingers awkwardly against the wall.

"How long has she been in labor?" Irina asks.

"She's been in active labor for several hours already," Ify replies. "But there's a problem. I checked with the ultrasound, and the baby is in breech position, feet down."

"Can you still deliver a baby that way?" Irina says.

He sighs. "I've only ever delivered horses. I have no experience with childbirth, other than holding my wife's hand during my own children's births. The books tell me, though, that this is a dangerous situation. It's early, so the baby's head is large in proportion to her body, and she may get stuck. The cord could get pinched," his voice breaks, "and Emma could hemorrhage, and there's nothing I can offer her other than expired medication. I've tried what the books recommend—turning the baby by pressing on Emma's stomach—but it didn't work. The usual solution to this problem is a c-section, but we have no anesthesia."

"Can I do anything?" Rafael asks.

"Get Julián, and go to the NICU in Eureka. The baby is early and will need some help breathing and staying warm. Bring back one of the NICU warming units. Yumi can tell you how to sanitize it. Grab a couple of the oxygen tanks and hookups too. Connect them to a battery generator." Ify scratches down a list of medication names on a small notepad. "Find these if you can . . . and look in the maternity ward for forceps." Ify scratches a picture for Rafael.

Rafael looks at Irina. It's clear on her face that she doesn't want him to leave, but she knows he has to. She kisses him and sends him off into the night.

Rafael bangs on Julián's door until he hears footsteps inside. Julián answers in nothing but boxer shorts, his hair disheveled. Rafael explains the situation to him. Julián asks him to wait while he dresses. Rafael hears him conversing with someone in his bedroom before he re-emerges with Shasta behind him. It occurs to Rafael how little they all know of each other's lives, despite being close friends.

"How can I help?" Shasta asks.

"Take the car to the pharmacy in Fortuna and look for these." He scrawls a copy of the list of medications for her.

He and Julián speed to Eureka. Rafael retraces the path to the NICU by memory. He and Julián disconnect the warming unit and carry it awkwardly down the stairs to the waiting car and bungee it inside the open trunk. They return for several oxygen tanks and a pair of what Rafael assumes are forceps.

In the hospital pharmacy, they find two of the four medications Ify had listed. They stop at two other pharmacies before finding one of the others. They make a final stop at the wind turbine charging site to get two battery-powered generators.

In Emma's bedroom, Irina crouches awkwardly on the floor as Emma kneels on her hands and knees. Tina rubs Emma's back with shaking hands as her wife cries in pain.

A few hours later, Rafael and Julián arrive with the warming unit and the oxygen tanks. They follow Yumi's instructions to sanitize the warming unit; then they connect it to a battery generator in the spare bedroom, leaving the generator off until it's needed. As they work, they can hear Emma's cries from the other room. Rafael feels queasy. Shasta brings them several of the medications on the list, including the one they're missing.

Hours pass. Rafael falls into restless sleep on the couch in the living room just before dawn. At breakfast time, François arrives, looking distraught.

"Emma is in labor?!" he asks Rafael.

Rafael gives him all the updates he's received. They sit on the couch together. François cries openly, and Rafael is suddenly certain that François is the father. Rafael wraps his arms around François, who sobs into his shoulder.

Irina stays by Emma's side, though she feels on the verge of collapse. Emma shifts positions without relief. With Emma's permission, Ify has Emma lie down on the bed as he inexpertly tries several maneuvers from a book with nothing to guide him but roughly sketched diagrams and written instructions. He repeats this several times without success. Time lengthens. Hours pass. The noon sun shines into hell through Victorian stained-glass windows. Ify checks again, then reports that the baby's feet have emerged but that the baby is in distress and the amniotic fluid is stained with meconium. Tina leaves to use the bathroom. Rafael finds her sobbing in the downstairs hallway.

"I should have said no to this," she cries into his already wet shoulder as he holds her tightly. "I should have fucking said no. I'm going to lose her. I won't live without her. I can't even remember my life before her."

Before he can formulate a response, she pulls away abruptly to re-join her wife in the bedroom.

The day grows late, and shadows stretch across the bedroom. Emma lies in her bed, exhausted and wracked with pain. Ify reassesses and says that labor seems to have stalled.

"Please," Emma sobs. "Save her. Cut me open, do whatever you have to do. Just save her."

"I can't do a c-section," Ify says. "That's out of the question."

"Obviously!" Tina almost shouts, "but you have to do something!"

"I'm doing everything I can," Ify says, pulling Irina and Tina into the hall. "I'm not an obstetrician. I'm not even a doctor! I don't know what else to try."

His voice breaks as he begins to cry. "I'm so sorry, Tina. I think the cord might be prolapsed, and I don't know what else to do."

"Do whatever you have to do to save Emma."

He takes a deep breath and returns to the room to try a different maneuver with Irina pressing on Emma's stomach as tears run down both their faces and the daylight fades from the room. It doesn't work, and Ify tries to use the forceps. Finally, the baby emerges, but when she does, there's no sound but Emma's sobs. Emma goes silent, and time stands still as Ify tries resuscitation. Tina cries silently as she holds her wife. There is so much blood. Irina can't breathe, but she also knows she can't leave.

"I'm sorry," Ify says in a broken voice. "I'm so sorry."

Irina cleans the baby and wraps her tiny body up in a blanket as Emma delivers the placenta. Emma reaches for the bundled body of her child and clutches it to her chest, sobbing. Tina holds them both tightly. Ify turns away, wiping his tears furiously with his forearm.

Irina flees out the door, down the stairs, and into the living room, where François and Rafael are sitting miserably.

"It's over," Irina says, "The baby . . . ."

She isn't sure how to finish the sentence. She's sleep deprived and horrified. She collapses against Rafael, burying her head in his shoulder. Upstairs, she hears Emma's loud sobs resume. She feels lightheaded and realizes suddenly that it's been almost twenty-four hours since she's eaten. Small black dots encroach on her vision, and then the world goes dark.

She wakes in her own bed. For a moment she's sure she's had a terrible nightmare—except that she's still wearing sweaty blood-stained clothes. Her heart races. Her thoughts swirl. She tries to tamp it down, but her mind keeps returning to memories of Emma's labor. That bleeds into other memories: Clara's final days in the hospital, the sounds of Sam's shovel hitting dirt. She can't breathe. Then Rafael is beside her, holding a cup of apple cider to her lips as she drinks it slowly, then crawling into bed beside her and wrapping her in his arms. She turns to face him, burying her head against his shoulder, and their tears commingle. They fall into troubled sleep.

Irina wakes as the first tendrils of light reach into the sky. She slips out of bed, changes into clean clothes, and goes to look for Matteo and Miranda, wanting to be reassured of their presence. Miranda is asleep in her bed with Jing on one side of her and Matteo curled up on her other side. Buddy sleeps at their feet. Irina stands in the doorway for a long time, looking at them, praying a silent prayer of gratitude, until Rafael steps behind her and wraps his arms around her. She turns to him, closing the door behind her.

"I need to go to Eureka," she tells him.

"Irina, you need to rest. Whatever you want, I'll get it; just please go back to bed."

Irina reluctantly agrees to let him go to Eureka in her stead, but she has no intention of going back to bed. She gives him a short list of items to buy. As soon as he's left, she scratches a note for Yumi, who's asleep on their couch, and goes next door.

"You should be resting!" Ify says as soon as he sees her. "Go lie down. There's nothing more you can do here."

Irina waves him off. "How is Emma?"

"She's devastated. And she's still bleeding a lot. I don't know if that's normal, so I gave her some medication in case she's hemorrhaging. I have no idea if it will work though. We also have to keep a close watch for infection. I tried to follow Yumi's instructions on sanitizing as closely as possible, but this isn't a sterile setting."

Irina nods. She opens the door to the bedroom. Inside, Emma sleeps with Tina curled up in bed next to her. In a chair a few feet away, François dozes in an uncomfortable-looking position. The baby's body is tucked in the bassinet beside the bed.

As Irina enters, Tina's eyes flutter open. She asks about Jing in a whisper. Irina tells Tina she's sleeping peacefully.

Emma wakes; for a moment she's disoriented; then she looks around and Irina can see her realization. Irina knows that feeling—the momentary forgetting, then the crushing memory of reality. She takes Emma's hand.

At 6:00 a.m., Benoit arrives with breakfast. No one is very hungry, but Ify pushes them to eat. Benoit stays with François until it's time to make breakfast for the rest of Ferndale. Emma falls back asleep just before Rafael returns at 7:30 a.m. He's unhappy to find Irina not resting. They exchange terse words about it in the hall before he departs to get the children ready for the day.

Irina steps back into the bedroom with the bag of items Rafael had brought. "Have you given her a name?" Irina asks Tina.

"Selah Marie."

Tina watches as Irina carefully unwraps the tiny bundle and presses Selah's small hand into an inkpad, then onto a piece of watercolor paper. Irina repeats this with Selah's feet, marveling at how tiny and perfect her toes are. She tries to keep her tears from falling on the paper and ruining the prints there. She gently washes the ink off of Selah's cold skin. The air-dry clay is a little stiff, but she's able to get decent impressions of Selah's foot and hand. She sets them aside to dry.

"Are you going to dress her?" Tina asks.

"I think we should let Emma do it, if she wants."

Tina nods. "Thank you," she says tearfully.

"Someone did this for me," Irina says. She doesn't even remember who. "Is there someone from your church you'd like me to bring?"

"Emma and François usually lead our services. He's already prayed over her."

Irina struggles to remember what to do next. She'd handled most of the arrangements for Clara's memorial service and cremation. Sam had been too devastated to manage it, and Irina figured it was her penance for causing the accident.

"Do you want me to make an announcement to the community?" Irina asks.

Tina nods. "But please tell people not to stop by."

Irina doesn't need to make an announcement, though, because by breakfast everyone already knows. The cafeteria is quiet, except for the children, who seem oblivious to the adult melancholy that surrounds them.

The next day, they bury Selah in the old cemetery on the outskirts of town. They all pass tombstones adorned with faded artificial flowers and personal mementos as they walk up to the top of the hill where the cemetery stones fade into the pine forest. Emma sits in a decaying lawn chair that had been left there by some now-deceased mourner, watching as Irina and Ify lower the small box into the ground. Her face is blank and her eyes are tearless as François reads funeral rites from a prayer book while she looks out over the town in the valley below them.

François modifies the words, because they don't quite fit for the death of an infant. Tina weeps silently beside her wife, leaning on Rafael. The autumn rains begin as they walk back down the hill to Ferndale.

That night Irina and Rafael lie in bed, listening to the downpour. The weight of the past few days and the impending anniversary of her own daughter's death sit heavily on Irina's chest, making it hard to breathe. She shifts uncomfortably to her side, and Rafael turns to look at her. In his hazel eyes, she sees her own sorrow and fear reflected.

"You were right," she says through her tears, "I shouldn't have taken this risk. I'm so sorry."

He brushes her tears away with his thumb. "Ify said that what happened to Emma was rare. You'll be okay."

He's trying to convince himself as much as her. He desperately wants to believe his own words. "We'll figure something out," he says.

+++

Irina spends as much time with Emma as she can among her other responsibilities. Often they just sit together in the October dimness of Emma's living room. Sometimes they read passages of books aloud to each other or put together puzzles without looking at the pictures on the boxes—something Irina's Aunt Hannah had done with Irina after Clara's death.

Irina sits with Emma as Emma attaches the hospital-grade breast pump to herself. Irina asks her again if she's really sure she wants to continue to do this.

"There's no formula," Emma says. "Lots of women can't breastfeed, and what I'm doing could save another baby's life. I'm going to do it for as long as I can."

Tina had objected stridently to this plan, believing that it would only make it harder for Emma to move through her grief. But Emma held her ground, and Ify had supported her, even going so far as to return to the hospital to get the pump and to ensure that freezer space would be set aside to store the breastmilk. To Irina's knowledge, she's the only other pregnant woman in Ferndale, but Ify's devotion to this plan makes her wonder if he knows something she doesn't.

+++

On the second Friday of October, the Ferndale representatives depart for the autumn trade show. Irina waits in the passenger seat as Rafael asks Tina one final time if she's really sure she wants to come along. She nods, then gets into her car with Jaya, who, after winning the apprenticeship lottery, had recently been selected to become Tina's deputy. Shasta and Ify get into the last car, and they depart with vehicles full of goods that Julián and the Council have approved for trade.

"How's Emma?" Rafael asks Irina as they drive through the verdant mountains.

"About as expected, I think, but it's hard to tell," Irina responds. "I don't really remember what I was like after Clara died. There's this big, disturbing gap in my memory during those first couple of months. I only remember flashes. And everyone grieves differently anyway. So even I don't really know what to expect."

"What parts do you remember?"

It hurts, physically, to go back there in her mind, to remember those stark, surreal days after Clara's death, her desperation and devastation. It's a room in her house that she's closed off and almost never visits.

Finally she says, "I remember that Halloween, driving home from work and seeing the kids out in their costumes and just feeling despair."

"You were already back at work?!"

"I only got a couple of days of bereavement leave. I had to burn all my vacation time just to get two weeks off."

"Jesus."

"I actually thought being at work would be better than being at home in that silent house, surrounded by reminders of her. But nowhere was better. I ended up taking a leave of absence from my job that spring."

"I'm sorry." He squeezes her hand.

"I remember talking to another woman in a child-loss support group I went to. She'd lost her little boy, and the father hadn't been in the picture. She had a crappy job, no money, no family, very few friends. And I thought, at least I have Sam, and Kylee, and my family, and enough money to get by. It was this strange island of gratitude in a sea of grief. I remember getting the explanation of benefits from my health insurance company in the mail. A fifty-thousand-dollar hospital bill that my insurance brought down to 'only' ten thousand dollars. Fifty thousand dollars not to save the life of my child . . . ."

Irina is still filled with anger at the memory of that bill. In hindsight, her rage at that unfairness is a large part of what had driven the politics in the Charter she'd drafted.

"I remember moments when I had enough perspective to think that I might recover someday," she continues. "But mostly I felt despair. I didn't think my life would ever improve. That's where Emma is now, and I don't blame her. She told me that

Ify cautioned her against getting pregnant again. He thinks there may have been some issue with her uterus or cervix that caused the early delivery."

"That's awful."

"I feel like I should be able to help her more," Irina says, feeling tears threaten. "But nothing I say reaches her. Sometimes I wonder if my presence actually makes things worse for her because I'm still pregnant."

"You're doing the best you can. You can't fix this for her."

Irina wipes her eyes with her sleeve.

"How are you doing?" he asks, mindful of the recent anniversary, her concerns about the pregnancy, and the nightmares she often has about Selah's birth.

"I don't know. Okay, I guess." He takes his eyes off the road for a moment to assess her. She doesn't look okay.

"I just have to make it through the next three months," she continues, her voice wavering a little.

"Have you talked to Charlotte?"

Irina nods, "Yes. And I'm trying to get Emma and Tina to join me for Charlotte's Child Loss Support Group. How is Tina? She talks to you."

"Not good. She's upset about the baby, worried about Emma, and concerned about her marriage," he replies.

"It's a hard thing for a marriage to survive."

Rafael knows this. Even the miscarriage had nearly torn apart their marriage. Rafael regrets that he hadn't done a better job of supporting her then, though he knows she doesn't blame him. "I told her she should talk to you, because you and Sam survived losing Clara."

Irina nods. "How are you?"

"I'm managing my anxiety," he replies, but she can see the worry on his face. It radiates off him, even when he tries to hide it for her sake. Aside from her pregnancy, they're headed into another winter, and their infrastructure issues remain.

For a while they're silent; then she changes the subject to something lighter—the upcoming Halloween party. The hours and scenery pass by.

At the fairgrounds, Tina implements her new security strategy. Everyone will camp together with their trade goods in a single large arena with night guards posted at the perimeter. Gail and Irina watch as Tina briefs the night guard volunteers.

"I was sorry to hear that Emma lost the baby," Gail says. "How are you doing with everything?"

Irina's instinct is to say 'fine,' but her emotions are close to the surface, so she says, "Not good. We have no doctor, and Ify is terrified to oversee any more births."

Gail listens with empathy. "Rick and Amy are also worried about Amy's pregnancy."

They catch up for a while about their respective communities and their concerns for the upcoming winter.

"Thanks again for sending Rafael to build the wind turbines and water sanitizer with us," Gail says. "Everything is working well."

"I'll let him know," Irina watches his setting up their tent with fondness. His tendency to worry and take on too much is the other side of his kindness, she knows.

That evening, when Tina returns from her guard shift, Irina is still awake, sitting by the fire, staring into the flames. As Irina pokes the logs with a stick, Tina settles onto the ground a few feet away from her.

"How are you doing?" Irina asks her.

"Pretty fucking awful, to be honest. We lost our baby, and now I feel like I'm going to lose my marriage," Tina pauses. "Rafael said you lost your daughter, but kept your marriage. How?"

It's a clear night, and Irina looks up at the stars as she tries to remember.

"I think it was kindness, faith, and patience," she says finally. "You have to accept that you're going to grieve differently. Emma is probably like me—her grief will be all-consuming. You have to just stand there with her in the devastation and not flinch. Don't try to fix it or change how she's feeling. Just be sad together or sit with her when she's sad, even if it's uncomfortable. Be patient and have faith that she'll come back to you. It might take a long time, and she might be different, but the core of her and your marriage will still be there."

The fire casts flickering shadows on their faces as Irina recounts the things that Sam had done for her, his patience and steadfastness. She feels a sharp stab of longing for him. She still has moments of confusion about loving Rafael while missing Sam. She suspects that will never quite resolve.

She tells Tina about one particularly moving and influential thing Sam had done when Irina was lost in the wilderness of grief. He'd put Irina in contact with a woman named Cecily who had lost her own child a decade before and now ran a café and a program for troubled youth in his honor.

Irina sat at a table in the busy cafe across from Cecily two weeks after Clara's death, picking at her nails as Cecily recounted her own story.

"I can't give you a map through the mountains," Cecily had said to Irina, "but I can tell you that there is something worthwhile on the other side."

Irina had never seen Cecily again, but the woman's words had stuck with her.

Irina looks at Tina in the firelight and says, "When I asked Cecily how her marriage had survived, she said that after her son died, she realized that she and her husband could never divorce, because there would never be another person in the world who would truly understand what it was like to love—and to lose—Ivan. That realization kept her fighting for her marriage even when things got really hard."

The fire before them crackles as Tina digests Irina's words.

"Marriage is so fucking mysterious," Tina says finally. "You have to learn to love a new version of the person every couple of years or so, and they have to learn to love a new version of you, too. There's no way to predict how you'll both change over the course of a lifetime. You just have to place your bet and stay at the table. When Emma and I started dating, I thought: here's this beautiful girl, my best friend. I thought we knew everything about each other. But life happened and several times we've had to relearn each other all over again."

Tina looks up at the sky, blinking back tears. "Does it ever get better?"

Irina remembers her conversation with Rafael that first October. "The proportions change. You feel sad less often. It takes a long time, though."

"I wish that I could fix this," Tina says. "I hate the idea of being pregnant, but if I could do it, I would."

"You can't?"

"I have really bad polycystic ovarian syndrome. Maybe with modern medicine I could have gotten pregnant, but even that wasn't a sure thing. We figured it would be fine, since Emma wanted to carry our children."

"I'm sorry," Irina says. She wants to take Tina's hand or wrap her arms around her, but isn't sure how it will be received. She's never been as close to Tina as Rafael is.

Tina sighs with frustration and says goodnight abruptly, departing to her tent and leaving Irina to watch the fire in the company of her memories.

+++

The conference is, by all accounts, a success. Ferndale's representatives manage to trade for almost everything on their list, and the training slots are completely filled. By Gail's count, they have almost three hundred attendees.

"Seven percent of the remaining state of California, if you believe the Pandemic mortality estimates," Gail says. "We're really doing something here!"

For the first time since Selah's death, Irina feels her grief and anxiety lift just a little bit. On the final morning as they pack their tents, Rafael tells her that he'll need to get Sunshine and go to Redding in December.

"Why?" Irina asks.

"Because I've traded her."

"What!?"

"I've arranged for an obstetrician to come to Ferndale for four months to train us on maternal care and delivery. In exchange, we'll trade her Sunshine, four cows, and three months of my time making wind turbines for her family."

Irina is momentarily dumbfounded, then very angry. She drags him into a small building away from the tents and closes the door behind them.

"The Council didn't authorize that trade!"

"I only found out about her when I got here, so it wasn't possible to get pre-approval." He tries to keep his voice even.

"How do you know that she's actually a doctor?"

"The Monastery medic, Brother Nicholas, is the one who told me about her. She's delivered several babies for women from neighboring communities. Brother Nicholas, Ify, and I vetted her."

"Ify is involved in this?!"

"Yumi is pregnant. And even if she wasn't, Ify doesn't want to feel responsible for another death. What happened with Selah wrecked him."

"Yumi is pregnant?"

He sighs. "They were going to tell everyone, but after Selah, they thought it would be kinder to wait a while."

"This wasn't a good trade, Rafael. Sunshine is one of our most valuable assets, and we need her. We need you too. You can't leave for three months."

"I have to."

"You can't. And you can't trade away community property without talking to the Council. Can't you see how this will look?! It is so clearly self-interested! We have ethics rules for this very reason. You can't use community resources to benefit yourself personally. You know this."

He shrugs. "I do, but I don't care. If they want to take a recall vote and kick me off the Council, that's fine. I never wanted to govern. If they won't let me trade her, I'll leave the community, take the horses, cows, and the chickens and go back to the House by the Sea. That's the rule you made, right? Anyone can leave with whatever they brought. I brought the horses, so I can leave with them."

She stares at him, aghast. "You would do that?"

"I'll do whatever I have to do to protect you."

"You don't have to protect me! I'm a grown woman, capable of taking care of myself. I don't need protection!" She's almost shouting at him, and it takes all his willpower not to raise his voice in response.

"In this case, I do have to protect you," he replies. "You're forty-two years old. By any pre-Pandemic measure, this is a high risk pregnancy . . . ."

"You've never mentioned my age before," she says to him with narrowed eyes.

"It was never relevant before!" he replies. "But it is relevant in pregnancy. That's just science, Irina."

She knows that he's right, though she hates to admit it.

"Ify isn't qualified to manage risky deliveries, and I don't want anything to happen to you," Rafael says. "I can't control all the variables, but I can at least try to control this one. I want an actual doctor to attend the birth of our child. I probably shouldn't have agreed to another pregnancy, but I was obviously a willing participant. And now I need to do whatever I can to lower the risk."

"You didn't say that you thought it was too risky!" she argues.

"I did, but you disregarded it. I don't know if you realize how indomitable your will is when you set your mind to something. Only an idiot would try to stand in your way. I value our marriage and my life too much for that," he sighs and runs his hand through his hair, his voice heavy with emotion.

"I'll be fine! What happened to Emma was . . . ."

"I know, I know . . . most women throughout history have given birth," he replies with irritation. "But many of those women had qualified midwives or family members to help. And many of them died anyway."

"I don't need you to lecture me about risks or choices I make about my own body!" Irina exclaims at him.

"It's not just about you, Irina!" he nearly shouts. "It's about our children too. Our family. If I lost you, if our children lost you . . . . You have to think about them. You have to consider what would happen to them if something happened to you. You have a responsibility to them."

"I know that!" she replies, her anger boiling over.

He pauses for a moment to calm himself, then decides to try a different argument. "Think about Emma and Selah. Maybe if there had been an actual obstetrician in that room, Selah would have survived. Even if you're willing to risk your own health, think about the baby, our baby. Why take that risk?"

She looks stricken at his words, and he continues, "If the price for trying to keep you and our child safe is that I have to leave Ferndale, I accept that."

She considers how difficult it would be for him to have to leave the community he'd built with his own hands, the sacrifice he would make on her behalf. They're both quiet for a few moments, trying to calm their emotions. He looks at her earnestly with tears in his eyes.

"I don't want to lose you," he says again. He touches her stomach. "And I don't want to lose our child."

She'd been so focused on his perceived breach of her own autonomy that she hadn't even considered that he was also trying to protect their child—all of their children, really. Something in her shifts. She takes several deep breaths to release her anger, then says, "I'm sorry. I know you're trying to help. I just wish you'd talked to me about this before you made this trade. Why didn't you?"

"Because I figured you'd say all the things you just said."

She sighs. "We'll have to take it to the Council when we get back. This doesn't look good."

"But it will be beneficial to the community," he says, "and we can train others and even offer midwife services ourselves."

"I'll help you prepare the best arguments on the drive home," she concedes reluctantly.

+++

Two nights later, Rafael presents his "proposal" at the Council meeting. Julián, who'd privately agreed to Rafael's trade when they had returned from Red Bluff, grills Rafael as they had prepared. Rafael doesn't flinch. Irina has prepared him as she would prepare a trial witness. The entire Council is a part of the ruse. Irina feels guilty about this piece of theater, but they need some veneer of legitimacy for Rafael's unauthorized and self-interested trade.

"Why can't pregnant women from Ferndale just travel to Redding like women from other communities have done?" Julián asks Rafael.

"Because it's more than one hundred fifty miles away, and pregnancy and delivery are often unpredictable," Rafael replies. "Having our own trained midwives will allow us to handle circumstances like we saw last month . . . ."

He looks at Emma and Tina, who have already been warned that this conversation was coming.

". . . if we have our own midwives, we won't have to pay exorbitant rates for another midwife's services. It will help to ensure our self-sufficiency. The upfront cost is high, but the long term payoff is higher. We may even be able to gain resources from this if we're skilled enough to offer midwifery services."

"You don't only think this is a good idea because your own wife is pregnant?" Julián asks.

"Many women of childbearing age will end up getting pregnant at some point," Rafael says. "It would be prudent for us to plan for that and try to do whatever we can to ensure their safety. Also, Dr. Cunningham has said that she can instruct our doctors on how to insert IUDs for effective birth control, and she's offered to help train members of our community on natural birth control methods as well, which will cut down on unintended pregnancies. So even for women who don't intend to have children, this will be helpful."

Irina watches him. He's a more convincing actor than she would have expected. So is Julián, who makes a compelling show of contemplating whether or not they can really spare the horse. He ultimately proclaims that they can, despite his private proclamation that they really cannot.

The audience seems convinced. Rafael calls the vote. Unanimous in favor. Irina lies in bed that night, contemplating this sham. Another moral compromise. Not their first and likely not their last.

+++

Irina is grateful when Gail, at least, gets her Tribe to agree to contribute two cows in exchange for Amy's having her baby delivered by Dr. Cunningham in Ferndale and two apprentices' being trained with Dr. Cunningham. This makes Rafael's questionable trade a little less costly. At the beginning of December, Rick arrives with the two Tribal apprentices and cows. Then he and Rafael depart with Sunshine and the cattle for Redding. It will take them at least a week to drive the cattle there from Ferndale with Rafael on a bicycle and Rick riding the horse. Jaya will drive to pick them, Dr. Cunningham, and the bicycle up from Redding when they arrive there; then they'll stop and pick up Amy on their way back to Ferndale.

When Dr. Cunningham completes her four months in Ferndale, Jaya will drive her and Rafael back to Redding, where Rafael will spend three months building wind turbines for Dr. Cunningham's family. Despite conceding that Dr. Cunningham's assistance will be helpful to the community, there's little that Irina likes about this plan. She dislikes the idea of Rafael and Rick's traveling alone, especially with such valuable assets, she still resents the terms of the trade, and she hates the idea that he'll be gone for three months the spring after their baby is born. Rafael does his best to reassure her, but he can feel her displeasure.

360

Irina dislikes Dr. Addie Cunningham even more when she sees her. She's a frosty blonde with ice blue eyes, a lean figure, and an aloof air. She reminds Irina of the popular girls who picked on her in high school. Irina knows it's unfair to judge a person based on appearance, but she reminds herself that it's more than appearance she's judging. She's still bothered by the unfairness of the deal Dr. Cunningham struck with Rafael, and, in a larger sense, she's troubled by a doctor's hoarding lifesaving knowledge for profit. Dr. Cunningham's insistence that everyone call her Doctor is also grating.

"I don't go around calling myself Irina Karrigan-Delgado, Esquire," she complains to Rafael later.

"You don't have to love her," Rafael replies. "She just has to deliver the baby safely."

The situation is even more uncomfortable because when Irina goes to Dr. Cunningham for her first exam, the room is crowded with Ify and the apprentices. It's worse than the hospital room full of residents that Irina had endured in her twenties when she'd been hospitalized for mononucleosis complications, because these are people she'll have to sit with in the cafeteria.

Dr. Cunningham snaps on a pair of gloves and declares that, because this is Irina's first appointment, they'll have to do an internal exam. Irina had missed this part of the prenatal experience with Matteo, so she'd forgotten the various degradations associated with pregnancy.

"Can they leave?" Irina asks, gesturing to the apprentices.

"I'm being paid to teach them," Dr. Cunningham replies. "That would defeat the purpose. And they'll be there at the birth, anyway."

Irina submits reluctantly. Dr. Cunningham narrates the exam to her audience, then does a sonogram and declares that everything looks fine. She confirms Ify's untrained assessment that the baby is a boy. She is thorough, Irina admits, but Irina still doesn't like her.

"It was humiliating!" Irina tells Rafael later as they sip mint tea in their living room. He rubs her feet and does his best to empathize but makes the mistake of agreeing that this is a necessary part of the training.

"I guess you'd be happy to submit to a prostate exam in front of a crowd for the sake of medical expertise?" she asks, narrowing her eyes. He blanches, and she rolls her eyes. "I figured."

The next day after Irina finishes her breakfast food service shift, Dr. Cunningham stops her in the parking lot in front of the high school and says, "I know you don't like me, but I'm here to help."

"If that was true, you wouldn't have charged such a high fee," Irina says, irritably. She's achy, underslept, and entirely uncomfortable.

Dr. Cunningham looks at her. "I have three children and an extended family I have to provide for. We don't have the advantages you have—electricity, horses, prepared meals. I have a skill, and I've been trading that skill to feed my family. What Ferndale asked from me was far beyond what I would ordinarily do. I'm going to be away from my family for four months."

"Then you're taking Rafael away from his family for three months," Irina replies.

"He offered! Because he understood that while I'm here, I can't attend any other births or bring in any other income."

"How do I know that Rafael will be safe with you?" Irina asks.

Dr. Cunningham laughs. "Because there are ten of us and almost two hundred of you. If anything happened to him, I know you'd send in your cavalry, but you'd shoot me yourself."

She's right. Irina is as protective of Rafael as he is of her. Still, "Your demands were too high."

Dr. Cunningham scoffs. "I bet you plan to share what I teach you with everyone else too and even offer midwife services yourselves?"

Irina reluctantly concedes that this is, indeed, the plan.

"Which means that I lose some of my income. So, yes, Ferndale has to make this worth my while, and I won't apologize for that. You're an attorney, and you seem both tenacious and shrewd. If you were me, you would have negotiated the best deal for your people."

"You could just join us."

The doctor laughs ruefully. "I don't share your politics or your optimism about human nature."

+++

While the rest of the town sleeps off the New Year's celebrations, Irina lies in bed, trying to deny the mild contractions she feels. She breathes to calm herself. The baby is a few weeks early but not dangerously early. A half hour passes. Rafael still slumbers peacefully beside her. The morning sunlight slants through the window. She hears Miranda and Matteo beginning to stir in their room down the hall. She's gripped alternately with terror and excitement. Rafael wakes and sees the worry on her face.

"Are you alright?" he asks, the anxiety obvious in his voice.

"I think I'm in labor," she replies. He leaps immediately out of bed and begins pulling on his jeans.

"I'll get Dr. Cunningham," he says.

Irina shakes her head, "You've watched too many movies. It doesn't work like that. Early labor takes hours."

"Shouldn't I just let her know so she can plan her day?"

She can feel the nervous energy radiating off him. "Fine, but I really need you to be calm right now, alright?"

Rafael thinks this is profoundly unfair since she knows that he doesn't operate well under pressure, but he's smart enough to know that it's not the time to argue. He finishes dressing and gets the children ready for the day. At breakfast, he quietly informs François of the situation and asks him to keep the children until Irina has the baby.

Dr. Cunningham sits at the edge of the cafeteria with a book in her hand, as always, holding herself apart from everyone else. When Rafael tells her that Irina is in labor, she asks him a series of questions that he has no answers to—how often are the contractions? For how long? Have they gotten stronger? She grows a bit impatient and ends up just going back to the house with him. Dr. Cunningham does a quick exam, then sends Rafael to get the interns immediately.

"Is that really necessary?" Irina asks.

"You don't like me, but you're going to have to trust me," Dr. Cunningham replies. "You're having this baby soon."

The crowd has barely assembled before the doctor declares that it's time to push. Irina is sobbing in pain, and Rafael feels deep concern and almost physically painful empathy. As Irina squeezes his hand and cries out, he loves her more than he'd thought possible.

Rafael had been present for Miranda's birth, but he hadn't been required to do anything. In fact, out of modesty, Helena had kept him from seeing any of the gruesome details. Dr. Cunningham, however, has other plans for him, commanding him to grab one of Irina's feet. He balks at the blood.

"If you're going to faint," Irina says testily, "please warn me."

For all of the worry they'd both invested in this, it's over shockingly quickly. There are a handful of actual pushes; then, suddenly, a baby. Headfirst, he slides into Dr. Cunningham's waiting hands. He looks a little blue, and there's a moment of silence . . . then a wail. Irina and Rafael both cry in relief as Dr. Cunningham hands Irina their little boy. Rafael cuts the cord. The placenta is delivered. Stitches are painfully administered. The apprentices watch, and Irina doesn't give a damn. She sees nothing but the baby and the man beside her. For a moment, every misfortune and sorrow fades away, and there's only joy and redemption.

They name the baby Javier, and he rests in Rafael's arms as Irina slumbers. Rafael marvels at how immediately he loves a creature whose existence he'd previously been profoundly ambivalent about. He'd been depressed when Miranda was born, so he hadn't been able to truly appreciate all the small details of her. He regrets that, as he notes every wrinkle of his son's hands and toes, his slightly smooshed face, his shock of dark hair. He whispers a grateful prayer in his mother tongue for the second chances he's been given.

+++

The winter rains go on and on. The days remain dark, and they have to run the refrigerators and freezers almost exclusively from generators charged at the Eureka wind turbine. Rafael is technically on leave, but he's pulled into Council meetings repeatedly as they discuss the possibility of stringing electric lines from the Eureka wind turbine and Ferndale. It had taken several months to run lines five miles from their new coastal windmills to Ferndale, and they'd blown out several refrigerators in the process because they'd stepped down the power incorrectly. He suspects that stepping down the power from the much larger Eureka wind turbine will be more complicated. The Council asks Mark and his two apprentices to conduct a feasibility study and report back.

Rafael and Irina are both relieved when the riskiest postpartum weeks have passed and both she and Javier are healthy. The newborn schedule, though, is grueling, and Irina marvels that she managed to care for Matteo alone after losing Sam. Rafael, mindful of her story about nearly jumping off the bridge with Matteo, consults with Charlotte, and they resolve to keep a close eye on Irina and to try to give her opportunities to rest.

So Rafael often wakes to feed Javier pumped breastmilk in the middle of the night so Irina can sleep a little longer. Because Helena had gone back to working night shifts almost immediately, he'd done this with Miranda too, though he hadn't been in a state of mind to appreciate that time. Despite his exhaustion, Rafael enjoys his quiet hours with Javier.

Miranda and even Matteo try to take care of Javier. Miranda seems to regard him as her babydoll and takes great pleasure in feeding him bottles while holding him on the couch. Irina, aware that this will be her last baby, dotes on Javier. Despite her IUD birth control and commitment to never get pregnant again, she often finds herself tearful over the transience of babyhood. She tries to absorb every detail of Javier—the scent of his hair, the softness of his skin, the intensity of his newborn stares. She often wakes in the night just to listen to his breathing, to reassure herself of him, to try to capture every moment in her memory. She's moved by Rafael's uncomplaining, usually unnoticed devotion to doing all of the little things that ensure their children's thriving.

Irina doesn't blame Emma and Tina for avoiding her, Rafael, and Javier. She hears from Tina, tipsy on whiskey, that Dr. Cunningham had confirmed, as best she could with only an ultrasound and physical exam, that Emma likely has some kind of uterine anomaly and should probably not try to get pregnant again. Tina cries as she reiterates her fears for her marriage. There is little advice Irina can offer, except to wait.

In February, Amy and Rick's baby girl is born. A few weeks later, another Ferndale baby boy arrives; then, in March, Yumi and Ify's daughter. Emma's foresight and perseverance in pumping breastmilk pays off when Yumi is unable to nurse sufficiently.

Julián reports at the Council meeting that their food supplies are holding. Mark's update isn't as positive. Because the Eureka wind turbine only generates 100kw and it is already beginning to show the effects of inexpert maintenance, the amount of effort required to run power lines that distance doesn't seem warranted. Their power problems seem intractable.

Two weeks before Founders Day, Rafael and Dr. Cunningham depart. Irina cries as she watches him go. He's thoughtfully arranged for others to help her in his absence, but still, she worries about his safety and her ability to manage everything on her own.

They talk several times per week on the radio, but they both know that anyone could be listening, so they have to be careful about what they say. Irina is thrilled to see him at the May trade conference. They set their tent up on the outskirts of the fairgrounds and spend every free moment there together. She still feels uncomfortable in her postpartum body, but she does her best to banish those feelings as he shares his vivid dreams of her. As they lie beside each other, he asks for all the details about their children and recounts his progress with the wind turbines at Dr. Cunningham's settlement.

"You were right about bringing Dr. Cunningham to Ferndale," Irina says to him the night before he's set to depart again. "I'm glad you stopped me from taking that risk."

He's gratified to hear this vindication, even if it is months after the fact. "I love you. I meant what I said: I can't bear to think about losing you."

"I know," she replies. "I'm glad we had Javier, though. Thank you for agreeing to that, even though you had concerns."

Two more months, she reminds herself, as they depart the next morning and go their separate ways.

The days drag on. Irina oversees the trial of a woman accused of scavenging in Ferndale houses and not turning the property over. The jury finds her guilty, and Irina gives her an extra labor sentence. She rejects the idea of a trial for a woman caught in adultery. She plows fields, cares for her children, visits Emma as often as possible, and goes hunting whenever she can.

Her friends stop by often, but still she misses the unique intimacy that she and Rafael share. She thinks about her marriage, and she is surprised to find that she doesn't believe the adage that all happy families are alike. Her marriage to Rafael is a happy one, yet it is profoundly different from her happy marriage to Sam. She and Rafael argue far more, he's more obstinate and generally unafraid to confront Irina when he disagrees with her, yet he's also more passionate and more likely to engage her in intense, intellectually-stimulating discussions.

Neither is better, she concludes: just different.

Finally, in July, Rafael returns to Ferndale with suntanned skin that makes his hazel eyes stand out all the more. Irina watches him with hungry eyes until they are alone.

Chapter Twenty-Three

Two months later, Irina sits unhappily in the judge's chair in the City Hall, listening as Tyler Robinson, a former paralegal who is now serving as the community's part-time prosecutor, outlines the case against a woman named Vera Russo, who's been charged with failing to meet Ferndale's minimal work requirements.

Tyler lays out the facts of the case in his opening statement: Vera had previously been found guilty of failing to meet the community's work requirements, and after a jury trial, Irina had sentenced her to extra labor. Vera had spent the intervening months drinking and had failed even the pretense of serving her sentence. Six different members of the community had complained about her failure to contribute. Tyler calls several witnesses who testify to Vera's frequent drinking, her long absences from work, her refusal to meet her community service and defense training obligations.

Vera, with the assistance of Dominic Romano, Ferndale's part-time defense attorney, testifies, claiming to have a chronic pain disorder and argues that in the absence of pharmaceuticals, drinking is the only way to make the pain bearable. Tyler grills her about her drinking and the fact that she'd been too unwell to go to work but not too unwell to show up at the community's holiday gatherings, to bike to the beach, or to engage in several softball games.

The attorneys make their final arguments; the jury briefly deliberates and hands down a guilty sentence. Despite her personal reservations, Irina is left with no choice but to give Vera the Charter's mandated exile sentence.

Afterward, she retreats to her office. This isn't the first exile sentence she's issued, but the other had been far less ambiguous. The first man she'd sentenced to exile that July had beaten his girlfriend—who very nearly followed him into exile until Tina and Charlotte were able to talk her out of it.

Irina is staring out the window deep in thought when Tina appears at her door. Irina frowns. Given that Tina was the one who had insisted that the exile penalty for 'non contribution' be added to the Charter, she's hardly the person Irina wants to see at the moment.

"I bet you're feeling guilty about today's trial," Tina says as she sits down in the chair in Irina's messy office. "But you shouldn't."

Irina purses her lips, and Tina continues without waiting for a response. "Everything falls apart if we allow people to get the benefits of Ferndale without contributing. If you let someone profit from everyone else's work without also working, all the trust we've created here evaporates. If people see someone not working but still getting benefits, they're going to think they can do the same thing. In fact, they're going to think they *should* do the same thing. If people can just skate by without contributing, it actually becomes irrational to work."

"But exile is a death sentence," Irina argues.

"99.9% of humanity just died by chance, not because of any poor choice or selfishness or character flaw, just by pure chance," Tina points out. "Unlike all those people, Vera had a chance to reform. You gave her a compassionate sentence the first time, and she didn't even try."

Irina looks unconvinced. Tina sighs with frustration and says, "You tell me . . . why should we support someone who contributes nothing to the community? Why are we obligated to do that? How is that fair to everyone who does work hard?"

"Your Christian faith doesn't require you to engage in acts of charity?" Irina asks testily.

"Acts of charity? Yes. Acts of stupidity? No. I don't think I'm obligated to prevent people from suffering from the consequences of their own bad choices. Jesus, Irina, you know as well as I do that most of the people in the world—pretty much everyone, in fact—are suffering by no fault of their own. We're obligated to help them. Our resources are limited, and we should prioritize helping the people who actually contribute, not helping people who are too lazy to show up to work."

"What if she really was sick?"

"Then she could have gone to Shantal and asked for a different job assignment! We have all the 'reasonable accommodations' you put in the Charter. There are job roles for people who are sick or have disabilities or are homebound. She didn't ask for that, did she?"

"No," Irina replies reluctantly.

"Look, I understand alcoholism," Tina says. "Some people might even argue that it's a thing I know from personal experience. But I'm at least a functional alcoholic. That's all we're asking from everyone here: be functional. Drink as much as you want, but show up to work. Contribute. It's a fair ask. I came back from the Marine Corps with PTSD, and I still fucking showed up to work. So, no, I don't feel bad for her. You shouldn't either."

She can tell that Irina is still unhappy about the sentence, so she concludes, "And anyway, your hands were tied. The Charter says that if the jury finds her guilty, you have to exile her. And I'm the one who's responsible for that provision. Not you. So you can put it on my tab."

Tina gets up and departs without saying goodbye. Irina watches her go, feeling both irritated and a little comforted.

An hour later, she hears Javier wake from his nap in the room next door, and she goes to retrieve him. She's just about to nurse him when there's another knock on the door. Irina opens it to find Aditi, who had been selected as the community's new midwife, and Ify.

"How did it go?" Ify asks.

"Guilty. Sentenced to exile," Irina sighs.

"Unfortunately, we have more bad news for you," Ify says. "You know Gracie Jennings?"

"Redhead? A couple of years older than Miranda?"

He nods. "Twelve years old. And pregnant."

"What? How?" Irina asks.

"She told me that her father impregnated her," Aditi says, looking slightly sick. It seems cruel to Irina that it should be Aditi, a former captive and sexual-assault survivor herself, who has to deal with this.

"Are you sure?" Irina asks. Javier fusses, and she puts on a cover and begins nursing him, figuring Ify and Aditi, who had both attended his birth, are unlikely to be bothered by this.

"Her descriptions were pretty specific. She thinks he may have also sexually abused her friend, Nellie Parker," Aditi replies. "Tina is talking to Nellie now."

"Shit." Given Irina's prior work, she really shouldn't be surprised by this, but she still is. Their community is small and tight-knit. It's shocking that someone so dangerous managed to sneak into their midst. They discuss the details for a while until Tina arrives and confirms that Nellie has also accused Jim Jennings of rape.

Irina sighs, "A private trial then, but I expect everyone will already know by dinnertime."

By early afternoon, Rafael is standing in Irina's office, asking her about the rumor he'd heard. She confirms that it's true, and they spend a half hour obsessing over any and all interactions Miranda has ever had with Jim. Unable to contain their mutual anxiety, they pull Miranda out of school to talk to her. Irina has asked children these questions many times, but it's different with her own daughter. They're relieved when Miranda has no idea what they're talking about. They see Gracie that evening at Tina and Emma's house, where she's staying while the trial is pending. She's an especially quiet pre-teen, a fact that Irina had noticed before but never really considered. Irina blames herself a little for never suspecting the abuse. She has enough knowledge to recognize the patterns, if she hadn't been so caught up in her own life and her other work.

Emma, who's grown a bit more quiet in the face of her own grief, works to draw Gracie out. Irina talks to Gracie about the details of the trial, assuring her, as she herself had been assured, that her life will improve after this is over.

Aditi and Irina are able to get in touch with Dr. Cunningham on the radio. Gracie holds Emma's hand while they discuss her options.

"Termination is legal under our Charter," Irina says. "Are you able to do that?"

"I've never performed an abortion," Dr. Cunningham tells them. "I could read up on it and try, but that's a big risk."

"What about the abortion pill?" Aditi asks.

"The newest pills would likely have been manufactured that spring before the Pandemic, more than five years ago. They're very expired by now. We can try, but I have no idea what will happen. That's also risky."

"And birth?" Aditi asks.

Dr. Cunningham sighs. "Risky, as well. Her body is undeveloped. There are a lot of potential complications. We can use medications to try to control hemorrhaging and treat infection, but those are also expired and antibiotics are really hard to come by these days. There are no good options here. I'm so sorry."

Aditi looks at Gracie, who is silently crying in Emma's arms. "What do you want to do?"

"Birth," Gracie replies. "I want to have the baby."

"If you can come and pick me up when she goes into labor, I'll attend the birth. And in the meantime, you can bring her to me for exams," Dr. Cunningham says. "At no cost."

Irina warms to Dr. Cunningham a little, but she can't shake her horror at the idea of a twelve-year-old's giving birth. She'd been lucky that Javier's birth was easy. Gracie likely won't have the same good fortune.

They thank Dr. Cunningham, and Irina returns to her own home next door, where Rafael has just finished getting the children to bed. They sit for a while in the living room. He asks how she is, but she tells him that she isn't ready to talk about any of this yet, so he eventually departs for bed.

After midnight, Irina is still awake, staring at the fire, trying to untangle her thoughts and her own history.

+++

The next day, Irina has just finished nursing Javier in her office when Tina appears again in the doorway, flanked by Emma and François. Irina puts Javier in his playpen and invites them in. They're barely inside the room before Emma says, "We want to adopt Gracie and the baby."

"Did Gracie agree to this?"

"Yes," Emma says. "They'll be raised as sisters. It will give them a more normal life. We're uniquely qualified because two of us are Gracie's teachers and the other is an adult who's very familiar with the details of Gracie's case."

"All three of you will be co-parents then?" Irina asks.

"We already had an arrangement in place for Selah," François replies. "I can move into the unoccupied house next door; then I can help with Gracie and the baby."

"The trial isn't over yet," Irina says. "I can't take away custody until Jim's found guilty."

"It's a foregone conclusion," Tina says, "and we wanted to be the first to talk to you."

Irina nods. "We'll still have to give other members of the community the opportunity to apply for adoption, and the Council will have to approve it."

Emma looks a bit crestfallen at that statement, but Irina reassures her, "I don't think there's anyone else here who will try to adopt, especially once they hear that you're trying. But we do have to maintain an appearance of fairness."

Two days later, Irina again sits in the judge's chair on the stage in the Ferndale City Hall, and Jim sits in a chair before her. She's reminded of the phrase "the banality of evil" when she looks into his bright blue eyes. He's affable and even tempered. He denies everything, saying that Gracie had probably been assaulted by one of her classmates or someone else in the community. When Tyler asks Jim why he thinks the girls are accusing him, Jim rambles on about how girls influence each other, just like the Salem witch trials. The jury takes no time at all to deliberate and find him guilty, leaving Irina with the choice she'd been dreading: death or exile.

She's barely put Javier down for a nap in the next room and closed the door to her office when there's a knock.

"Come in," she says. To her surprise, Julián steps through the door.

"I'd like to talk to you about the sentence," he says in English. She invites him to speak in Spanish, but he declines, knowing that her Spanish is far worse than his English. Irina gestures to a chair, and he sits.

"How familiar are you with the history of my country?" he asks her. She shrugs.

"El Salvador was plagued by gang violence for decades . . . , gangs that were exported from the United States," he says. "The gangs in El Salvador were brutal. Rape was a casual act to them, murder was costless, and life was cheap."

He takes a deep breath, and his voice wavers slightly with his next statement. He looks down at the desk, away from her. Irina has never seen him show this much emotion. Even at Selah's funeral, he had been characteristically stoic. "When I was sixteen, my sister was raped by one of the gangs and left for dead on a road outside of our town. Then men who raped her were never arrested, never tried, never punished."

"I'm so sorry," Irina says.

"Those gangs were in El Salvador because United States law enforcement decided that violent gang members were too dangerous to stay here, so the gang members were exiled back 'home' to El Salvador. What happened to my sister is what happens when dangerous people are banished instead of eliminated. I hope that you'll consider that when you make your decision."

Irina nods. "Thank you for telling me this. I'll think about it."

He gets up and departs quickly. He's just left when Tina opens the door and lets herself in. "Got a minute?"

Irina nods and Tina steps inside, closing the door behind her. "Tough day," Tina says as she sits. She pulls a flask out of her pocket and offers it to Irina.

Irina balks at first—it's barely 4:00 p.m., and she'll have to pump and dump—but Tina says, "You're going to need it for this conversation," so Irina takes a small sip, the whiskey burning her throat.

"Any idea what you're going to do?" Tina asks, taking a long drink from the flask Irina hands back.

"I'm weighing my options," Irina says, wondering where this is going.

"Well, I'd like to weigh in favor of the only option that makes sense."

"And that is?"

"Don't be naive, Irina."

"I'm not naive," Irina says defensively.

"Which is why I'm sure you know that the only safe option here is execution." Tina takes two more long sips from the flask. "I think you and I are alike. We both grew up in fucked up situations. Dads with anger problems. Moms that didn't protect us. But I think it's more than that too, isn't it?"

Irina stares at her blankly.

"Why did you include a provision for execution of sex offenders in the criminal code?" Tina asks.

"Because of my work as a prosecutor," Irina replies reflexively.

Tina scrutinizes her. "That's the only reason?"

Irina squirms in her chair, and Tina continues, "Well, let me tell you my reason for voting in favor of it; then maybe we can have a more honest conversation."

She takes another drink and offers the flask to Irina, who takes a long sip, figuring that Tina is right, and she's going to need it.

"So I had this mentor when I was in the Marines. About ten years older than me, a few ranks higher, but boy does he get me. He had a Black mom and a White dad, just like me. They were real shit parents, just like mine. He was raised by his White aunt and uncle in the Republican suburbs, just like me. Spent his entire life being an outsider, never fitting in anywhere, dealing with racism and bullshit. And I think, 'this guy understands me.' He believes in me; he sticks up for me. He gets me a promotion."

Irina can already sense what's coming next, but she's powerless to change the end of this story.

Tina takes another drink. "So one night we're out drinking with everyone, and we're the last ones left. We're having a great time, like we usually do. I'm not feeling too great; whatever I drank is really hitting me, so he offers to drive me home. And you know, I don't trust anyone. But I trust him, because he gets me, because we're coming from the same place, because we're friends. So I get in his fucking car, and I black out. And when I wake up, I'm in the backseat, and he's on top of me. Inside me."

Tina says all of this in a flat, matter-of-fact voice. It's a delivery Irina is familiar with. The same way she had recounted her father's abuse to Rafael. The same way she had told Rafael the brutal details of Clara's death. At some point, there's dissociation.

Tina continues, "And he says to me 'you're just a lesbian because you've never been fucked by the right guy.' Sometimes I still remember it when I make love to my wife. How fucked up is that?"

Irina knows how a statement will stick in the mind. She recalls what the social worker said about Clara climbing mountains.

"But here's the really fucked up thing: I didn't do anything about it. I was too much of a goddamn coward to report him. He said no one would believe me. And everyone liked him, so he was probably right. He used a condom, so there was no evidence anyway. So I didn't tell anyone but Emma, and I didn't tell her till I was home. Two years later he gets court-martialed. Turns out he drugged and raped two other women. Both were Black women he mentored. Both had difficult childhoods. Same pattern. And I could have stopped that if I'd just spoken up."

"It's not your fault," Irina says, "Reporting a sexual assault is a miserable process. It probably wouldn't have worked, and it could have made things even worse for you."

"Maybe. But I should have done it anyway."

Irina moves to the chair next to Tina and takes her hand. For a moment she thinks Tina is going to pull her hand away, but she doesn't.

"I'm so sorry," Irina says.

"Why did you include that provision in the criminal code?" Tina says, looking at her intensely. Irina reaches for the flask and takes another long drink.

"Because my father was an alcoholic, and he used to bring his alcoholic friends home with him, and once my mother was in the hospital there was no one to protect me. One of them came into my room and . . . ; I haven't even told Rafael this . . . ."

It had taken a year of couples counseling before Irina had told Sam. She likes to tell herself that she's never told Rafael because she's moved past it now; it's not relevant to their marriage.

She's pretty sure, though, that the real reason is because the story still makes her feel deep shame.

"It only happened a few times," Irina says. "He only touched me and made me touch him a few times. It's not like he raped me."

"It's not a pissing contest," Tina says. "That's fucked up."

Irina is quiet for a moment; then she says, "I looked him up years later. He was in prison for molesting two other girls."

"I think we understand each other," Tina says. "And I think you know what you have to do here. People like Jim don't kill, but they do ruin lives."

Tina offers her the flask one last time, and Irina takes another drink. "You should probably tell Rafael what happened to you. It sucks to carry that alone."

Irina nods with tears in her eyes. Tina gets up. "I know this isn't how we did things in the modern world, but we're not in the modern world. Sexual predators don't change, and we don't have the resources to imprison him for life. We've got a duty to protect the people of Ferndale and the other people outside."

She says goodbye and closes the door as she leaves.

That night as they sit in their living room after their children have gone to sleep, Irina asks Rafael, "What would you do?"

He's quiet for a minute. "Even for a murderer, the death penalty is questionably moral. It's terrible to take a life, even one that's deserving of being taken."

"I don't think I'm the right person to make this decision," Irina says, trying unsuccessfully to tame the anxiety that threatens to envelop her.

"Because you used to prosecute these cases?"

She sighs, "Because I was one of these cases."

"What do you mean?" His eyes are focused on her intently, and she has to look away to tell him what happened. She can't bear to see his pity. She recounts her story with the same blunt flatness that Tina had used. He is, at the same time, surprised and not surprised. She'd been very wary of him and everyone else at first. He'd just chalked it up to her bad experience with the man outside of Grants Pass and her former career as a prosecutor.

"I'm so sorry," he says, wrapping his arms around her. For a moment, he's a little bit hurt that she's never trusted him enough to tell him this. Then he realizes it isn't a matter of trust. He's never told her the more humiliating incidents of bullying he'd experienced in school or the insults Helena had hurled at him. Even in the most intimate relationships there has to be some allowance for a private inner life.

She seems to read his mind. "I'm sorry I never told you."

"You weren't obligated to."

"It didn't seem relevant. I spent years in therapy to resolve this. It did fuck me up for a long time, though. In college I . . . ," she wants to take back the words, but she's already started the sentence, so she finishes it, ". . . in college I slept with a lot of people. I think I liked feeling that sexual power over men, and I needed the approval. I married one of them, and it was a disaster . . . ."

She'd told him in passing that she had been divorced before meeting Sam.

". . . it caused a lot of problems with Sam. The number of men I'd been with made him feel insecure, and I was always a mess. I would pull him in and push him away. It was part of why we had to get counseling."

Irina is the most sexually forward woman Rafael has ever been with. He'd always chalked that up to her generally assertive personality and the fact that she, unlike anyone else he'd ever been with, except Helena, is North American. He'd also assumed that it was because she desired him. But this new information casts her forwardness in a new light. Is it, instead, related to her being sexually abused as a child? He's not sure what to do with that thought, other than keep it to himself and try to sort it out later.

As though she can sense his troubled thoughts, she says, "I don't want you to treat me differently because of something from three decades ago that I've already dealt with."

"Okay."

"Having a healthy sex life is really important to me," she says, her voice wavering slightly. "I had to work for years to be where I am now with you. I don't want anything to change."

It is a point of strange pride for her, a hard-fought victory, not only because of what her father's friend had done but also because of the religion she'd been steeped in as a teenager. When she was twelve, after her first Sunday School class, where she'd heard the teacher's admonitions on abstinence,

Irina had stood in the barn, crying into the neck of her favorite horse. Aunt Hannah had found her, and Irina had confessed her fear that if she wasn't perfect and pure, no one would ever really love her. Irina has always suspected that Hannah guessed the deeper nature of her distress and took the matter to Abuela Mariana, which was part of the reason her grandparents allowed her to avoid church. It had taken Irina three decades to reach a place of peace about this, and she's proud to have arrived here.

"It won't change," he says, bringing her knuckles to his lips. Still, he needs some time to adjust to this.

"Ignore what I said earlier," he tells her, "about the sentence. I think you might actually be the right person to decide this, because you know what's at stake."

She nods, though she isn't sure what the right thing to do is in this instance. She hopes the answer will come to her. She stays up most of the night, considering the awful details of the trial and what Julián and Tina had told her. She falls asleep briefly and wakes at dawn, resolved.

At breakfast, Irina stops by the job board, where temporary community jobs are posted for residents whose normal roles aren't filling all their hours. Irina figures she'll have some free time now that the trial is over, so she takes a few tear-off slips from the 'hunting' and 'plowing' fliers. Ify walks over and asks her to join him in the hall.

In a hushed tone, he says, "Jim was found hanging from a bedsheet rope in his cell this morning." He pauses. "But I'm not sure that he killed himself."

"What do you mean?"

"I'm not a coroner," Ify disclaims, "but he had marks on his hands like he'd tried to pull off the sheet that was used to hang him."

"So you think someone else killed him?"

"I can't be sure. Maybe he just regretted his decision at the last moment. Or maybe it's just an instinctive reaction. I don't have the expertise to know."

Irina sighs, unsure of what to do with this information. She returns to the cafeteria and sees Tina leaving through the other door. Irina runs to catch up with her.

As they walk through the parking lot, Irina says, "I heard that Jim hung himself."

"I heard that too."

"Strange thing is, Ify said there were markings on his hands that looked like he tried to pull the rope off. Like maybe someone killed him."

Tina shrugs. "Maybe. I guess whoever did that solved your problem, though, didn't they?"

Irina stops. Tina stops beside her, and they stare at each other for a minute.

"What did you decide, anyway?" Tina asks.

"It doesn't matter now," Irina says.

"Guess it doesn't. I've got to fill out some paperwork on Jim's suicide and file it with Shantal. See you later."

Irina stares after her. She returns to the cafeteria, where Rafael is just finishing breakfast with their children. After dropping off the children at school, she tells him about her conversations with Ify and Tina.

"You think Tina killed him?" Rafael asks. "Why?"

Then suddenly he recalls his conversation with Tina in the warehouse after that first trade conference. Tina had kept her word to him. But he can't tell Irina this, and Irina can't tell him what Tina had told her the day before. So they both demur.

"Should I do something about it?" Irina asks him.

He shrugs. "I'm not sure what you would do. She probably did the right thing, and she's the Head of Security."

There's a mechanism in the Charter to remove Tina from her position, or they could have a recall vote to remove her from the Council, but given their close friendship and Tina's standing in the community, it would be painful. Irina is also fairly certain that even if she could prove this accusation, most of the Council and the public would side with Tina. She and Rafael part ways with a promise to discuss this more later in the day.

That night, as he lies in bed waiting for Irina, Rafael wonders whether anyone can ever truly know another person. It strikes him that even after several years together, there are still parts of Irina that are unexplored territory. It took her forty years to meet him, and it could take another forty for him to fully know her. Still he wants to know her as much as he can.

She crawls into bed with him and runs her hand suggestively up his thigh as she kisses him. He stills, and she stops and looks at him. Her eyes narrow. "You promised this wouldn't change things between us."

He had, but it's difficult not to ask himself troubling questions about it. "I know. I'm sorry. I just need to know that you're okay with this, that it's what you want, that you're not reacting to what happened to you."

She sighs. "Are you reacting to what happened to you with Helena? With your classmates? With your childhood?"

"Yes, I guess," he concedes.

"So am I. I'm reacting to the sum of my experiences. No one can separate themselves entirely from their bad life experiences, but I'm old enough, and self-aware enough, to react in a way that's healthy and rational. At least most of the time."

As usual, her arguments are compelling, and her touch even more so. He shelves these doubts, knowing that they'll probably reappear again later, and he'll have to work through them anew.

He leans into her, trusting that they know themselves and each other well enough to navigate this territory together. They touch each other with practiced hands. She moves slowly over him, looking into his eyes as she does, and his anxieties quiet.

The next day in the Council meeting, Tina, Emma, and François officially petition to adopt Gracie and her unborn child. As Irina had predicted, no one else tries to adopt after they see Emma and Tina's petition.

Tina waits for Irina after the meeting. Irina tells Rafael she'll meet him at home; then she and Tina walk down Main Street past the dark storefronts.

"I think we need to do something more for Gracie," Tina says. "Everyone here will know what happened to her. She'll feel isolated and outcast."

"I don't know what we can do about that, though," Irina says. "That's the downside of living in a small community."

"We should work with Charlotte to form a support group, then announce it together, publicly acknowledging what happened to us so Gracie isn't alone and other people are more willing to come forward and get support," Tina says. Irina is surprised at Tina's change of heart about counseling. The child-loss support group must have made some difference for her or Emma.

Still, this feels like an act of vulnerability that Irina is not quite ready for. "I don't know . . . ; I only just told Rafael. This isn't a thing I'm ready to tell everyone. It's not something I identify with."

"You and I have the luxury of not 'identifying with' this. Gracie doesn't. Aditi and Jaya don't. You don't have to join me, but I think it will make a difference if you and I, as leaders, do this."

Irina sighs. "I'll make the announcement with you, but I really don't want to go into details."

"No details, then."

+++

In the final Council meeting of September, Charlotte, Irina, and Tina make the case for two more counseling positions. Julián negotiates this down to one position, citing the continued need to focus on basic survival. He reports to the Council that the river level is lower this year than the prior September.

"I'm pretty sure we're in a multiyear drought," he concludes.

"Climate change?" Emma asks. "But how? All the people are gone."

"It'll take hundreds of years to reverse climate change," Ify replies. "In the meantime, we'll continue to have droughts, forest fires, and extreme weather."

"We have to reduce our water consumption," Julián tells them. "We can't continue to grow rice, and we may need to grow less corn and wheat. There are other grains, like millet, rye, and amaranth, that require less water. We should look for seeds for drought-resistant crops at the trade convention."

The Council agrees to create two more full-time agriculture positions to assist Julián in researching and transitioning to more drought-friendly crops.

Tina nods at Irina, and they stand together to address the audience and announce the support group. Irina is mostly quiet, watching with admiration as Tina bravely addresses the crowd.

When Irina attends the first support group meeting, she's surprised to find many members of the community there—not just Tina, Gracie, Nellie, Aditi, and Jaya, but also Shasta, two other teenage girls, and several other women Irina knows in passing. Charlotte has already started the meeting when the door opens and Benoit steps quietly inside. At first Irina assumes that he's looking for a different meeting, but then he sits down in one of the chairs and joins them.

The winter rains start in October, and the river fills again. At the fall trade conference, Julián and Shasta trade for several varieties of drought-friendly grain and vegetable seeds. The fall harvest, winter-wheat planting, and Thanksgiving are celebratory community events, despite everyone's expectation that the winter will be long, dreary, and marked by intermittent power failures.

On Christmas Eve, after tucking Miranda in bed and checking on Javier and Matteo, Rafael and Irina sit in their living room in the glow of the fire and holiday cheer. Rafael checks his watch—9:15 p.m.—and invites Irina to walk down the street to Ferndale's small radio station with him for her Christmas present.

The night is cold and clear. The brightly-colored Victorian buildings along Main Street are studded with Christmas lights. They'd even resurrected the town's old tradition of lighting a giant Christmas tree on the hill south of town. The Council had approved this extravagance of electrical power after Emma and Irina had made a passionate argument in favor of joy and festivity. "More than survival," Irina is always reminding Julián and Tina. So Rafael and Irina walk in the romantic, nostalgic glow of the Christmas lights and the nearly full moon.

The room before them is filled with radio equipment and has a small sound booth in the back. He pulls up a chair and asks her to sit down; then he turns on the generator and the equipment. He tunes the radio to a frequency and checks his watch again.

"Say hello," he tells Irina. She looks at him with confusion, then speaks her name and a greeting into the radio microphone.

A voice that she hasn't heard in years replies.

"Aunt Hannah?" she says in disbelief. Her tear-filled eyes meet Rafael's, and he smiles. "I didn't think that I would ever get to talk to you again!"

"Me either! I couldn't believe it when I spoke to Rafael."

"You survived! You're all there?" Irina asks.

"Most of us. We survived because of what you and Sam told us. We stayed isolated here for two years."

"How is everyone?!"

"They're fine. Good actually. Isaac got married last fall. And Ruth is expecting a baby in a few months. The cattle are fine. The weather hasn't been so great, but we're hanging in there. And you? Rafael said you had a baby?!"

"Two, actually. One during the Pandemic, and one last year."

"I was so sorry to hear that Sam passed."

Irina cries as she recounts the story of how Sam got sick.

"I'm so sorry, Irina. We all loved Sam."

They're both quiet for a minute, then Hannah says, "I'm glad that you've remarried, though, that you made a new life for yourself after everything. And you built a whole town! Tell me about Ferndale."

Irina spends the next hour telling her aunt about how she'd come to Ferndale and fallen in love with Rafael, the town that they've built together, the challenges they'd faced. Hannah catches her up on all the family updates.

It's approaching midnight when they finally wrap up the conversation with a promise to talk again the following week.

"How did you do it?" Irina asks Rafael as they walk home. "How did you find a small group of people a thousand miles away?"

"I figured out a way to send our radio signal to a satellite," he replies. "The satellite acts like a repeater and sends the signal back to earth, so we can talk to people at much greater distances."

This idea sounds magical and romantic to Irina, like something out of a movie. He continues, "The equipment was always here, but until last year, I could never figure out how to get it to work. Once I got it working, it took me six months to make contact with someone in St. George. They asked around and found someone who knew your family. Last month your family borrowed the radio from the person I talked to originally and contacted me."

"You worked on this for all that time? For me?" she asks.

"For you, yes, but I hope that we can also use it to share information and connect with people at greater distances. It should work for a couple more years . . . until the satellites start to fail . . . ."

Another decaying piece of infrastructure. He imagines the satellites falling out of orbit and feels a stab of melancholy. Some days he feels like he's surrounded by entropy.

"Thank you," she says softly, taking his hand and stopping him beside her in the street. She looks at him with renewed appreciation for his sense of vision and dedication to her and this town. She reaches to touch his cheek. "I don't think anyone thanks you enough—I don't think I thank you enough for all the work you've done here."

She kisses him under the warm glow of the Christmas lights, then walks home hand in hand with him and undresses him in the firelight of their bedroom.

+++

In late January, Aditi and Tina drive to pick up Dr. Cunningham when Gracie goes into labor. Irina waits anxiously in the hallway, occasionally fetching items at Dr. Cunningham's or Emma's request. The labor stretches on for a miserable twenty-four hours. Halfway through, the power fails, and Dr. Cunningham has to deliver the baby, Penelope, by candlelight just past midnight. As Gracie falls into exhausted, painful sleep, Emma holds Penelope to her breast and nurses her tearfully. She's kept pumping breastmilk this entire time, supplying Ify and Yumi's daughter and supplementing for another baby that was born the prior summer. Dr. Cunningham stays for two weeks, checking Gracie continually for any signs of infection or hemorrhage. Finally, she declares that the riskiest period is over. She departs with admonition to Tina and Emma that they need to watch Gracie for signs of postpartum depression.

Winter's long stretches of cloudy, rainy days don't provide enough sunlight for the solar panels or enough wind for the wind turbines they'd built on the coast, so they have to run the refrigerators and freezers off the battery-powered generators charged at the Eureka wind turbine. Many evenings, the community eats dinner by candlelight in the chilly high school cafeteria. The last of the lead-acid car batteries fail, and the electric construction engines limp through what Mark declares will likely be their final spring planting.

Still, they carry on. Javier takes his first steps and says his first word—"dada," and Irina is only mildly jealous. Ify and Irina adjust the currency distribution in response to unexpected inflation. Julián and Shasta get married just before the first new grain crops are planted. The four hundred and seven residents of Ferndale celebrate their third Founders Day. Ferndale and the Six Rivers Tribe put on another successful trade and training conference, even better-attended than the last. Summer arrives with longer days and consistent electric power.

Chapter Twenty-Four: July 2038

The first Monday of that July, an extraordinary sight greets the residents of Ferndale: a luxury SUV with a combustion engine drives down Main Street, its headlights cutting through the dim of the morning fog. Irina leaves the desk in her living room and joins several other residents to watch from the sidewalk as the SUV pulls up next to the Administration Building. The engine stops and a man steps out of the driver's seat. He's very tall and movie-star handsome in his early forties with shiny black hair, olive skin, and dark eyes. He's dressed in expensive-looking business casual attire that's still in excellent condition. Irina has a surreal, momentary feeling that the vehicle and its inhabitant have emerged from a time warp. He's so perfectly coiffed, and the car itself is spotless.

Tina, who'd been talking to one of the shopkeepers at their town thrift store, walks over to Irina. They watch the man walk into the Administration Building, greeting people as he does.

"This is weird," Tina says. She and Irina walk around the vehicle, surveying it. "I thought gas didn't work anymore."

"Maybe it's not gas," Rafael says, walking up behind them. "Maybe it's ethanol."

"Why don't we have that?" Tina asks.

"Technically, we do have ethanol—Julián's moonshine. But it's very energy intensive to produce, and it still requires an acid battery to start the engine," Rafael responds, a bit defensively.

Irina leaves them to go to the Administration Building. Inside, the man is filling out the usual forms. He frowns at the patchiness of the ink. They've used a lot of new arrival forms over the past few months and haven't had time to find the right toner cartridge. He looks up and sees Irina standing there. He shakes her hand with a grip as firm as her own.

"Ro Gupta," he introduces himself. "I've heard your broadcasts. You must be Irina."

Irina isn't sure how he guessed that, and the feeling of surrealism only increases. She tries to be friendly, though, engaging him in the normal welcome conversation and learning that he's traveled all the way from San Jose.

"I think the trip will be worth it," he smiles. "I estimate that there are only around 4,000 people left in the entire state of California, and ten percent of them are here. You have power, a constitution, a legal structure. You're decades ahead of everyone else."

"We're not alone in that. The Native tribes and the religious orders have the same," she says.

"But they're not inviting people to come and join them. You are. You've had the vision to open this place up to everyone, and I want to help with that! I'd like to meet with the Council to talk about what we can build together."

"That would be great," Irina replies. "Our meetings are Thursdays at 7:00 p.m."

"I'd like to meet with you all privately. I think you'll want to hear what I have to say," he tells her.

"I'd love that, but all official business has to be conducted in the open," Irina replies as diplomatically as she can manage. He looks at her with a puzzled expression but lets the topic drop, choosing instead to ask her detailed questions about the town's infrastructure and government, which fills up an hour of time until Irina departs for an appointment, leaving Ro in Shantal's care.

+++

The next afternoon, Ro appears at Irina's office. She invites him in and gestures to the chair. As he sits, he says, "I was hoping to talk to you about my work assignment. I was assigned to agriculture, but I think I'm better suited to an engineering role."

"All of the engineering roles are currently filled, and we really do need people in agriculture. If you want, though, you can petition the Council to create a new engineering position."

He hands her a piece of paper that feels thick, textured, expensive. It's not the kind of paper used in Ferndale. She looks at it. A résumé.

Bachelor of Science, Yale Engineering School. Harvard Business School MBA. Staffer on the Senate Commerce, Science, and Transportation Committee. CEO of Centeotl Technologies, Irina reads. It occurs to her that she knows virtually nothing about the educational backgrounds of anyone else in their community. It hasn't been relevant.

"So you see the problem, right?" he asks. "My skills aren't being put to good use pulling weeds and picking vegetables. I know how to make technology that will be useful to this community."

"My understanding was that you would spend some time on assignment with the engineers, helping them develop that technology," Irina replies. Rafael had talked to her excitedly about it earlier that day.

"Overseen by someone far less qualified than I am."

Irina narrows her eyes at him as he continues speaking, "I thought that, as someone with a similarly credentialed educational background, you might sympathize. Rumor is you graduated from one of the best law schools in the country."

Irina has never mentioned that to anyone in Ferndale.

"No one here is any better than anyone else," she says. "The work we do on behalf of our community is all that matters. If you heard me on the radio, you should already know that."

For a moment, they stare at each other. Irina senses that this is a test of dominance, so she doesn't avert her eyes, even when the silence becomes uncomfortable. Finally, he says, "I'll take it up with the Council on Thursday, then."

He thanks her curtly and leaves. She stares out the door after him, feeling unnerved.

That evening she, Julián, and Rafael converse in Spanish on the back patio of Rafael and Irina's house while the kids play in the yard.

"It was weird," Irina tells them. "He knows things about me that he shouldn't."

"And he doesn't know some things he really should know," Julián remarks. "He seems entirely unfamiliar with gardening tools, how to hoe out a field, what vegetables are ripe. Really basic stuff. I'm not sure how he survived this long."

"Maybe he farmed other things in San Jose," Rafael says. "Using ethanol-powered equipment."

"Maybe," Julián says, "but I agree with Irina that something doesn't feel right."

That Thursday, Ro arrives at the Council meeting, holding a stack of binders while clad in a dark blue suit of the slim cut that Irina remembers being in fashion before fashion ended. When the public comment section of the meeting arrives, he's first to stand. He hands several folders to the crowd, then steps unselfconsciously up onto the stage and hands a folder to each of the Councilmembers.

"I'd like to share some ideas about how we can modernize Ferndale," he says, addressing the audience more than the Council. "I've been working for the last four years to design an ethanol engine that doesn't rely on an acid battery for its ignition. Inside these folders, you'll see plans for a factory that will produce these engines, as well as a separate plan to make the ethanol that will fuel them. It won't be hard to modify existing gasoline engines to run with ethanol."

Rafael looks at the diagrams and says, "I've considered ethanol before, but even with pre-Pandemic technology, it was energy intensive to produce, barely creating more energy than it required."

Ro fixes Rafael with a hostile stare. "Then it was done incorrectly. I can show you the correct way. This will bring back combustion engines that will enable travel, farming, and electricity generation."

"How much water does it require?" Julián asks. They're all aware that it hasn't rained since May.

"Only what's required to grow the corn."

"That's a lot," Julián says. "There's a reason we transitioned away from corn to more drought-friendly crops."

"I think," says Rafael, "we should embark on this prudently. We plant a small crop of corn and invest some resources in producing engines with Ro's help. We'll see how it goes and re-evaluate next year."

"This is an opportunity for exponential growth!" Ro exclaims. "And you're choosing caution?!"

"It's also an opportunity for catastrophic failure," Rafael responds.

"Where did you get your degree?" Ro asks. "What are your qualifications to be deciding this?"

Rafael looks momentarily taken aback before recovering. He silently thanks Irina for all the opportunities she's given him to improve his debate skills. "My qualifications are that I've been in this town for more than four years building things and solving problems."

"And in four years, what have you accomplished?" Ro replies. "Some refrigerators and lights? This will bring back modernity!"

There's an uncomfortable silence. The thirty or so members of the audience watch with interest. Council meetings rarely offer this level of conflict and engagement.

"My recommendation remains the same," Rafael says. "Start small, scale up if it works. Ro can work with my engineering team to build the engines and . . . ."

"That's a full-time role," Ro interrupts. "And no one else can occupy it."

Rafael shrugs, "A fair point."

"I guess we can create a 'Head of Fuel Innovation' position," Irina says.

"And apprentices?" Ro asks. "I need a full staff."

"And we need to remember that we're in the middle of a drought and should be focusing our resources on diversifying our food production," Julián says. "Our summer crops could fail. If we're creating new apprenticeships, they should be for foraging and hunting."

They take a vote. Unanimous in favor of the role without apprentices.

That night, Rafael and Irina lie in bed. She feathers light kisses down his neck and reaches to take his shirt off, but he's unresponsive.

"What's wrong?" she asks him.

Rafael sighs, "Ro is right. I haven't been able to accomplish much here. I've been working for four years with almost no improvement. Our power is still unreliable. I still haven't found a solution to our battery problem."

"He's preying on your insecurities. He's that kind of guy. I knew plenty of them in law school and dated several of them in college. You can't let him see you sweat."

"Irina, I was a poor, 5'7" tall nerd in a rich kids' school. I'm quite familiar with the operating system of bullies. He's right, though. I've been stuck on this problem for years. Maybe we should let him try to solve it."

"I don't think he'll solve it, though," she says. "Like you said, this requires a lot of energy in order to produce negligibly more energy."

"For me, it would. But maybe he knows something I don't know. We'll see."

+++

Ro shows up at each of the next three Council meetings. At the third, he brings a stack of handouts. During the public comment period, he gets up and distributes them to the audience and the Council. "This is a news story about an offshore wind farm that's supposed to be nearby."

Rafael looks at the paper. "We've already investigated this. It was never completed."

"Are you sure?" Ro says. "Because it says here that a company was selected to begin this project in 2018."

"How long have you lived in California, Mr. Gupta?" Ify asks.

Ro looks confused by the question. "I moved here a couple of years before the Pandemic."

"Well, you've clearly never experienced the California permitting system," Ify says. "You can't hang a bird feeder in your yard without ten levels of approval. Everything requires impact assessments, public comment, months—years!—of discussion before approval."

"That sounds familiar," Ro says pointedly.

Ify sighs. "Permitting reform failed, Mr. Gupta, and we're living with the consequences. We've investigated this and found that it's a dead end."

"But what if you were wrong?" Ro replies.

Rafael shrugs. "I've looked, but if you want to check it out, I can show you the site. You'll see there's nothing there."

The following Monday morning, Rafael and Mark wait beside the blue EV. Ro arrives a few minutes late without apology. He opens the car door and sits shotgun, without even offering the seat to Mark. Mark and Rafael exchange glances in the rearview mirror as Rafael starts the car.

"So, Rafael," Ro says as they cross over the anemic Eel River. "What did you do before the Pandemic?"

Rafael can already guess where this is going. There's no evading, so he leans into the punch, "I did landscaping in Seattle."

"I know it's hard when you first arrive here as an immigrant. My parents struggled for a few years too, but they were smart, so they worked it out. By the time I was five, my father had gotten re-certified in medicine and my mother as an engineer. What did your parents do?"

"My mother was a nanny, and my father owned a cocoa plantation."

Ro nods. Rafael can sense that these questions are information-gathering, not a courtesy. He turns the tables.

"I heard you came here from San Jose," Rafael says to Ro. "What's it like there?"

"Well, I knew this Pandemic was going to be serious, so I found a renewable energy project and tapped into its grid," Ro says. "But the rest of San Jose was the same as everywhere . . . , sent back to the stone ages. People scratching out a living on amateur farms, raiding houses for weapons and whatever canned goods are left at this point, fighting for scraps like animals."

"If you had such a good setup, why leave?" Mark asks from the backseat.

"Because I had hoped that we could form a partnership to fulfill my vision. I didn't think you would be so hostile to any kind of progress. I figured you'd be happy to be offered the opportunity to have unlimited power, transit, farming equipment that doesn't rely on horses . . . ."

Rafael glances in the rearview mirror and sees Mark roll his eyes. Rafael chooses not to engage with Ro's antagonism and, instead, recalls Julián's prior remarks about Ro's apparent lack of survival skills. "So how did you survive for the past five years?"

Ro shrugs. "I had foresight. I stocked up on MREs months before anyone else even knew the name of the Virus."

"You're in pretty good shape for a guy who lived off of MREs for five years," Mark remarks. It's true that Ro has the physique of a man who works out daily and has excellent nutrition.

"I supplemented with farming, like everyone else," Ro says with a shrug.

"Oh?" Rafael asks. "What were you growing down there in San Jose?"

"The usual things. Corn, beans, vegetables," Ro replies vaguely. "So where did you get your degree again? You didn't really answer when I asked you in the Council meeting."

"In Venezuela," Rafael replies. He senses that Ro is about to turn the questioning back around, so he tries to find something he assumes Ro will be happy to bluster about at length. "Irina said that you were an entrepreneur?"

"Among other things," Ro replies. "Most recently, I ran a startup focused on designing a better ethanol engine. We were poised to get some big venture capital funding—household names, names even you would recognize—but then the Pandemic happened. I ended up figuring the engine design out on my own, though, which, again, is why I came here. I thought Ferndale would have the vision and resources to transform what's left of the world . . . ."

"Was that your first start-up?" Rafael asks, trying to keep the conversation going.

"Of course not! I'd built and sold my first company by the time I was twenty-eight. By thirty-five, I'd already built and sold a second company. This would have been my third."

"What kind of companies?"

"Well, the first one was a dating app. I'm sure you've heard of it." He names the app, and Rafael and Mark both shrug. "Anyway, it revolutionized the dating app market . . . ."

He rambles on for several minutes, giving them his elevator pitch about using technology to systematize and optimize romantic pairings.

"And yet you're still single," Mark observes from the backseat.

"I never found anyone who shared my vision and ambition," Ro replies. "And, anyway, I've been focused on my work. That's my legacy. I don't have time for romantic or familial entanglements."

"It's certainly true that children keep a person from getting things done," Mark agrees.

As they pass over the bridge across the bay, Ro relaunches his questioning of Rafael. "Irina is your wife, right?"

"Hence the matching hyphenated last names." Rafael smiles. "Were you married before the Pandemic, or did you meet after?"

"We met in Ferndale." Rafael wonders where this is going. It seems unlikely that Ro is benevolently interested in Rafael and Irina's romantic origin story.

"Before or after the Charter drafting?"

"Met before. Married a few months after."

"Then it must have been interesting to work on the Charter together."

"It was." A seed of suspicion grows in Rafael's mind about Ro's motives for this line of questioning.

"I read that you two had some disagreement about the Economic Charter."

He must have reviewed the legislative history that Emma wrote, Rafael concludes. "We did, but we resolved it."

'What's in that legislative history?' Rafael wonders. He's never looked at it. Did Tina slip in that joke about his reasons for voting the way he did? Surely she wouldn't have.

"Two married couples drafted the Charter, right?" Ro asks.

"Yep. Along with two other people."

"And now you all run the town."

"Until next spring; then the Council leadership starts to turn over."

Ro nods, "I've heard."

Thankfully, they arrive at the wind turbines a few minutes later. As he always does, Rafael remembers the tryst he and Irina had here. Ro gets out to look around. When he's about fifty feet away, Mark says, "What an asshole. Just like those guys who used to bring their fancy cars in for service and look right through me."

"I know what you mean," Rafael says. He remembers the sensation of being invisible, of standing, sweaty, in the afternoon sun as the owner of the expensive house he'd landscaped walked by without even acknowledging him.

Ro spends an hour inspecting the area, but he's still dissatisfied. "Are you sure there's no other site around here?"

Rafael shrugs, "We've looked all along the coast and found nothing else, but you're welcome to borrow the car and do your own reconnaissance."

Ro takes the keys and leaves. Mark rolls his eyes.

Mark and Rafael hook up the generators they've brought to charge. Mark notes that the lithium generator batteries seem to be losing capacity. Rafael knows. He has a couple dozen internal clocks operating in his mind at any time, all ticking down to the zero hour when various aspects of their infrastructure cease to function.

"What about the wind turbine battery?" Rafael asks. "How much time do you think it has?"

"It still seems to be functioning at full capacity."

Rafael looks at the large shipping container that houses the battery. They both walk over to it, and he asks, "Is this a lithium battery?"

Mark shakes his head. "It's not like any battery I've ever seen."

Rafael opens up the back of the shipping container and steps inside, where he sees rows of battery cells that, upon closer inspection, do look a bit different from what he's used to. On the back wall of the shipping container, he sees a sign: "Iron flow battery?" he reads aloud. Mark shrugs. In his small notebook, Rafael jots down the name of the company and the Oregon address at the bottom of the sign.

Ro returns a couple of hours later and summons them to the car with a frustrated sigh. Mark looks at Rafael and shakes his head.

+++

At the next Council meeting, Ro argues that they should send out boats to look for the offshore wind turbines. Julián points out that it's a big ocean, and it would take a while to search, even if they contain their search to the approximate area highlighted in the picture of the news story Ro had distributed.

"If you don't take big risks," Ro replies, "you don't get big rewards."

"We have some people assigned to deep sea fishing, right?" Ify asks.

From memory, Shantal rattles off the names of eight people. The Council grants Ro a week of two sailors' time to search for the windmills.

"Even if they were there, though," Rafael says, "six years in ocean air without maintenance would likely render them inoperable."

"A competent engineer could get them running again," Ro replies. Rafael shrugs.

After the meeting, as Rafael and Irina walk home, she asks, "Am I a bad person for hoping that his boat sinks?"

"Only because there are two other people on it."

"Well, then, I hope he falls overboard."

+++

After an unsuccessful hunt for wind turbines, Ro appears again at the Council meeting to complain about how a week with a non-motorized sailboat wasn't enough time to do a thorough search. Ify assures him that the fishing crews will continue to watch for the turbines.

Rafael moves to the next item on the agenda.

"Now that we have enough ethanol, Mark and I are planning to go up to Oregon to investigate the battery company I briefed the Council on last week," he says.

"You should take me with you," Ro says, speaking out of turn. "Aside from the fact that the SUV you'll be driving is mine and I manufactured the fuel, I'm more familiar with renewable energy technology than anyone else here. I'm the only one who can figure out how these batteries work."

Rafael really doesn't want to go on a multi-day buddy road-trip with Ro, but he has to admit that Ro has a point. Mark and Rafael have looked at the flow battery many times but still aren't sure how it works. When Rafael had mentioned flow batteries in an engineering meeting the prior week, Ro had seemed familiar, at least, with the concept.

Rafael makes a mental note to find something to listen to in the car so he won't have to spend twelve hours conversing with Ro.

"Are we certain that we'll have enough fuel to get to Eugene and back?" Ify asks.

"I'm certain. My engines are the most efficient ethanol engines ever produced. We could probably even get to Portland and back on a single tank of fuel," Ro replies.

"It's about three hundred and twenty miles to Eugene," Rafael says. "So just to be safe, we're going to tow a trailer with a large tank of extra fuel."

"It's not necessary," Ro replies.

"Just a precaution," Rafael answers. He really doesn't want to get marooned with Ro along the road. "Better to be safe than sorry."

After the meeting, the Councilmembers walk back down Main Street.

"There are a lot of places to hide a body between here and Eugene," Tina jokes.

"I dealt with plenty of worse people at boarding school," Rafael replies. "It'll be fine."

The next morning, Rafael and Mark wait in the SUV. Mark makes himself comfortable in the front passenger seat, while Rafael shuffles through Irina's downloaded playlists on her old phone, trying to resist the urge to violate her privacy by looking at her old texts or photos. Ro arrives five minutes late, instinctively heads for the driver's side door, and scowls when he finds Rafael there. He gets in the backseat without comment. Rafael cues up a downloaded podcast and hits play. It's an episode from the beginning of the Pandemic, and listening to it is eerie but fascinating. The host and his guest, an epidemiologist who'd written a series of public health articles about risk during Covid, discuss the Covid pandemic and how it's impacting this new pandemic. They talk about the comparative danger of this virus versus Covid, speculate about its origins, and analyze the government's belated response.

"I hate this guy," Ro comments about the podcast host. "He thinks he's so clever, but he's not. Also, his wife is a total socialist."

Rafael, whose wife has also been credibly accused of being 'a total socialist,' is amused.

"People always think that the main problem with socialist economic systems is that they disincentivize hard work," Ro says, talking over the podcast. "And that *is* a serious problem. If you don't compensate the hardest working, smartest people, what incentive is there to work hard, to do a little extra?"

"Other than the satisfaction of having contributed meaningfully to your community?" Mark asks.

"Almost no one really cares about that," Ro says, rolling his eyes. "People care about the social status and the consumer goods that money buys. If you do more—if you're smarter, more innovative, if you take bigger risks—you should be rewarded. That's only fair."

"But that's not how it actually worked. You're wrongly assuming that the people who made the most money were the ones who were doing the most useful things or working the hardest," Rafael remarks. During the Founding, he'd had some of the same thoughts that Ro is articulating, but time has vindicated Irina's approach, so he's happy to defend it. "Instead, the richest people were often just the ones who got lucky or designed products that were actively harmful but were addictive enough to be highly profitable or engaged in anticompetitive corporate practices that shut out the competition or had good enough connections to be handed venture capital with little actual oversight."

"I think you're overgeneralizing," Ro replies. "Anyway, as I was saying, the real problem is that socialist systems assume that the government knows best—that the government knows anything really. The truth is that government just isn't well-positioned to assess what people need and want. It's always going to guess wrong. But the market is always going to guess right, because it responds directly to supply and demand. If people want more of something, they'll pay more for it, which will incentivize manufacturers to make more of it."

Ro continues sermonizing on this topic until Rafael gives up on the podcast and turns on Irina's old playlist. He's surprised to find that Mark has a good singing voice. The miles roll by.

+++

When they return the following week, Rafael reports their findings to the Council. "The good news is that there are a lot of materials to manufacture the batteries at the site. The even better news is that these batteries, unlike lithium or lead-acid batteries, are made of materials we can find pretty much anywhere, so we could still manufacture them once we run out of the materials at the site. If we can figure out how to build the flow batteries, it would solve our battery problem for the foreseeable future. The bad news is that we haven't figured that out yet."

Ro had been reluctant to give up on this effort, despite making no progress over the course of the week. Rafael, though, has a plan: "I'm going to use the radio with the satellite connection to see if we can find someone who can assist us."

406

The Council agrees, and calls Ro to the stage so he can update them on the modifications he's making to the combine's original combustion engine.

"And you believe it will be ready in time for the harvest?" Julián says.

"Since I've been putting in so many extra hours, I'm certain it will be," Ro replies. "Those hours, by the way, have been entirely uncompensated."

"Everyone is compensated at the same rate, Mr. Gupta," Ify answers. "As discussed in the Charter."

"That's hardly fair," Ro objects. "If someone else works forty hours and I work sixty, shouldn't I get paid more?"

"We all put in extra hours. We do it because we care about our community," Rafael replies with mild annoyance. "I have three children and a more-than-full-time job, but I'm still sitting here in this chair listening to you at . . . ," he checks the clock on the wall, ". . . 9:07 p.m. Ify, how often do you have to make nighttime house calls?"

"At least once a week. Often more," Ify answers.

"Tina, how many evenings do you offer security training?" Rafael asks.

"Mondays and Wednesdays," she replies, "and some Sundays."

"Yael, how many evenings a week do you offer self-defense classes?" Rafael asks their new martial arts instructor, Yael Feldman.

"Three, sometimes four," Yael replies.

Rafael nods. "And Shasta, how many times do you have to do inventory work on evenings or weekends?"

"During harvest time? Constantly. The rest of the year? Occasionally," Shasta replies.

Rafael calls on several more members of the audience to emphasize his point. Ro listens with annoyance.

"Everyone is equally compensated because everyone's work is essential to our survival," Ify concludes. "And we don't want to send the message that some people are more valuable than others."

"That is, again, clearly discussed in our Charter," Irina points out. "And emphasized in our radio addresses. If you didn't like that, you shouldn't have come here."

Throughout the fall, Ro complains regularly to Rafael about the fact that he now has to pay to rent his own car. Rafael finally tells him that he's free to take the car and leave if he'd like. In October, Irina is livid when she finds out that Ro is paying a woman in the community to clean his home. Rafael points out that as long as he isn't paying her for anything sexual, it's a permissible exchange of services. Ro complains to Ify about how it's a waste of time for him to be doing mandatory food service and agricultural work. Ify shrugs and cites the Charter.

Ro is a regular fixture at the Council meetings, often targeting Rafael, who, despite his privately expressed insecurities, remembers Irina's admonition not to waver and patiently avoids rising to the bait.

After Rafael and Irina have undressed and gotten into bed together one night after another frustrating Council meeting, Irina looks into Rafael's eyes earnestly and says, "I'm proud of you, you know, for not backing down with Ro. You're doing a good job."

"Our marriage has given me plenty of opportunities to hone both my patience and my arguing skills," he jokes. She cuffs him on the arm. "And anyway I have a brilliant wife, three mostly lovely children, a beautiful home, a ragtag group of friends, meaningful work, a position of reluctant leadership within my community, and," he gently takes her earlobe between his teeth as he runs his hand enticingly down her breast and over the swell of her hip, "very good sex. Who gives a damn what he says? I'm winning."

+++

The week before the harvest, with Mark's help, Ro finishes retrofitting the combine, and he and Mark demonstrate it before a gathered crowd of Ferndale residents. Irina and Ify give a speech thanking Ro, Mark, and the other workers for their hard work; Ro spends fifteen minutes talking about this great accomplishment before the crowd, inserting not-so-subtle digs at the Council's lack of commitment to his work. The Councilmembers watch from the edge of the crowd.

"Did we make it a crime to be an arrogant motherfucker?" Tina asks, watching Ro gladhand members of the crowd like a politician or movie star.

"Unfortunately, being insufferable is entirely legal," Ify replies. This is the first negative thing Irina has ever heard Ify say about anyone.

"What about a recall vote for an ordinary citizen? Can everyone get together and vote him off the island?" Tina asks.

"Sadly, no, but we really should have included that," Irina says with a sigh.

"Even if we could remove him," Rafael says, "it would be unwise. He's given us useful technology. Next season we should slowly increase the amount of crops dedicated to ethanol. We move forward, but don't bet the farm."

To reward Ro for his efforts, the Council grants him two apprenticeship slots, but he's both publicly and privately unhappy with the quality of the four apprentices generated by the lottery.

"I should be able to pick whatever apprentices I want," he tells the Council.

"This is the way our system is set up," Irina replies. "It ensures that everyone has an equal chance to pursue a job they're interested in."

"In order to do my work, I need to be able to select the most qualified and intelligent people from the community. This shouldn't be left to chance!" Ro says.

"Even before the Pandemic, Mr. Gupta, who was and was not given an opportunity was largely a matter of chance," Ify replies, arguing against the very same points he'd made during the Charter drafting. "People who were lucky enough to be born into wealth or with advantageous familial connections got opportunities the rest of us could never have. It was always a matter of random chance. Our system is just a fairer kind of lottery: a pure lottery instead of a birth lottery."

"You can also still select for the most qualified or intelligent applicants," Irina points out. "You can pick the best two of the four apprentices; if you're unhappy with all four, you can redraw from the lottery in a few months."

"But that's so inefficient," Ro complains.

"Efficiency isn't the only factor that matters," Irina answers. "Fairness and egalitarianism are also important considerations."

The Council turns to preparations for the first Council transition the following Founder's Day.

"We've been relying on drawing of paper lots," Shantal says, "and that works well enough for apprenticeship lotteries with a limited number of people, but right now we have more than three hundred registered candidates for the Council lottery, so we should consider a more efficient system: a random number generator."

"Do we have something like that?" Ify asks.

"We do," Shantal says, approaching the laptop where Emma is taking the Council's notes. Shantal asks to borrow the laptop; then she pulls up Excel.

"We set it to pick a number between one and, say, three hundred . . . ," she says, typing the values. Then she hits F9 with flourish. Fifty-seven appears in the column. She hits it again: two hundred forty-two. A third time: Ninety-five. The Council agrees that this method works for the Council lotteries going forward.

Chapter Twenty-Five: April 2039

At the Founders Day picnic, the Council thanks Tina and Emma for their service. Rafael leans over to Irina. "I can't believe we agreed to this rotation order. We could have left the Council now and spent our evenings playing with our children and engaging in other recreational activities."

"Everyone agreed that the best order for transitions would be the reverse order of when we arrived in Ferndale," she replies, so Rafael will be the very last person to rotate off the Council.

They stand before the assembled residents of Ferndale. Rafael, nominally (and to his constant annoyance), the Chair of the Council, hits the F9 button on the Excel spreadsheet, and it produces a number: two hundred ninety. Shantal consults her printed spreadsheet.

"Ro Gupta."

+++

"Well, this is going to suck for you," Tina says, sipping her moonshine on Rafael and Irina's patio, where the founders have gathered. "I'll think of you when I'm at home drinking moonshine and making love to my wife and you're sitting in City Hall dealing with that asshole."

Rafael already has a growing headache. "Kind of a strange coincidence, right?"

"You think he rigged it?" Tina asks. "I wouldn't put it past him. It's worth investigating."

"We don't have probable cause for any kind of search," Irina says, "and we have to consider how it would look if we launched an investigation against our very first new Councilmember."

A few days later, Tina appears in Irina's office and closes the door behind her.

"So I did a little poking around," Tina says, "and Ro has a bunch of property he hasn't turned over, including a bunch of hard drives, some ethanol, and an ethanol-powered generator."

Irina looks at her, aghast. "Did you illegally search his house?!"

"The door was unlocked."

"It doesn't matter!" Irina exclaims, exasperated. She thinks for a moment. "Were these things readily visible from the outside of the house?" Tina shakes her head. "Then we can't use it. A hunch isn't probable cause for a search, and even if we did have probable cause, we need people to have faith in our system; this is a crucial moment. If things go awry with the very first Council transition, how will that look?"

Tina frowns and walks out of Irina's office without another word.

+++

The following month, Ro rejects all four of his apprentices, demanding that he be given the opportunity to redraw a new set of even more candidates. The Council reluctantly allows him to draw six new names. Given Ro's treatment of his previous apprentices, only one person registers for the lottery, so the other five names have to be drawn from the larger pool of residents.

Ro spars with Rafael and Julián again over the amount of corn they've dedicated for his ethanol project. One day he appears with a vial of liquid.

"With the help of my best apprentice and some basic materials I gathered from the Cal Poly Humboldt chemistry lab, I've been able to produce our first antibiotic: penicillin!" he proclaims proudly.

Ify calls Yumi up to the stage from the audience.

"It's theoretically possible that this might work," she says, "but it seems risky. Still, I guess if the risk on the other side was death and if the patient consented to this . . . treatment, we could try it out, ethically."

"My office is at the forefront of efforts to bring back modernity!" Ro says. "I deserve more resources and better apprentices."

The Council agrees to create another apprenticeship lottery position to work with Ro on developing facsimiles of modern medications.

+++

In September, Rafael and Julián stand on the bridge over the Eel River, staring at an alarming sight.

"The river is gone," Rafael says in shock.

"Not entirely gone," Julián replies. "There's still a lot of water underground, but, yes, this is a big problem."

"We need to let the Council know," Rafael says with a sigh. "And consult with Rick and Gail."

That night on the radio, Rick and Gail say they do have some ideas, but they'd rather not discuss them over the public airwaves. So they suggest discussing this at the October trade conference.

Rafael and Irina decide that their children are old enough to go to the conference, and since they have the ethanol-powered SUV, there's enough space to bring them along. They load up the kids, camping gear, and Buddy and set off for Red Bluff. The children have rarely been in a car, so they're entranced by the scenery that speeds by as Irina drives.

"I do have a bit of good news that I'm going to announce at the Council meeting next Thursday," Rafael says, as Irina negotiates the tight mountain turns. "I've finally found a chemical engineer who wants to come here. She worked for a mining company in western Montana, and she's going to leave once the snow clears from the mountains next summer."

"That's excellent news!" Irina agrees. "You feel a little better about the battery situation, then?"

"I'll feel much better if we can figure this out. This would solve a lot of our problems."

They stop for lunch at an old ranger station and let the kids explore the mountainside for a little while. Irina and Rafael marvel at how big they're all getting. Miranda had gotten her first period the summer before, but when Irina had tried to talk to her about it, she'd insisted that Jing had already told her everything she needed to know. Irina had persisted, though, knowing that pregnancy is still a risky endeavor for women in their community. Pre-teen hormones have made Miranda surly and withdrawn some of the time, but on this day, she seems to be in good spirits. Matteo has turned from a toddler into a little boy. He has little time for Irina now and prefers to spend his days tagging along with Rafael on engineering projects or collecting insects and butterflies with several friends in the fields and forests near their house. Even Javier is usually more interested in exploring than staying near his parents. He basks in whatever attention his siblings give him, following them clumsily.

"You were right about having a child," Rafael says, watching Javier and Matteo chasing a butterfly. "I'm glad we did."

She takes his hand. Beside her, Buddy lazes in the grass. He's getting old, Irina realizes, with sadness. They'd recently celebrated his tenth birthday. Still, he sometimes has enough energy to keep up with the children. She hopes he has some good years left.

That evening Rick, Amy, and Gail join Irina, Rafael, Julián, Shasta, and Tina by the fire.

"We need to drain the reservoirs and get rid of the dams," Rick says matter-of-factly.

"If there are dams, can't we use them to harness power?" Rafael asks.

"They're too far to be useful, and even if they were closer, they're too outdated to provide power," Rick replies. "They were actually slated to be destroyed years ago, but the process kept getting delayed. Native tribes commented on the project numerous times. These dams divert water from the Eel River into the Russian River, and they block fish from reaching the best breeding areas. Also, they're already disintegrating, and it would be better to do a planned destruction than to wait for them to just burst unexpectedly one day. Getting rid of them benefits Ferndale and the ecosystem."

They talk for a while about the logistics of dam removal—they'll have to make sure that they drain the dam slowly enough to prevent any damage to the roads or bridges downstream, and they'll need to ensure that any towns downstream that could be flooded are actually empty. They will also need to prepare for a possible temporary influx of water in the river near Ferndale, and they'll have to find a way to create enough explosives to actually destroy the dams once they've drained the reservoirs.

"Maybe we can get our chemical engineer, Aurelia Gomez, working on that when she finishes with the batteries," Rafael says. He tells Gail, Rick, and Amy about the plan to try to build iron-flow batteries. "Aurelia said she'll probably need someone to get into the company's computer systems so she can get schematics and other information about the batteries. If you can help with that, we're happy to share the technology."

Gail and Irina agree to take the matter to their respective Councils.

The rains come in late October, and with the help of Ro's retrofitted ethanol generators and the allotment of corn he'd been given to produce ethanol, they make it through the winter without power failures. Ro selects one apprentice and redraws four more applicants from the pool of unapprenticed residents.

He continues to agitate for more apprentices, more corn, more scrap metal for his projects.

When a baby gets a severe and potentially deadly blood infection, Ify and Dr. Cunningham—whom they had rushed to pick up from Redding and had paid dearly in exchange—are forced to use Ro's homemade penicillin. To everyone's surprise, it works, and Ro begins producing more of it.

Chapter Twenty-Six: April 2040

They gather for their fifth Founders Day. The remaining Councilmembers thank Julián for his service. Rafael uses Excel to generate a random number: two hundred seventy-five. Shantal consults her list. "Brandon Sterling."

Rafael has met him in passing. He's assigned to building maintenance but has occasionally been pulled into Rafael, Mark, or Ro's engineering projects because he has some engineering expertise. Rafael has found him to be quiet and somewhat socially awkward, the kind of man who mostly blends into the background. In the Council meetings, Brandon says little, but he always votes with Ro. Two months after Brandon joins the Council, Tina arrives in Irina's office, with Shantal in tow. Tina closes the door, and both of them sit down.

Tina hands Brandon's intake form to Irina; then Shantal speaks, "Brandon was the one who came up with the idea of using a random-number generator. He was helping me fix the printer, and we started talking about the election. He suggested Excel, then showed me how to use it."

"So the claim is that he suggested the number generator, then somehow fixed it so that Ro would get elected, then waited a year and fixed it again so he would get elected?" Irina asks. "That sounds circumstantial."

"What if they knew each other Before?" Tina asks.

"Do you have reason to believe that they did?" Irina says.

Tina points to the intake form. "They're both from the Bay Area, they both have engineering expertise, and Brandon arrived just a few months before Ro."

Irina doesn't conceal her skepticism. "It's not enough. If you really think there's some conspiracy here, we should wait until we have some evidence."

"I'll keep digging," Tina says.

"Please do it legally, okay?" Irina says. Tina smiles but doesn't respond.

Aurelia contacts Rafael on the radio in July to let him know that she's in Eugene waiting for him. Ro argues that he should go along, but Rafael stubbornly refuses, saying that he'll take Mark and Jaya instead because Ferndale can't spare Ro and his work on the ethanol engines.

Privately, he tells the other founders, "This is the first encounter that Aurelia will have with us, and I want it to be a good one. We need her to join us here in Ferndale. Ro's demeanor doesn't lend itself to good first impressions."

As usual, Brandon backs Ro's proposal to go to Eugene, but the others outvote them.

This summer, at least, Julián reports to the Council that the river is as high as it had been two summers before. Ro uses this information to push for a larger portion of the corn crop, arguing that they can afford to grow more fall vegetables to make up for it, now that the water isn't a concern. Rafael attends the Council meeting via radio and votes down this proposal, cautioning Ro once again that they need to move carefully.

Ro is visibly angry. "You weren't so careful when you traded away one of Ferndale's most valuable resources so you could get a doctor for your wife."

Irina pales as he continues, "I spoke with Dr. Cunningham when she was here, and she said that Rafael and Ify made the trade at the Conference that year, which is, according to the Council records, before the Council agreed to any such trade. Interesting that two members of the Council whose wives were both pregnant would unilaterally agree to such a deal, and none of the rest of the Council would exercise any oversight of the unauthorized trade."

"The trade was beneficial to the community as a whole," Rafael replies over the radio. "It was discussed and debated openly in the next Council meeting. If the Council hadn't agreed to it, it could have been canceled."

Ro looks out over the audience. The room is so full that people are standing in the back. Council meetings have grown progressively better-attended as he's stirred up more controversy.

"I'll leave it to you to decide," Ro says to the audience, "whether this Council has actually served you well. In the three years before I arrived, things were stagnant. You struggled with power issues, you had no modern medicine, you had an insular Council of people who were committed to serving their own interests and their narrow vision of what this town could be. In the two years that I've been here, I've brought you the best innovations from modernity: engines that allow for electricity generation and long-distance travel—if you're ever allowed to use them—medication, and the possibility of unlimited electric power from the wind turbines I'm still certain are off the coast, waiting to be rediscovered. I'm offering you technology that was cutting edge, even for its time. They're not even offering you a contemporary lifestyle. My parents came to this country because it was the land of opportunity, because this was a place that rewarded you if you worked hard . . . ."

"It rewarded some people who worked hard," Irina interrupts. "It ground others under its heel."

"Was it that bad?" he asks her. "So bad that a little girl from Southern Utah who was removed from her father's care couldn't get into one of the finest law schools in the country? So bad that an immigrant child from Nigeria couldn't go on to attend Cornell Veterinary School? So bad that people like Rafael and Julián and my own parents took great risks to come here? This was the greatest country in the world. We invented the telephone, the airplane, the internet, the automobile, GPS technology, moon landings, and reliable electricity. And that was because we had an environment of freedom that was conducive to innovation. What you've created here is conducive only to stagnation."

There's a buzz in Irina's ears. She tries to gather her best arguments, but he continues, "Your legislative history notes that the Ferndale Charter was meant to evolve with the circumstances. I would argue that the circumstances now necessitate changes. We should be rewarding innovators, maximizing economic freedom, allowing people greater choice about how they live their lives, and getting rid of the ridiculous apprenticeship system. This town is large enough now that we don't need a proscribed list of professions from an inexpert Council."

Ify's eyes widen as they meet Irina's. Is Ro calling a referendum vote to amend the Charter? He stops just short of it. "I would encourage you all to think about it," Ro says to the audience. "What future do you want: do you want to continue to live in cold houses, hold jobs that are chosen for you instead of by you, receive no compensation for your extra work or ingenuity? Do you want to survive, or do you want to flourish? Do you want to live in a free society or not?"

He sits down. There's a stunned silence in the room and on the ham radio. Irina wonders suddenly if Rafael is the only one listening to this public broadcast. She hopes so. It's Ify who finally speaks, "You're mistaken, Ro, about the freedom that was offered in the pre-Pandemic United States. That 'freedom' was for the few, and it was always at the expense of many others, both here and abroad, including in my own home country. You speak about the boundless technological growth of the United States without considering who was sacrificed in the name of that growth. Who mined the coal that powered the factories or the lithium used in the batteries? Who was displaced and murdered by the government that took this land in the name of manifest destiny? Who fought to serve this country's supposed interests in the Cold War and the Middle East? Who did the backbreaking agricultural labor that helped to establish the country in its beginning? Always the few benefited disproportionately from the work of the many, while the many struggled to afford healthcare, housing, childcare, and education. And always those few have thought that they were uniquely deserving of the fantastic, disproportionate benefits that accrued to them. Sometimes they let a couple of us slip through the cracks to give the others hope, but the game was always, always rigged. What we've built here is different, and it's better. We've created a system where everyone has a good quality of life, all work is valued, everyone has an equal chance to get the job they want. And we've built a community, which is something that most people were struggling to find under the individualistic system you're describing."

A hush falls over the room. Irina has nothing to add to Ify's words. From the radio, Rafael proposes that they conclude the meeting. Everyone files out in stunned silence, and Irina and Ify walk wordlessly into the night.

Later, Irina lies awake, worrying about what might happen if Ro calls for a referendum. Would the people of Ferndale reject the economic charter? It seems like the economy the founders set up has been working, but there's no way to tell if Ro's arguments are getting traction. His arguments—that their economic system is stifling their progress, that the system forces people into roles they don't like, that they could move forward more quickly if they just took more risks—reflect her own occasional doubts. She wishes that Rafael were here to talk through these worries. In his absence, she snuggles up against Buddy, pulls out her favorite book, and reads until her eyelids grow heavy.

+++

The next afternoon, the founders take their lunches to-go and meet in Tina and Emma's back yard.

"Ify," Irina asks, "have you ever told anyone here where you went to school?"

"Most definitely not. That would be bragging," Ify replies as he eats his salad.

"Neither did I," Irina says. "He could have heard about my childhood from anyone in our support group, but I've never told anyone here where I went to school."

"That information would have been online, though, right?" Emma says. "On social media?"

"I did have a professional profile online. But the internet's been gone for years," Irina replies.

"What did you spend your time doing before the internet died? Once you knew that everything was really going to collapse?" Emma asks, as she hands Penelope a sippy cup. "I spent a lot of time researching and downloading anything I didn't want to lose. Tina said that he has a bunch of hard drives in his house. Maybe he downloaded a different kind of survival information."

"Information about people?" Irina asks.

"He does spend a lot of time asking nosy questions, doesn't he? Clearly he believes that knowledge is power," Emma replies.

"Maybe," Irina says. "Our bigger problem, though, is that I think people are starting to agree with his arguments."

"You think so?" Ify asks. "I'm not sure they are."

"He has given us ethanol engines and an antibiotic," Irina argues. "We haven't offered anything new in a while."

"We offer them security, childcare and education for their children, three healthy meals a day, professional counseling, medical care, basic electricity, community, and hope," Emma says. "You shouldn't discount that."

"Maybe," Irina replies, "but we need to do something more, something big. We need to show that we can still solve problems. Hopefully Rafael's battery idea works. Julián, where are we on the dam removal?"

"We've scouted the two dams and ensured that there's no one living downstream," Julián replies. "Rafael was going to talk to Aurelia about explosive options. Rick says September would be the best time to do it because that's when the water levels are lowest and the flooding would be more minimal."

"We need to change the lottery mechanism before the next selection," Tina says.

"We will, but we shouldn't do that yet," Irina says. "He would know we're on to him, and if he has tampered with the system, he could destroy the evidence before we can get it. We still have no probable cause to search his home or his computer."

"So we just wait?!" Tina says.

"We wait strategically," Irina replies. "We wait to provide some compelling evidence of our competence. We wait to figure out a way to get probable cause to search Ro's house. We wait until we can talk to Amy, because if there's evidence of some kind of interference with the random-number generator, we're going to need someone with the technical expertise to recognize that."

"We can't contact her over the radio?" Tina asks.

"We know Ro listens to the radio," Irina says. "Anything we say, he could hear. We'll talk to the Tribe when Julián and Rick meet to blow up the dams."

"We shouldn't wait too long," Tina says. "He could call for a referendum or get someone to ask for a recall vote for you, Rafael, or Ify."

"I'm confident he won't," Ify says.

Irina doesn't share his certainty. Waiting, though, still seems like the most prudent option.

When Rafael returns, he briefs the Council on the battery progress.

"Aurelia is fairly certain that she'll be able to reverse-engineer the technology, but it will take time," Rafael says. Not wanting to reveal Amy's existence to Ro, Rafael leaves out the part about her help.

"How much time?" Ify asks.

"Weeks? Months, maybe?" Rafael replies.

"And where are we on the dam destruction project?" Ify asks.

"Aurelia is confident that she'll be able to build explosives from relatively easy-to-find ingredients. She's sent a list of materials and likely locations," Rafael replies. "Julián and Shasta have agreed to leave tomorrow to start gathering the supplies."

After the Council meeting, Rafael feeds the fire in his and Irina's living room, and the two of them sit on the couch with cups of tea. Rafael says, "When I stopped to pick Amy up, Gail said that a lot of people heard about our very contentious Council meeting. The Tribe is rooting for us and said that if there's anything they can do to help, we should let them know. The Sisters and Brothers said the same and so did Dr. Cunningham and several other people I stopped to see on my way back."

That solidarity warms Irina. Rafael continues, "There are a lot of people who admire what you and Gail have done with the trade conference. I don't think it's overstating things to say that the trainings have saved lives and prevented resource-based conflict."

"I hope so," Irina says, "but I'm worried that people here are starting to agree with Ro. His arguments are compelling, even to me."

He takes her hand. "We've always been honest with each other. When you first proposed the economic plan, I wasn't sure it would work. I made a lot of the same arguments Ro is making. But I can see now that this was the right approach. What we've set up here is good. People are fed, and their physical needs are met, but beyond that, we've created a place where people take care of each other, where they have a sense of community. We did what we set out to do, and I think people can see that."

+++

Ro uses the final August Council meeting to advocate for more Charter changes. He argues that government by lottery is a terrible idea that resulted in exactly the situation they're in now: questionably competent leadership with no expertise. If they really want good government, they need a system of elections without term limits, which will allow leaders to really grow knowledge over time. Rafael, Irina, and Ify reiterate all the arguments that had been made in favor of the government-by-lottery system during the Founding. As he had before, Ro doesn't actually call for a referendum to amend the Charter; he just invites his audience to consider his words.

Afterward, the founders sit on Rafael and Irina's back porch, drinking Julián's moonshine, and Irina remarks, "Those Free Speech limits Ify and I wanted are looking pretty good right now."

"We can't compromise our principles for one bully," Rafael says.

"But we could just drop him off in the mountains a couple hundred miles away and let nature take its course," Tina points out.

"Tempting," Irina says.

"That's not who we are," Rafael says. He and Tina get into a heated philosophical debate over whether the ends justify the means. Irina pours herself more moonshine, and a strong longing descends on her. She recalls the evenings that she and Rafael spent together in the House by the Sea, sitting on the patio and exchanging confidences. She remembers those heady first weeks when the founders had dreamed up this society, and she longs for that comparative simplicity. Those days are now wreathed in the ethereal glow of nostalgia.

She'd known that someone like Ro would show up. It was the reason she'd felt such trepidation about inviting others here. There would always be people who believed that they had the right to rule over others, people who would fight for dominance, people who expect others to do their hard work for them, to clean up their messes.

"The woman who cleans his house!" Irina exclaims suddenly. The others turn toward her, and she explains, "Ro pays a woman to clean his house. She may have seen the illegal property he has. That could be our probable cause to search his house."

"The invisible help," Rafael says, thinking of his and Mark's experiences with men like Ro. "Do we know who cleans his house?" Tina asks.

"No, but Shantal may. She makes it her business to know everyone else's business," Irina says.

+++

"Lucia Hernandez," Shantal says the next day when Tina and Irina ask her about Ro's house cleaner. "Arrived here a year ago, thirty-one years old, one child, former house cleaner in the Sacramento suburbs, assigned to work in agriculture, but she likes having some extra income to buy gifts for her son. I can introduce you."

Irina says. "I know her. Our sons go to school together."

"Can we trust Lucia not to tell him we talked to her?" Tina asks Irina as they walk to the school that afternoon.

427

"We kind of have to," Irina says. "I don't know another way we can establish probable cause to search."

They wait outside the school and, when Lucia approaches, they pull her aside. In an empty classroom, after advising Lucia of the need for secrecy, Tina asks her if she's seen the hard drives or generator in Ro's house.

"I've seen some hard drives in his office, I think, but he doesn't usually ask me to clean that room," Lucia replies.

Tina and Irina step back into the hallway, and Tina asks, "Enough for probable cause?"

"I think we need the generator," Irina says. "He can claim that the hard drives are just sentimental property that wasn't required to be turned over. But an ethanol generator is clearly community property. If he has one and didn't turn it over, that would be a violation of the Code."

"Can you look again for a generator?" Tina returns to the room and asks Lucia. "We think that he's illegally keeping community property in his home."

"I can try," Lucia says. "I'll let you know if I find it."

+++

A few weeks later, Rafael retrieves Aurelia from the battery site, and the two of them, along with Julián, Shasta, Rick, and several other members of the Tribe, depart in ethanol vehicles to destroy the Potter Valley Dams. As they drive through Miranda, CA, Rafael thinks again of Helena. He's been surprised to find himself in a happy marriage with Irina. After Helena, he hadn't thought that he was capable of having a real partnership or being a good husband, yet Irina seems satisfied with him. After five and a half years, some of their passion has burned off—though they're still able to summon it on plenty of occasions and had, in fact, done so just the night before. Infatuation has been replaced with a deep and abiding admiration.

That their marriage is a loving partnership of equals is both deeply mysterious and very simple to Rafael. What are the odds, he wonders, that two random strangers, thrown together at the end of the world, might be so compatible? Astronomically small. And yet . . . what if love is partly a choice? What if it's really as simple as that marriage book—to which they've returned many times—says? What if love is just a matter of kindness, grace, and attention? Though he sometimes fails to tell Irina so, he's profoundly grateful for their marriage, which is the last thing he would have expected to bloom from the ruins of the world.

Highway 101 is as beautiful as Rafael remembers, though a few places are burned out from forest fires. It winds through pine mountains and valleys of golden fall grasses. He drives carefully, trying to conserve fuel. They've taken the smallest, most efficient cars, but to get to the dams and back will bring them to the edge of their fuel range. He's relieved, though, that if they do run out of fuel, he can radio for someone from Ferndale to drive out and refuel them. Things have gotten easier over the past few years. With Mark's permission, Rafael rolls down the windows and lets the mountain breeze pour into the car. Mark sings along to The Killers. Rafael feels content.

At Rick's suggestion, they start with the lower dam. Rick points upstream. "There's your problem," he says. "There's a diversionary tunnel there that takes water out of the Eel River and reroutes it to the Russian River. The tunnel entrance should be high enough that if we destroy the dam, the water will miss the tunnel and take the lower course to the Eel River instead. It's not a perfect solution, though. We're still going to face historic droughts for the foreseeable future."

Rick consults a printed document from Gail's legal files—a description of the dams and their proposed removal procedure, saved from when the Tribe had commented on this project more than a decade ago. Rafael, Mark, and Aurelia follow him to a small building beside the upper part of the fish ladder. He turns a large needle valve, and water begins to rush down the fish ladder at an increased rate. They move to a building below the high spillway, and he repeats the process there, turning the mechanical valve controls to slowly fill the large pipes that will drain the reservoir, then turning the valve for the large pipes. The team moves to higher ground to watch the reservoir drain. The water pours out of the pipes and over the stones in the valley below. Rafael imagines the water's flowing freely under the bridge near Ferndale. It feels cathartic.

That night, they camp on a hill above the dam. As the sun sets, Rafael and Julián sit by the fire with Rick.

"We've got a little bit of an issue with one of our new Councilmembers in Ferndale," Rafael tells Rick after Aurelia and Mark have departed to check the reservoir from a higher vantage point. He details their problems with Ro—their suspicion that he fixed the Council drawing, his strange biographical knowledge of several of the Councilmembers, his consistent push for potentially unsustainable policies.

Rick listens attentively. When Rafael finishes speaking, Rick asks, "What ask should I take to the Tribal Council?"

"I think we'll need Amy's help to prove that he manipulated the computer program," Rafael says. "And probably her testimony at his trial if there's any technical evidence that he stole the Council seat."

"That seems doable . . . as long as you don't think there will be any danger for her?" Rick responds.

"I don't think Ro is actually dangerous. And, anyway, Tina can manage him if he is a threat," Rafael answers. Given her strong dislike of Ro, Rafael is certain that Tina would relish the opportunity.

"I'll take it to Amy and the Council then. I don't anticipate they'll say no," Rick says. "If they approve it, Amy and I can meet up with you at the trade conference."

They camp for two more days as the reservoir slowly drains; then they set several small charges on the spillway dam and move back to higher ground to watch the explosion. Aurelia counts down and they cover their ears for the blast. A small portion of the spillway blows apart, and a rush of muddy water moves through the resultant passage.

They wait another day to monitor the progress of the drainage; then they drive forty-five minutes to the larger, upper dam. There, they pry open the doorway to the control room and, after a bit of searching, locate two successive release valves. Mark consults an old operations manual they find in the office there, and they follow the directions to open the valves. The water shoots out of the release valves in a high pressure arc, making rainbows in the late morning sunlight.

They spend several nights camping there, watching as the muddy bottom of the lake along the shoreline is slowly revealed. Rick declares the mission a success, and they make plans for Mark and Julián to return in a month to blow up what's left of the dam so the water can finally flow freely.

+++

In Ferndale, Irina and Emma sit on neighboring benches, watching Javier and Penelope play in the grass. At Irina's request, Rafael and Tina had built a bench for Selah next to Sam and Clara's bench. The benches are surrounded by flowers Emma and Irina had planted together.

"How are you?" Irina asks Emma, mindful of both of their impending bad anniversaries.

"Better; then not better. It comes and goes."

"It always will." Irina still sometimes feels that old ache, especially on the anniversaries of Sam and Clara's births and deaths. Sometimes she still struggles with guilt about her role in Clara's death, and occasionally she feels bad about how much her life has moved on, how happy she often is.

Emma nods. "Gracie's doing well, though."

"I saw her in the school play last spring. She seemed surprisingly comfortable up on stage," Irina says. Benoit had directed the high school's first play and also directed and acted in Ferndale's first post-Pandemic production in its small theater. Both had been well-received.

"I think the support group has been really helpful for her. It's good for her to see that there are other women—like you, Tina, Aditi, and Jaya—who've overcome abuse and reclaimed their lives. It's important to have examples so you know what's possible." Emma pauses. "Can you do me a favor?"

"Sure, anything."

"Can you take François with you to the trade conference this month? I think he's lonely, and his opportunities to meet someone here are very limited."

To Irina's knowledge there are only three other gay men in Ferndale: two are married to each other, and the third is three decades older than François. She feels a bit guilty for never thinking of this before. She remembers the aching loneliness of losing a spouse and longing for companionship. "I'll bring him along. Maybe we can plan some kind of regular social event at the trade conference too. I'm sure he's not the only person who'd like to meet someone."

Many of Ferndale's residents have coupled off—Benoit and Aditi had just married, in fact—but there are others whose ages, personalities, or backgrounds have made it harder for them to meet someone. The ethanol vehicles open up the opportunity for more residents to attend the trade conference. Irina adds this to her list of future projects.

"Also, you should try to talk to Miranda," Emma says. "She seemed withdrawn in school this week."

Irina had noticed, but her other familial concerns had taken a backseat to preparing for Rafael's impending departure for the dam project. She adds this item to her list as well.

That Saturday morning, while Emma babysits, Irina rents one of the EVs so she and Miranda can hike to some mineral springs in a redwood forest nearby. As they drive over the Eel River, Irina is pleased to see the swollen river rushing past. Rafael and the others must have succeeded. Under the boughs of the redwoods in the chill of the morning air, Irina and Miranda strip down to their bathing suits. Irina notices Miranda's new self-consciousness, her uncertainty about her body and herself, and she feels deep empathy. She wonders if this is an inherent part of womanhood or if it was another product of modernity that she should have tried harder to banish from Ferndale. They sink into the spring water, scrunching their noses at its sulfur smell. Irina tries to engage her daughter, asking her about school, the next play that Benoit is going to put on, and her classmates, but Miranda seems troubled by something. Irina knows better than to press, so she just waits. Finally, as they're about to get out and hike back to the car, Miranda says, "Are we going to have to leave Ferndale?"

"Why do you think we'd have to?" Irina asks.

"Kitty told me that she heard her mother say that Ro is trying to get us kicked out."

A flood of anxiety hits Irina. She wants to grill Miranda, to ask her if she thought that Kitty and her mother were supportive of this idea or if other classmates had mentioned it. She knows, though, that right now what Miranda needs is reassurance, not to be bombarded with her mother's own anxieties. "He's just a bully. Your father and I have a plan to deal with him."

Miranda seems somewhat placated by this, but Irina's worries follow her through the day. She checks with Lucia, who reports that Ro has always been around when she'd been cleaning, so she hasn't been able to investigate yet.

Rafael and the others return the following week after dropping Aurelia back off at the Eureka battery site. They report their success to the Council. Ro presses again for a larger percentage of the corn crop. Rafael, Ify, and Irina agree to double the amount of ethanol corn, but Ro still isn't satisfied. Ro produces several articles he'd found in Rafael's office while he was using the ham radio there. They detail the steps for making ethanol.

"You had plenty of information about how to make ethanol engines, yet you deliberately kept it to yourself! You chose to slow this town's progress!" Ro says, holding the articles up before the audience.

Rafael merely shrugs, used to Ro's antics, and says, "I've already reported in prior Council meetings that I had knowledge of ethanol but that it didn't seem like a good use of our resources, given how energy and water-intensive it is to produce. I also didn't know how to convert regular engines to run on ethanol or how to get around the battery problem."

"If you were a better engineer, you might have," Ro says.

"Maybe," Rafael says, doing his best to sound bored and unconcerned, "or maybe I would have continued to focus on water purification, repairing the Eureka wind turbines, figuring out our battery issues, building our coastal wind turbines, setting up basic communications infrastructures, or any of the other projects I've completed over the past five years."

Afterward, Tina pours Rafael a drink and reiterates her offer to drive Ro out to the wilderness and drop him off. Irina, impressed by Rafael's show of calm confidence, waits impatiently to take him to bed.

"It's strange that Ro didn't want to go to the trade conference, right?" Emma asks. The first agenda item at that evening's Council meeting had been to finalize the list of Ferndale representatives for the conference. Everyone had expected that Ro would push to be included, but he hadn't. "He usually loves having crowds of people listen to him talk."

"Maybe he wants to avoid someone he thinks might be there," Julián says. "We should ask around about him at the conference."

Two days before the conference, Tina arranges for Mark to summon Ro from his home while Lucia is cleaning. Mark temporarily disables one of the ethanol vehicles they'd planned on using to travel to the conference so Ro will be occupied fixing it. "He's terrible at delegating," Mark tells Tina. "He doesn't think anyone can do anything as well as he can, so he'll fix it himself."

The plan works, and Lucia presents Tina and Irina with several pictures she'd taken with a battered smart phone.

"Probable cause?" Tina asks.

Irina nods, "Now all we need is Amy and a bit of luck."

Chapter Twenty-Seven

Irina stands with Rafael at the conference, watching the crowd at the community dance she and François had organized. They'd connected fairy lights to an ethanol generator and strung them over an indoor horse arena. Someone had connected a surprisingly good, downloaded playlist to Rick's karaoke machine, and the music carries over the sound of conversation and laughter.

Irina is pleased to see François dancing and conversing with several men. Jaya is talking flirtatiously with a young woman by the potluck table. Julián and Shasta are already tipsy on the moonshine he'd brought and are dancing with surprising grace. Rick and Amy are laughing as they dance clumsily. Tina watches it all with wary eyes, searching for security threats.

Irina sees the man from Grants Pass inviting a woman to dance. "Should I warn that woman?" she asks Rafael.

"I'm not excusing what he did to you," Rafael replies. "It was awful. He scared you and threatened you, but when it came down to it, he wasn't a rapist. We have to make some allowances for people to make mistakes and learn from them. Are you a killer? Am I? Are we defined forever by the worst thing we've done in a moment of desperation?"

Irina has always figured that Tina lied to her about missing her shot at the thief during that first trade conference, but this is the first time Rafael has acknowledged the truth.

"You gave me grace when I told you about the mountain man," Rafael continues. "Maybe extend that same grace to everyone else."

"Even Ro?"

"Yes, when the time comes, probably even Ro." Rafael offers his hand to her. "Do you want to dance?"

"Of course."

They spend several songs in each other's arms before François breaks in. He motions for them to follow him outside, where Tina and Julián stand with another man, who introduces himself as Liam Martin.

"François told me that you know Ro Gupta," Liam says. "I know him too."

They sit down on some benches nearby, and Liam continues, "Before the Pandemic, I lived in San Jose with my boyfriend. He was an EMT. We both got sick. I survived, but he didn't. I spent the next year scavenging grocery stores and nearby apartments. Then one day I got on my boyfriend's battery-operated radio, and I heard a guy talking about a settlement fifty miles south. He said he'd found a small wind farm at a state park and hooked into its grid—so he had lights, refrigerators, hot water, everything. It sounded too good to be true, but I figured I had to check it out, so I rode all the way down to the middle of nowhere. Sure enough, there was a settlement with power. At first it seemed like paradise."

The laughter and music carry from inside the pavilion as he continues, "It was Ro I heard on the radio. He said he was developing a way of retrofitting regular car engines to ethanol engines.

He made it very clear, though, that he owned our community. He could turn the power off anytime he wanted, and none of us would have been able to figure out how to turn it back on. He was a jerk, but he was a jerk who provided us with electricity, so most people went along with it. He had grand plans about how we were going to 'restart the modern world.' He worked on perfecting the engine with some kind of special ignition system, and we worked on everything else."

"That explains why he can't even identify a garden hoe," Julián remarks.

"And gardening was the problem. There's very little rain there. We were relying on two little creeks that dried up during the summer. After two years, he figured out the engine and started demanding more and more of our crop for ethanol production. It was a pretty small community, though, only about forty people, and we couldn't keep up with what he wanted. When the corn crop got a blight, we started to go hungry. He hadn't balanced our crop selection. People started talking about throwing him out. He always claimed, though, that we just weren't working hard enough. Then two and a half years ago, he just disappeared. He torched his engines and the wind turbines. We've never been able to get the power back on. Some of us left; others stayed."

He looks at Rafael. "I thought I could come here and learn something useful for my community. I was hoping to see your presentation on wind power. I heard you on the radio last spring, but I wasn't able to replicate things without actually seeing it in person."

"That's actually how we started talking about Ro," François says. "Liam asked me about Rafael's windmills and the ethanol presentation he's going to give tomorrow."

"When Ro left, you couldn't replicate what he did with the engines?" Rafael asks.

"That was another power play. There was only one other guy he ever let work on the engines with him, and that guy left with Ro," Liam replies.

"Brandon Sterling?" Tina guesses. Liam nods.

"It's kind of amazing Ro didn't learn from his mistakes the first time," Liam says.

"Guys like him never do. It's always someone else's fault," Tina replies.

"Liam asked me if he could come to Ferndale for a while and spend some time learning about our power generation and the ethanol engines," François says.

"I think that sounds like a fair trade in exchange for this information," Irina says. "Liam, would you testify to this if we put Ro on trial?"

"Sure."

"If you wouldn't mind staying in Fortuna for a week or two, we should be rid of Ro soon."

+++

That Monday, they return to Ferndale, leaving Amy, Rick, and Liam in Fortuna temporarily. Early Tuesday morning, Irina, Jaya, and Tina knock on Ro's door to execute the search warrant. Irina has never been to his home, but she isn't surprised to find that he's claimed a huge house on the outskirts of town.

He opens the door shirtless in a silky set of pajama pants, his six-pack abs wasted on all three of the women in front of him. "It's very early, ladies."

Tina holds up the warrant and tells him to move aside. She and Jaya step inside the house and go straight to his office.

"We have reason to believe that you're illegally withholding community property," Irina informs him. He shrugs. Tina and Jaya emerge from the office with the generator, laptop, and two boxes of hard drives.

"Looks like a community-owned generator," Tina says.

"I work from home sometimes," Ro replies. "I use it to power my laptop so I can work on the engine schematics."

"And the hard drives?" Jaya asks.

"Personal files. I was a photographer in my past life, and I liked to store my photos in the highest resolution. I also have an extensive movie and music collection."

Mark knocks on the door. Brandon stands uncertainly beside him. Tina says, "Bring him in so he can look at the laptop."

She turns to Brandon. "Shantal said you had computer expertise? I need you to look at the laptop and tell us if there's anything weird on there."

Then she tells Ro to write down the password for the laptop so Brandon can look at his files. Ro scrawls a long series of letters, numbers, and symbols on a piece of paper. Tina types it into the lock screen, and the desktop appears. Brandon spends a half hour clicking on various windows and looking at files before declaring that there's nothing there.

Ro smiles. "If there's nothing else, I'd like to get dressed and get on with my day. I've got lots of essential work to do for the community."

Tina scowls at him. She picks up the laptop and the paper with the password as Jaya picks up one of the boxes of hard drives, "We're going to confiscate these for now. We'll return them when we complete our investigation."

"Fair enough. I'll look forward to hearing about the conclusion of your investigation at the next Council meeting," Ro says, smirking.

While Mark walks back to town with Brandon, Tina and Jaya load the boxes, laptop, and generator up into one of the EVs and drive with Irina to Tina's office, where Amy is waiting. Tina hands her the laptop and the paper with the password. Amy taps in the password, then spends a little time clicking around.

"Wow . . . he must really think you guys are idiots," Amy remarks after a few minutes. The other three women look at her blankly. "This is so obvious, guys," she continues. "Look."

She points to the file extension on an Excel file she's opened up: *.xlsm*.

Blank stares greet her, so Amy continues, "Modern Excel files usually have an .xlsx extension. This one has an .xlsm extension, which means that it contains macros/VBA."

She may as well be speaking Mandarin. Amy clarifies, "It means the file has been altered. Look."

She hits the F9 key, and a number comes up. She hits it again. Same number. A third time. Same number. "You see?"

"Can I see the laptop you use for your Council drawing?" Amy asks. Irina jogs down to the Administration Building and returns with it. Amy says, "Whose laptop was this originally?"

"Mine," Irina says. "It was the only laptop Rafael found that didn't have a password."

"But you added a password?" Amy asks.

"I added a PIN number," Irina replies.

"What's Matteo's birthday?" Amy asks.

"January 24."

Amy types in the numbers. The computer unlocks. "You guys *are* idiots!" she exclaims. "Literally anyone can guess that!"

No one speaks. Amy rolls her eyes. "I can't believe you had such lax security for something so important."

"We're not computer people . . . ," Irina says.

"Obviously," Amy interrupts with an eye roll.

". . . and it didn't seem like the kind of thing that anyone would be interested in doing," Irina concludes.

Amy raises her eyebrows. She pokes around on Irina's laptop for a little while.

"He at least assumed you were intelligent enough to look at your own laptop. The altered file isn't here. But since it was so easy for him to get in and load it onto your computer, he probably just loaded it when he needed it and deleted it after, then saved the code on his own computer to do it again next time. Seriously, guys, this is an embarrassing level of security incompetence. I kind of expected better from you."

"We're going to go back to a paper-based system," Irina volunteers.

"That's probably a good idea, given your lack of technological expertise." Amy shakes her head.

"Is this enough to arrest him and Brandon?" Tina says, looking at Irina.

"It is if Amy can testify at the trial," Irina replies.

"You mean if I can embarrass you at the trial?" Amy says, smirking. "Yes. I've cleared my schedule."

Tina and Jaya leave. Amy looks at the boxes of hard drives. "Are you as curious to know what's on there as I am?"

Irina agrees, and they plug one of them into Ro's laptop. Amy silences the audio and clicks on several files, then says, "On its face it looks like useless stuff. Photos, videos," she makes a face, "some very distasteful porn. But there's far more space taken up on this laptop than those files should require."

She spends a few minutes checking folders, then says, "A hidden directory."

She clicks on it, and it expands. She clicks on one of the folders. It takes a long time to load. Once it loads, she types in a search term and calls Irina over. Irina's younger face stares back at her along with the professional profile she'd originally written a decade and a half ago and updated regularly until Clara's death and her resulting leave of absence.

"Looking at that degree, I would have assumed you were clever enough not to use your son's birthday as a PIN number," Amy says. "What's Ify's full name?"

"Dr. Ifeanyi Igwe."

Amy searches and pulls up his profile. She searches for Rafael and nothing comes up. Julián and Tina's names also yield no results. Emma's name turns up a short profile.

"But how did he know ahead of time what profiles would be useful?" Irina asks.

"He didn't. There are more than 500 million files in this folder. He downloaded every profile on the site and compressed the files."

"You can store all of that on a single hard drive?"

"You can probably store five times that much. There are tons more files on here. I'm betting he used some kind of web crawler to download any information he thought would be useful before the internet went down. There could be things on here that will be helpful to us." Amy clicks on several more large files that take a long time to load. "Court dockets for family and civil court. News story archives. Criminal cases. A lot of prepper videos and blogs. It will take forever to go through all of the files on these hard drives, but we should invest the time."

Tina returns and reports that Ro is in one room and Brandon is in another.

"Everything we have is still circumstantial," Irina says. "Ro could claim that he has that program for any number of reasons. There's no evidence it was ever used on my computer. They can still argue that all of this was a coincidence."

"You think people will buy that?" Tina asks.

"I think we need to have a really strong case. I'm a Councilmember going after another Councilmember who has publicly ridiculed me and my husband. This has to be beyond dispute. We need Brandon to testify against Ro."

Irina considers for a moment, recalling her time as a prosecutor, then says, "I've got an idea."

The room where Brandon sits, guarded by Jaya, is barely large enough for the table and four chairs. Irina and Tina sit down across from him.

"We know you lied to us about the computer," Tina says. "We know the number generator was your idea, and you and Ro stole two Council seats. And we know you and Ro worked together at the settlement near San Jose."

"So, that would be obstruction of an investigation and corruption," Irina adds.

"There's no incentive for me to talk to you," Brandon says. "The penalty for either of those things, if you could prove me guilty, is exile, and I don't want to stay here anyway."

"It's true that the penalty is exile," Irina replies, "but the criminal code doesn't specify where we have to exile you to."

"We could take you to a little island and drop you off there," Tina says. "Or we could drop you in the middle of nowhere in the mountains. Alone, with no supplies. Just you and the mountain lions."

"Or," Irina suggests, "we could take you back to the community you came from near San Jose. I'm sure they'd be happy to see you."

"'Exile is so open ended," Tina says.

"A lot of discretion," Irina agrees. "Or you could tell us where you want to go, and we can tell you if that's possible and what it will cost you."

He glowers at them. Finally, he says, "I want to go to Fort Bragg, and I want a horse, fishing gear, and enough seeds to start a garden."

"No horse, but you can have the rest," Irina says.

"A goat then. You can spare one."

"Fine, a goat, if you're sufficiently forthcoming," Irina agrees.

Later, after Brandon confirms their suspicions, signs a statement, and promises to testify in the trial, Irina and Tina visit Ro in the other room. They both sit down in chairs across from him. Ro smiles at them insolently. "This is clearly a politically-motivated witch hunt. Is a generator really worth all this drama?"

"This isn't about the generator," Irina tells him. "You're being charged with corruption. You conspired with Brandon to steal two Council seats."

"That's an entirely speculative accusation, and, again, politically-motivated," he looks at Irina, "You've hated me since I arrived here, despite the many contributions I've made to this community. You're just trying to oust me so you can refill my seat with someone who will go along with all of your ridiculous, restrictive policies, someone who will yield to you, like Rafael did during the drafting of the Charter, like all of the Founders did. . . everyone except you, Tina. I read the legislative history—you were the only one brave enough to really fight back during the Charter. You don't believe in this system, but they force you to do their dirty work."

Irina senses a sudden change in Tina's demeanor and a little tendril of self-doubt unfurls inside her. What if he's right? What if she'd forced everyone to adopt a system of government and way of life they didn't actually want?

"Your trial is in two days," Irina says, with more confidence than she feels.

"Fair enough," Ro replies. "But you're mistaken about who'll be on trial."

Afterward, Tina and Irina stand in Irina's office. Irina can sense Tina's anger, so she tries to clear the air, "Is Ro right? Do you feel like we make you do the dirty work for the community?"

"That's an insulting assumption. I make my own choices. The world needs nice, sensitive people like Rafael and Emma, but the world also needs people like me who make the difficult choices and do what has to be done to protect those nice, sensitive people and their 'civilized' world. I'm happy to be able to protect you all from your impractical bleeding heart moral hang-ups," Tina says.

"But you didn't agree with a lot of what's in the Charter," Irina says.

Tina shrugs. "I didn't, but I think things were going pretty well here until Ro showed up."

That evening, the founders gather in Rafael and Irina's backyard in a somber mood.

"Ro's right," Irina says. "It won't only be him on trial, it will be us and the town Charter. He's going to blather on about how incompetent we are, how bad our system is, how he's our savior."

"We couldn't just cut a deal with him so he'll leave quietly?" Emma asks.

"That would look even worse," Irina says. "A trial gives us legitimacy. We just have to keep the trial on point, stick to the facts. Any reasonable jury will find him guilty."

"But even when the jury finds him guilty, we'll just be releasing him back into the wild," Tina says, "Because we didn't make corruption an executable offense."

"I don't think he'll be a physical threat to us," Irina replies.

"That's not the problem," Tina says. "The problem is that he can find a radio and continue spewing lies and bullshit."

"At some point," says Ify, "We need to trust the people of Ferndale to evaluate the evidence for themselves. They can see the good we've done here."

"I hope you're right," Irina says doubtfully. "But I can think of a lot of examples in recent history where people believed the lies of demagogues and podcast prophets."

"People believed those things because they lived in a toxic political milieu. They were primed to believe lies because they didn't trust their leaders or each other," Ify replies. "We set out

446

to create something different here, and I think we've succeeded."

Irina isn't convinced, but she's tired and she wants the comfort of Rafael's arms, so she concedes the point and they all break for the evening.

Later, as Rafael and Irina lie in bed, she recounts what Ro had said to her about the Charter drafting. Then she tells Rafael the concern that's been bothering her all evening. "You told me once that I had an indomitable will and that it was hard to fight against that."

"You do, and it is," he replies, "But we've had plenty of fights over the important things. There were times when I backed down, but there were also lots of times that you did."

"You don't think I steamrolled everyone during the Charter drafting?"

"That's not how I remember it at all. I remember a lot of robust disagreement and concessions all around. People like Ro always try to get into your head. He's so sure of his own reality that he makes you doubt yours. Don't let him. This is the path we all agreed on, and it was the right one."

Chapter Twenty-Eight

Irina asks Tyler to judge the case, since she was involved in the investigation and plans to serve the prosecutorial role. Ro refuses Dominic's help, claiming that he can represent himself more skillfully and that he doesn't trust anyone associated with Ferndale to assist him.

Shantal draws a six-person jury, using numbered paper slips. She does a careful public audit afterward to be sure that no one has manipulated the results. Irina isn't particularly familiar with any of the six jurors. She prepares her witnesses and anxiously awaits the trial.

Everyone is granted a day of administrative leave for Ro's trial, and most of Ferndale's three-hundred-thirty adult residents crowd into the largest venue in town: an old church that had been converted to a performance hall. The residents squeeze into the red fabric seats and extra folding chairs or stand against the walls, gossiping and speculating about the trial.

Between the crowd and the giant woodstove in the corner of the room, Irina is already sweating through her green dress. She stands on the stage and shuffles her papers nervously. Rafael squeezes her shoulder and wishes her luck, then sits in the front row of the audience. Ro, Tyler, and Irina take their seats on the stage.

"We're here today for the trial of Ro Gupta, who joined our community two and a half years ago after leaving his last community for dead," Irina begins her opening statement. "You'll hear evidence about how he mismanaged his last community, coercing the people there into engaging in risky farming practices that ended up causing a famine. When he was confronted with the results of his bad behavior, he destroyed the community's infrastructure, potentially dooming them to death, and fled to Ferndale, where he manipulated our Council selection process in order to steal two seats—one for him and one for his former colleague, Brandon Sterling. Together, Ro and Brandon intended to take over our Council so he could repeat the same mistakes here that he made in his last community. He intended to use Ferndale to promote his own ambitions, even if it might cost the lives of the people here."

She goes on, detailing the story that Liam had told about how Ro threatened the people in his last community. She describes the computer program Ro had used to fix the Council selection. Then she sits down, looking out at the audience members, trying to gauge the reception of her arguments. As Ro stands and speaks, Irina gazes at the room's huge stained glass windows, which glow in the morning sunlight, and she tries to keep from rolling her eyes.

"We're actually here today because I had the audacity to confront the town's Founders, to challenge their convoluted, protectionist, self-interested system," Ro begins. "In retaliation for my courage, the Founders of this town—an insular group, which, arguably, conducts lots of Council business in their backyards over drinks in contravention of their supposed open meetings laws—conspired together to create a story about how I tried to take over the Council. The real story is that since I arrived here, I've worked tirelessly to benefit this community with no extra compensation. If, in fact, I am exiled after these proceedings, the vehicle that will drive me to my new home will be of my own design, a product of my hard work, stolen from me by the unappreciative, small-minded Founders of this town."

He turns toward the jury. "Consider what I've selflessly given you: technology that will fuel transport and more efficient harvests, medicine that will save lives, a chance at a better future. It's clear that the Founders feel threatened by what I've been able to offer this community. They like to keep you trapped in a prison of their making. So they've concocted an unlikely story about my manipulating the Council selection system—a system they designed!—in order to steal Council seats. It's convenient for them, though hardly dispositive for their case, that Brandon and I knew each other in San Jose.

But, as you'll hear, we'd had a disagreement and parted ways after leaving our last community. My only crime is trying to promote progress, trying to improve this town, trying to break the Founders' stranglehold on this place. And the only process that's fixed here is this sham trial. You'll watch today as those very same Founders present the evidence that they collected, the collection of which was also approved by them and will be used to prosecute me under the Code that they wrote. I guess I should just consider myself fortunate that one of them isn't the judge for this trial . . . ."

He looks at Irina, who summons all her willpower to keep a neutral expression on her face. "I've asked you all to consider whether you want to continue to live under this system—their system—before, and I'll ask you to consider that question again during this witch hunt," he concludes.

Irina calls Amy to discuss the evidence on Ro's computer. Amy recounts what she'd discovered, pulling up the file on a projector. She explains to the jury why the file extension signals that the file was manipulated. She hits the button to generate the same number several times over.

"But did you also find this file on the laptop that was used for the Council drawing?" Ro asks when he's given the opportunity to cross examine her.

"No, but . . . ," Amy starts to reply.

"Did you find any evidence of its having been used on the Council selection drawing?"

"That wouldn't be provable, since you deleted it off the Council laptop," Amy replies.

"So you say," Ro replies with a smirk. "A convenient argument for you."

Ro changes the subject. "You're a self-proclaimed computer expert. Have you ever heard of red teaming?"

"Yes," Amy answers.

"Can you explain to the audience what that is in plain terms?"

"It's when you stress-test a system. You assign a group of people to design ways to attack the system so that you can identify your vulnerabilities and fix them."

"Interesting," Ro replies. "We'll come back to that later."

He looks at Irina, then back at Amy. "And you're friends with the Founders of Ferndale, right. In fact you benefited from the questionable arrangement they made with Dr. Addie Cunningham that I talked about in the Council meeting a while back? She delivered your baby here in Ferndale, correct?"

"Yes," Amy admits reluctantly. "We're friendly, but that has nothing to do with this."

"You actually came here to Ferndale from Six Rivers just to assist the Founders with their case, right?"

"I'm the only computer expert around, so my assistance was necessary," she replies.

"The only computer expert affiliated with the Founders," he says. "I heard that there's someone else with computer engineering expertise over in the Convent community."

Amy shrugs, "Not that I've heard of."

"Well you should get on the radio more," Ro replies, "try to expand your network a little, make some new, less corrupt friends."

"Objection, argumentative," Irina says in a bored voice.

"Sustained," Tyler says. He looks at Ro and says, "Stick to asking questions. Save the opinions for your own testimony and your closing statement."

"Noted . . . ," Ro replies, "from the judge who works with the prosecutor . . . and the defense attorney."

"It's a small world," Tyler replies. "In a community of three hundred adults who eat together, work together, and even shower together, you're unlikely to find someone who isn't connected to the Founders. Stick to questions."

"But you could have brought someone in from outside, right?" Ro asks. "From the Convent? The Monastery? One of the other communities around here."

"They're all, as you accused Ms. Smith of being, allies of the leadership here," Tyler says. "Let's get back to the trial."

Irina calls Brandon. He sits down before the jury and stares at Irina impassively. "How long have you and Mr. Gupta known each other?" Irina asks him.

"Since shortly after the Pandemic. I heard him on the radio, advertising his community. I was one of the first people to arrive there. After that, we worked together for several years developing the ethanol engines that Ferndale is benefitting from. But we had a falling out after we left the community in San Jose. We came to Ferndale independently, months apart. Until I won the Council lottery, we barely spoke," Brandon says. Irina is momentarily confused. This is not the answer they'd gone over the day before.

"Did you suggest the Excel number generator to Shantal?" Irina asks, trying to get things back on track.

"Yes, because she said she wanted a better solution for the Council drawings."

"Did you install the fake number generator program on the Council computer at Ro's direction?" Irina asks.

"I have no idea what you're talking about," Brandon says with a shrug.

"I have a written statement here where you admit to installing—then deleting—the fake number generator program at Ro's direction in order to ensure that Ro, then you, won the Council lottery," Irina says, walking over to the table, shuffling through her papers, and holding up his statement. Irina reads the relevant portions of Brandon's statement out to the jury.

"I only said that because you threatened to kill me," Brandon says. Irina's eyes widen. Ro smirks in his seat.

"I did no such thing," Irina replies.

"You told me that you could drop me off on an island. Or in the mountains with no supplies. Or I could cooperate with you and you would give me supplies and drop me off wherever I wanted."

"Prosecutors cut deals with defendants all the time," Irina points out. "They promise reduced sentences for witness testimony. That's standard practice."

"Seems corrupt," Brandon replies with a shrug. "Anyway . . . I only gave that testimony because I was coerced. Like I said, Ro and I had a falling out before we arrived here."

Flustered, Irina calls Liam to the stage. Liam recounts the history of the San Jose settlement, Ro's mismanagement, Brandon's loyalty to Ro, and their disappearance.

"So your claim," Ro says during cross examination, "is that there was a blight that had nothing to do with me; then, when people started saying they wanted me to leave, I left?"

"You left, after you destroyed our power source, torched the engines and the ethanol, and left us for dead," Liam argues.

"You have absolutely no evidence to support that accusation!" Ro retorts. "Because I didn't do that."

Liam rolls his eyes and replies, "Yeah, I'm sure it was just a coincidence. And the blight was mostly a problem because you demanded that we grow too many crops for your project and too few to feed ourselves."

"Did I threaten you with force if you didn't grow the crops I wanted?" Ro asks.

"No, but you had literally all the power in the town. You held that over our heads." Liam looks at the jury. "You all know as well as I do that having electrical power can be the difference between life and death. Electrical power is heat. It's air conditioning. It's refrigeration. When electrical power fails, people die."

"That seems overblown," Ro replies. "San Jose has a mild climate, right? Only a little more extreme than Ferndale. Surely you could have survived without central heating and air. Did I ever beat anyone? Did I ever physically punish anyone in any way?"

"No," Liam admits reluctantly. "But the threat of being expelled from the colony was always on the table."

Ro shrugs. "My town, my rules, just like the Founders here. I was the one who got the power systems set up. I invited you all there, and it was fair for me to ask you to leave if you didn't work. Ferndale does the same when people don't contribute."

"Objection, argumentative," Irina says again.

"Sustained," Tyler agrees. Ro rolls his eyes.

After several more minutes of questioning, Liam departs the stand and Tyler looks at Ro. "The Defense can call witnesses now."

"I call Rafael Karrigan-Delgado to the stand," Ro says.

"Objection. Mr. Karrigan-Delgado's testimony isn't relevant," Irina says.

"It is relevant," Ro argues. "The only reason we're here today is because the Founders are trying to exile me by framing me for something I didn't do."

"Overruled," Tyler says reluctantly.

"Mr. Karrigan-Delgado, where did you get your degree?" Ro asks.

"The same place as the last time you asked me," Rafael replies.

"So, not in the U.S.?"

"No."

"And did you ever get recertified here? Did you ever go back to school and get a degree in engineering from a school that's actually accredited here?"

"No."

"Was your degree in electrical engineering?"

"No."

"Did you ever actually practice any engineering?"

"Not until I arrived in Ferndale."

"Which might explain why you still haven't been able to solve Ferndale's electrical problems," Ro remarks.

"Objection, argumentative," Irina says.

"Sustained," Tyler replies. "Try to keep things cordial, Mr. Gupta."

"So despite your lack of qualifications and despite the fact that there are more than three hundred adults here, you've never found anyone who was more qualified to serve as Ferndale's engineer?" Ro asks.

"Objection, relevance," Irina says. "What is the purpose of this line of questioning, Mr. Gupta?"

"To lay the groundwork to show the jury that Mr. Karrigan-Delgado—your husband—was intimidated by me and, hence, you were intimidated by me, and you both conspired, along with Ms. Jones-Macy and the rest of the Founders, to oust me. Also, to show the Founders' stranglehold on this town. I'm clearly more qualified to be this community's engineer than Mr. Karrigan-Delgado is, yet he maintains the position."

"Because of the way our Charter is set up," Irina says.

"In order to consolidate your own power!" Ro argues.

"Objection sustained," Tyler interrupts.

Irina can see that Rafael's confidence is flagging. His eyes meet Irina's, and he recalls all the times she's reassured him. Her love bolsters him. He sits up a bit straighter.

"I've read the legislative history of the Charter," Ro says to Rafael. "Have you?"

"I was there. I don't need a recap," Rafael replies, regretting the fact that he had neglected to look at the document since the last time Ro brought it up. He wonders again what Emma had included there.

Ro goes over to his table and pulls out a binder. He pages through it and reads off the records of several conversations during the Founding, including Rafael's unexpected concessions to Irina on abortion and the economic system.

"It sure looks like your wife influenced your vote in the Charter drafting," Ro remarks.

Irina is about to object, but Rafael speaks instead. "Is my marriage on trial? Or are you on trial?

Ro reads several other parts of the legislative history where Irina had pushed her own vision for the Charter. "It sort of seems like your wife doesn't take disagreement very well, right?"

"Objection, argumentative. Also possibly sexist," Irina says, looking at Ro. "When you try to push and persuade people, that's being assertive and visionary. But when I do it, that's disagreeable, controlling, and corrupt?"

"There's nothing sexist about it. You clearly like being in control, and you don't handle dissent well," Ro replies. "Which is why you steamrolled everyone during the Founding and you're engaging in this ridiculous witch hunt against me."

"Objection argumentative, again," Irina says.

Rafael doesn't wait for Tyler's reply. He looks at Ro with narrowed eyes and says in a voice cold with rage, "My wife is the one who wanted to include other people in conversations about the Charter. We were presented with a perfect opportunity to create the kind of community you created: dictatorial, top-down, and hierarchical, serving only our own interests. Instead we created a democratic system in which we dole out cafeteria food, pick up trash, plow the fields and scoop the innards out of the game we hunt . . . and we get paid the same salary as everyone else here. And we both sit in Council meetings and listen to your drivel and actually take it into consideration."

Irina has rarely seen Rafael this angry. She's moved when she realizes that he'd been motivated to defend her and their marriage.

"It's clear," says Ro, ignoring Rafael's argument completely, "that you don't have the expertise necessary to really lead this community. I arrived here and challenged you, so you and the rest of the Founders—especially your wife—are trying to eliminate me and consolidate your power."

"If power was what we wanted, we wouldn't have created a system that transitions all of us off the Council within ten years," Rafael replies. "I may not have your gilded résumé, and I may have made mistakes along the way, but, unlike you, my mistakes have never caused my community to go hungry. We've been careful stewards of this town, and we expect that others who come after us will be too. I do despise you, but I don't need to frame you—the evidence is clear that you stole the Council seats."

"You may claim not to want power, but you set up a system where no one else really gets a say," Ro remarks. "Other than the six of you, no one here ever voted on this Charter."

"They voted with their feet by joining us," Rafael says. "We've been open about who we are, and people chose to come here."

They spar for a while longer, and Rafael holds his own. Ro takes the stand and denies everything. He agrees with Brandon's account that they'd gone their separate ways and both happened to arrive in Ferndale. He reiterates that his prior community had asked him to leave; he hadn't abandoned them.

"When I'm told that I'm not wanted somewhere, that my contributions aren't appreciated, I leave," Ro says. "Like a lot of visionary leaders before me, I was blamed when something unexpected and out of my control went wrong. But everyone in that community had agreed to take that risk. Everyone thought that it was worth it in order to work toward creating a better world. To get great rewards, you have to take big risks, and sometimes things go wrong. I thought they shared my vision, but I was mistaken, so I left."

"After you torched the wind turbines and other infrastructure," Irina remarks.

"They caught fire from lack of maintenance," Ro replies. "A foreseeable risk when you exile your only qualified engineers."

"Is that a threat?" Irina asks.

"No. It's a statement of fact. When you put unqualified people in charge, bad things happen," Ro says, looking at the jury. "That's what I've been trying to prevent here in Ferndale . . . , which brings us to the red teaming idea that I discussed with Ms. Smith earlier. The program on my computer was actually something I was working on to show all of you the flaws and vulnerabilities in your system. I was planning to do a demonstration before the Council this winter."

Irina calls Amy back to the stand to refute this, and Amy pulls up the file again and shows it to the jury.

"That's a blatant lie," Amy says, gesturing to the information about the file. "This file was created a month before the first Council drawing."

"I was thinking ahead," Ro replies. "It didn't occur to me that you would use this to frame me. I underestimated how aggressively the Founders would work to eliminate a political inconvenience like me. I'm the only one brave enough to question the Founders, to point out the flaws in the Charter, to try to push this town forward against the wishes of its incompetent, backward leadership."

By 5:00 p.m., Irina is exhausted. She closes the trial by reminding the jury of the simple facts: Ro and Brandon mismanaged their prior settlement, they left everyone there in a perilous position, they came here and pretended not to know each other, then colluded to fix the Council drawing so they could continue the same bad policies that resulted in the collapse of their prior settlement. Ro reiterates his prior denials of guilt and accusations against the Council.

After the jury leaves to deliberate, the founders gather in one of the anterooms of the performance hall.

"I hope I didn't screw that up too much," Rafael says as soon as the door is closed.

"You did great," Irina says, taking his hand. "I was the one who screwed up, trusting Brandon."

"I think the case was still strong enough," Ify says.

"Even if the jury finds him guilty," Irina says, "We've lost credibility. Our very first Council transition was poorly executed, and Ro has publicly questioned us and the Charter. People will lose faith in Ferndale and our leadership."

They're all silent for a moment, reflecting on that. Then Ify says, "We should put the Charter to a one-time ratification vote."

"That's a hell of a risk!" Irina exclaims.

"Before Ro came along, very few people attended our Council meetings," Ify says. "Why do you suppose that was?"

"Well," Irina answers, "it could be one of two things. The first is what often happened in pre-Pandemic America: people stopped believing in government, so they grew apathetic and didn't show up to engage with it. The second possibility is that our government was functioning well enough that people just didn't think about it. They showed up for things that were particularly important or interesting to them, but otherwise, they trusted us to manage things."

"Which do you think it was?" Ify asks.

"I don't know," Irina replies honestly.

"I know which, and I think Ro does too," Ify says. "That's the reason he's never called for a referendum vote to change the Charter or pushed anyone to try to do a recall vote. He's not stupid; he has a keen sense of his own power. If he thought he could win those fights, he would have tried."

"Just because he couldn't get two thirds of the vote doesn't mean we can," Irina points out.

"At some point you have to have faith, Irina. Like Rafael said, every one of these people chose to be here. They believe in what we're doing."

"And if we hold a ratification vote on the Charter and we fail? Then what?" Irina asks.

"We can stay here," Ify says.

Irina makes a face. "I think if they vote down our system, they probably don't want us here."

"Then we leave and start over again somewhere else," Ify says. "It's a big, mostly empty world."

"We leave together, then?" Irina says, looking around at the group. Everyone agrees.

"But I don't think we'll have to," Ify says. "Have a little faith."

A little while later, there's a knock on the door. Jaya stands outside. "The jury's done deliberating."

They return to the performance hall, where the audience is buzzing with anticipation. Everyone who has a seat takes it; the rest stand and whisper to each other around the periphery of the cavernous room under the backlit glow of the massive stained-glass windows. The forewoman of the jury hands Tyler a piece of paper.

"Guilty," he reads. He continues, "In accordance with our criminal code, the penalty for corruption is exile."

That night, the founders gather at Ify and Yumi's house. The atmosphere of celebration is subdued by the question of a Charter ratification vote.

"Where should we send them?" Rafael asks about Ro and Brandon.

"There's a dry island off the Oregon coast that sounds good," Irina says.

"I don't think there's anywhere that's far enough for them not to be a threat to us," Tina says. "I could take care of it, though . . . ."

"No," says Rafael. "Ro gave us some useful technology, and he may create more. People like him can exist; I just don't want to live in their world anymore."

The next day they hold a trial for Brandon, who's also convicted of corruption and sentenced to exile.

Because attendance has gotten so large, they hold Thursday's Council meeting in the same performance hall where they'd held the trial.

Rafael reports, "Aurelia got one of the batteries working. If we send a team up there to help, she thinks she can have several batteries assembled within a few weeks. Each battery is the size of a shipping container, but Mark thinks he can retrofit a tractor trailer engine to run on ethanol. It will take almost all our fuel to haul all the batteries and materials here and to the Tribe, but it will be worth it."

Privately, he'd stressed the importance of moving all the battery materials because Ro is aware of their location.

"The next order of business," Ify says, "is to draw two new Councilmembers. Anyone who would like to be part of the drawing can register with Shantal by next Tuesday. We'll draw names—the old fashioned way, with paper—next Thursday."

"We'll also be holding a special vote," Irina says, looking out over the audience, "We've heard the concerns that Ro expressed during his trial, and we want to address them. Tomorrow night, we'll gather here to do a special one-time vote to ratify the Charter."

A murmur moves through the crowd as she continues, "This isn't our government. It's yours. And you should have the right to decide if this is a system you want to continue to live in."

That night, Irina leans back into Rafael's arms on their living room couch.

"What if we have to leave?" she asks as they both watch the fire. "I don't think I have it in me to rebuild again."

"I think Ify is right," Rafael replies, "We won't have to. If we do, though, we won't be doing it alone, and I can't think of a better group of people to rebuild with."

+++

The founders sit on the stage, looking out over the crowded performance hall as Shantal explains the mechanism for the Charter vote. She has a roster of adult residents. Each person will submit a secret ballot one by one as she checks them off on the roster. The entire process will be public. Afterward, Shantal and her administration team will count the votes publicly, and the paper ballots will be available for anyone's inspection.

Irina stands to give the speech she had prepared. At the same time, though, Aditi stands up in the front row of the audience.

"I'd like to say something in favor of the Charter," Aditi says.

Ify lightly touches Irina's arm. "I think we should let them speak. They've heard all of our arguments before. Let them tell each other why this is important."

Irina sits and invites Aditi to speak.

"My sister and I decided to come here to Ferndale because we were struggling to survive on our own. Most of you know that on our way here, two men kidnapped us and held us captive for a month before Irina and Tina found us. Despite how terrible our journey was, I'm still glad we came here. The people in this community have taken care of us and taken care of each other. Not only have our leaders ensured that we're safe and fed, but they've helped us to thrive with friendship, care, and support. This place has allowed me to find a new profession, to help others and contribute in a way that feels meaningful. I don't want to go back to the way that things were before the Pandemic, when it was 'every person for themself,' when some people were thriving while others struggled. I love what we've built here, together."

François stands. "I also love this town. I've always felt accepted here, and I really appreciate the support that you all gave me, Emma, and Tina when Selah died. I'm honored to teach everyone's children, to get to see them grow in a place that's filled with love and collaboration. I don't think this kind of community is possible when you live in a system where everyone competes for resources instead of cooperating together. I don't want to see our Charter change."

Mark stands next, he smiles. "Like a lot of you, I came here because I needed childcare. But what I've found here is so much more than that. I used to worry constantly about how I would give my kids a future—how I would afford a house in a good school district, how I would pay for their education, how they would manage in a zero-sum world. Now I don't worry about that at all, because I know they'll have a future here, that they'll be on equal footing with every other person in this town. I wouldn't change a damn thing about the Charter."

Person after person stands to speak. Two people argue openly against the Charter, reiterating Ro's arguments and complaining about the assigned job rules and mandatory public service. Most of the audience listens politely, but there's clear hostility to those views. Everyone else expresses their support for the Charter and their founders. Ify dabs his eyes with a handkerchief that Yumi hands to him from the side of the stage. Irina and Emma cry openly. Irina thinks she even sees a tear in Julián's eye, though he's quick to wipe it discreetly away with his knuckle.

The night grows late and Shantal announces that it's time to take the vote. One by one, the residents of Ferndale cast their secret ballots. Everyone waits anxiously while Shantal and her team tally them before the crowd.

When they reach the magic number—two hundred and eighteen—Irina breathes a sigh of relief, but they keep counting. In the end, three hundred and twelve people vote in favor of the Charter.

"It was never a question," Ify says afterward as they toast with Julián's first batch of rye whiskey. "These people had to travel hundreds of miles to get here; they're invested in this. And we have been good stewards."

They declare the next day a public holiday; everyone gathers for a barbeque on Main Street. Irina announces that they'll exile both Ro and Brandon to a small, empty town in the Sacramento Valley and that anyone who wishes can go with them; they just need to let Shantal know so transportation can be arranged. Shantal reports that thirteen people have decided to leave with Ro and Brandon. Irina wonders about the identities of the other fifteen people who voted against the Charter, and how Ro had coordinated with Brandon to recant his testimony, but she puts those worries out of her mind and reminds herself again of the Charter's overwhelming victory.

Later that week, Tina stands beside Ro's ethanol SUV and says to Irina, "It's not too late to change our minds about this. I could drop him in a desert somewhere instead . . . ."

"No, I think Rafael is right. Ro may end up being useful to us in the future. I just don't want to live with him."

Tina nods, then gets in the SUV. Ro glowers at Irina from the back seat. Irina smirks and waves as the car pulls away.

Chapter Twenty-Nine

Using old-fashioned paper lots, two new Council members are selected. Benoit is one of them; the other is a woman named Khadija Brown-Davis who works in animal husbandry. Ify and Irina are both familiar with Khadija from her work with Lily, and Emma remembers her testimony about her near starvation. They know her to be kind, patient, and attentive to the needs of the animals she works with.

That evening, Irina has her regular conversation with Aunt Hannah on the radio. These conversations have become more and more logistically difficult over time as the satellites have begun to fail, and Irina anticipates that soon they will cease forever. The thought makes her deeply melancholy.

"How are things there?" Irina asks, expecting the usual family and ranch updates.

"We're going to have to leave Utah," Hannah says.

"Our family has been there for nearly two hundred years!" Irina replies, "Why would you leave?"

"Without air conditioning and modern water systems, this part of Utah is uninhabitable," Hannah says.

"Where will you go?" Irina asks.

"Now that things have stabilized in Ferndale, we were actually hoping to join you, if that's okay with you. We could bring some of the cattle and horses."

"That's a thousand miles!"

"Our ancestors did it."

"If you think you could make that journey, I would love to have you here," Irina replies. She knows there will be complications, given her family's religion, but they've managed to integrate people from all kinds of backgrounds into Ferndale. The Council had even added Jewish and Muslim holidays to the official calendar the prior year to accommodate adherents to those faiths. Irina is confident that people of good will can find a way to coexist together.

The cattle, too, could pose problems, but there's a lot of empty space between Ferndale and Eureka where they can graze, and if they do end up being too environmentally intensive, they're still a valuable trade good, helping to provide an additional bulwark against hunger for the town. The horses will diversify Ferndale's horse stock and help reduce the town's dependance on ethanol engines and electric machinery for work and travel.

"We'll leave early next spring before it gets too hot," Hannah says. "It will take months to get to you, but I'm sure it will be worth it. I've missed you, and I can't wait to meet Rafael and the kids and see the life you've built for yourself. I'm really, really proud of you, Irina."

"Thank you," Irina says through her tears.

+++

Ferndale's engineers and mechanics spend the next few weeks working on equipping a tractor-trailer truck with an ethanol engine so they can retrieve the iron-flow batteries. They're able to use the schematics on Ro's laptop, as well as the knowledge of his many former apprentices, to modify the engine and create an acid-battery-free, magneto ignition.

Mark, Rafael, and Rick depart for Eugene during the first week of December and return with Aurelia three days later to a hero's welcome. They drive down Main Street with the tractor trailer towing the huge iron-flow battery. They take the battery to the coast, where they plan to connect it to the existing handmade wind turbines and another thirty or so wind turbines they'll build in the following months. Then they return to haul the rest of the batteries and components to Ferndale and the Six Rivers Tribe.

Irina joins them on their final trip to Eugene to pick up the last battery. While the others wait an hour south at the battery company in Eugene, Irina and Rafael stand in the doorway of her house in Salem. The yard is choked with weeds, but the house looks surprisingly intact. She reaches for the doorknob and opens the door to her old world.

There's the living room with the pictures of her, Clara, and Sam; the fireplace that she and Sam had sat in front of so many times that Pandemic winter; the bank of windows that overlooks the emerald hills of the Willamette Valley; and the kitchen window where she had held up notes to Sam before he'd gotten sick.

She walks down the hall to Clara's room and opens a door she hasn't opened since that October when Clara died. Inside is a time capsule of Clara's life. Clara's favorite doll lies in the unmade bed, where she had been on the morning of the accident. Irina picks her up and tucks her into a bag she carries. She takes several framed photos off Clara's desk, along with a couple of drawings that were pasted to the mirror. Their edges are curled from the Pacific Northwest humidity, but the marker lines are still familiar. Irina traces them gently with her finger. From the closet, she retrieves two of Clara's favorite t-shirts.

In Irina and Sam's bedroom, Rafael sees several post-it notes, little handwritten proclamations of love, stuck to the mirrors and dresser drawers. It occurs to Rafael that despite the magnitude of his love, he rarely tells Irina how he feels about her. Memento mori, he thinks. He doesn't want to miss the opportunity to tell her what she means to him, everything he's grateful for.

Irina takes several of the notes and adds them to her bag. From her closet, she retrieves her favorite pieces of clothing. She takes some jewelry, old journals, photo albums. Rafael bags those things up.

He looks at the pictures of Irina through the years and feels a strange longing, wishing, impossibly, that they had known each other when they were young.

He follows her to the car, where she retrieves a small shovel, Clara's urn, and the grave marker Rafael had carved for her; then they both walk to the backyard. The grass has entirely overgrown Sam's grave, but she finds it instinctively. She digs a shallow hole, then she opens the urn and pours half of the ashes in. She covers the ashes, then uses the shovel to hammer the marker into the ground nearby.

She wraps her arms around Rafael and for a moment they stand together. Rafael sends a silent prayer of thanks to Sam for having the patience to help Irina learn to love, for standing with her through Clara's death, for anchoring her here in the world with Matteo, for ensuring her survival until Rafael could meet her.

Irina breathes a final, resolved goodbye to her old life and her past self; then she and Rafael turn and depart for home.

Chapter Thirty: April 2041

On the sixth Founders Day, Rafael pulls the paper lot that signifies the end of the founders' majority on the Council. He reads off the number, and Shantal announces the corresponding name: Maeve Willis, a nurse who works with Ify and Aditi in Medical. Rafael and Irina are both familiar with Maeve and relieved to work with another person who will likely be a good Council member. Everyone thanks Ify for his excellent leadership and congratulates Meave enthusiastically; then they sit in lawn chairs and on picnic blankets to enjoy the meal that Benoit had prepared for them.

Irina and Rafael sit on Clara and Sam's bench, watching their children play.

"My family is probably in Las Vegas by now," Irina says. "But they're going to have to get through hundreds of miles of dry desert before they reach California."

Irina imagines her family moving slowly toward her across a desert plain, as their ancestors had nearly two hundred years before. Mindful of the settlement history of the United States, Irina had drafted up a territorial agreement with Gail and the Six Rivers Tribe. She'd then successfully advocated for it to be added to the Ferndale Charter so it would be far more difficult for any future Council to reverse. Tina had also convinced the leadership of Ferndale and the Six Rivers Tribe to sign a mutual aid and defense agreement.

"They're resourceful, and they have each other," Rafael replies as he wraps his arm around her and she leans into him. "They'll make it here safely."

"Liam told me his community is going to join us in time for spring planting," she says, "which should help ensure that we're prepared when my family arrives."

"Julián was inspired by his rye whiskey, and he thinks we should be able to turn more drought-friendly crops, and maybe even our compost waste, into ethanol. With the ethanol-fueled farming equipment, we won't have to worry as much about going hungry," Rafael says. "And . . . I'm hoping that now that we've trained other communities on how to make ethanol, we can start to make agreements for fueling stations around the state."

"You've done an amazing job with everything," Irina tells him. "On a related note . . . I have something for you, to congratulate you on the fact that you only have two more years to serve on the Council before we can get back to spending our evenings 'playing with our children and engaging in recreational activities,' as you put it."

He smiles as she hands him a messily-wrapped package. He slowly unwraps it, taking care to peel the tape off instead of tearing the paper. Inside, Irina has framed the worn flier she'd found seven years before on the door of the Walmart. Rafael's unadorned words, scrawled with Sharpie and desperate loneliness, blur before his eyes as a wave of emotion overtakes him.

Irina has kept that flier tucked into her favorite book all these years. The week before, she'd seen a frame in the thrift store, and she'd realized that the flier—the genesis of everything they've built here—deserved to be memorialized.

"Thank you for this," Rafael says, his voice heavy with emotion. "And thank you for coming here, for building Ferndale with me."

"You would have built it anyway," she says. "You were already working on it."

"You told me once that in law there can be two essential conditions for an outcome."

"*Sine qua non*—without which, none."

"*Sine qua non*," he agrees, taking her hand. "You're that for me and for Ferndale. None of this would have been possible without you. Maybe people would have followed my fliers here and maybe there would be a town, but it would have paled in comparison to what you and I have built together."

"Thank you," she says. He gently brushes a tear from her cheek with his thumb, then presses his lips to hers, kissing her deeply. When they pull back, she leans into him again and surveys the picnickers before them.

"What do you think will happen now that we no longer control the Council?" she asks him.

"We still have a lot of challenges. We need to figure out running water and improve our electricity generation. Hopefully the droughts improve and we continue to avoid forest fires. I don't think Ro will cause any more problems, but Tina is a bit more pessimistic about that. Tina is always telling me that there are bad people out there, but I think we've done a good job of avoiding the worst kind of post-apocalypse in our corner of the world. We've done what we could do to optimize for the best outcome, now we just have to wait and see."

"Like parenting."

"And marriage and love and pretty much any human endeavor. In all those systems, you can improve your probabilities, but there's always a little magic you can't account for."

They watch Miranda pointing out a bald eagle nest to Matteo and Javier, and Irina thinks of all of the magic she hadn't accounted for over the past eight years. She considers the distance she's traveled since that moment she stood on the bridge over the Willamette River with Matteo in her arms, contemplating the end of their existence. Is it possible that she, like the phoenix, has been reconstituted into something better than or at least equal to what she once was? She likes to think so. She's built something beautiful for herself, for Matteo, for the other residents of Ferndale. There are still moments of sorrow when she is reminded of her losses, but they're far outnumbered by days of joy and purpose.

"I don't know what happens next," she says, squeezing his hand and looking out over the town they've built, "but I know that I'm looking forward to the rest of the story."

Epilogue: April 2041

The young man waits anxiously at a dusty table inside the abandoned donut shop. As the first rays of sunrise illuminate the derelict buildings and empty parking lot, he picks at his fingernails and regrets every choice that brought him here. He considers getting back on his bicycle and riding away, but there's nowhere for him to go, and, anyway, he senses that there's an opportunity here to protect a few people he cares about and avert a potentially deadly conflict.

He gazes at the shop around him, the empty cases that still bear neat labels: "Glazed," "Rainbow Sprinkles," "Apple Fritter." He longs for donuts and every other modern convenience that's now lost to him. The donuts remind him of Sunday morning, church, coffee hour. That reminds him of his dead father, mother, and siblings. He's alone in the world now and at the mercy of everyone higher up on the food chain . . . a category which seems to include every other man left in the world. He runs his hand through his sandy-blond hair nervously, his fingers catching on the scar on his scalp, a reminder of how far down the food chain he is: a scared rabbit in a world of coyotes and wolves.

The headlights of the Tesla catch his eye, and he watches the car move silently down the deserted four-lane highway toward him. He tamps down his instinctive fear and tries his best to get himself in character for this encounter. He's armed with a handgun, but he's certain they'll be better armed. And they have backup. He has no one.

He watches the car pull into the parking lot ten feet from him. The doors open, and the two men step out, laughing. The passenger peels off his night vision goggles and tosses them carelessly onto the seat of the car before closing the door.

The young man recognizes the red-haired driver, but the other man, who has dark hair and a jagged scar on his cheek, is a stranger. That seems as ominous as the spring storm that's encroaching with the sunrise. Both men have handguns and assault rifles. They both move through the world with ease, barely bothering to check their surroundings as they stride across the parking lot toward him.

The dark-haired man throws open the shop door, and they cross the room. The legs of the metal chairs scrape on the floor as the two men pull them out and sit down across from the young man at the table. The young man waits for them to speak first.

The dark-haired man speaks, not even bothering with a greeting or introduction. "We're under new leadership. Marcus is the Director now. Your instructions have changed."

"Toby is dead?" the young man asks.

"Died last Wednesday." The red-haired man doesn't specify the cause, but the young man doubts that it was natural.

"That's too bad, because I'm sure he would have been interested in the biggest update from Ferndale," the young man says.

The two men look at him expectantly, and he continues, "Maeve Willis just got on the Ferndale Council."

"They use some kind of weird lottery system, right?" the dark-haired man asks. "Did you rig it?"

The young man shakes his head. "Nope. Someone apparently already tried that last fall and got sent out. Ferndale fixed the drawing so it can't be rigged. This was just random chance."

"Well, that's awful unlucky. Do you think Ferndale is going to become a threat? Should we tell the new boss?" the red-haired man asks.

"I don't think they're going to be a problem," the young man replies. "I doubt Maeve Willis is going to be able to convince Ferndale to do anything, even if she tries. Rumor is that she and the others are having a tough time fitting into Ferndale's weird culture. And, anyway, Ferndale isn't going to be interested in getting into a conflict with a town a couple of hundred miles away. They're busy planning community dances, talking about their feelings in support groups, and discussing how they're going to accommodate kosher and vegan food restrictions in their communal cafeteria. Tell Marcus that Ferndale isn't a threat. It's a hippy commune."

"But they're well-armed . . . or at least they claim to be in their radio broadcasts," the red-haired man points out.

The young man plays to their political sentiments. "Guns don't kill people. People kill people. And the hippies in Ferndale aren't actually going to pull any triggers."

"They're mostly harmless," the young man concludes, quoting a book he'd read the prior autumn. The other two men, of course, don't catch the reference.

"We heard they execute lots of people," the red-haired man replies. The young man has heard that rumor too. It's at odds with what he's seen of the town, but he isn't inclined to test his assumptions, so he's been careful to avoid Ferndale's detection.

"We'll let Marcus know what you told us," the dark-haired man with the scar on his cheek says. He produces a folded piece of paper from his pocket and slides it across the table to the young man. "Your new instructions."

The young man skims the note, trying his best to keep his face from revealing his distress about these new orders.

"Marcus said to tell you that he'll honor Toby's agreement with you. You do this, and he'll set you up wherever you want. You don't . . . , and you'll spend the rest of your days looking over your shoulder," the red-haired man says. "It's a small world . . . not a lot of people left. And most of them know each other."

"You can't get very far very fast on a bicycle," the dark-haired man agrees. "And anyway, there's nowhere to go."

They all look out over the desolate world outside the window. The young man tries to stay in character and keep a neutral expression on his face. "I'll check in on the radio when I get back to Ferndale," he promises.

The dark-haired man smirks. "We'll look forward to hearing from you then. Stick with the new codes in the note I gave you. And we'll meet you back here in two months."

The red-haired man stands and says, "We've gotta hit the road. We're going hunting. We got a final gift from the old boss: a little piece of intel about a promising hunting ground along I5."

The young man's stomach sinks. He can only imagine what that means. He hopes that their quarry is well-enough armed to fight them off or at least smart and swift enough to escape them. He watches the two men stride back out of the donut shop and get into the car. The sky opens up just as they depart down the highway, headed toward I5.

He watches the rain pelt the parking lot. After twenty minutes the storm moves off to the south, and he retrieves his bicycle from where he'd leaned it against the empty counter. He walks the bike out to the misty parking lot, puts on his backpack, and rides west toward Ferndale.

Author's Note

I started writing this story in December 2019, nine months after my husband and I lost our infant daughter—our only child—to meningitis and sepsis. A politically-well-connected bully had pushed me out of my dream job, so my husband and I were forced to make a long, expensive move back from the West Coast to Washington, DC. We were broke, we were struggling to conceive, our marriage was in shambles, and I'd become estranged from many of my friends and family after my daughter's death. I could see no real path forward for myself. In that mindset, I started writing the story of a woman whose world was as hollowed-out as mine felt.

The trouble was, I couldn't figure out how she could possibly recover and rebuild, because I couldn't figure out how *I* could possibly recover and rebuild. I wasn't sure what Irina's path forward was, because I wasn't sure what my path forward was. Then in February 2020, the first whispers of the Covid pandemic started circulating, and I set the draft down and walked away from it.

I didn't pick the draft back up again until April of 2023. By that time, I had two sons, my marriage had miraculously recovered (though that wasn't so much a miracle as it was a lot of hard work on both our parts), and I was living an admirably happy life in the Virginia suburbs, visited often by friends and family. I could see a path forward for Irina because I had already walked that path myself.

So this note and this story are a long way of saying that wherever you may find yourself, whatever bad circumstances you might be in, you should hang around and wait for the next chapter. There's a good chance that things can improve. I can't give you a map through the mountains, but I will tell you that there's likely something worth seeing on the other side.

Acknowledgments

The biggest thank you of all to my very first, most dedicated beta reader and cheerleader, Nathalie—my partner in poorly considered adolescent antics and dangerously chaotic golf cart rides, the person who shared my love of X-rated X-files fanfic (which eventually inspired me to start writing my own love stories), the one who has been reading all my shitty first drafts since sixth grade. This book is dedicated to two people we both cared about who passed on, but my stories have always been written *for* you.

My second biggest thank you to my husband, Omar, the one who stood with me in the fire after our daughter died, the man who may bear a bit of a resemblance to a certain Venezuelan engineer, my partner in every sense of the word, the person who encouraged me to keep writing these stories, who gamed out plot arcs with me at happy hours and on hikes in a half a dozen states, who traveled with me to Ferndale to check out all the spots I'd researched. I believe in love because of you.

To my amazing beta readers, Ashley, Susan, Gary, Maria Emilia, and Tom, thank you for all of your feedback, for making this book better with your recommendations, and for encouraging me to move forward with it. To my editor and publisher, Ran, for all of your time and attention to this story and your dedication to helping me make it the best story it could be. This book is so much better for your work on it. To my au pairs, Mafe and Andrea, because without good childcare, literally nothing else can get accomplished. I'm fortunate to have people I can trust to take care of my children. To the people of Ferndale, who generously made time to help me, and inspired many pieces of this story—including the very specific anecdote about a sidewalk concert. Special thanks to Ronda and Bill; Paul and Cary at Old Steeple; Lee, Cathy, Cheryl, and Deb at the Ferndale Museum; and Julie at the Bureau of Land Management. To my many technical experts who answered all my dumb questions about electricity generation, ham radios, plot points, and government structures. Thank you Chuck, David, Andy, Emily, Alex, and Daniel. To my family for their encouragement, especially to Mom, Amy, Ed, and Jana.

And of course to my sons, for being the force that animates my days and gives me purpose . . . and for inspiring a lot of Matteo's antics.

About the Author

Genevieve Carr is a lawyer and policy expert who lives in Northern Virginia with her husband and two sons. In her free time, she enjoys traveling, hiking, biking, gardening, photography, and passionately discussing politics after a glass (or two) of wine.

Find out more about *The Town at the End of the World* book series, sign up to be a beta reader, and find discussion questions at www.GenevieveCarr.com.

Your opinion matters to me, so if you enjoyed Book One of *The Town at the End of the World*, please spread the word by posting a review on Amazon, Good Reads, Barnes & Noble, and other sources to which you have access. Reviews are enormously helpful to the reading community, and your support really does motivate me to keep writing. Thank you!

—Genevieve Carr—

Discussion Questions

1. If you were able to write a charter for Ferndale or another post-apocalyptic town, what kind of system would you create and why?
2. Did Ferndale live up to the Founders' goals? In what ways did the Founders succeed? In what ways did they fail?
3. Before the others arrived in Ferndale, was there a way that Rafael could have respectfully initiated a romantic relationship with Irina that would not have felt coercive, given their isolation and dependence on each other?
4. Do you agree with Irina's idea that grief doesn't reveal you, it transforms you? Have you experienced grief that changed you or the way you viewed the world?
5. Both Tina and Irina had an adult who "showed up" and had a profound positive impact on their lives. Is there someone like that in your life? In what ways did they show up? How did their support impact your life?
6. Did you agree with any of Ro's points about the downsides of Ferndale's political model? Are there other problems with Ferndale's model that you see?
7. Do you agree with Tina's stance that post-apocalyptic conditions necessitate some moral compromises? Should Tina and the others have shot the thieves at the trade conference and in the barn on the outskirts of town? Should the town have executed the man who was found guilty of incest? Should Irina have sentenced Vera to exile for not contributing? Why or why not?
8. What do you think about the power dynamics of Rafael and Irina's marriage? Is it an egalitarian marriage?
9. In what ways do each of the Founders' past experiences affect the system they create and the later decisions they make—for example, Irina and Tina's decisions about how to handle sex offenders? In what ways does your own history affect your political beliefs and ethical decisions?
10. Do you agree with Irina's argument that most parenting decisions don't really matter? How much of someone's personality is the result of nature (genetics) and how much is the result of nurture (parenting, societal influences, and experiences)?
11. In what ways is government by random selection (sortition), a better model than elections? In what ways are elections better? What system would you prefer to live under?
12. What are the strengths and weaknesses of Irina and Rafael's marriage? Is it a model of marriage you would aspire to?
13. Is a happy marriage a matter of chance, as a Jane Austen character remarked, or a matter of choice, as Rafael thinks?
14. In what ways could modern society be made more egalitarian? What would the costs or tradeoffs be?